THE COVERING

MISS CHEYENNE MITCHELL

Copyright © 2011, 2024 Miss Cheyenne Mitchell.

All rights reserved. No part of this book may be reproduced, stored, or transmitted by any means—whether auditory, graphic, mechanical, or electronic—without written permission of both publisher and author, except in the case of brief excerpts used in critical articles and reviews. Unauthorized reproduction of any part of this work is illegal and is punishable by law.

ISBN: 979-8-89419-007-5 (sc)
ISBN: 979-8-89419-008-2 (hc)
ISBN: 979-8-89419-009-9 (e)

Because of the dynamic nature of the Internet, any web addresses or links contained in this book may have changed since publication and may no longer be valid. The views expressed in this work are solely those of the author and do not necessarily reflect the views of the publisher, and the publisher hereby disclaims any responsibility for them.

THE EWINGS PUBLISHING

One Galleria Blvd., Suite 1900, Metairie, LA 70001
(504) 702-6708

This book is dedicated to The Lord God Almighty
Who has given to me the great gifts of creativity and imagination

SEPTEMBER, 1998

CHAPTER ONE

The fierce flashes of lightning accompanied by loud rumblings of thunder awakened me. It was four o'clock in the morning, the rain was coming down hard and I was terrified! Ever since I was a little girl I was afraid of thunder storms. Yet, I didn't know why. I was seventeen years old and still afraid of them. After all of the years of listening to my Aunt Margeaux telling me, "You'll grow out of it, Celia." Referring to my fear, I realized she didn't have the slightest idea what she was talking about, because the older I got the more afraid of the storms I seemed to get.

I got out of bed and put on my bathrobe and slippers then I started to walk throughout the house. I left my bedroom light off because I didn't want to awaken my sister, Drew. She was never scared of thunder and lightning. In fact, there were very few things that scared her. And as far back as I could remember I was always the timid one. While moving throughout the house I turned on the lights in each room that I came to. And my mind began to wander.

I was two years older than Drew was but if we got picked on in our neighborhood, as we often had growing up, it was she who defended us. And the size of the other child, or children didn't matter to her. It got to be a way of life for us wherever we moved to. And we moved quite a lot.

The last town that we lived in was a place called Wesbury, before that we lived in Sheriville, and before that we lived in a place called Prato. Other children would always taunt Drew and I because of our family, in particularly our grandfather. They thought our family members were strange, and that Drew and I were just as equally strange.

Sometimes things would get so bad that the other children would throw stones at us. One time when that happened to us I ran home as fast as I could. But Drew stood her ground and challenged all of the children to a 'fair one' one at a time. Fortunately, someone came along and stopped things from really getting out of hand.

As far as the taunting and the throwing stones at us went Sheriville was the worse place we had lived in. It was there that my sister got hit with a stone so hard it knocked her down, and one side of her head was bleeding. The children who were picking on us got scared and ran away after it happened. So I guessed they thought they had really hurt her badly.

A few people who saw what happened came to Drew's rescue as she laid there on the ground. And somebody called for an ambulance to take her to the hospital. The entire time I was hiding behind some bushes about a half a block away.

Drew ended up getting three stitches in her head and the scar could still be seen. Especially if she wore her beautiful, dark brown hair in a certain style. However, it didn't take away any of the beauty from her face. The scar was a small one at the very top of her forehead by her hair line.

It was always the same with us in each town that we lived in. The funny thing is that the same children who taunted Drew and I were previously our friends, because we played together every day. Yet, eventually everything would change, and always because of our grandfather and the rest of our family members.

My sister and I never could understand why other children called our grandfather a murderer. And they called the other members of our family names, too. We found out from a few of the children that their parents told them they were no longer allowed to play with us, as well as other mean, hateful things.

Things like *"Stay away from those two Bellis girls or you might end up getting hurt! They're a strange bunch of people and we believe that their family members are dangerous!"* Of course Drew and I never had a clue what they were talking about.

My sister and I always made lots of friends wherever we moved to. Still, in the end all of them would turn on us. Even some of the adults who talked to Drew and I would suddenly begin to scowl at us when they saw us.

People in the towns that we lived in seemed to change toward us after a series of mysterious disappearances. Disappearances which resulted in those missing people being found murdered. Unfortunately for us those people were last seen with one of our family members, and oftentimes it was our grandfather. Needless to say, we were very happy when our family decided that it was time for us to move on.

As soon as Drew and I got comfortable in a town we would have to leave there. When we moved it was always for the same reason. The people suddenly hated us but my sister and I never knew why. We never knew what we had done to those people, or what our grandfather and the other members of our family had done to them to make them suddenly hate us.

When we moved from Prato I was four years old. But before we left there a crowd of people from the town surrounded our house demanding that our grandfather come outside to face them. All of them had some kind of weapon in their hands but I didn't see any guns. Our grandfather never did go outside, and during the night our family quietly left town.

After a while we faced the same problems in Sheriville because a little boy who used to be friends with my sister and I was found murdered. Strangely, I still wondered years later about what happened to Tommy Lee Stone. It was after that when we moved to Wesbury.

We were living in Wesbury when Drew and I started going to school. We were happy there, too, at first. Yet, when things turned sour again we had to move away. The one good thing that came out of leaving there was that we never moved again, but the bad thing was that our grandfather left us forever.

My sister and I overheard the adults in our family talking one night. We learned that there were sixty people in Wesbury and in Suffic, a nearby County, who had been missing for quite some time. After a terrible thunder storm on the night before we were run out of town thirty of those people were found dead, and buried in shallow graves, twenty of them were found in Suffic and ten of them were found right there in Wesbury. Mysteriously, every one of the bodies was missing its' heart, and the heads had been nearly decapitated from some of the bodies.

Our grandfather was the last person to be seen with a lot of those people as well as some of the other thirty people who were still missing. I recognized some of the women when I saw their pictures in the newspaper because they had been to our house. However, I never saw them again.

Every one of the victims had been torn apart as if by a wild animal, I overheard the Sheriff telling our parents when he came to our house to question our grandfather. The strange thing was that there were no wild animals where we lived.

The Sheriff questioned our family members, too. And all of them told him they didn't know anything about the murders. They also told him that our grandfather wasn't at home at the time, and that they didn't know when he would be returning. It was an outright lie.

Our grandfather came home just minutes before the Sheriff knocked on our front door. He was hiding in the basement. The Sheriff and two of his Deputies decided to park outside in front of our house and wait until he got home.

Sheriff James Turner was affectionately known in our town as "Big Jim". He was a middle aged man with very kind eyes. His hair had turned gray almost overnight. Also, I heard that he had been the Sheriff in Wesbury for nearly thirty years, and he was a widower. The people in town said that he had been devoted to his wife and his four children who were all grown and had moved away. "Big Jim" looked sad to me most of the time, and there was a reason for that.

I heard the people in Wesbury say that his children rarely came to visit him, or even telephone him since the death of their mother. Sadly, "Big Jim" had never seen any of his eight grandchildren either. It was suspected that his wife, Ann Marie, died under suspicious circumstances in the beginning.

She had her usual cup of tea one night before going to bed, but that time it was laced with arsenic. Naturally Sheriff Turner was the prime suspect. Yet, eventually he was exonerated of any wrongdoing in the matter, but his children were still suspicious of him. It didn't matter that there was a rumor around town that their mother was dying of cancer.

Ann Marie mentioned to a few people in town that she was thinking about taking her own life, because she didn't want to be a burden on her family in the last stages of her illness. Everybody in town figured that she committed suicide, even the Sheriff, and in the end the Coroner ruled her death as just that, a suicide. Still, "Big Jim's" children would not accept that. It was a terrible shame that they felt better believing their father killed their mother than to accept the fact that their mother killed herself.

Every Christmas Sheriff Turner would get dressed up in a Santa Claus suit, and entertain the children at the local hospital. He would hand out lots of toys and goodies to them. He was a kind man to everyone who knew him and his love of children was obvious. I felt sorry for his grandchildren because they had no idea what a wonderful man they had for a grandfather. Anybody who knew him would never believe he was a killer.

My sister and I were awake on the night that "Big Jim" came to question our family. We heard him when he left and went outside with his Deputies, too. Oddly, our parents told us to go to bed, and it was two whole hours before our regular bed time. That's when we knew something was horribly wrong. Furthermore, we knew that our grandfather wasn't hiding in the basement for no reason.

Drew and I went upstairs to our bedroom. We heard our parents go downstairs to the basement where our grandfather and the rest of our family were. My sister got into bed like our parents said. But I listened to what they were talking about in the basement through a vent in our bedroom wall. I could hear all of them as if I was in the same room with them.

"If you stay here, Papa," I heard my mother say to our grandfather, "they will destroy you. So you have to leave here, in fact maybe we all do." "But, Kate," said Aunt Jada, "what about the babies?" She always referred to my sister and I as "the babies" although we were big girls. "They have to go to school you know," she continued, "we can't just pick up and go like we used to."

When I heard her say that I knew our family had moved around quite a lot, probably since before Drew and I were born. And the only reason they had been in Wesbury as long as they had was because we were going to school.

Even at the age of seven it was obvious to me that if they were not run out of a town, they just moved somewhere else when things got too bad for them. I kept my eyes and ears open for any clues. Still, I never knew what any of them had done to make people so angry at them, and at Drew and I.

Our family's moving around so much explained why I was a grade behind other children my age in school. I was in the first grade when I should have been in the second grade, and Drew was in Kindergarten. I continued to listen to their conversation in the basement that night.

"I won't hurt my granddaughters like that, Kate," I heard our grandfather say to our mother. "I'll just have to find a way out of this mess. If I have to leave here I will, but Celia and Drew are not going to be dragged around from place to place anymore." We didn't think much about it at the time. But as we grew older my sister and I started wondering. Also, we couldn't help wondering if our grandfather, or the rest of our family did have something to do with those terrible killings.

That night Sheriff Turner and his Deputies finally got tired of waiting for our grandfather so they left. It was then that our grandfather saw his chance to get away, but it was a mistake. He should never have left our house. I went to bed after I heard him leave, but I was determined to stay awake until he returned home. I had a horrible feeling that he was in grave danger, yet, against my will I fell asleep.

I was awakened around dawn by the sorrowful moans and sobs of my mother and our aunts. Immediately I wondered if our grandfather was alright. So I got out of bed and went downstairs to the living room where the sounds were coming from. It was so dark down there that I could barely see any of them.

All of the shades on the windows were pulled down, and the curtains which happened to be black were drawn. Drew and I were used to our family members being in darkened rooms during the day time. They liked the rooms so dark that they would be almost black, and we could never understand that.

"Why are you crying, Mama?" I asked my mother as I walked over to where she was sitting. "What's the matter?" I put my arms around her neck as she held me tightly. And Papa who was sitting next to her gently stroked my hair. "Your grandfather is gone, Celia, baby," he told me.

"No!" I cried and the tears came easily because our beloved grandfather couldn't be gone. Why did he want to go away and leave us? "Yes, sweetheart," said Papa, "he's gone." Then I saw Drew coming down the stairs. Papa walked over to her and picked her up. Then he told her the same thing that he told me about our grandfather.

Our family members enveloped Drew and I as if they were trying to shield us from something. "Why did Grandfather leave us, Papa?" my sister asked our father. After that everyone in the room stopped sobbing, except me, and there was complete silence.

Suddenly with great rage and anger Aunt Jada cried, "He was murdered! They murdered him those rotten sons of bitches! We ought to kill every last one of them for what they did!" "Jada, please!" cried my mother reaching for my aunt's hand. Aunt Jada pulled away from her angrily. Of my mother and her sisters it was Aunt Jada who had the bad temper. When she got angry she could also be violent, and it scared Drew and I sometimes.

She put her face in her hands and started sobbing softly. Her husband my uncle, Marcus, tried to comfort her. "Who would kill Grandfather, Mama?" I asked my mother and I saw the tears in her eyes. She hugged me closely but she never did answer my question. It seemed like she couldn't talk about it right then for some reason.

As best as my sister and I could figure out, by listening to Aunt Jada rant and rave, the people in Wesbury had cornered our grandfather. It happened somewhere between our house and the outskirts of the town then they killed him. There was nothing that the Sheriff, or his Deputies could do to stop them either. I guess there is nothing that you can do with an angry mob.

Aunt Jada was like a madwoman. Her whole countenance changed right before our eyes, and it was scary! Aunt Margeaux, with her head resting on Uncle Wilhelm's shoulder, said nothing and she looked like she was in a daze. Papa held Drew and I on his lap and I couldn't seem to stop sobbing. I went on long after my sister and the others stopped. I couldn't stand the thought of being without our grandfather.

"I want you to listen to me, darlings," Papa said to Drew and I. "Sometimes people hate what they don't understand. But it's more accurate to say that they fear what they don't understand. And in their minds it's better to destroy something like that than to tolerate it. One day you'll understand but your grandfather is where he will always be able to watch over you. Okay?" Drew nodded her head but I didn't want to hear it. I wanted our grandfather there with us not somewhere else watching over us. I cried for many days after that, too.

There was no funeral service for our grandfather because his body was never recovered. I thought that was strange, too. Drew and I would've settled for a nice memorial service. However, our family members made it clear to us that he was gone and we were moving on. Neither our parents nor any other member of our family ever talked about that terrible night, and after that we left Wesbury. My sister and I liked it there in the beginning. But we were glad to leave there, then our family came to live in Hardelle.

After I got older I asked Mama why things always changed so suddenly for us everywhere we lived. All she said was, "Honey, don't worry about anything that people say, because you know that we love you and Drew very much, and that's all that matters." Her 'explanation' did not satisfy me at all, because she never really answered my question. It was easy for her and the other adult members of our family to say something like that. But it wasn't so easy for Drew and I because it hurt to lose our friends and not know why we lost them.

Our grandfather's name was Damion Carbell and he was tall, dark and handsome. We never knew how old he really was. But he surely didn't look old enough to be our grandfather. He was a kind, gentle man and very loving to my sister and I. Also he would play games with us when he awoke in the evenings, too.

Our grandfather always had a gift for each one of us. It was nothing big just a small toy or trinket. And he would leave each one of us a brand new, gold dollar coin on our individual bureau dressers once in a while, after he came home from one of his 'all-nighters' as he called them.

In the eyes of my sister and I our grandfather was the most wonderful man on the face of the earth, after Papa that is. Still, even we had to admit sometimes that he was very enigmatic. Also, he was a ladies' man and he never went out with the same woman twice. He would bring a woman home with him in the evening and they would stay upstairs in his bedroom all night. Yet, we never saw or heard from any of those women again.

One night Drew and I thought we heard a woman scream upstairs in his bedroom. "Oh, they're just playing around," Mama told us. It didn't sound like it to us. As young as we were we could certainly tell the difference between someone playing around, and someone who was being hurt. My grandfather may have been strange but there was never any doubt in our minds that he loved us.

My sister and I desperately wanted to question our parents about our grandfather. But we didn't because we knew we would never get a straight answer from them so why bother? We tried once after he'd been gone for a few years. But all they did was rattle on about things that we hadn't even asked them about. We wanted to know what he did to make people angry enough to want to kill him. And we wanted to know what happened to our former playmate, Tommy Lee Stone.

They found Tommy Lee faced down in a ditch with his throat ripped open, and his heart torn out of his chest one week after Drew got hit with that stone. He was the one who hit her. His body was so torn up that his family had the casket closed at the funeral. I couldn't imagine anyone murdering a child like that. *"Whoever did that to him must be a monster!"* I thought. It was even more disturbing that his killer was never caught.

Mama was the oldest of our grandfather's three daughters, and her name was Kathleena, Kathleena Carbell-Bellis, and they called her Kate for short. Our aunts were named, Margeaux, who was three years younger than Mama and, Jada, who was a year younger than Margeaux. Aunt Margeaux was married to a guy named, Wilhelm Anderson, and Aunt Jada was married to my uncle, Marcus Walker. My father's name was, Omri Antoine Bellis, and ever since I could remember all of us lived in the same house together.

Aunt Jada was somewhat of a "hot-head" but she was the most beautiful of the three sisters. She had long, curly, dark brown hair, olive- colored skin and big, green eyes. Aunt Margeaux was dark complexioned with long hair that was dyed dark red, and she had light brown eyes. My sister and I thought she was pretty, and in a way she looked like a witch but a pretty one. She had a sweet disposition and was usually quiet most of the time.

I did recall Aunt Margeaux and Aunt Jada having a bad quarrel once when I was a little girl, and things had really gotten out of hand between them. I thought they were actually going to fist-fight, and I was surprised when Aunt Jada backed off suddenly before they came to blows. Aunt Margeaux was the quiet one. However, I had a feeling that if she got really angry she was far worse than Aunt Jada ever could be.

Mama had a coffee and cream-colored complexion, long, jet black hair that was down to her waist and hazel eyes. All three sisters were tall and slender like models. I looked like my mother except my hair was not as long as hers' was, and Drew resembled Aunt Jada.

My father as well as my uncles were all dark-complexioned with dark brown hair and eyes. Also, they were tall and handsome. Papa was the only one who kept his hair shoulder-length and pulled back. Sometimes he would put it into a pony tail, and have the rest of it cut short and waved. It looked really good on him.

Papa was a very kind man, however, he could also be very intimidating, and our uncles were nice guys, too. Our father and our uncles could have passed for brothers because they looked so much alike. It seemed eerie to me how much all three of them looked like our grandfather, too, especially Papa.

Mama never talked to us about her mother, except to say that she died when she and her sisters were young women. She told us that her parents never had any sons, only the three daughters. We never knew Papa's family at all and he never spoke about his family.

To tell you the truth my father was just as much of an enigma as our grandfather was because the two of them were a lot alike. *"They should've been father and son,"* I thought, *" instead of father-in-law and son-in-law."* I would always think about our grandfather, even many years after he left us and I missed him very much.

Our aunts and uncles treated my sister and I like we were their children, too. They had a say in everything that we did right along with our parents. Also, they were very good to us. They never failed to show us plenty of love and affection. We had enough love in our home to share with hundreds of children.

Drew and I often wondered why our aunts never had any children of their own. And my sister, who was always outspoken, decided to ask Aunt Jada about that one day. "Why, sugar plum," she said to Drew, "I already have two children, you and Celia, so I don't need anymore."

Once in a while I would notice that Mama looked very sad. I would be doing my homework or something and so would Drew. When suddenly I could feel eyes watching us, and when I looked up she would be staring at us. I knew she wanted to tell us something, but she couldn't bring herself to do it. She would quickly turn away from me when I caught her watching us. Yet, my sister never noticed it but I would tell her about it when we were alone, and she thought nothing of it.

Somehow I knew that whatever it was that Mama wanted to tell us she never would. It made me wonder about our family more and more as I got older. There was nothing that Drew and I wanted more than for our parents to tell us about our family. You would think that they would be glad to tell us about our family and about our heritage, because that is what normal families did. But all of them acted so strangely, and my sister and I would never have guessed why in our wildest imaginations.

CHAPTER TWO

Our family members became more cautious than ever after what happened to us in Wesbury, and the lives of my sister and I changed…..for the worse. As I look back I guess it was inevitable, simply because we were getting older. Things that we never paid any attention to before started to peak our curiosity.

Our parents laid down rules for us, and they were rules that to us never made any sense. We were not allowed to have any friends over to our house after it got dark. Nor were we allowed to spend the night at any of their houses. It made things rather difficult for Drew and I when we moved to Hardelle.

As soon as Drew and I got to Hardelle we started attending school, and naturally we made new friends. We could invite them over to our home during the day time, but under no circumstances were they to come inside our house. We would have to entertain them outside on the front or back porches. Which was fine in the summertime, but when the weather was cold it became rather hard to say the least. And we were not allowed out anywhere for very long either, except for school.

Needless to say Drew and I had very few visitors. We didn't keep a friend for very long either. Also, we missed out on a lot of birthday parties, sleep-overs, as well as other gatherings that we were invited to. However, I don't think that our parents realized that sooner or later we were going to challenge their unusual and bizarre rules.

I was old enough to go out on dates, but no one was allowed in our house during the day time and definitely not after dark. So neither

Drew nor I kept a boyfriend for very long. If they wanted to come inside our house to play records, or anything else that normal teenagers did they couldn't, not at our house. And they had better use the bathroom before they left home because they wouldn't be able to use ours. It was all so ridiculous to us.

It was during the day time that our family members slept because they stayed in the streets all night long. They never met any friends that Drew and I did bring home. However, we knew that Caroline kept them well informed about all of our associates and activities.

To make things more comfortable for Drew and I, and to help us cope with their foolish rules our family had Caroline. It was our grandfather who found her and hired her when Drew and I were toddlers. She came from a place called Kingstown, and she had known our family for a long time. I had to admit that things were a lot more bearable for my sister and I because of her. Caroline was our Housekeeper and Baby-sitter but you would have thought she was our mother, too.

She participated in anything for the benefit of the town, children or teenagers. Also, she made sure that Drew and I were well fed and well dressed. She took care of us when we were sick, or if we were in any kind of trouble, too. All of the things that our parents did not do Caroline did for us. She ran our home as if it was hers' which was fine with our family and with us. It was especially nice to have her around near the end of the month when we rarely talked with our family members.

My sister and I noticed how Caroline took care of other things for us, too, as we got older. Because we never had to be bothered with anybody picking on us anymore. If someone was bothering us we would come home and tell her all about it, and she would say, "Okay, girls, I'll see that the problem is taken care of."

After that she would ask us all kinds of questions about the person, or persons who were picking on us. Such as their names, addresses and what they looked like, and we knew she told our family members everything that we told her. After that we didn't see the people who were bothering us anymore. It was as if they had dropped off the face of the earth, or something. No one else that we talked to knew what happened to those people either.

Randi Ames and Donnie Ross were two such people because Donnie liked my sister and Randi knew it. A few of her friends at school were always telling her that they saw him talking to Drew. He thought he was the hottest thing in our school as well as in Hardelle. But to me he was ugly because he had a freckled face and red hair that looked like his head was on fire. My sister and I couldn't stand him and he knew it, too.

Randi knew that he fooled around with other girls behind her back, but she was too stupid to leave him alone. Drew didn't want him and she let him know it in no uncertain terms. Yet, he kept trying to come on to her. My sister even went to Randi once and asked her to make him stay out of her face. But when the deal went down he had the poor girl believing that Drew was chasing after him.

I couldn't understand Randi because she was a pretty girl. She wasn't fat just a little on the plump side and kind of short. I knew she could do better than Donnie if she wanted to. But there is an old adage that says that 'love is blind'. In her case I guessed it was true because she thought every girl in our school wanted that ugly, two-timing bastard, and she wouldn't hesitate to fight over him either.

Drew rejected all of Donnie's advances every chance she got. Therefore, he told Randi a lot of lies about my sister and naturally Randi believed him. Even though my sister tried to tell her the truth. I think that Donnie enjoyed seeing her fighting with other girls over him, too.

One day Drew and I were walking home from school when Randi and Donnie ambushed us. We were covered with scratches and bruises all over our arms and chests from the fight. But we did get in a few good licks before somebody came along and broke it up. When Caroline saw us that afternoon she became hysterical. I guess that our bruises and scratches looked much worse than they really were, so we told her what happened.

"You can bet your asses," said Caroline angrily, "that those two will never bother you two again!" She cleaned and dressed all of our 'war wounds' after that. "I'll see that they never cause you two anymore trouble," she promised us.

Three months after that day posters all over Hardelle were still displaying Randi's and Donnie's pictures. And there was a small reward posted by their families for any information about their whereabouts, and asking if anyone saw them to call the Sheriff. A lot of people in Hardelle thought they ran away together, but for some reason I doubted that. When Drew and I talked to Caroline about it all she said was, "Whatever happened to them I'm sure that they deserved it." Her statement surprised us because unlike other people in town it was obvious to us that she knew they hadn't run away together. "Maybe she knows something that we don't," Drew said to me. "Yeah,"

I replied with my mind wondering, "it sounds like it. Doesn't it?"

Caroline was a beautiful woman, and she told Drew and I that she was in her thirties. She was medium height and had long, dark brown hair and light brown eyes. Also, she was slightly plump. Both of her parents were killed in a car accident when she was six years old she told us. And she had a younger sister who was killed in the accident, too. Also, she had no other family members except an older brother that she had not seen, or heard from since the funerals.

When I was almost three years old she turned eighteen years old. So she left the orphanage that she'd been living in for most of her life, and one of the matrons there gave her $100.00. She wanted to find herself a job and a place of her own. One night after she had been walking from place to place all day long looking for work, and not finding anything she met our grandfather. Since she had no luck finding a job she thought she would have to return to the orphanage. Without a job, or a place to live $100.00 was not going to last very long.

The somber thought of going back to the orphanage depressed her terribly. But she felt that she had no other choice. She sat down on a bench at the bus stop to wait for the bus that would take her back there, and started sobbing. That's when she met our grandfather she said. She learned that he had been following her, and watching her that night as he sat down on the bench beside her and asked her why she was crying.

At first she was wary of the handsome stranger who seemed to come out of nowhere she told Drew and I. But as he kept talking to her she started to relax then he took her to a cafe nearby, and bought her something to eat. Afterward he offered her a job as a Housekeeper for himself and his family at a salary she would never have gotten working on any job. So she accepted his offer.

"Your grandfather was the kindest, sweetest man that I have ever known," she told Drew and I. Although we agreed with her we couldn't help wondering why he was following her that night in the first place. *"Dear Grandfather,"* I thought. He had foreseen mine and Drew's need for Caroline in our future, and I recalled his kindness, too. My sister never talked about him so I guessed that was because she could barely remember him. However, I had fond memories of our grandfather no matter what other people had said about him.

Caroline stayed with us for many years. But after our grandfather left us in Wesbury she returned to Kingstown where she had lived for most of her life. It was not hard to figure out from the way that she talked about him that she had fallen in love with him, and his leaving us was painful for her, too. Yet, I couldn't understand how she stood by watching in silence as he went from one woman to the next.

One month after we moved to Hardelle our parents contacted Caroline, and asked her if she would come back to live with us. She agreed so I guess she was over our grandfather by that time. I continued walking throughout the house.

There was no one at home as usual except Drew and I. I knew that Caroline had gone out to the guest house where she lived. My sister and I spent a lot of time by ourselves in the big, old Victorian-style house where we lived. Especially toward the end of the month because that was when our family members spent a lot more time away from home, and always during the night. We never knew what time they came home in the mornings. However, we tried many times to stay awake and see, but it was no use because we would always fall asleep.

I could only remember one time that I was awake when our family came home from one of their end-of-the-month rendezvous. I was twelve years old, and I pretended to be asleep when I heard all of them come into the house that morning. It was just before dawn and I had been awakened earlier because it was a night just like that one. There was a bad thunder storm that awakened me and I couldn't get back to sleep.

To make matters worse I had gone to the bathroom around three o'clock that morning, and when I came out of there a strange man was standing at the foot of the stairs looking up at me. At first it was so dark I couldn't tell who, or what it was until he moved and I saw his arms, legs and hands. I ran into my bedroom, slammed the door shut, jumped into my bed and pulled the covers over my head because I was terrified!

Later that morning just before dawn I heard our parents and the others come home. Our parents came into our bedroom and kissed my sister and I on our foreheads, and they thought I was asleep. I don't think I will ever forget the horribly pungent odor that I smelled on them. It was awful and it smelled like something dead. I would never be able to describe that horrible odor to anybody, or ever forget it.

When Drew and I awakened in the mornings our family members would be fast asleep. We always checked on them to be sure that they were in their bedrooms, except for my uncles who slept in the basement. We never ventured down there for any reason. It was the one area of our house that our parents forbid us to enter, and they made that very clear to us.

It would be so dark in their bedrooms that we could hardly see them lying there. And it never mattered how high the sun was outside their bedrooms were completely dark. We did not know anybody whose family members stayed in darkened rooms all of the time like ours did. Neither Drew nor I could ever recall having seen the shades pulled up on their bedroom windows during the day in order to let some light into their rooms. They were always pulled down as if they were deliberately trying to keep all light out. They would be sound asleep and nothing could awaken them.

For example, my mother had a stupid cuckoo clock that she put on the wall in our hallway upstairs. And if you accidentally bumped against the thing a little wooden bird would come out of its' house. The noise that it made was unusual and deafening instead of a normal cuckoo bird's noise. It was the craziest thing that my sister and I had ever heard in our lives.

One morning I was in a rush to get to school because I was running late, and I accidentally bumped into that impractical cuckoo clock and it went off. The noise was horribly loud. Everyone on the block had to hear that noise. Even Drew who was halfway down the block heard it. She came running back to the house to see what happened. Caroline had to come upstairs and shut it off by thumping it a few times. Yet, believe it or not, not one member of our family stirred, and it was unbelievable.

I looked at Drew and she looked at me. We couldn't understand how they slept through such an ostentatious racket. I mentioned that to Caroline after she turned it off, because every one of them should have heard that thing and awakened. "Honey," said Caroline, "some people can sleep through anything and they're just heavy sleepers that's all." *"Heavy sleepers my ass!"* I thought.

There were more strange things about our family members, too. Our parents painted the walls of their bedroom black, and the woodwork was painted a dark red color. Aunt Jada and Aunt Margeaux's bedroom was on the first floor. They painted the walls of their bedroom an ugly, dark gray color, and the woodwork was painted black. The basement where Uncle Marcus and Uncle Wilhelm slept was dark anyway. Yet, they painted all of the windows black.

Drew and I couldn't figure out what was going on with our aunts and our uncles either. We assumed that all married couples slept together like our parents did. But Uncle Marcus and Aunt Jada slept in separate bedrooms, and so did Aunt Margeaux and Uncle Wilhelm. It was only occasionally that our aunts slept with their husbands. It was not very often, and never during the days heading toward the end of the month, which was when all of them stayed out all night.

"Maybe they're having affairs with other people or something," Drew said to me one day. "I don't know," I told her, "but it's strange that they're married and only sleep together sometimes." We could have understood it better if we knew that they were seeing other people. However, my sister and I had our suspicions about that but that's all we had. There was no evidence to support our suspicions. However, we saw something one night that we would never forget.

It took a lot of begging and pleading with our parents, but they allowed Drew and I out one evening. Of course we had to lie to them. So we told them that we had to visit a friend of ours named, Lana, because we had to study for a very important exam at school the next day. We came home earlier than we expected from Lana's house that night.

We were two blocks away from our house, but we could see our front porch clearly. We saw Uncle Marcus on our front porch with another woman. He was openly caressing the breasts of a strange, young woman that we had never seen before. Our mouths dropped open in shock.

"Do you see what I'm seeing?" asked Drew as we walked toward our house. "I sure do," I said. "Maybe we were right about them having affairs with other people after all, Celia," she continued, "look at the way he's touching that woman." "I can't believe he's that bold," I told Drew. "I wonder where Aunt Jada is?" "I don't know," said my sister, "but if he's on our front porch doing that to some woman she can't be anywhere around." "I didn't think he would be that stupid," I said still stunned, "to bring a woman right to our house. So evidently he doesn't give a damn if he gets caught or not." Uncle Marcus was a horrific ladies' man like our grandfather was.

We got a further shock after that when Aunt Jada opened the front door, and let Uncle Marcus and the strange woman into our house. Our mouths fell open again and we were stupefied. "My God," cried Drew, "what the hell is going on here, Celia?" "You're asking me?" I replied. So instead of going home like we planned we walked past our house.

Drew and I went to the park a few blocks away, because we didn't want to embarrass our aunt and our uncle by coming home sooner than they expected. "Actually," said Drew as we were walking past our house, "it's kind of kinky. Don't you think so, Celia?" I looked at her as if she had suddenly grown two heads.

As we were walking we heard a woman scream and it was a horrified scream. A scream of sheer terror, and it came from the direction of our house. My sister and I looked back at the house then at one another. "No," said Drew shaking her head, "we must be hearing things, Celia." "Sure," I told her, "if you say so." We hadn't imagined anything because both of us heard a woman scream. Then there was nothing but silence. It was a dead kind of silence, too. We kept on walking toward the park.

When we got there we found a bench and sat down, and we sat there until two o'clock that morning. It was well past our curfew by then but we didn't care. "I guess we'd better be getting home now,

Celia," said Drew checking the timepiece that Papa gave her on her last birthday. "I guess so," I said. So we got up to leave.

I saw the man out of the corner of my eye and turned to face him. He was tall, all dressed in black and had a very sexy voice, also he seemed very familiar to me. "It's about time that you girls headed home," he said. We didn't say anything. I could barely see his face because it was so dark, and there was some kind of veil covering him. Then I remembered the man that I saw at the foot of the stairs when I was twelve years old, and I knew it was him.

The park was well lit at night so there was no logical reason why I should not have been able to see him clearly, but I couldn't then he spoke to us again. "I see that you have been taught not to talk to strangers," he continued, "and that's a good thing." Drew and I began to leave the park then something he said startled me.

"I want both of you to get home right now," he said. "You know that your parents don't like you out on the streets at night because it's dangerous. You're supposed to be at your friend's house. Aren't you?" Quickly I turned around to face him but he was gone. I became frightened and I began to tremble all over.

"What's wrong with you, Celia?" asked Drew curiously. I looked at her strangely and when I did I realized something. She had neither seen nor heard the mysterious man. I began to tremble more and started walking faster toward home. "Are you alright, Celia?" asked my sister trying to keep up with me. "I'm fine," I lied. She noticed that I had suddenly become very quiet. "There *is* something wrong with you," she insisted. "What is it?" "Nothing," I lied again, "let's just hurry up and get home." "Okay," she replied eying me.

When we got home everything was quiet there. The light was turned on in our parent's bedroom so we knew they were home. "What's up with them I wonder," said Drew. I shrugged my shoulders. However, it was peculiar that they were at home that early at night during the end of the month. I knocked on their bedroom door because I wanted to talk to Mama about the stranger that I saw in the park. She opened her bedroom door.

"Mama," I said to her, "can I talk to you about something?" "Sure, honey," she said sweetly, "what's troubling you?" I told her about the man in the park. All she did was smile at me. But it was a smile that told me that she knew something that I didn't. And it was something that she would never tell me then she put her arm around my shoulders.

"Are you okay, sweetheart?" she asked me. "No," I replied, "he scared me." "Well, honey," said Mama, "it sounds to me like you really had nothing to worry about. He wasn't there to harm you or your sister. You see, it's just like I told you girls. It can be dangerous out there on the streets at night. You never know what might happen so it's best if you're safely inside the house. Right?" I nodded my head. Yet, I knew there was something that she wasn't telling me. I had no idea at the time, but I was destined to encounter the dark stranger again.

Our family members slept their days away no matter what time of the month it was. But it was only during the last ten days or so of each month when they went out at night, always returning home before the sun came up. Like a ritual when the sun went down in the evenings they would awaken, and they would spend a little time with Drew and I. However, they had more time for us during the first few weeks of the month when they stayed home at night.

During those times before Drew and I went to bed they would hold long conversations with us about anything that we wanted to talk about, anything but our family, or our heritage that is. They would play games with us, or we would listen to the radio together. And sometimes we would play records and dance. We would have regular parties with just my sister, Caroline, our family members and I. It was the only time that our household really seemed normal.

It was only during the end of the month that they had little time for Drew and I, because they were busy getting themselves ready to go out into the night any other time. Our parents always spent a little time with us regardless of what time of the month it was. But usually all of them were gone from our house not two hours after they awakened.

Now I was in the kitchen. I walked over to the window and looked outside. The rain was coming down harder and I could hardly see anything. All of the lights were off in the guest house so I gathered that Caroline was asleep. I was probably the only person in the whole town who couldn't sleep because of my fear. "Why am I so afraid of these things," I asked myself, "and nobody else in the family is?"

I tried to recall when my fear of thunder storms first began. Every time I did I would remember the night that our grandfather left us. There was a bad storm that night, too. And he had a lot of trouble with the law and with the people in the town, because of those missing people who were found dead after that terrible rain that occurred on the night before. Then another loud crack of lightning lit up the sky and I shuddered.

CHAPTER THREE

As I walked throughout the house I began thinking about the Baptist church down the street from where we lived. The former Pastor, Reverend Sam Daniels, and his wife, Miss Becka, used to be friendly with Drew and I. They were very nice people, too. Rebecca Daniels looked like she was a bit older than her husband. She looked like she might be in her late fifties, but he looked somewhat younger.

I guessed that he could not have been more than forty five years old. Neither one of them had a gray hair in their heads, although I suspected that Miss Becka dyed hers'. She was short and stout and he was a big, tall man. They didn't have any children, and they had lived in Hardelle for a long time.

The Daniels' were well liked by everybody in town. Drew and I met them one day while we were in the General Store, and we liked them both immediately. The Reverend became the Pastor of The Hardelle Baptist Church of Christ when the former Pastor, Reverend Lee Wheats, passed on. I heard that he was one hundred and one years old when he died in his sleep one night. It was hard for me to believe that he was still pastoring a church at that age. I never knew him personally, but people said he was in very good shape for a man his age.

Drew and I went to the General Store that day for Caroline, but we ended up buying a lot of junk for ourselves. After we paid for everything and ate it we remembered what Caroline sent us there for. Unfortunately we spent all of our money and some of hers', too. So we didn't have enough money left to pay for what she wanted.

Miss Becka and the Reverend were in the store at that time. I noticed how she had been watching my sister and I. We had a problem and I guess she could tell so she came over to us, and introduced herself. Then she asked us what was wrong so we explained our dilemma to her.

"Is that all?" she exclaimed smiling. "Well I have more than enough change in my purse so I can help you girls. Alright?" We nodded our heads all smiles then she opened her pocketbook, took out some change and gave it to us. We thanked her and were very grateful that she came to our rescue. "What are your names?" she wanted to know. "My name is Celia," I told her, "and this is my sister, Drew."

"Well," said Miss Becka, "I'm very glad to meet you both." After that her husband came over to us, introduced himself and started talking to us, too. He was a loud man but still very nice. Ever since that day every time they saw Drew and I they would stop and talk to us.

Through our conversations with the Daniels' we learned that the Reverend was Miss Becka's second husband, and they were married for twenty one years. She was a victim of domestic violence during her first marriage she confided in Drew and I. And she had no children from either one of her marriages. It was suspected that she couldn't have any children due to the horrible abuse that she suffered at the hands of her first husband. She told my sister and I all about the abuse, too.

Miss Becka told us that during her first marriage she was hospitalized forty seven times, and we were astonished! "How did you ever get away from that terrible man?" Drew asked her anxiously. "The last time he put me in the hospital," said Miss Becka, "I almost died. But I had some very good friends who helped me get away from him. They helped me with the divorce and with getting my life back together, too. That was nearly twenty five years ago." She chuckled softly. "I can look back now," she continued, "and laugh about it, because I was so timid and afraid to leave him. But it certainly wasn't funny at the time. I thank God for saving my life and for sending me a wonderful new husband."

For the life of me I couldn't imagine anybody mistreating her. In fact, I couldn't understand anybody treating another human being like she had been treated by her first husband. She showed Drew and I some of the scars that she had from that abuse, too. They were horrible ones.

The Daniels' invited my sister and I to services at their church. So we told them that we would come but we really didn't mean it. Then one Sunday morning out of the clear blue we decided to go to their church. The people in the congregation were very nice to us, and the service was nice, too. It may be hard to believe but Drew and I had never been to church before.

As far as we knew our family members had never set foot inside a church either. Our parents were married by a Justice of the Peace they told us, and so were our aunts and uncles, even our grandparents. None of them had ever been to church. It was another weird thing about our family that I added to a list of strange and oddball things I began to mentally prepare.

Drew and I were glad that we went to church that Sunday, and we ended up joining the congregation. Of course we were candidates for baptism. All of the members of the church congratulated us and hugged and kissed us because they were very happy for us. When our parents awakened that evening we told them all about it, but we certainly didn't expect them to react the way that they did.

They actually broke down and cried. At first by their reaction my sister and I thought we did something wrong, and Drew immediately tried to comfort them. She put her arms around both of them. But I was so shocked by the way they reacted I just stood there staring at them.

"Oh, Mama, Papa," cried my sister, "we're so sorry for upsetting you because we didn't mean to. Don't you worry. We won't go back there again and we won't let them baptize us either." Suddenly Papa looked at her and said, "The hell you won't!" Drew and I were taken aback and I know it showed on our faces. "We're happy that you're going to be baptized, darlings," said Mama calmly. "And it's something that we should've done for you a long time ago."

"Then why are you so upset?" I asked them confused. "We're not upset," said Papa, "we're ecstatic for you. We didn't think that you would want to go to church because we never took you, or talked to you about it." "You will never know how happy we are for both of you," added Mama. My sister and I were very bewildered by their behavior, to say the least.

We could understand them being happy for us, but to break down the way they did truly had us puzzled. It was as if something that they were hoping for but never thought they would see had happened for them. But I started to wonder, *"Why haven't they ever taken us to church?"*

Our parents told the rest of our family members about us joining church, and you would've thought that Drew and I had found some long lost treasure, or something. There was a lot of crying, hugging and kissing one another and us because they were overjoyed. They continued to celebrate by taking us to the movies that night. However, when we returned home they didn't hang around very long, and they all headed out of the front door, and into the night within minutes. *"Well,"* I thought, *"so much for that."*

Through Caroline our parents made sure that we attended church faithfully. They sent her shopping with us so we could buy a lot of new clothes and shoes, too. Yet, on the Sunday that Drew and I were baptized not one member of our family was there, only Caroline. We were very disappointed with them. We could tell by the look on Caroline's face that she knew how we felt, but there was nothing that she could have done about it.

Our family members never promised us that they would make an effort to be there so we couldn't get too disappointed with them. Still, I thought any parent would want to be present at their child's baptism. Yet, Drew and I had to keep reminding ourselves that our family members were a bit out of the ordinary. And they were not like other families in Hardelle, or anywhere else that we knew of for that matter.

Our family members may not have shown up but I did see the strange man again. I was standing in the pool of water with Reverend Daniels. The stranger was standing in the back of the church in the vestibule just before you entered the sanctuary. He was looking directly into my eyes, and smiling because I could see the smile on his lips.

He was still covered in that dark shadow that always accompanied him, too. When Reverend Daniels lifted me out of the water I looked to the back of the church again, but he was not there. It was then that I mentioned seeing him to Drew.

"Who is he I wonder?" she asked me. "I didn't see anybody back there." "I don't know who he is," I told her, "or why I am the only one who sees him." It was eerie but I tried not to let it bother me, and I didn't mention seeing him to my mother. Then we had a problem and I knew it was coming.

It wasn't long before the Daniels' wanted to meet our family, which is why we never joined any auxiliary in the church. All of the members of the auxiliaries knew everyone's family. It was the way they did things in any church I guessed. Also, it was why we hurried out of there as soon as the service was over on Sunday. I knew Miss Becka noticed how we never hung around after the service was over like the other members of the congregation did. Then one Sunday she was waiting outside on the church steps for us.

"Girls," she said, "the Reverend and I would like to come over to your house, and meet your family so we can invite them to services, too." I had just left the Lord's house but I had a lie all ready for her on my tongue. Yet, before I could say anything Drew answered her. "Sure, Miss Becka," she said, "I'll tell them tonight when they get up."

"Oh?" said Miss Becka with a funny look on her face. I knew by the questioning look on her face that she was wondering why our family members didn't get out of bed until evening. "They work at night," I lied looking into her eyes. "Oh I see," she said. Drew looked at me strangely with her eyebrows knitting together, then the Reverend joined us.

"Well, girls!" he said in his loud voice. He always talked a little loudly as if he might have a hearing problem, or something. I found out later on that he did because he was deaf in one ear. "Did Sister Daniels tell you that we want to meet your family? We've wanted to talk to you about it for a while now, but you're always out of here so fast after service on Sunday." "If it's alright with you girls," said Miss Becka, "we can come over tonight before they leave for work." "That's a wonderful idea!" exclaimed the Reverend. "What do you say, girls?!"

"Is it alright if we call you about it first?" asked Drew. "You sure can, honey," said Miss Becka. She wrote their address and telephone number on a piece of paper, and gave it to Drew. After that we said our good-byes and hurried down the street toward our house. "Why did you lie to her, Celia?" Drew asked me.

"Think about it, Drew," I said, "do you really think that our family wants to meet the Pastor and his wife? We're talking about people who have never entered a church in their lives. And people who sleep in darkened rooms all day and ramble the streets all night. They don't even want to meet any of our friends." "I don't see why not," she said. And she truly couldn't see anything wrong with them meeting our strange family.

I had a bad feeling about it in the pit of my stomach. I couldn't explain it and I don't know how I knew it, but it was not a good idea. It could've been the fact that our family didn't want anybody other than Caroline and us in our house day or night. I just couldn't understand what was going on with them.

They slept all day every day until the sun went down. Therefore, meeting them during the day time was out of the question. Although I couldn't put my finger on it, it just didn't feel like the right thing to do where the Daniels' were concerned. I had bad feelings about it but I kept them to myself. It was the beginning of a lesson that I would learn and practice, to always trust my instincts.

Drew was anxious and excited about asking our parents to meet the Daniels', and she couldn't wait until they awoke that evening. However, I didn't share her enthusiasm because I knew something wasn't quite right with our family members. Yet, I just didn't know what it was.

When we walked into the house that afternoon we smelled the wonderful aroma of the dinner that Caroline was preparing for us, and Drew told her about the Daniels' request. As long as I live I will never forget the way that she looked at my sister. It was as if she thought Drew had completely lost her mind. Then Caroline sat down in a chair.

"I don't think that's a good idea, girls," she told us. "Why not?" asked Drew. Caroline looked at us, and there was a solemn expression on her face. I could tell that there was something that she wanted to tell us but she couldn't. Because I had seen the same look on my mother's face many times.

"What is it, Caroline?" I asked her softly. She put her face in her hands and shook her head. "Caroline?" I asked again. She looked at Drew and I and her face was filled with concern. "It's not my place to tell you girls anything, or speak to you on any matter regarding your parents, and your other family members," she said, "unless they tell me to. So you'll have to discuss this with them." "Sure," said Drew. "Okay, Caroline," I replied. So we waited for our parents to awaken.

Just like clockwork that evening we heard them as well as the others moving about. "They're getting up," said Drew still excited. Then she noticed the look of concern on my face. "Are you okay, Celia?" she asked me. "Yeah," I said flatly, "fine." I followed her up the stairs. She didn't even let our parents get out of their bedroom before she burst into the room.

"Mama! Papa! Guess what?" she cried. "My, my," said Mama, "what's got you so stirred up, honey?" When Drew told them that our Pastor and his wife wanted to meet them their smiles vanished. "What's the matter?" my sister asked them when she saw their faces. It was Papa who spoke.

"I'm sorry, honey," he told Drew, "but we can't allow them to come here, and you know the rules." "But," said Drew, " this is our Pastor and his wife, Papa." I could see that she was becoming upset. So she turned around, and faced me pleading with her eyes for me to back her up. I didn't let her down. "Yeah," I said, "why can't you make an exception for once?" Drew smiled at me.

She felt that she had an ally and I could tell that our parents were taken by surprise. Because usually Drew was on her own when it came to challenging our parent's crazy rules. I believe they thought we were trying to gang up on them.

"The answer is NO!" said Papa harshly. He walked out of the bedroom after that and Mama stood there looking at us sympathetically. Drew and I looked back at her hoping that she would be on our side but she wasn't. "One day you'll understand why we can't do that, girls," she said softly. "No," cried Drew, "we'll never understand you!" She was very upset. "No wonder people treat us like we're from another planet or something! You're crazy and they think Celia and I are crazy, too!" Mama held her arms out to us, but Drew stormed out of their bedroom and I followed her.

Both of us were angry with our parents. However, I wasn't quite as angry as my sister was. *What are they so afraid of?* I wondered. Deep down in my heart I knew that our parents would have given anything to be able to say 'yes' to us that night. But for reasons that only they knew they couldn't. I knew their hearts were broken because of that.

For the next week my sister refused to talk to anybody in our house other than Caroline and I. But I remained civil to everyone since I wasn't as angry as she was. Yet, I never expected Drew to do what she did on the following Sunday. I didn't know anything about it because she never told me what she planned to do. But I knew that something was wrong because I could feel it.

Miss Becka usually stopped us after church service was over on Sunday. But that Sunday she only waved good-bye to us when the service was over. Then she went over to some other members of the church, and started talking to them. *"Good,"* I thought, *"she's not going to bother us today."* I should have known that something was wrong.

Drew who usually talked my ears off was very quiet that Sunday. She was still quiet that evening when our family members awakened. One by one they gathered in our living room like they usually did before they went out. My sister was talking to all of them by then, but with answers that only required a one or two word response. However, I could tell and so could they that she was still a little upset with them.

I hated to see our family members looking so forlorn. I could see the hurt in their eyes whenever they looked at Drew. She was angry with our aunts and uncles, too, because they always supported any decision that our parents made regarding us.

I could easily understand the hurt they must have been feeling. All of them gave love to my sister and I so freely. I often wondered where my sister inherited her bad temper from, and why it passed over me and went to her. She reminded me of Aunt Jada sometimes. *"Maybe it runs in the family on Mama's side,"* I thought.

Aunt Jada and Uncle Marcus wanted to play a game of cards with us that night, but Drew refused to play so I played with them. My sister was reading a book. It was one that we had read so many times that we knew it by heart. Therefore, I knew she wasn't really interested in it. Suddenly a noise that was rarely ever heard in our house startled me, not only me but everybody else in the house, too. It was the doorbell.

Everyone looked at one another in surprise. However, nobody moved to answer the front door. Finally Caroline made a move to see who it was, but Drew was a little faster than she was. "Come on in," we heard her tell the person at the front door. "Hello! How are you?!" Reverend Daniels said in his loud voice. "Hi, Drew," said Miss Becka.

They came with Bibles, Communion wine and wafers. I was shocked! But it was nothing compared to the looks on the faces of our family members and Caroline. If I hadn't known better I could have sworn that every one of them, except Caroline, was scared to death.

Our family members stared in the direction of the front door waiting. *"They look like they're scared to death,"* I thought as I looked into each one of their faces. It was not my imagination either because they were scared! My two aunts were sitting next to our parents, but our uncles hastily retreated to the basement.

I knew Drew could be daring, but I never would have thought she would challenge our parent's authority the way she did that night. I found out later on that she had telephoned the Daniels', and told them it was alright if they wanted to come over to our house that night. They stood on the front porch until Drew closed the front door. "Come on inside," she told them.

The minute that Miss Becka stepped into our living room that night she became ill. It was so sudden that I got frightened for her and so did Drew. She became nauseous at first then she dropped the Bible that she was holding, and grabbed her head with both of her hands. "Oh, my God! My God!" she cried as if she was in terrible pain. Reverend Daniels could hardly keep her on her feet. Even he put his hand to one side of his head once as if he felt pain there. "I'm so sorry, folks," he said quietly. I had never heard him speak that softly since I met him.

"I don't understand this," he said," we were both fine a moment ago." In the meantime poor Miss Becka was getting more and more pale. She began to sweat profusely, she couldn't talk and her eyes were wide open with fear. "I'm really sorry for this," Reverend Daniels said to our family again. Drew and I did not understand what was happening to them, and nobody in our family said a word.

To make matters worse not one of them got up to help poor Miss Becka. They just sat there and watched as she became horribly sick right before our eyes. "We'd better go now," said the Reverend turning around and heading toward our front door to leave. Finally he got Miss Becka to their car and to mine and Drew's astonishment she seemed to get better once she left our house. My sister and I walked over to the passenger side of their car where she was sitting.

Before they drove away Miss Becka was able to speak again. "I'm s-so s-sorry, girls," she said to my sister and I as we stood there beside their car. She could hardly breathe. "I'm b-burning up! I-I don't know what came over m-me in there, please forgive me." "It's okay, Miss Becka," I said, "you better go home and lay down." "I-I sure will, honey," she replied. She unbuttoned her blouse at the top almost exposing her breasts. She laid her head against the passenger's seat and closed her eyes.

The Reverend opened the car door on the driver's side to get in. He couldn't seem to apologize to us enough. "We really did want to meet you folks tonight," he said looking past Drew and I as we stood there. He was speaking to someone behind us. "We're so sorry," he said again. We didn't know Aunt Margeaux was standing there until we turned around to see who he was talking to.

My aunt was standing behind us on the front stoop staring at Miss Becka. Drew and I looked at her as the Reverend looked at her strangely. We saw the expression that was on his face before he got into his car to drive away. There was only one way to describe a look like that. It was terror and it was easy to see that he could not wait to get away from our house. We knew he would not be coming back again. Drew and I had never seen such a horrifying look in Aunt Margeaux's eyes before, and it was truly terrifying!

After the Daniels' left Drew and I went back up the steps to go inside the house. Aunt Margeaux was still standing there staring at the back of their car as they drove away. "Are you alright, Aunt Margeaux?" Drew asked her, but she didn't answer her. I don't even think she heard my sister talking to her. My mother came outside, took my aunt by the arm and almost had to drag her back inside the house.

"Good grief!" cried Drew. "What the hell is wrong with her, Celia?" "Did you see her eyes, Drew?" I asked. "I sure did," she replied. We would never forget the way that my aunt looked at Miss Becka. She almost didn't look human anymore. Her light, brown eyes had turned so red that they looked like two pools of blood, and her countenance had changed completely. She looked evil and threatening. For the first time in our lives my sister and I were afraid in our own house. I think our parents knew it, too, and so did the others. Somehow Drew and I knew that our aunt had not meant for us to see her like that.

When we went back inside the house we didn't say anything to anybody. We just went straight upstairs to our bedroom. To our surprise our parents said nothing to my sister about what she did. We had seen Aunt Margeaux looking like some kind of demon from the pit of hell so what my sister did was the least of their worries. That night my sister and I did something that we never did before. We locked our bedroom door.

A few minutes later Mama knocked on our bedroom door. She called to us, too, as she turned the knob to enter our bedroom, but we didn't answer her. Our bedroom door was locked so she knew that we didn't want to be bothered. After a while we heard her go back downstairs.

Drew and I knew they were downstairs talking about us because our aunt allowed us to see something that night that she should not have. I don't know how I knew that but I did. And it was something that would haunt us for a while, too. "Celia," said Drew as we laid awake most of that night, "she really looked like a monster." I couldn't have put it better than that. "Why do you think her eyes turned like that?" asked my sister. I didn't have a clue and I told her so. We kept our bedroom door locked that night and for many nights after that, too.

Our parents were hurt by that but we could not forget our aunt's horrifying, red eyes. We kept seeing those terrible eyes in our heads every day for weeks after that, too. I tried my best to convince myself and my sister that we were being silly, but it didn't work. We knew Aunt Margeaux loved us dearly and that she would never harm us. It was just the fact that we had never seen anything like that before. It took us both a long time to get to sleep that particular night, too. And for that reason we didn't wake up until one o'clock on the following afternoon.

Caroline didn't awaken us for school that morning. I guess she realized how upset we were about seeing Aunt Margeaux's terrifying, red eyes on the night before. I think she knew we had a lot of trouble getting to sleep all night so she left us alone that morning. Of course our parents had a hand in that decision. Caroline never did anything concerning Drew and I without their approval first.

That following afternoon Drew and I got up, bathed and dressed then we went downstairs to see what Caroline had fixed for lunch. She was sitting at the kitchen table reading the newspaper. So I looked in each pot that she had on the stove to see what was in them. Suddenly, I heard a glass crash to the floor and break. It splattered and a piece of it stung me on my leg so I turned around quickly to see what happened. "Oh, no!" cried Drew. "Oh, no, no!"

She had gotten a glass from the cupboard, and the orange juice from the ice box, and both were all over the kitchen floor. Caroline started to clean up the mess. Drew dropped the glass and the juice when she saw the photographs in the newspaper that was laying open on the kitchen table. I followed her stunned gaze. There near the top of the page were the photographs of Reverend Daniels and Miss Becka. The headline over their pictures read: "PREACHER AND WIFE SLAUGHTERED INSIDE THEIR HOME". Drew sat down in a chair and so did I. We were shocked beyond belief because it was so unbelievable. Caroline said nothing as she held us in her arms.

The Daniels' were murdered in their beds some time during the wee hours of that morning. A nephew of theirs' who came to visit that morning found them. One phrase of the story under the headline stuck in my head and would not go away. I heard it over and over again in my mind for weeks after that, and until well after the Daniels' funerals. "TORN APART AS IF BY AN ANIMAL". *"Why do they always say that?"* I thought, because there were no wild animals where we lived. The Associate Pastor, Reverend Bernard Dykes, took over the congregation of the church after that. But Drew and I never went back there anymore.

CHAPTER FOUR

A powerful flash of lightning followed by more thunder jarred me from my reverie. Now I was in the den so I turned on the light. Then I went into the living room and turned that light on, too. "I guess I'll read a book," I said to myself, "since I can't get back to sleep."

"Couldn't sleep huh, sweetie?" I nearly jumped to the ceiling I was so startled! "Oh, honey, I'm sorry. I didn't mean to scare you anymore than you already are." It was Caroline, and she was sitting there in the dark smoking a cigarette. I was so preoccupied with my thoughts that I hadn't even smelled the cigarette smoke. There was a glass of whiskey in her other hand, although she rarely drank alcoholic beverages.

"What are you doing here?" I asked her. "I thought you would be in the guest house." She looked at me and smiled. "Why don't you let me fix you some warm milk, Celia, honey?' she asked me sweetly. "It will help you get to sleep." "Okay," I replied. So I followed her into the kitchen.

"I thought you would be scared by the storm," said Caroline, "so I came over in case you woke up." "I guess I'll always be afraid of thunderstorms," I told her. "No you won't, sweetheart," she said comfortingly, "you'll grow out of it. " She sounded just like Aunt Margeaux. "I'm glad that tomorrow is Saturday," continued Caroline, "you don't have anywhere to go, and you can sleep as late as you want to. I'll see that you're not disturbed." I knew she would do just that.

Caroline was like a 'watch person' for our family for lack of better words. She watched over the others as they slept during the day time, and she took care of Drew and I. We didn't think she ever slept. Her lovely face was the last one that we saw before we went to bed at night, and the first one that we saw in the morning when we awoke.

I looked out of the kitchen window while she fixed the warm milk for me. The whole town was dark except for the lights on the streets, and one other house where all of the lights were on. *"It's probably somebody like me,"* I thought, *"who can't get to sleep because of the storm."*

Hardelle was a quiet place. I never bothered to find out how many people lived there, but I don't think it was more than eighty five hundred. Only our house and one other house in the area that was three blocks away stood by itself, and the rest were mainly twin houses. The people were mostly upper middle class. However, there were some well-to-do families.

The people in Hardelle were for the most part friendly, and many of them had lived there for a long time. Some of them moved away at one time, but they returned when they found out how it was living in the big cities. I could hardly wait until I graduated from school. Because I was leaving Hardelle and I wasn't coming back because I wanted to see for myself how it was living in the big city.

I never said that to my family anymore after the few times that I told them that, and it hurt their feelings. I did not want to upset them. Still, I planned to leave there after graduation because I wanted to see how it was living on my own for a while.

Hardelle had everything that any other small town had including crime. Not only the Daniels' were massacred inside their home, but another family was slaughtered in the same way. The whole town went into shock over that terrible tragedy, and all over Hardelle people were scared after that. Nobody hardly ventured out alone at night the way they used to before the murders, that is no one except our family.

There was a lot of pressure on Sheriff Tom Jackson to find the killer or killers of those people. But neither he nor his Deputies knew what direction to go in, and the murderer never left any clues, not even a fingerprint.

It was the Mackrey family. They were nice people, too, and everybody in town liked them. Andy Mackrey was eight years old, and he delivered newspapers. But he had a twin brother named, Alvin who stayed in trouble. Their parents considered putting him away after they woke up one night, and he was standing over them with a butcher's knife in his hand. He was always in fights, and he would pick up anything that was handy to hurt you with.

One day Alvin took his father's gun to school and shot a teacher. The reason he said he did it was because the teacher gave him a detention for being late to class. He was always late. The teacher was shot in the leg, and went back to work after he got better. But Alvin was sent to reform school. Their sisters, Mavis, who was fifteen years old, and, Cynda, who was thirteen years old worked as volunteers at the local hospital. Also, they regularly visited the elderly people in Hardelle, too, and would stop by their homes to run errands for them.

Their mother, Brenda, and their father, Charlie, were always working in the five churches in Hardelle, or involved in something to improve the town. They tried to make things better for people who were in need, or had a hard time making ends meet. So Brenda and Charlie Mackrey organized a committee that arranged for whole families to be able to eat, or pay their bills when breadwinners were out of work, or too sick to work for a while. They called it "The Community Basket". Also, they set up a food distribution drive twice a week.

"The Community Basket" was like a fund that the people in Hardelle contributed money, food and clothing to once every month, and everybody participated in it. When a family fell on hard times, like so many people had lately, they could always turn to The Community Basket for help for as long as their hardship lasted. It was a wonderful thing that helped many families, and even our family contributed to it because they had to.

It didn't matter if they never bothered with the people in the town, which they didn't, or if they ever needed it. It was part of the arrangement that the committee had set up with everyone. It was a very good idea because it helped so many people who had fallen victim to the politics of the day. Furthermore, no one ever knew when they themselves might need it.

Another thing that Brenda and Charlie Mackrey did in Hardelle was to organize the older members of the town into committees that chaperoned dances for the teenagers. We had The Hardelle Teen

Center which was a place where children, and teenagers could go when there was nothing for them to do.

It was set up by the Mackreys with donations from the well-to-do families in Hardelle. They held dances there, played games such as pool, tennis, backgammon, chess, basketball and other games. They also had a big indoor swimming pool that was open all year round. Sometimes the Chaperones would bring in a great book to read to us, books for teenagers as well as children's books for the children.

Drew and I went to the Teen Center almost every weekend. Especially on the weekends that came near the end of the month, which was when we were left by ourselves a lot, and we would get tired of having only Caroline to talk to.

Lana Mackrey was the oldest of the Mackrey children, and my best friend. We would meet each other every morning on our way to school. It would be Drew and I, and Lana and her sister, Mavis. I was a grade behind other students my age. So Lana, who was a year younger than me, was in the same grade that I was. I missed her so much. She was the only real friend that I ever had outside of my sister, and Caroline up to that point in my life.

When I told Lana that Drew and I couldn't spend the night at anybody's house and why she understood. "Some parents are like that, Celia," she told me. "Don't worry about it. They love you and they do things like that because they don't trust other people around their children." She was so understanding. I had put off telling her about the weird rules that Drew and I had to live by every time she asked us to spend the night with her and Mavis. Finally, I told her the truth.

I could tell Lana lots of things, things that I did not want anybody else to know, not even Drew. She shared things with me, too. She told me about her Uncle Lewis who was her Dad's younger brother. And how he had been molesting Alvin from the time that he was four years old. But they didn't find out about it until Alvin was seven years old, and had the courage to tell his parents about it. "No wonder that kid has serious problems," I told Lana after she confided in me.

She and I felt that Alvin needed to have psychiatric counseling, but all her parents wanted to do was keep it quiet. Lana and I thought that was a terrible mistake because Alvin definitely needed some kind of therapy. After the incident at school with the teacher the State authorities stepped in and took Alvin away from them. Lana was happy about that. "Maybe now he'll get the help that he needs," she said. Needless to say, not only did they take Alvin away from them, but Uncle Lewis was prosecuted for what he did, and got a ten year prison sentence. I felt that he should have gotten more time than that and so did Lana.

There were many nights when Lana and I would be on the telephone for hours. Caroline thought I was in bed asleep and her parents thought she was asleep, too. It caused us a lot of headaches if we had to go to school the next day. We would be running late and tired and sleepy all that day.

Lana was a little stout and average height. She had short, curly, black hair and light gray eyes. I guess you could say she was average-looking. She was well liked in our school and in the town. I rarely ever saw her get angry about anything. She was always calm, polite and friendly. There were many times that she wanted to meet my parents. But she knew from all that I told her about them it wasn't possible. However, she accepted Drew and I for who we were as did her sister, Mavis.

Lana was out on a date with a guy named, Jimmy Seevers, on the night that her entire family was murdered. She and I had made plans earlier in that week to go to the movies that night, and I told my parents about it. Also, I told them that I would be home after midnight because it was a late show. When Lana canceled out at the last minute I was disappointed. However, I knew how much she liked Jimmy. She had been waiting for him to ask her out for a long time, and he was one of the most popular guys in our school, and truly very nice.

Naturally I had to tell my parents about the change in our plans. Mama looked as disappointed as I felt. "So Lana's going to be home tonight?" she asked me. "No," I replied, "she has a date with a guy that she likes who goes to our school." "Why that's great!" she cried. I didn't want my imagination to get the best of me, but I could have sworn that she looked and sounded relieved.

"Well," said Mama, "since Lana has a date don't you think that you're overdue, honey?" I looked at her. I knew she and Papa wanted my sister and I to go out on dates like other girls our age did. But it was no big deal to us. Besides, as soon as we told a guy that he couldn't come over to our house after dark they left us alone anyway, and who could blame them? It was crazy and just as Drew said they thought we were crazy, too. "I'm not interested in anybody right now," I told my mother. She smiled at me. Strangely, after that I felt very depressed.

Mama had an uncanny ability to know when Drew and I were feeling badly. So she put her arms around me, and held me tightly pressing her face against my hair. Since the day that I lashed out at my parents, telling them that I was leaving home when I finished school, they went out of their way to shower my sister and I with more love and affection, if that was possible. She hugged me so hard I squirmed uncomfortably in her arms. Our parent's strength astounded us. Mama let me go tenderly stroking my hair.

"When you're ready," she said lovingly, "you'll have more dates than you can handle, you'll see." *"You're right,"* I thought, *"until they find out how weird my family is."* I thought about Lana again.

Her parents, grandparents, her brother Andy, and her sisters were all killed on that horrifying night. We heard that there were body parts all over the Mackrey home, and Lana was the one who came home from her date with Jimmy and found them. I don't think anybody in Hardelle will ever forget her terrifying screams which were heard for blocks. People who were awakened by her screaming came running to her house from all directions that night.

After those horrific killings nobody in Hardelle felt safe anymore, and everyone feared that the killer, or killers would never be caught. According to the town newspaper every one of Lana's family members were torn apart as if by some wild animal. That phrase was always used whenever the news people described murders that occurred in the towns where our family and I lived no matter how unbelievable it was. What kind of wild animals would do that to people?

Lana was so torn up about the tragedy that she had to be hospitalized. In fact, she remained in the hospital for quite a while. After a couple of weeks she started to talk about the murders a little. I would visit her at least twice a week after school. When it first happened all she did when I came to see her was stare into space, or she would break down and start sobbing suddenly. I felt so sorry for her because she and her family had helped so many people. Yet, nobody could help her, or Alvin who was still away in reform school. Neither one of them made it to the funerals.

The Nurses at the hospital told me that Lana needed time to come through the horrible tragedy on her own, and there was nothing that anybody could really do to help her. When they decided that she was ready to be released from the hospital she went to live with her father's sister, Jennifer, who also lived in Hardelle. Jennifer was devastated by the murders, too. However, she knew she had to be strong for Lana's and Alvin's sakes. Caroline finished fixing the warm milk for me.

"Here you are, honey," she said giving me the cup of warm milk. "You drink all of this and you'll sleep like a baby. I promise." I took the cup of warm milk and sipped it. But there was something that I tasted in it, and I didn't know what it was. "Did you put something in this, Caroline?" I asked her. "Yes, honey," she replied, "it's an old, secret recipe that I learned at the orphanage many years ago. It will help you sleep."

I sat down in a chair in the living room by the window. A loud crack of lightning lit up the sky, and I shuddered as I moved away from the window. Caroline put her arm around my shoulders. "Don't be afraid, sweetie," she said guiding me over to the couch. "It's just God's Way of letting us know that He's still in charge of things down here." She chuckled softly. I wondered how my sister could sleep through such a terrible storm like that one, and how our family members could be outside in it.

"You know, honey," said Caroline, "when I was a young girl in the orphanage the Matrons there would make us turn off all of the lights, and radios whenever there was a storm like this one. We had to sit down in one spot and be quiet until it was over, or just go to bed." "Why?" I asked her. I could feel my eyes getting heavier and heavier and I never did hear her answer to my question. When I awakened I was in my bed, and it was nearly two o'clock in the afternoon.

"It's about time that you woke up," said Drew. "What are you trying to do sleep the whole day away? Do you know what time it is, Celia?" She was sitting on the side of my bed. "Are you alright?" she asked me. "I'll bet you were up all night again scared. Weren't you?" That was my sister. I wasn't even fully awake yet and already she was talking my ears off. I guess she was like that because all we had most of the time was each other to talk to.

"Caroline fixed me some warm milk last night," I told her, "or rather I should say this morning. She mixed some secret recipe of hers' in it to help me sleep, and before I knew it I was out like a light. I don't even know how I got to bed." I looked down at my bed as if it was some strange thing that I had never seen before. "Uncle Wilhelm brought you up here," said Drew. "I saw him around dawn."

"Is everyone else at home?" I asked her. I must've been a little groggy from the warm milk to ask such a silly question. The expression on my sister's face confirmed that. "Where else are they going to be, Celia?" she asked me. "Are you joking? You know they're here."

She pondered something for a minute then said, "I wonder where they go every night during the last eight, or ten days of the month." "I don't know, Drew," I told her. "We'll probably never know that." "We should follow them one night," she continued. "That way we can see for ourselves where they go, and what they do all night." I didn't realize how serious she was, but the night would come when we would follow them.

My instincts warned me. I don't know what came over my sister and I on that night and I don't think I ever will know. I should've stopped Drew but my own curiosity had taken control of me. I wish that somebody, or someone would've stopped us, something or someone that would've made us stop and think before we acted.

I called it my instincts but it was common sense trying its' best to get through to me. I know that I could've been the stronger one and insisted that we didn't follow our family members on that fateful night. My sister and I saw something, and it was something that would be burned into our memories for the rest of our lives. A horror that we would never break free of no matter how hard we tried.

CHAPTER FIVE

It was a beautiful, sunny afternoon. I listened as Drew continued to talk to me, and she was still talking to me as I went into the bathroom. I was always happy that our house had partial, indoor plumbing because a lot of people we knew didn't. When I came out of the bathroom she was still talking. I started to get dressed and I could hear Caroline downstairs in the kitchen. Whatever she was cooking smelled delicious, and she was an excellent cook. She tried to teach my sister and I how to cook but we were never interested in learning.

Drew followed me as I looked in on our parents who were sleeping like babies. As usual their bedroom was so dark we could hardly see them lying there. Aunt Margeaux and Aunt Jada were sleeping soundly, too, when we looked in on them. "So," said Drew, "what do you want to do today, Celia?" "I haven't any idea," I replied, "the day is almost over anyway." "Let's go down to the Center and see what's going on down there," she suggested. "Alright," I replied.

I really didn't feel like being bothered with anybody that day, not even her. But she insisted that we get out of the house together. I knew that if I had said 'no' and stayed home she would have stayed home, too, and talked my ears off all day. I loved my sister dearly but I just wanted to be alone.

"How did you sleep, honey?" Caroline asked me as Drew and I entered the kitchen. "I fell asleep so fast," I told her. "What did you put in that warm milk you gave me?" "Ah-h-h," she said, "I'll never tell." She smiled slyly. "What's for lunch, Caroline?" asked Drew. "I made some beef stew, and some homemade rolls, honey," she told Drew. "Are you hungry?" "Yeah," replied Drew. "Me, too," I said. "Well," said Caroline, "sit down and I'll fix you some." We sat down at the kitchen table as Caroline fixed our plates, and the stew was delicious.

Drew and I devoured the beef stew as well as the homemade rolls. Suddenly my sister asked Caroline, "Why don't Mama, Papa and the others ever sit down to eat, Caroline?" Caroline was surprised by her question, and so was I. I don't think she knew what to say, but secretly it was something I had been wondering about myself.

"What makes you think they never sit down to eat anything, honey?" Caroline asked Drew. It was I who said, "Well, they don't." "It's just that you girls have never seen them when they're eating," replied Caroline. "Oh come on, Caroline," said Drew, "as long as we've been in this world Celia and I have never seen them eating anything. Don't you think at some point in our lives we would?" Caroline got up from the table calmly. She walked over to the kitchen sink, and began washing some dishes. "Caroline?" asked Drew puzzled.

Suddenly Caroline turned around to face us, and there was an expression of anger on her face. Drew and I had never seen her angry before. "Now you two listen to me very carefully," she said softly holding back her anger, "no two children have more love on the face of this earth than you two do. But all you ever do is gripe and bitch about all of the faults that your parents, your aunts and your uncles have. From now on any questions that you have regarding your family members you will address to them not me. Do you understand?"

Drew started to say something but Caroline cut her off. "I said..... do you understand?" she asked us again. We nodded our heads too scared to open our mouths. Then she turned around and began to finish washing the dishes in the sink.

Needless to say we were taken aback by Caroline's anger at us. It was something we had never experienced from her before. But we would learn in the future that her anger was not directed at us. It was anger at our family members, and rightly so. Because any questions that my sister and I had should have been answered by them not her. She had a right to be angry.

Drew and I got up from the table after we finished our meal, and were ready to leave the kitchen. "I'm sorry, Caroline," said my sister. I apologized to her, too. We had no right to put her in the position that we had. Yet, as far as us not seeing our family members eating Caroline didn't lie to us. However, it would be a while before we learned the true meaning of what she said.

Before we left the kitchen we put our arms around Caroline to hug her. She smiled weakly. We knew that we had upset her. "We're going to go down to the Center," I told her, "so we'll see you later." She didn't say anything but continued to smile at us as she washed the dishes. I wasn't sure but I thought I saw tears in her eyes. I figured that she would tell our family members about our questioning her when they awakened. Drew and I left the house and headed down the street to the Teen Center.

"I don't think we should ask Caroline anymore questions about them. Do you, Celia?" Drew asked me. "No," I replied, "I don't think so either." We tried for a long time to keep our curiosity to ourselves. But it was only a matter of time before we went to Caroline again with more questions.

When we arrived at the Center that afternoon it was very crowded. It looked like every child and teenager in town was there, and we saw a few faces we had never seen before. "I wonder where they're from?" whispered Drew, nodding toward a group of unfamiliar faces. As if they heard her two girls in the group turned around and looked at us. Then they walked over to where we were standing.

"Hi," said one of them cheerfully, "my name is Lila Birch, and this is my sister, Dara." She and her sister shook hands with Drew and I. I could tell right away that Lila was very outgoing, but Dara was more laid back. "Hi," I said, "my name is Celia Bellis and this is my sister, Drew." "We're happy to meet both of you," said Lila smiling. "Same here," I told her returning her smile. Neither Drew nor Dara said much of anything, and I think that they were 'sizing' one another up.

Lila was not what you would call pretty but she certainly wasn't unattractive either. She was a little shorter than I was, and she had dark brown eyes, sandy brown hair and a fair complexion. Her personality was a bubbly one that Drew and I liked immediately. Dara on the other hand was gorgeous. She was tall like Mama and our aunts, and she had big, dark brown eyes and dark brown hair that was frosted with an ash blond color, and her complexion was fairly dark like our Aunt Margeaux's.

I didn't know why but I got the impression that Dara was very distrusting of people for some reason. She was just the opposite of Lila, very quiet. It seemed like she was lost in her own thoughts, things that she couldn't share with anybody else. Yet, she and Lila were very nice and it wasn't long before we became good friends.

Drew and I learned through our conversation with them that Lila was a year younger than I was, and Dara was a year younger than her. They enrolled in the same school that Drew and I attended. Their parents were recently divorced, and their father had legal custody of them. After the divorce they moved to Hardelle where Mr. Birch grew up. They had been living in Hardelle for seven days, and had just finished unpacking, and getting their house in order on the afternoon that Drew and I met them.

One day when the four of us were at the Teen Center one of the Chaperones brought in a book to read to all of the teenagers there. Most of the Chaperones were excellent readers and story tellers, too. The book was a scary one and very good. The entire time Drew, who was rarely ever quiet, said nothing and neither did Dara. They were completely absorbed into the story just like the rest of us were. It was a first believe me since my big, brave sister who feared nothing hated scary stories. If they were really good like that one was it scared the shit out of her. I knew that night she would be the one who would be up all night scared.

The story was about a serial killer in a small town who turned out to be a monster in every sense of the word. When it was over Lila and Dara invited us out for pizza. On our way to the restaurant we talked about the book.

"Wasn't that horrible how that woman murdered all of those people?" asked Lila excitedly. "It sure was," I replied. "How could anybody be so wicked and evil?" "I remember something like that," she told me. "It was a long time ago in the town that we moved away from, and our aunt was one of the victims, too." "Wow!" I cried. "Where did you move away from?" "A place not far from here called Wesbury," she answered.

"Wesbury?!" cried Drew surprised. I was surprised, too. "Yeah," said Lila, "do you know it?" "That's where we came from, too," replied my sister. "Then you must remember all of those killings that happened there around ten years ago," said Lila. "No," replied Drew, "what killings?" Of course she didn't remember them but I did.

"Do you recall any killings happening there, Celia?" asked Drew curiously. "I remember a little bit about them," I replied. "Why didn't you ever tell me about them?" she wanted to know. "I don't know, Drew," I said. "I guess I just forgot." "I don't know how you could forget something like that," replied Dara. "Well," said Drew to me, "tell me what you remember, Celia." "Nothing much," I lied to her.

The truth was that I recalled a lot about those murders in Wesbury, especially that our grandfather was accused of being the killer. I remembered the night that he left us, too, but I didn't tell them that. "Well," said Drew, "tell me what you do remember, Celia." "I don't recall that much about them, Drew, " I said becoming irritated. "Okay," she said. "Why are you getting so hostile about it?" I didn't say anything else about what happened in Wesbury and I hoped that Lila and Dara wouldn't either. Then we arrived at the small pizza shop.

We sat down in one of the booths in the restaurant and ordered a large pizza and some sodas. During our conversation the subject turned to the boys in town, then we talked about our families. When Lila and Dara told us about their parents it was a horror story from start to finish. After hearing their story Drew and I began to realize how blessed we were. Our family members may have been strange, but we always knew how much they loved and adored us.

They told us that their father was a Dentist. But he rarely practiced because he was usually too drunk. Also, they told us that he acted like he didn't care about anything anymore, and that they were practically raising themselves. At first I couldn't understand why any judge gave him sole custody of Lila and Dara. But after they told us about their mother we understood completely.

Since the two girls were old enough to understand her their mother let them know that she never wanted any children. Every chance she got she told them what a mistake they both were, and how they had ruined her life. Drew and I thought that was terrible, and we couldn't imagine our mother saying something like that to us. They told us that their mother had one love affair after another during the course of their parent's marriage.

Eventually their father found out from one of their neighbors what was going on behind his back. As soon as he left for work in the morning, and the two girls left for school, whatever current boyfriend their mother had at the time slipped into the back door of their home. Drew and I were even more flabbergasted when they told us that she sold Dara into prostitution. She wanted to buy one of her men a leather jacket that he wanted for his birthday, but she didn't have the money because their father accounted for every penny spent in their household. So she used Dara to get the extra money that she needed.

The man raped Dara repeatedly during a week when she was home from school sick. She was thirteen years old at the time. When Dara ended up getting pregnant their mother got rid of the baby, and Dara nearly died. She threatened Dara not to tell her father or she would kill her. Yet, all of this came out during the divorce proceedings anyway. "God," I said, "if our mother thought someone was trying to hurt one of us she would kill them, and so would our father." I didn't know at the time just how true my words really were. Lila and Dara continued to tell us their story.

Their mother's name was, Annabelle, and after seventeen years of marriage filled with one love affair after another she started sneaking around with the next door neighbor. Dr. Birch didn't know that anything was going on between the two of them for a long time, and neither did the neighbor's wife. What hurt the most was that the four of them had been good friends.

Often they went out to dinner together, they had a Pinochle club they were all in, and they had cook-outs together. All of that time their mother and the neighbor's husband were screwing each other's brains out. When the neighbor and Dr. Birch both turned up with a venereal disease neither one of them wanted to acknowledge how they got it.

I could understand Dr. Birch not wanting to believe that his wife had given him a sexually transmitted disease. But I figured the neighbor got just what he deserved. In fact, Lila and Dara told us that his wife nearly left him because of it when she ended up getting it, too. To me, according to all that they told us, it sounded like the man's wife suspected that something was going on between her husband and Annabelle all along.

At a party one night at the neighbor's house Dr. Birch happened to go to the washroom, and that's when he caught his wife and the neighbor making out in one of the bedrooms. Before that discovery Dr. Birch was already getting drunk on the weekends, and crying on everybody's shoulder about his sister, Selma Ann. After he found his wife and the neighbor in bed together he started getting drunk every day. Sometimes he went on drinking binges for days at a time, then he would dry out for a while.

It was Annabelle who initiated the divorce proceedings Lila told us. "Boy, did she have a lot of nerve!" said Drew disgustedly. In spite of all that she had done they told us that their father did not want a divorce. He was willing to try to work things out with their mother, but she didn't want him anymore. I didn't say anything, but to me it sounded like she never wanted him in the first place.

"He must have loved her very much," I said to Lila and Dara. "I guess," said Dara. The neighbor's wife wasn't so understanding in the end. She filed for divorce without hesitation after Dr. Birch told her what had been going on, and she left Wesbury after that, too. Annabelle had the audacity to move into the neighbor's house. I couldn't believe it. They ended up getting married as soon as their divorces were finalized.

Subsequently, a terrible scandal erupted in Wesbury over the illicit affair. Therefore, Dr. Birch, to protect Lila and Dara, decided to return to his hometown of Hardelle. Their mother and her new husband remained in Wesbury and chose to ride out the scandal. Drew and I thought Annabelle was a wicked woman. Lila and Dara told us that they didn't care if she lived or died.

She never bothered to telephone them, or asked to see them. "We don't care if we ever see or hear from her ever again in life," said Dara angrily. *"How awful!"* I thought. But Drew and I would have felt the same way if we had been in their shoes. Anybody would have understood how those two girls felt about their mother, if you wanted to call that a 'mother'.

Dr. Birch's sister, Selma Ann, was only twenty one years old when she was murdered Lila told us. She was their father's only sister and he had no brothers. Dara told us that Selma Ann was very pretty, and that she looked a lot like her. She lived with them in Wesbury, and they recalled how much she loved them and how she liked to have fun. "Before she was killed," said Lila, "she told us about this new boyfriend that she had. After four years of being with a guy who beat her up all of the time we were glad that she found somebody nice."

"He was an older guy," said Dara, "and she thought he really cared about her. She told us that he was really nice to her, too. Evidently he had money because he would buy her expensive gifts." "We never did get to meet him though," said Lila. "Every time we thought we would meet him he would always come up with some kind of excuse why he couldn't meet us." "He was a night person," added Dara, "because she never saw him during the day time." I didn't say anything but I thought that was very curious. I don't know why but suddenly I remembered how Caroline told my sister and I that she met our grandfather.

We sat in the pizza parlor that evening talking about ourselves, and our families. Drew and I felt sorry for Lila and Dara because of all of the horrible things they had been through. We felt sorry for their father, too. On top of dealing with the death of his sister he had to cope with a wife who was obviously rotten to the core. When Drew and I told them about our family they thought we were making it all up. We knew it was hard to believe that people could be that strange. In spite of that they told us they would have gladly traded places with us.

"Maybe Caroline is right after all," I thought. Drew and I spent so much time bitching and griping about our parent's rules and our family's strange ways. We failed to appreciate the fact that we had never known abuse of any kind. All we ever got from any of them was love and affection. It was something for us to be thankful for instead of complaining about all of the time.

Suddenly Drew got very quiet and I knew that she was thinking about our family just as I was. At that moment I wanted to run home, and throw my arms around all of them and never let go. We wouldn't have traded our family for anything on earth. Yet, we were destined to have more run-ins with our parents. It was beginning to get dark and time for my sister and I to get home. So we walked Lila and Dara home then went home ourselves.

When my sister and I got home that evening our family members had already gone out for the night. I thought we would get into trouble with them for questioning Caroline earlier that day. But we never heard anything about it because Caroline hadn't mentioned anything to them about what happened. We discovered that we had a true friend in Caroline Saunders that day, and she would be loyal to Drew and I until the day that she left us forever.

CHAPTER SIX

The first time that Drew and I went to Lila's and Dara's house to visit them their father was drunk. Dr. Allan Birch was a fairly young man but he looked much older than he was. He was a good Dentist they told us. However, because of all of his problems he became an alcoholic.

Before we got inside their house good that day he wanted to know who we were, who our family was, and where we originally came from. When we told him Wesbury he looked at us very strangely. In a slurred voice he asked us, "How long ago did you live in Wesbury?" "About ten years ago," I told him. "Well," he said, "in that case you should remember all of those murders that happened there." "I can only remember a little bit about them," I told him, "because I was just a little girl."

"Damn shame," he muttered to himself, "my sister was one of those women that they found torn to pieces." Then his voice grew louder. "HER NAME WAS SELMA ANN!" he said as if he was talking to someone we couldn't see. "DO YOU REMEMBER HER?!" Drew and I just looked at him as he poured himself another drink. I had a feeling that the death of Selma Ann had played the largest role in his drinking so much. He was definitely a man who was in a lot of pain. He left the room after that and retreated up the stairs to his bedroom with the bottle of whiskey he had. Lila and Dara looked embarrassed.

Dr. Birch recently rented some office space for his practice in a newly erected building in Hardelle. The building wasn't very big. It only had five floors, but it was the largest building in town. Also, the new building had offices for the Sheriff's Department, and space for three lawyers offices, three doctor's offices and a couple of other Dentist's offices. The offices for the employees of the courthouse would be there, too.

Dr. Birch didn't open his office for business right away. He was closed a lot of times when he should have been open because he was too drunk. He hired Millie Taylor to be his secretary, and she was thrilled to get the job.

Millie was middle-aged and fairly nice looking. Also, she was a widow and never had any children. Her husband committed suicide six months earlier so she had no life insurance money to live on. She was working nights at a local variety store. And on three different occasions the store was robbed while she was working there by herself. She was afraid and nobody could blame her. Yet, she kept working there because she needed the money.

When Dr. Birch put a notice in the General Store asking for a secretary Millie jumped on it. She told him that she had experience so he hired her right away. After that she didn't know if she should quit the job at the store or not. She came to Dr. Birch's office every day since the day that he told her to be there at eight o'clock in the morning. But for two weeks in a row he wasn't there and the office was closed. It was Dara who told him about Millie, and that what he was doing to her wasn't right. So after that he got himself together.

Dr. Birch was a completely different person when he wasn't drinking. He was kind, soft-spoken, intelligent and very loving to Lila and Dara. Finally he opened his office for business. The people in town thought he was the best Dentist that they ever had in Hardelle, and they called him Doc B. He gave the other Dentists pretty stiff competition, too. Needless to say Millie was very happy.

Doc B. treated Millie very well. She came to work early and left the office very late sometimes. She loved her job and she was paid well, too. It didn't take long before there was talk around town about her and Doc B. They were seen together long after the office was closed. My sister and I saw nothing wrong with that, and neither did Lila and

Dara. They were both adults and neither one of them had anybody special in their lives.

After a while Doc B. seemed to be getting his life in order. However, he still got drunk now and then, but he was sober far more than he was drunk. When he was intoxicated all he did was cry over Selma Ann and his ex-wife. He would completely ignore Lila, Dara, Millie and his practice. All this did was reinforce Lila's and Dara's hatred of Annabelle. They saw all over again how much pain she caused their father as well as them.

After hearing Drew and I constantly talking about Lila and Dara, Caroline knew we had become very close to them. She was very instrumental for us with our parents where they were concerned. And for the first time in our lives we were allowed to bring our friends inside our home. The only condition was that they had to be gone by a certain time, and our family members didn't want to meet them. It was another oddball thing to add to my mental list.

"Why don't they want to meet Lila and Dara, Caroline?" Drew asked Caroline one day. "I guess they have their reasons, sweetie," replied Caroline. "Don't worry about it. Just be glad they're allowing you to do this because it's a first for them you know." "I guess you're right," said Drew. "I still would like to know why," I said. "Because usually parents do want to meet their children's friends." Caroline just smiled at me.

Another thing that was good for Drew and I was that we could spend the night over Lila's and Dara's house if we wanted to. But only with our parent's approval, which was definitely a first for my sister and I. I don't have to tell you that we were absolutely thrilled! We had Caroline to thank for that, too. However, Lila and Dara could never stay overnight in our house we were informed. As usual no reason for that was given to Drew and I. We didn't think it was fair, and we let them know it.

One evening against my better judgment my sister and I confronted them about it, or rather I should say that my sister confronted them. In my heart I felt they had done well by allowing us to have friends inside our house. And I felt good about them letting us spend the night out sometimes. Yet, Drew didn't think it was enough.

"Why can't they spend the night with us sometimes?" my sister asked our parents one night referring to Lila and Dara. I was too pusilanimous to say anything. "We have never allowed strangers into our home overnight, girls," said Papa adamantly. "And I don't see any reason whatsoever for that to change now. We're trying our best to be more reasonable with you and Celia. So your friends will just have to understand. Okay?" Mama didn't say anything and I had to agree with Papa because they were getting better.

Drew looked at Mama pleading with her eyes for a better reason. But my mother still said nothing, instead she tried to comfort my sister and I as usual. Drew turned away from her. I smiled at her then followed my sister. I saw tears in Mama's eyes and Papa shook his head sadly. I guess they felt that no matter what they did for us it would never be enough. I felt badly for them but I didn't understand why we just couldn't live a normal life like other teenagers we knew did.

I followed my sister into our bedroom. She was sobbing softly as she laid across her bed so I sat down on the side of her bed. "It'll be alright, Drew," I told her calmly. "Why don't you ever say anything to them, Celia?" she asked me. "I'm always out there on a limb by myself." "Do you really think it would do any good?" I asked her anxiously.

"Celia," she said, "Lila and Dara are our friends. We have never had any real friends except Lana, and you know that! You never open your mouth and say anything. You just go on letting Mama and Papa do this shit to us. You're the oldest so act like it!" "I know, Drew," I said. "But I already know what I'm going to do after I graduate from school so I don't worry about it anymore."

"Oh yeah," she said, "in the meantime we'll have lost two more friends. Don't you see that we will never keep any friends as long as we're in this house?" "Don't say that, Drew," I replied. "They are getting better. Don't you think?" "Hell no!" she cried a little angrily.

My sister was right. I didn't want to lose Lila and Dara as friends. But what could we really do about it? "Well," said my sister breaking into my thoughts, "is that all you have to say about it?" "I don't know what else you want me to say, Drew," I told her. "I know I should back you up with Mama and Papa. But I guess I just don't want to hurt them." "What?!" she cried incredulously. "Hurt them? What about them hurting us, Celia?"

I could see the hurt she was feeling in her face and it was the first time I had ever truly seen it. "You do whatever you want to, Celia," she told me. "But I'll be damned if I'm going to let them cause me to lose anymore friends because of their stupid rules. Sometimes this place feels like a prison." "Oh, Drew, no," I said, "you don't mean that." "Oh yes I do," she shot back at me. "I can't wait to get out of here. In fact, I might just run away from this damn house and never come back. That'll make them sorry." She got up from her bed and went into the bathroom as I sat there. In the back of my mind I could understand the frustration that our parents were probably feeling.

I heard the water splashing in the bathroom and knew Drew was washing her face. She came back to our bedroom a few minutes later. Although it was still early she had changed into her pajamas. She got into bed, turned on the radio, laid back against the pillows and stared at the ceiling.

"Drew, are you going to be alright?" I asked her softly. She ignored me lost in her own thoughts. "I'm going downstairs for a while," I told her. "I'll see you later. Okay?" She didn't say anything. I had never seen her that upset with our parents before. I knew then that if they didn't lighten up on us my sister would run away from home.

Drew was so upset with our parents that again she refused to talk to any of our family members for a few days. I went along with them because I did feel that they were trying to do right by us. I didn't let much of anything bother me by that time because I knew what I planned to do. I made up my mind not to let our parent's ridiculousness bother me.

I could not see it and neither could my sister but our parents knew what they were doing. Their rules seemed senseless to us. We didn't know it at the time but those rules were for theirs as well as our welfare, and the welfare of others.

CHAPTER SEVEN

Drew changed after that night and she started staying away from home more and more. When school let out she would go home with Lila and Dara and stay there until late in the evening. I would stop over there, too, but only for a little while. Caroline questioned me about her whereabouts for a few days then she stopped. A few times Drew even spent the night at their house without our parent's permission.

At first they didn't say anything which surprised me. I think they were trying to let Drew get over her anger at them. But when she kept on staying away they sent Caroline to talk to Doc. B. I went with her that day to show her where they lived. When we got there all three girls had gone out so I stood there on the front porch silently while Caroline and Doc B. talked.

"I'm really sorry about this, Miss Saunders," Doc B. told Caroline. "But I was under the impression that Drew had permission to stay overnight with us." "Well," said Caroline, " she doesn't. So her parents and I would appreciate it if you wouldn't allow her to stay overnight anymore, unless they or I say it's alright." "That's no problem, Miss Saunders," said Doc B. "Thank you," said Caroline. We headed back home after that. Of course when Lila, Dara and Drew returned to the house he told my sister about Caroline's visit, and what she said to him. Also, he made it clear to Drew that he was a little upset about it.

Caroline and I hadn't been home for half an hour before Drew stormed into the house. She was very angry and went completely berserk that afternoon. I had never seen her like that before. She was like a madwoman, and for a minute I thought she was going to attack Caroline.

"You had no right to do that!" she shouted at Caroline. "How dare you go behind my back like that!" "Now you listen to me, girl," Caroline said becoming angry, "I acted on behalf of your parents at their request." "In that case," said my sister, "I'll see them when they get up this evening. They won't interfere in my life anymore." "Now you just take it easy, little girl!" shouted Caroline getting angrier. "Your parents have every right to do what they think is best for you and Celia whether you like it or not. And that's the way it is until you are grown. Do you understand me?!"

Drew rolled her eyes and stormed upstairs to our bedroom. We heard the door slam shut. I felt sorry for Caroline as she sat down in a chair shaking her head sadly. Our parents had certainly put one hell of a responsibility onto her shoulders, and in my opinion it was not fair.

Drew may have been angry with our parents and Caroline but I was furious with her! She had no right to take her anger out on Caroline, who was only doing what she had been told to do by our parents. I hoped Mama and Papa would put her in her place if she tried that nonsense with them. However, I was in for a surprise and a big disappointment. After a few minutes Caroline got up and went into the kitchen to prepare our dinner. I started to do my homework.

Drew waited for our parents to awaken that evening. When she heard them stirring she burst into their bedroom without even knocking first. I ran up the stairs to see what was happening. I was smiling to myself. Our parents would surely straighten her out for being so nasty. When I got to their bedroom door they were staring wide-eyed at my sister, and she was poised as if she was ready to attack both of them. I couldn't believe what I was witnessing.

"Drew!" cried Mama. "What the hell has gotten into you?!" "As if you didn't know," said Drew angrily. "I know what you did to me Mama and Papa." Our parents didn't look surprised. "How dare you send Caroline to my friend's house, and tell their father not to let me stay there overnight anymore? How dare you?" Drew continued.

By then our aunts, our uncles and Caroline were all standing in the hallway.

"Now you just wait a damn minute here, young girl!" shouted Papa. "Who the hell do you think you're talking to like that?!" In all of my seventeen years neither Drew nor I had ever seen our father as angry as he was then. I watched in amazement as his eyes changed from their usual dark brown color into a light almost yellowish color. I thought I was seeing things.

"No, Papa," cried my sister who was in tears by then. "I'm telling you both right here and now. You always interfere with Celia and I having any friends, but not anymore. From now on we do whatever we want to do and you can't do anything about it." I wished she would've spoken for herself, and left me out of it.

"Drew," shouted Papa, "who the hell do you think you are?!" He walked over to my sister and slapped her across her face with the back of his hand so hard she fell to the floor. "Oh no!" cried Mama as she fell to the floor, and threw her arms around my sister. Papa quickly thought about what he had done. He reached down to help Drew up from the floor apologizing to her.

"I'm leaving here!" shouted my sister. "Don't you worry it won't be long!" She pushed Papa's hand away and got up from the floor by herself. She rushed past all of us in the hallway, went into our bedroom and slammed the door. Mama was still sitting on the floor. Papa leaned over a table shaking his head. I could see that our parents were devastated by what happened.

The rest of our family members, Caroline and I crowded into their bedroom. Our uncles helped Mama up from the floor. Then she sat down on the bed and my aunts sat down beside her. Papa sat down in a chair by the window looking outside. He kept shaking his head as if he couldn't believe what had happened.

Since Drew and I were born neither one of our parents had ever laid a hand on us. I was hoping that my sister would get what she deserved for being so nasty, but I didn't expect anything like what happened. Suddenly she came out of our bedroom, rushed down the stairs and out of the front door. Everyone went to the bedroom window and looked out because we wanted to see where she was going. It wasn't in the direction of Doc B.'s house, so we had no idea where she was going.

"Omri," said Uncle Marcus, "Wil and I will go after her and bring her back home." "No," said Papa, "let her cool off. She'll come back on her own." Mama was sobbing softly. "Maybe we have been a little too strict with Celia and Drew, Kate," said Aunt Margeaux. "They're getting older now and they have minds of their own." "At any rate," said Uncle Wilhelm, "we all know we can't have her running around out there at night. Right?" I saw a strange look on all of their faces when he said that.

There was a very important reason why Drew and I could not be out on the streets at night. Everybody in Hardelle already knew that it was dangerous since the murders. But there was something else I saw in their faces. "That's right, Omri," said Aunt Jada, "you guys go after her."

Our parents didn't go out that night, only our uncles went out to look for Drew. They were gone for hours but they never found her. None of our family members went out of the house at night after that, except to look for my sister. They were beside themselves with worry over her, too. Drew couldn't be found anywhere. Sheriff Jackson and his Deputies searched for her, too, but they couldn't find her either. She hadn't shown up for school, or at Lila's and Dara's house. Nobody knew where she was.

Mama cried the entire time that my sister was gone and Papa was nervous and jumpy. Night after night they went out looking for Drew but they never found her. Caroline would help the Sheriff look for her during the day. When our family members awoke in the evening they would look in our bedroom to see if she had come home. Then one by one they looked to Caroline for any news about her. It seemed like all of them were on the verge of having nervous breakdowns. The days kept passing with no word about my sister.

I tried my best to stay cheerful for the sake of our family but I was worried, too. I didn't know what I would do if something happened to my sister. She was my best friend, too, just like Lana was. Then I got angry with her. *"How dare she do this to me!"* I thought.

It was the fourth night that Drew had been gone, and just when I thought Papa would explode she telephoned. I answered the telephone when it rang, because nobody else was in any kind of shape to talk to anybody. I was happy to hear her voice on the other end of the line. "Drew," I cried, "where are you?!"

Our parents and the others ran over to where I was, and Papa snatched the receiver from my hand. "Drew, honey," he said, "where are you? We've been worried sick about you. We can work this out, sweetheart, just come home. Please!" Mama was standing next to him wringing her hands nervously.

"Drew?!" shouted Papa into the receiver. He took the receiver away from his ear and looked at it. Then he looked at Mama and shook his head. Drew hung up on him. Mama started sobbing softly and Papa held her in his arms. The look on their faces was heartbreaking. I went upstairs to my bedroom and laid down across my bed. "At least she's alright," I said to myself.

When the telephone rang again I heard Papa snatch it up before it finished the first ring. "Hello!" he shouted into the receiver. "Drew?!" But that time it was not my sister. "Just a minute please," I heard him tell the person on the other end of the line. "Celia, honey," he called to me. "Yes, Papa," I answered. "It's for you," he said. I picked up the telephone receiver in my bedroom. "Thank you," I told him then he hung up the phone downstairs.

"Hi, Celia," said Lila on the other end of the line. Before she could say anything else I asked her, "Lila have you and Dara seen my sister? She's been gone for four days and we don't know where she is." "Celia," said Lila calmly, "meet me in front of my house in twenty minutes. Okay?" "Why?" I asked her. "What's wrong?" "Nothing," she replied, "just come." "Alright," I told her. I hung up the telephone and went downstairs.

"Mama, Papa," I said to my parents, "I'm going over to Lila's house for a little while. Okay?" "Sure, honey," said Papa. Mama was still sobbing softly. "What time will you be back because it's getting late." "I'll only be gone for about an hour or so, Papa," I replied. "Alright, sweetheart," he said. Then I went out the front door, and headed for Lila's and Dara's house.

I wished that there was something that I could do to comfort our family. Still, I couldn't help feeling that it was their own fault that this happened. *"Maybe they do deserve this,"* I thought. They had made Drew's life and mine so miserable, and now they were paying for it.

None of them had been out at night for a while except to look for Drew that is. I could not help noticing how all of them would spend hours downstairs in the basement at night. And I began to wonder why and what they were doing down there. *"What's down there?"* I thought. I knew it was where our uncles slept, but what else was down there?

CHAPTER EIGHT

When I arrived at Lila's and Dara's house they were waiting outside for me. "What's going on?" I asked them curiously. "Come with us, Celia," said Lila taking me by my arm. "Where are we going?" I asked her confused. "You'll see," said Dara. I went with them, but I didn't know where they were taking me. We ended up at an abandoned church not too far from their house. It was the old Baptist church that Reverend Daniels had pastored.

The people in the congregation had raised enough money to build a larger church. And it was the one that they had now down the street from where I lived, and the same one that Drew and I joined. This small, dilapidated building sat unoccupied since they moved into the larger one. "Why are we coming here?" I asked them puzzled but they didn't answer me.

Lila pushed open the back door of the building. After we got inside Dara knocked on the wall three times and I knew that it was a signal to someone. To my shock and surprise from behind one of the walls came Drew. I was astounded that Lila and Dara knew where she was all along and never told me. "So this is where you've been hiding," I said. I walked over to her and hugged and kissed her because I was so glad to see her, and know she was alright.

"I've missed you so much, Drew," I told her. "Are you alright?" "I'm fine," she said flatly. "How are Mama and Papa doing?" "They're going out of their minds with worry about you, Drew," I said. "Good," she replied. "How is everybody else?" "They're okay," I told her, "but they're all worried about you, Drew, so when are you coming home?" "Celia," she said looking into my eyes, "I'm never going back there."

"You can't mean that, Drew," I said in disbelief. "I know we can work this out with them just like Papa said if you come home." "Whose side are you on, Celia?" she asked me. "Things are never going to change for us with Mama and Papa, never." "Why can't you just give them a chance, Drew?" I asked her. "A chance?" she asked incredulously. "Are you kidding me? They'll never change and you know it." "Well," I said, "if you're not going back home neither am I." At the time I really meant that.

Having my sister at home with me made life more bearable there dealing with our parent's rules. And without her I felt like I was all alone in the world. "You can bet your ass," said Drew, "when you don't come back home tonight Mama and Papa are going to tear this town apart looking for us." "Yeah," I said, "I know."

Drew told me that she had been staying in the abandoned church ever since she ran away from home. The weather was still fairly warm so she didn't have to worry about being cold at night. Lila and Dara brought her food and clothing to change into every day, and some blankets in case it did get a little chilly at night. She was taking a chance going to the service station down the street to wash up every day. My sister was determined that she wasn't going back home, and only Lila, Dara and now I knew where she was.

The four of us sat down in one of the old pews and talked. Lila and Dara stayed with us until well past midnight. They told us that Doc B. was on one of his drinking binges, so he would never even notice that they were not in the house. "He's probably passed out on the sofa by now," said Dara chuckling a little bit. Then after some time they got ready to leave us.

"We'll see you tomorrow," said Lila as they left. "Okay," we replied. Drew and I watched them from one of the church windows as they walked down the street toward their home. "You know that they'll probably send every Deputy in town out after us," said Drew. "Yeah," I replied, "you're probably right. But I don't think we have to worry about Lila and Dara telling anybody where we are." "They've been quiet all of this time," said Drew. "They won't tell anybody."

I felt badly because I told Papa that I would be home in an hour, and that was nearly five hours ago. I put the thought out of my mind. Drew and I made ourselves some pallets on the floor, then we laid down and talked until we got sleepy. "At least we're in a safe place," said Drew, "because no harm can come to us in a church."

The next afternoon Lila and Dara came to the abandoned church, and brought us some food and clothing. "Boy oh boy," said Dara, "you would think that you two were famous around here, or something. The whole town is talking about you. They think you might have been victims of the killer that is on the loose." "Oh really?" I said. "Yes," said Lila, "your whole family came over to our house last night after we got home. They were there earlier, but they couldn't get any sense out of our Dad. So they came back later when we got home, and they told us who they were."

"I feel so sorry for them, Celia," said Dara compassionately. "They really love you two so much. Your poor mother could barely stand up, and she was leaning on your father. We felt so badly for lying to them like we did." "Yeah," said Lila, "and I think they knew that we were lying to them, too." "Why do you say that?" asked Drew. "I don't know," replied Lila, "it's just that your father didn't seem to believe us when we told them we hadn't heard from you two." I was not surprised by that. It wasn't easy to lie to Papa and he did know that they were lying. After all their house was the last place where I told him I was going. However, I didn't tell them that.

After they told us about our family I felt worse than I did before, but my sister was as indifferent as ever. "I think I overheard one of your aunts say something about hiring a Private Investigator," said Dara. "Well," said Drew, "they were probably just saying that to scare you."

At the time it seemed like Drew and I were the adults, and our family members were the children who were being punished for doing something bad. I didn't like the idea that they were hurting so much, and I mentioned it to Drew. "So what," she said, "look how much they've hurt us, Celia. They deserve this." She was completely unmoved.

That night I saw another side of my sister that I had never seen before. We were definitely in control of the situation, or so we thought. But something was soon to happen to us and it was something that would let us know, without a doubt, that we didn't have as much control over things as we thought we did.

We were gone for eight days when strange things suddenly started to happen in and around the abandoned church where we were. On two different occasions I was awakened from my sleep because I thought I heard my father calling to me. But when I opened my eyes a huge wolf with red eyes was standing over me. I was terrified and even more terrified when it vanished right before my eyes. I started to awaken Drew but I didn't. I laid awake for the rest of that night too scared to close my eyes.

On another night I thought I saw the same wolf again when I was awakened by a thunderstorm. I woke up and there it was standing over my sister. I thought I was seeing things again because I was awakened from a very sound sleep, and I felt a little groggy. Suddenly the wolf was gone and my father was standing in its' place. He told me in a gentle voice, "Don't be afraid, Celia, honey because I'm here."

I went back to sleep and when I woke up that morning I chalked it all up to just being a dream. How could it have been anything other than that? Our parents had no idea where we were, or did they? When I thought I saw my father it seemed so real to me as if he had really been there. *"I must* have been dreaming," I thought. *"I HAD to be."*

It was the morning of the tenth day that my sister and I had been gone from home. Just before dawn I was awakened by a soft rapping on one of the church windows. It sounded like nothing of this world and I can never describe that sound to anyone. It was ghostly, eerie and inhuman and it seemed to pierce my brain.

I looked over toward the window in the direction of the eerie sound, and the mysterious stranger that I saw in the park, and in the church was there. I recognized him by the shadowy covering that was always over him. I could see a little bit of his face and body that time but only barely.

He was young and handsome with long hair that was pulled back into a pony tail. His eyes were so light that they looked like two balls of fire piercing the dark veil that covered him. He beckoned me to the front of the church. I was afraid because I didn't know who he was, or why he was bothering me.

I went to the front door of the church and opened it then I went outside onto the steps. I prayed silently that no one would see me. The stranger was there waiting for me. As close as I was to him the veil that covered his body still prevented me from seeing him clearly. It was such an inexplicable thing.

"Yes?" I asked him warily. "Celia," he said, "why don't you and Drew go on home? Your parents and the others are frantic over you both, and they won't be able to handle much more of this. It's really not fair to them you know. Give them a chance because I know things can be worked out for you and your sister. They are trying. Aren't they?" I always wondered how he knew so much about us.

I turned around to see if Drew had awakened because he was talking loudly enough to awaken her. But she was still fast asleep. Just like before I realized that nobody could see or hear the strange man but me. When I turned back around to face him he was gone and it unnerved me. I'd heard no movement from him at all, and he had been standing right in front of me. I went back inside the church and closed the door. Then I awakened my sister.

"What is it, Celia?" she asked me sleepily. "Drew," I said, "there was a man here a few minutes ago, and he said we ought to go home." "What man?" she asked. "I didn't hear anybody. When did this happen?" "A few minutes ago like I said," I told her. "Did you know him?" she asked me. "No," I told her. "But he is the same man I have been seeing." "You mean….. the one you saw in the back of the church that Sunday?" I never told her about seeing him in the park, or at the bottom of the stairs when I was twelve. "Yes," I said, "it was the same man."

"How did he know where we were, Celia?" she asked me. "And how does he know our names?" "I don't know, Drew," I said. "Do you think he's some kind of maniac, or something?" she asked. Before I could answer her she said, "Oh, my God! Maybe he's the killer that's been running around here!" "No," I told her emphatically, "he wouldn't hurt us." "How do you know that, Celia?" she asked curiously. "I just know it, Drew," I replied, "I don't know how I know it, but I just know he wouldn't harm us."

Suddenly something came to my mind that I had never thought about before. I realized that the man who kept coming to me had to be our grandfather, or his spirit. It was the only way that he would've known our names, and about our family's anguish about our being missing. It had to be him! When I told Drew that she didn't believe me, not that I could blame her, but there was no other explanation. Besides, it was the only thing that made any sense to me.

"Celia," said my sister, "it can't be Grandfather because he's dead." "I know that," I said. "Well," she replied, "if you really believe it was him that means you've been seeing a ghost." "Think about it, Drew," I told her, "nobody else knows that we're here, except Lila and Dara. And how else could he know so much about us, and our family?"

She did think about it and as she did my big, brave sister suddenly became fearful and frightened. She knew I was right. There was no other way to explain this strange and mysterious man's appearances. But why he only appeared to me was the real mystery.

I could barely remember what our beloved grandfather looked like anymore. Yet, I knew it had to be him who wanted us to go home. As willful and stubborn as my sister was she agreed with me. It was time for us to go home. Of course the fact that she was afraid played a huge role in her decision. We waited until it started getting dark before we set out for home, and on our way there we stopped at Lila's and Dara's house to let them know.

"Oh, thank God," exclaimed Lila, "your parents have been walking these streets every night looking for you two." "I think they've been watching our house, too," said Dara, "and us." "W-we weren't going to come to the church tonight because of that," Lila added nervously. "Really?" said Drew. "Yes," said Dara, "we didn't want to take the chance that they would follow us."

"I got up around two o'clock this morning to get a drink of water," said Lila, "and when I looked out of my bedroom window there were two men and two women staring at our house. They saw me in the window and they looked right into my eyes. It was scary!" "What do you mean?" asked Drew. "Well," replied Lila, "a dark-skinned woman and another younger woman who resembled Drew were looking up at my bedroom window. It was dark outside but I'm sure they were your aunts. I think they knew that we knew where you two were."

"You're probably right," I told her. "Anyway we're going home now so thanks a lot for all of your help. You're real friends to help us out the way you did." "Don't worry about it, Celia," said Lila, "you would've done the same thing for us." "Well," said Drew, "we'll see you guys later." "See you later," they told us. Then Drew and I started out for home.

The first thing that I wanted to do when I got home was to find a photograph of our grandfather because I knew he was the man who kept coming to me. *"Why doesn't he come to Drew?"* I wondered. It was just about dark so we hurried down the street. We didn't want to be out past the curfew that the Sheriff issued. But we were already ten minutes past it.

When we reached our house Drew thought it was best if I went inside first. So I turned the knob and opened the front door. Immediately I could hear the sobbing of my mother and our aunts, even Caroline was sobbing. It sounded like there was a funeral going on in there. They were sitting in the living room. Maybe all of them thought they would never see my sister and I again.

In the back of my mind a stunning revelation hit me. If Lila and Dara had not confessed to our whereabouts soon the consequences for them would not have been good. Drew and I saved our two dear friends from a very ugly horror. And I just knew I was right about that because I could feel it. Call it instinct, intuition or whatever else that you want to, but there was no doubt in my mind that I was right about what I was thinking.

CHAPTER NINE

When my sister and I walked into the living room our family members shrieked with joy, and we were smothered with hugs and kisses. They held us so tightly we could hardly breathe, and we didn't think they would ever let us go. Our faces were so wet from all of their tears that it looked like Drew and I were crying, too, but we weren't.

Papa held us at arms' length to look at us. You would have thought he had never seen either one of us before. Mama and our aunts began to feel all over our bodies as if they wanted to be sure we were really there. "Oh, my girls," cried Mama holding onto us. Papa telephoned Sheriff Jackson to let him know we were home, and that we were alright. He thanked him for all of his help, too.

The first thing Papa said when he got off the telephone with the Sheriff was, "Where were you girls hiding from us?" By the look on his face lying to him was useless, and without any words he could easily get his point across. In other words don't lie to him because if you did he would know you were lying. He and Mama let us know from the time that we were old enough to understand them that there was nothing we couldn't tell them.

They made it clear to both of us that we were never to lie to them about anything, and we never did. Papa stood in front of us with those piercing, dark eyes of his waiting for an answer to his question. It was Aunt Margeaux who came to our rescue.

"Oh, Omri," she said, "what does it matter? They're home now where they belong." She and Aunt Jada hugged us again. "Oh, it matters alright," said Papa looking at Drew and I. He had a sly smile on his lips as he waited for an answer to his question. By the look that he gave both of us we were not going to get away without giving him one either. If we told him the truth we knew we would never be able to use that old church as a hideout again. So we had no other choice but to tell him the truth.

"We were hiding in the old Baptist church on Grapel Street," said Drew looking into our father's eyes. He smiled and his eyes softened as he looked at both of us because he knew we were telling him the truth. "That was pretty clever," he told us, "because we never would've looked for you there, never!" My sister and I were confused. *"What was so clever about it?"* I wondered. Drew looked at me, and I knew she was thinking the same thing that I was.

Then Uncle Marcus asked us a very odd question. "Did you see anybody while you were there?" he asked. Papa was still looking at my sister and I. It made us uneasy and he knew it. We looked at one another again. *"Why would Uncle Marcus ask us a question like that?"* I was thinking.

"I didn't see anybody," said Drew, "but Celia did." My father turned his gaze to me alone. "Who did you see, honey?" he asked me softly coming closer to me. He was an ominous presence in our home just as our grandfather had been. He never failed to let my sister and I know how much he loved us. But he didn't play around with us when it came to serious matters like our running away from home.

When my sister and I ran away it threatened our family's peace of mind where we were concerned, and the peace of our household as well. In his own way Papa was letting us know not to do it again, ever! We remembered what Lila and Dara told us, but we were seeing first hand how what we did had affected our family.

Papa was standing in front of me looking at me intensely with those dark eyes of his still waiting for an answer to his question. I knew for sure if we had not come home when we did he would have torn the whole town apart until he found us. And God help anybody, or anything that got in his way.

"I saw a man at the church," I told my father. "Oh?" he said. "He called to me from the church window one morning." "What did he want?" asked Papa. "He told me that Drew and I should go home because all of you were so worried about us." "Did you know him?" asked Papa. "No," I replied, "but I've seen him before and I told Mama about it." "Yes," said Mama smiling at me sweetly, "I remember that, sweetheart." "I saw the same man when I was twelve, too," I blurted out, "and at the church when Drew and I got baptized."

All of our family members had smiles on their faces as I told them about seeing the mysterious man. It was as if they knew something that Drew and I didn't know. "I thought I saw you, too, Papa," I said, "a couple of times. I thought I heard you calling me, and there was a huge wolf standing over Drew and I. I thought I was seeing things because it vanished, and you were there instead. You told me not to be afraid because you were there."

"You didn't tell me about all of that, Celia," said Drew. I just looked at her and said nothing. "Do you believe you really saw me, honey?" asked Papa. "I think I was dreaming, Papa," I replied. "Because you didn't know where we were so you couldn't have been there. Right?" He gently caressed my face.

"One day," he said, "you and your sister will understand how powerful love can be." "Wait a second," said Aunt Margeaux, "I have something I want to show you, Celia, honey." She went into her bedroom to get something. A few minutes later she came back with a photograph in her hand, and gave it to me. "Is that the man that you saw, honey?" she asked me. I couldn't be sure if it was the same man or not, because he was always covered by that strange veil, and the photograph itself was worn and faded. However, deep down inside me I knew it was my grandfather who came to me.

It was easy to see that the photograph was very old by the clothing that the man was wearing in the picture. And in the photograph there were horse and buggy-drawn carriages in the background on a cobble stone street. The man in the photograph was dressed in an old-fashioned dark or black, three piece suit and a dark overcoat. "That could be him," I said unsure. "Who is he?"

Aunt Margeaux put her arm around my shoulders. "You were so young, honey, when Papa left us," she began, "but that's your grandfather." Drew wanted to see the photograph, too. She had no recollection of our grandfather and mine was hazy. We had never seen any photographs of him, or any of our other family members for that matter. "But Grandfather is dead, Aunt Margeaux," I said. "How could it have been him?" Nobody answered my question, and Papa was still looking into my eyes smiling. Drew looked at me and what our aunt said finally hit her like a ton of bricks.

"Oh, my God, Celia!" cried my sister frightened. "I told you! I was right! I knew it! You saw a ghost!" She was visibly shaken by then, so Mama put her arms around her trying to soothe her. "Now, now, sugar plum," she told Drew, "you know your grandfather would never harm you or your sister. Don't you?" "I don't care," cried Drew shaken up a bit. "Oh, Mama I don't ever want to see him. Please make him stay away from me. Please!" "S-s-sh!" said Mama gently stroking my sister's hair. I realized then why our grandfather never came to her. He knew she would be too scared

I caught our parent's eying one another, and I thought Drew would be no more good for the rest of that night. "Apparently," replied Aunt Jada, "he has some kind of link with you, Celia. And if that's the case he'll be back again you can be sure of that." When she said that everything began to grow darker and darker around me. The last thing I saw were my father's eyes staring into mine. When I woke up I was in my bed, and it felt good since I hadn't been in it for a long time.

"Hi, there," said Caroline sitting on the side of my bed. "How are you feeling, honey?" "I'm alright," I replied sitting up in the bed. "What happened to me, Caroline, and how did I get to bed?" "You fainted, sweetie," replied Caroline, "and your Papa carried you up here." "I remember now," I said. "I talked to a ghost." "It seems so, honey," she said calmly. "And more than likely it was probably your grandfather." "Oh my," I said softly as I laid back down in the bed.

"Don't worry about it, sweetie," said Caroline still very calm. "Your grandfather would never harm you, or Drew. Always remember that." "I know now why he doesn't bother her," I told Caroline. "Oh?" she said. "He knows she's scared," I said. "But she is the brave one, Caroline, not me. I don't understand." "Maybe you have more bravery than Drew does in this area, Celia," chuckled Caroline softly. "Where is Drew?" I asked her. "She's downstairs talking with your parents and the others," she told me. "Do you want to go back downstairs?" I looked over at the clock on my bureau dresser and it was nearly midnight.

"Our parents are home?" I asked surprised. "You bet they are, sweetie," said Caroline. "They're staying in tonight. I guess it's a celebration of you and your sister's homecoming." "That's okay," I replied. "I'm really kind of tired and I just want to lie here in bed." "Okay, honey," she said. "If you need anything just let me know." "Okay, Caroline," I said. "Thank you." Then she left my bedroom.

I could hear music playing downstairs and a lot of laughing and talking. They were all having a little private party and Drew would tell me all about it later. As I laid there I thought about my grandfather. I fainted at the idea of talking to a spirit. Yet, I did know that he would never harm my sister or I. I never once sensed any kind of danger from him whatsoever.

Lila and Dara tried to make us understand how badly our family members were hurting while we were gone. But it was our grandfather who truly knew how much pain they were in. And it was obvious that he was always around us. I recalled what Papa told us on the day that our grandfather left us. He told us, 'that he was where he could always watch over us', so I knew it was true.

Also, I knew there was a reason why he always came to me. *"Maybe there is some kind of link between he and I, "* I thought, *" like Aunt Jada said."*

Weeks passed before Caroline told me that our grandfather came to our parents in a dream while Drew and I were gone. He told them not to worry because he knew where we were, and he would make sure that we came home soon. In his lifetime our grandfather was a man of his word Caroline told me. So we ended up coming back home just like he told our parents we would. It was just a matter of them waiting patiently. Still, it was confusing to Drew and I. *"Is he really dead?"* I thought.

"Why is that shadowy veil always over him?" I asked myself. I didn't mention that to anybody for a long time and I don't know why.

I just never said a word about him always being covered in a shadow when I saw him. It was as if he was trying to hide something from me.

I recalled that we never had a funeral service for our grandfather. *"Why wasn't his body ever found?"* I wondered. Questions like those went around and around inside my head all of the time. However, there were no answers and it was so frustrating to me.

CHAPTER TEN

Things did get better at home for Drew and I after we ran away from home. Our family members still roamed the streets at night. But we appreciated them letting us have friends in the house and that we could spend the night at Lila's and Dara's house. It was alright with our parents as long as they knew about it in advance. Also, if it was okay with Doc B. Yet, no one was allowed to stay in our house overnight. That was one of the rules they refused to budge on.

There was a condition to us having friends over at night, too. If they were coming over to our house it had to be after it got dark. They had to be gone by ten o'clock on weekdays and by midnight on the weekends. Our family members would never see them and they didn't want to. Needless to say, Drew and I thought that was crazy but we didn't bitch about it.

When our family members were not going out and we had company they stayed inside their bedrooms. It was truly a strange setup but my sister and I were grateful for what we got. We didn't know why none of them ever wanted to meet our friends. They just told us that they trusted our judgment. Drew and I were very happy for the changes and we realized that our family did want us to be happy.

One night for the first time since we were born Drew and I had dinner guests. Caroline usually fixed dinner only for us and herself. She was thrilled when we told her that Lila and Dara wanted to come over and have dinner with us.

"Wow!" cried Dara when she saw our house. "You didn't tell us that you guys lived in a mansion. Your family must be rich, huh?" Drew and I smiled. Our home was big but it certainly wasn't a mansion. And our family had a little money, however, I didn't think we were rich. Then again what did I know because there were so many secrets in that house.

Caroline out-did herself on the night that Lila and Dara had dinner with us. She made two different appetizers, two different kinds of meat, two different kinds of vegetables, two kinds of desserts and her famous homemade rolls. It was great! Lila and Dara raved about the dinner because it was so rare that they ever got a home-cooked meal. Like Drew and I neither one of them could cook and Doc B. wasn't a good cook either. Millie fixed dinner for them once in a while but they usually ate a lot of junk food.

Caroline waited on us like we were royalty and she sat down and ate dinner with us, too. Afterward she played a game of cards with us. Later the four of us sat outside on the front porch while Caroline cleaned up the kitchen. Around nine o'clock we went back inside the house, and Drew and I took Lila and Dara upstairs to our bedroom. In the hallway upstairs we passed by the door that lead to the attic.

"Where does that door lead to?" asked Lila curiously. "It goes upstairs to the attic," replied Drew. "Have you guys ever been up there?" asked Dara. "No," I said. "Why not?" she asked incredulously. "Because," I replied, "we've never had any reason to go up there. I don't think there's anything up there of any interest to us anyway." "Oh, I'll bet there is some very interesting stuff up there," said Lila. "Because people usually keep their pasts inside their attics, or in their basements you know."

"Yeah," said Dara, "you two should go up there and look around sometime. You might be surprised at what you find." "The door is always locked, " said Drew, "and only Caroline and our parents have a key." "Key!" cried Dara. "Where I come from, girls, you don't need a key." "Oh?" I said confused.

It was then Dara told us that she had spent some time away. It was in an all girls' school for troubled teenage girls. She was there from the time that she was thirteen years old until that previous year. Drew and I were totally surprised because neither she nor Lila ever told us anything about that.

"I had a lot of problems," said Dara, "after I was raped and ended up getting pregnant." "She was always in some kind of trouble after that," added Lila. "It ranged from breaking curfew, running away from home and skipping school to shop-lifting, so good ole Mother dear put her away." "Gee," said Drew, "I'm so sorry , Dara." "It's alright," said Dara. "It was an experience and at least I got a chance to get away from her." Of course we knew she was referring to Annabelle.

"While I was there," continued Dara, " I learned a lot of things from the older girls and one of them was picking locks." "That's right," said Lila chuckling softly. "No lock has ever been made that Dara Birch can't open." We chuckled together.

Dara asked Drew and I for a hairpin. Neither one of us had any but Mama had plenty of them on her bureau dresser. So I went into her bedroom, got a hairpin and gave it to Dara. "Are we ready?" she asked us. We nodded our heads. We knew what we were doing was wrong, but our curiosity won out over our good sense. We heard Caroline downstairs in the kitchen so we closed our bedroom door in a way that she would think we were in the room, just in case she happened to come upstairs.

The three of us watched as Dara skillfully opened the lock on the door with the hairpin. Then we went inside closing the door behind us, and walked up the two flights of stairs to the attic. When we reached the top of the last staircase we were in another small hallway. At the end of that hallway was another locked door so Dara picked that lock, too. We opened the door and went inside.

All of us were amazed by the size of the attic, and it was full of all kinds of things that our family had once used. There was old clothing, shoes, coats, handbags, jewelry and a lot of furniture that looked like it was very old, and there were fur coats, too. We were fascinated!

"These things look like they're real," said Drew holding two beautiful, golden rings in her hand. I didn't know very much about gold, silver or any other precious stones but the rings, earrings, necklaces and a few old timepieces did look genuine. Also, we found a brooch that we knew had to be very old. Dara and Lila found an old music box and fell in love with it. "I wish we could keep this," said Lila. "But we can't take anything out of here. Your family is probably saving these things for you two." "Look at this," cried Dara turning the music box over.

At the bottom of the music box there was an inscription that read: *"With love on our special day, Love Danielle."* The date under it was June 21, 1765. "That's nearly two hundred years ago," said Lila. "I wonder who Danielle was." "Well," said Drew, "one thing is for sure whoever she gave it to is dead and so is she." "Evidently it was something that she gave to her lover," I said as I held it in my hands. I wound it up and it played a sorrowful tune that made me feel sad suddenly. I sat down in an old chair still holding the music box.

Suddenly the room began to darken around me, but I could still hear the sad song playing from the music box. I was all alone in the room because my sister and the others had mysteriously vanished. "I was so lonely and sad," a tiny voice said to me softly. I didn't know where it was coming from then I heard it again. "I was so unhappy but I loved him," said the same tiny voice penetrating the darkness that had engulfed me. Then I heard a different voice and it was my sister.

"Celia," she said, "are you okay?" I could hear her voice but I couldn't see her. "I can't see you, Drew," I told her. "Where are you?" "I'm right here, Celia," she said touching my hand gently, but I could hardly see it. The darkness that covered me suddenly disappeared after that and the room became bright again. I saw my sister's face and I saw Lila and Dara. "What's the matter with you, Celia?" asked Drew. She was looking at me strangely as all three of them stared at me.

"What happened to me?" I asked them. I was still holding the mysterious music box but the music had stopped playing. "Are you sure you're alright, Celia?" asked Lila. "I felt so much sadness when I was listening to the song from the music box," I told them. "It was like I wasn't here anymore but somewhere else." "Where?" asked Dara confused. "I don't know," I told her.

"Well," she said, "it sounds to me like you should put that music box away and leave it alone." Reluctantly, I did as she suggested but something kept drawing me to it. I kept my eyes on it the entire time we were in the attic, and I decided that I would take it with me when we left.

"I wish I knew who Danielle was," I thought, *"and who she gave that music box to. Why does it play such a sad song?"* I was so wrapped up in my thoughts that I didn't hear my sister talking to me. "Did you hear what I said, Celia?' she asked me. "No," I replied, "I'm sorry, Drew, what did you say?" "Celia," she said, "you're scaring me. Are you sure you're alright?"

"Yes, I think so," I replied. I couldn't shake what happened to me while I was holding that music box.

"I was saying that we can't ask Mama and Papa about the music box," continued Drew. "If we do they'll know we've been up here searching around." "Yes," I said, "I know that. But I would just like to know who Danielle was that's all because she was so unhappy." "Maybe," said Drew, "if we look around some more we'll find out something about her." "Yeah, maybe," I replied solemnly.

As it turned out my sister was right because we found some old photographs inside a trunk along with some other things. They were inside an envelope that had once been white but had turned yellow. "Here she is, Celia," cried Dara holding one of the photographs in her hand. "She could be your twin." "Who?" asked Lila. "Danielle," answered Dara, "the woman who gave that music box to her lover." She gave me the photograph. "My, God!" I said stunned when I looked at it because the woman did look a lot like me.

Danielle was dark and beautiful and the only difference between us was our skin color. She was dressed in an old-fashioned, lace, wedding gown and veil. She had long dark hair and her complexion was dark like Aunt Margeaux's. Also, she had big, beautiful, light eyes, too. A brooch was pinned to the front of her wedding gown, and it was exactly like the one that we found among the old jewelry in the attic.

When we compared it to the one in the photograph we knew it was the same one. We looked on the back of it and the initials 'D.B' were engraved on it. "This is an antique," exclaimed Dara, "and it's probably worth a lot of money." "All of these things are antiques," added Lila.

We turned Danielle's photograph over and on the back of it was written *"To Danielle With Love Your Husband"*. In the bottom right-hand corner was written *"Danielle Bellis-Carbell, June 21, 1765"*. "That must've been her wedding day," said Lila exuberantly. "She must be your great grandmother, Celia." Drew and I were puzzled. "Why haven't they ever told us about her?" I asked thinking out loud.

Contrary to what Lila said I believed that Danielle must have been my mother's great grandmother not ours. "Let's keep looking," said Drew, "we're bound to find more clues to help us put things together." She was right again because we found more than we ever thought we would.

There were other photographs of Danielle Carbell, and with our grandfather. There was no mistake because I knew it was him in the photographs with her. He looked a little older than he was in the picture that Aunt Margeaux showed us. Drew and I became more puzzled. Logically it wasn't possible for our grandfather to have been married in 1765 because it was nearly two hundred years ago.

"I don't understand," I said. "Celia," said Drew, "it can't be him." Yet, the photograph told me otherwise. It was him alright. I stared at the photograph as I sat down on the floor, and the darkness that covered me before came back again. "Oh no," I said almost in a whisper, "please, what do you want with me?" "Celia," cried Lila, "who are you talking to?" I had the same feeling of sadness again, only it was a little different that time because it was not as profound as it was the first time. She took the photograph from my hand.

When she did the darkness vanished as suddenly as it came. Lila and the others were staring at me again. "Celia," said Dara, "I think you should leave those photographs, and that music box alone because you're scaring me, too. It's like you go into a trance, or something." She didn't know how right she was. The sadness that came with the darkness seemed to overwhelm me.

Whenever the room darkened I would be there alone and the others disappeared. It was eerie but I would be somewhere else, and obviously it was somewhere that the others could not go. It was very scary!

Drew, Lila, Dara and I found photographs of our parents, our aunts, our uncles and of other people that we didn't know. Every one of them had the person's name written on the back of it as well as the date they were born.

There was a photograph of a man named, Larry Carbell, who was born on January 11, 1768. He had to be some relation to our grandfather, but who was he? What surprised us even more was the photograph of another man whose name was Richard Bellis. The date on the back of his photograph was February 12, 1763.

"Wow!" cried Dara. "These people lived before the Revolutionary War started! Richard Bellis had to be your great grandfather, Celia, or a great uncle, or something." I stared at the photograph. "Did you ever hear our family mention anything about these people, Celia?" asked Drew curiously. "No," I told her, "not a word. They've never mentioned anything about them." "Our father never talks about his family," Drew told Lila and Dara. "So we assumed that he didn't have any family." "Well," said Dara, "I think Richard Bellis was definitely a part of his family."

I put the photograph of Richard Bellis on an old table sitting by the stairway, and I didn't care what Lila and Dara said. I was taking the photographs and the music box with me when we left the attic. Since they had been up there for years I doubted that they would be missed.

Then we found a photograph of a different woman. She looked like a teenager in the picture and she was very pretty. I thought she looked a lot like Mama. We looked at the back of the photograph to read what it said. It read: *'Selena Bellis, wife of Oliver Bellis, born December 8, 1720, France'*. They had to be Richard's parents, and our father's great great grandparents. However, something didn't feel quite right but I just didn't know what it was.

Drew and I always wondered why our parents never wanted to talk about their families. Mama said very little about her mother, and Papa never told us anything about his family. "I hate to say this, Celia," said Lila. "But usually when people hide things like this there's a lot more that they're hiding." "What do you mean?" I asked her knowing exactly what she meant.

"Just what I said," she replied. "Maybe there's a reason why you and Drew have never been told about these people." "Yeah," said Dara, "you have to admit that you two do have a strange family." "Maybe if we keep on looking," said Drew, "we'll find some answers." We continued to search.

We looked at more old photographs. Also, we found more pictures of our parents and our other family members. Drew and I were stunned when we saw the dates that were written on the backs of them. "These dates have to be wrong," insisted Drew, and I could see that she was becoming upset.

We could tell that the photographs were old like the others were because the ink that was used in the writing on the backs of them was faded. In the photograph of Mama she had on a dress that we knew had to be from the eighteenth century. And on the back of her photograph someone wrote: *'Kathleena Carbell, born July 23rd, 1767'*. "How can that date be right?" I asked confused. In the photograph of Papa he was dressed in eighteenth century clothing as well. And on the back of his picture was written: *'Omri Antoine Bellis, born August 30th, 1764'*.

"Something is definitely not right here," said Drew visibly shaken as she sat down on the floor next to me. "You're telling me," said Dara. "That would make your parents nearly two hundred years old, and that's impossible." "You're right," said Drew. "Our parents can't be more than forty years old." It was true. We never knew how old our parents really were but neither one of them looked a day over forty.

We never asked our parents their ages, but common sense would tell anybody that they couldn't be as old as the photographs indicated. "Whoever wrote these dates must've made a terrible mistake," I said. "Yeah," said Lila, "but look at their clothing."

The clothing that they wore in the photographs was definitely from another era. Not to mention how aged the photographs themselves were. Drew was looking at me thoroughly bewildered as if she thought I would have some answers for her, but I didn't. I was just as befuddled as she was, and we were both as confused as Lila and Dara looked.

"This is really getting strange," said Lila. "Maybe we should put all of this stuff back and leave well enough alone." "No way!" cried Dara. "Are you kidding? We can't stop now." "I think that's up to Celia and Drew. Don't you?" commented Lila. "It's their house and their family not ours." They looked at Drew and I with empathy in their eyes. "Well?" asked Dara trying not to sound anxious. "Oh, what the hell," said Drew, "we might as well keep on looking, Celia. What have we got to lose now?" I agreed with her wholeheartedly.

CHAPTER ELEVEN

There was another large envelope inside the trunk, and Dara took it out and gave it to me. "Here," she said, "you open it." As I looked at the envelope in my hand I felt a knot in the pit of my stomach suddenly. Before I even opened it I knew there was information inside it that we would regret finding.

"Hurry up, Celia," said Drew on the edge of her seat, "open it and stop staring at it." I walked over to an old rocking chair, and before I sat down in it I noticed the initials 'K.B.' carved into the wood. It had belonged to Mama. I gently let my fingers glide over the letters. I could imagine her rocking my sister and I to sleep in that old rocker when we were babies. Lila, Dara and Drew each pulled up a chair and sat down.

I opened the envelope and took out the papers that were inside it. They were as old as the envelope itself. The first one was a deed to some property in a town called Wakling. "Have you ever heard of that place before?" I asked them. "I haven't," said Drew. "Neither have we," said Lila. "But when we get home I can ask my Dad if he knows where it is." There were other deeds to property inside the envelope, too.

According to the deeds our family owned property in places like Anders County, Walkersville, Sheriville, Kingstown, Prato, Treylor, Wesbury and Hardelle. Every deed was in the name of our grandfather, Damion Carbell, and his wife, Danielle, and each property had been owned by them since the 1700s. "Gee," said Dara, "to own all of that property your grandparents must've been rich." "Maybe," I said nonchalantly. It wasn't hard for me to know that our grandfather had purchased a lot of various properties for a reason, and whatever that reason was only he and our family members knew. Strangely, the deeds were only signed by my grandfather not he and Danielle. Therefore, it was obvious to me that he just put her name on the deeds, and I wondered why that was.

I remembered how our family used to move around a lot when Drew and I were little girls. Our grandfather bought all of that property so our family would have somewhere to go in case of trouble. There was no other reason that I could think of for him to do it. "Celia," said Drew breaking into my thoughts, "why do you think they bought all of that land?" "I don't know," I lied to her.

Since I was older than she was I recalled a lot more about our family than she did. She couldn't remember that whenever our family moved it was because they had to, not because they wanted to. "What are you thinking about, Celia?" asked Dara noticing that I was lost in thought. "Nothing," I lied again, "I'm just surprised to learn that we own homes in every town that we've ever moved to." "What else is inside the envelope, Celia?" asked my sister curiously.

I reached into the envelope and pulled out two documents that were folded together, and they were not very old. When I opened the first one I saw my name at the top of the page. The document was handwritten by a woman named Adria but there was no last name. "That's your birth certificate, Celia," said Lila. "Let me see it," said Drew taking the papers from my hand. "The other one is mine." We knew that Adria had to be the midwife that Mama had when she gave birth to Drew and I.

According to our birth records Drew and I were both born at home. She was born in a place called Anders County and I was born in a place called Wakling. We had never heard of either place before. "I'm going to keep mine," said Drew excitedly. "You always need your birth certificate because it's an important document." I agreed with her so I decided to keep mine, too. After that we got a real shock.

The next document that I retrieved from the envelope was another birth record, and it belonged to Mama. There was her name, Kathleena Carbell, printed neatly at the top of the page by a woman named Sara. It listed her parent's names as 'Mother: Danielle Bellis and Father: Damion Carbell'. Her date of birth was written as July 23, 1767. "Nobody could write the same mistake twice," I said. "And Mama's birthday is July 23rd, although we've never known the year." Drew looked at me and I at her. We knew as did Lila and Dara that it had to be a mistake.

Papa's birth record was with Mama's. I read it, and after I did I dropped the paper to the floor as if it had been lit by fire suddenly, and burned me. I got up, walked over to the attic window and opened it. I needed some air because I couldn't breathe and I was trembling.

"My God, Celia!" cried Lila. "What is it?!" Drew picked the document up and started to read it. "Oh my God!" she cried as she put her hand over her mouth in shock. Lila gently took the paper from her hand and read it. Dara looked over her shoulder as she did. After they read it they looked at Drew and I. They were both too stunned to say anything, but they would never be as stunned as my sister and I were.

Papa's name was written at the top of the birth record: 'Omri Antoine Bellis' by the same midwife that our mother had and his parents were also named. His mother's name was *'Danielle Bellis'* and his father's name was *'Damion Carbell',* and he was born on August 30th, 1764. It was the same date that we saw before on the back of his photograph. Our father's birthday was August 30th. According to their birth records our parents were brother and sister. It was more than obvious by then that all of the written dates couldn't be wrong.

"How can they look so young, Celia," asked Drew still stunned, "if all of this is true?" All I could do was shake my head in disbelief. There was no way we would ever be able to accept that our parents could be that old. It couldn't be true no matter what anybody said because it just wasn't possible. People didn't live that long and look as young as they did. Not to mention the fact that they were siblings.

In a strange and insensible way my sister and I felt as if our parents had betrayed us. Lila and Dara looked at us with sympathy in their eyes. I knew they were feeling sorry for urging us to keep searching until we found something. We found more than we bargained for. Also, it was obvious that our grandparents had not been married to one another when Papa was born, and that was a 'no no' in our society.

It was some time before our mother was born that our grandfather married Danielle.

We knew that Richard Bellis and Larry Carbell were their children, too. If it was all true it started to make perfect sense. It explained why neither one of our parents ever wanted to talk about their families. I began to wonder about Uncle Marcus and Uncle Wilhelm because they resembled Papa, and our grandfather a great deal. Lila came over to me and put her arm around my shoulders.

"Don't worry about it, Celia," she told me. "Even if your parents are sister and brother there's nothing wrong with you and Drew." "That's right," added Dara trying to sound comforting. "All of that nonsense about the blood being too close, and the kids being born retarded is bullshit, because there's nothing wrong with you two." "Oh yeah," said Drew smugly, "you mean...... nothing that we know about." She was hurt, embarrassed and upset just as I was. We thought it was sick for a brother and his sister to marry one another, and on top of that have children together. "How could they do that?" asked Drew ineffably with her voice choking up a little.

It seemed like my sister and I were always at odds with our parents for one reason or another, but this was huge. Mama had lied to us all of our lives because she told us that she didn't have any brothers. When in reality she had three brothers, and Papa never said anything at all about his family. Under the circumstances we really couldn't blame them. Because in my opinion they should've been ashamed of themselves. If Drew and I were in their shoes we wouldn't talk about our family either.

"No wonder they're so secretive about that," I said softly referring to our parents never wanting to speak of their families. They harbored a dark and morally revolting secret. But it was nothing compared to the other diabolical secret that all of them guarded.

As for our grandfather I recalled that he was a real ladies' man. I couldn't understand how any woman in her right mind would marry a man like that. I finally understood something about Danielle. *"No wonder she was so unhappy,"* I thought. Because I realized that hers' was the voice I heard when I was listening to the music box, and why it played such a sorrowful tune. *"What did he do to her?"* I began to wonder.

I walked over to the music box and held it in my hands. I turned the key and wound it up again then the sad melody began to play. As before I was lost inside the eerie darkness and the others had vanished. I fell to my knees overwhelmed by the sudden sadness that I felt and the blackness swallowed me up again.

Suddenly our grandfather, always covered in that dark veil, was standing next to me. I couldn't see anybody else. "I love you, Celia," I heard him say to me. I wasn't afraid. In fact, his presence was comforting to me. I felt all of the love that he and Danielle had between them and I felt their love for me. But there was overwhelming sadness and heartache in the midst of it. I felt someone take the music box out of my hands, the sad song stopped playing and the darkness was gone.

"Celia, are you alright?" asked my sister as she put her arm around me. She was the one who took the music box from me. "Yes," I replied, "I'm okay." She helped me to my feet. "What happened?" I asked her. "You fell, Celia," said Dara. "Then you went into some kind of trance like you did before."

"Will you please do me a favor, Celia?" asked Lila compassionately. "What's that?" I asked. "Leave that music box alone please," she said. I smiled at her sarcastically. It didn't matter what she or anybody else said. As far as I was concerned that music box was mine, and I was taking it with me when we left the attic. I was drawn to it as if it and I had some kind of connection with one another.

"I should never talk to them again," pouted Drew. "You can't do that, Drew," I told her. "Why not?" she asked. "Because," I said, "if you act that way they'll wonder why then what will you tell them?" "That's true," said Dara. "You can't say anything about any of this stuff because those doors were not locked for nothing."

"Just think about it," said Lila. "The first time you two ever have company in your house and it was their undoing. I don't think it's wise for you to let them know anything. Do you?" "You're right," relented Drew considering what Lila said. "But it's going to be difficult pretending we don't know about any of this stuff." "That may be," replied Lila, "but there is one thing we know for certain about your family."

"What's that?" I asked. "They adore you two," she replied, "and you should always keep that in mind." She was right of course because our family members loved Drew and I very much.

We found out a lot about our family in that attic. But there was more that my sister and I wanted to know about them. "I wish we knew why they go out at night during a certain time of the month," said Drew. "Or why they stay in the dark all of the time." "Yeah," I said, "they stay downstairs in the basement at night for hours when they don't go out." We desperately wanted to know why they did the things they did. When we were younger Drew and I never cared about their odd behavior, but we were not little girls anymore. Then we heard Caroline calling to us.

"Girls!" she shouted from downstairs. We hurriedly closed the trunk. Drew and I kept the birth records, the music box, the photographs and the deeds that we found in the attic. "Girls, where are you?" Caroline called again. We could tell that she was in the living room at the foot of the stairs. And if she had to call us again she would've come upstairs to see what we were doing.

"Quick, Drew," I said, "answer her." My sister ran down the stairs and flung open our bedroom door as if we had been in the room, then she answered Caroline. "We're right here, Caroline," she said. "It's almost midnight," said Caroline, "Dara and Lila should be going home now. Okay?" "Okay," said Drew. We had no idea that much time had passed by. We turned off the lights in the attic, locked the door, courtesy of Dara, and went downstairs to the second floor. Dara carefully locked that door, too.

"Boy, that was close," said Dara. "Yeah," replied Lila, "too close." I had no idea where I was going to hide my music box. Our parents rarely came into our bedroom looking for anything. But we knew that they still came in there every morning to kiss us. I had to find a hiding place. In the end I decided to keep it at the top of my bedroom closet behind some shoe boxes. We hid the documents and the photographs underneath the large doilies on our bureau dressers.

When we got downstairs to the living room Caroline hugged Lila and Dara, and told them good night then Drew and I walked them to the corner. We stood there for a few minutes talking while Caroline stood on the front porch watching. She waved to Lila and Dara. They liked Caroline and she liked them. "We'll call you when we get home," Lila told Drew and I. "See you later." My sister and I walked back to our house.

I told Caroline that Lila and Dara were going to telephone us when they got home to let us know they arrived safely. So when the telephone rang fifteen minutes later she let Drew and I answer it. Drew, Dara, Lila and I were on the telephone until two o'clock that morning. It reminded me of Lana Mackrey and I and how we used to do the same thing.

CHAPTER TWELVE

Lana came home from the hospital and was living with her aunt, Jennifer. Shortly after she came home I visited her. She had changed a great deal since the murders which was understandable. Naturally everyone felt sorry for her because they knew that she would never be the same again, after the horror she had been through. She talked like she was drunk, or something. Her voice was a bit slurred because of the tranquilizers she had to take. And sometimes she looked like she was in a daze. I knew she was thinking about her family. Yet, she wouldn't talk about what happened.

There were times when we would be talking and she would start to cry. It didn't matter what we were talking about. Our conversation could've been about the weather, and suddenly Lana would burst into tears. If she didn't take the tranquilizers like she was supposed to she would start screaming for no reason at all.

I didn't stay long when I visited Lana. Especially after the last time when she broke down while I was with her. I will never forget that night as long as I live because after that I knew my friend was gone forever, in mind and in spirit.

The last time I visited Lana it was Thanksgiving eve. We decided to go out for a walk that evening because the weather was unusually warm. I asked her to come home with me so we could get my sister because Drew missed Lana just as much as I had.

When we were almost at my house I saw my family members leaving for the night so I called to them. They turned around and waved to Lana and I. Aunt Margeaux was lagging behind the others. She was just coming down the front steps when I called to her. "See you later, Aunt Margeaux!" I shouted. She looked at me and waved. Suddenly Lana froze in her tracks and she had a horrified look on her face.

"The eyes," she whispered frightened. I barely heard her. "What did you say, Lana?" I asked her. She just stood there staring at Aunt Margeaux and my aunt stared at her, too. Lana became very agitated and she started trembling. "What's wrong, Lana?" I asked her. "It's alright. It's just my aunt, Margeaux. Come on I'll introduce you to her."

Aunt Margeaux was still standing there watching us. I took Lana by the arm trying to guide her toward my aunt. But she yanked her arm away from me so hard I almost lost my balance. I could easily see that she was scared to death for some reason.

"The eyes," Lana whispered again and after that she screamed! It was a terrifying scream from a terrified person, and all the while she was staring at Aunt Margeaux. "Lana!" I cried. "What is it? What's wrong?" No matter what I did I couldn't calm her down. People nearby came running over to us to see what was wrong. Lana couldn't be controlled. She was out of her mind with fear so someone ran to get Jennifer.

Lana fell to the ground still screaming. "The m-monster," she cried deathly afraid. "I-it's the m-monster!" She kept on screaming and pointing to where my aunt had been standing. But by then Aunt Margeaux was gone. Someone called for an ambulance and they took Lana to the hospital.

The doctors gave her a sedative when she got there. And when she calmed down Jennifer was allowed to take her home. Whatever happened to Lana that evening sent her over the brink into insanity. A few days later some people from an asylum came and took her away. I couldn't shake the fact that she was alright until she saw Aunt Margeaux that night. Afterward she became hysterical and I started to wonder why. Also, I felt a little guilty because if I hadn't insisted that we go out for a walk that night the whole thing wouldn't have happened.

She kept saying *the eyes* when she saw Aunt Margeaux that night. I recalled the night that the Reverend and Miss Becka Daniels came to our house unexpectedly, and Drew and I saw those eyes. *"But where did Lana see them?"* I wondered. I knew there had to be a reason why seeing Aunt Margeaux had terrified Lana so badly. *"Why?"* I wondered.

Neither Drew nor I had forgotten the night we saw Aunt Margeaux's horrifying, demonic eyes and we never would. Also, we would never forget how she looked at Miss Becka that night either. Later our Pastor and his wife were murdered inside their home. *"Is there some connection here?"* I wondered. When I told my sister what happened to Lana she began to wonder, too.

As far as anybody knew Lana had not seen the person, or persons who killed her family. *"If she did,"* I thought, *"why did they spare her and none of the others?"* Nobody knew for sure if she had seen the killer, or not because she hadn't said much of anything about the murders. When she did talk about them you had a hard time understanding what she was saying, because of the strong medicine that they gave her. She didn't make much sense.

As much as I tried to deny it I was sure that Lana had seen who murdered her family. She didn't scream and carry on like she did when she saw Aunt Margeaux for nothing. She was truly terrified! It was obvious that she'd seen my aunt before, and under circumstances that were not good.

I hoped one day Lana would be alright and become her old self again. Yet, deep down in my heart I knew it wasn't going to happen, and in the end I was right. It never happened and Jennifer had to have her committed. She telephoned me on the day that the people from the asylum were coming to get Lana so I could be there. I thought I would never stop crying because I was saying good-bye to my friend forever.

They had no trouble with Lana because they told her that they were taking her to see her family. Oblivious to the fact that they were all dead, except Alvin, she seemed happy as they lead her to the hospital's car. When they drove off I watched until the car disappeared from sight. I would never see Lana again.

Drew and I tried not to do it but after what happened to Lana we became very suspicious of Aunt Margeaux again. We knew she loved us and that she would never harm us. However, we felt like we couldn't trust her anymore. My sister and I knew that she had done something to Lana.

We talked to Lila and Dara about Lana and about what happened that evening. But the person we really wanted to talk to was Mama. It got to the point where Drew and I started keeping things to ourselves instead of talking to our parents. We felt like we couldn't go to them with our problems, especially after learning that Mama had lied to us. There were a lot of things that they could've told my sister and I about our family. However, they refused to tell us anything.

We wanted to talk to them about the things we found inside the attic instead of making our own assumptions, or relying on Caroline for answers. But we couldn't talk to them. In the first place if they wanted us to know anything the attic door wouldn't have been locked. But they must've known that sooner or later we would venture up there. Curiosity started to get the better of us. We couldn't go to our parents so we had no other choice but to go to Caroline.

She knew a lot about them. It was just a matter of her being willing to talk to us. It took Drew and I one month to muster the courage to confront Caroline, and finally the day came when we did.

We approached her one afternoon when we came home from school. When we entered the house she was sitting at the dining room table reading the newspaper. We hugged her as usual then we put our school books onto the table.

In my opinion the town newspaper wasn't worth reading. There was never anything worthwhile printed in it, mostly news about the murders that occurred in Hardelle and in surrounding Counties. Also, a lot of other junk that nobody really cared about. News traveled faster in Hardelle by word of mouth.

It used to be the same way with the newspaper in Wesbury. I could understand them always printing stories concerning the murders, especially since entire families were sometimes being slaughtered. There was one thing that was strange though. As suddenly as the killing began it ended just as abruptly.

I noticed that the murders occurred toward the end of every month. For eight or ten days there would be a rash of disappearances. Then the bodies, or the body parts of the missing people, or missing person would be found, and after that there was nothing for weeks.

That afternoon it was Drew who approached Caroline. She sat down at the table across from her. While I stood in front of the only mirror that we had in our house, other than the one in our bedroom, and the one in our bathroom. I started putting my hair into different styles waiting for my sister to begin questioning Caroline. We had already talked it over, and hoped she wouldn't bite our heads off for questioning her again.

With my eyes I signaled to Drew in the mirror to begin when she looked at me. She rolled her eyes at me. If I could have read her mind I knew she was probably thinking, *"Celia, you're such a coward!"* I wished I could have been as outspoken as she was but we were as different as night and day. I thought I would get braver as I grew older but I never really believed it would happen. I was chicken-shit and she knew it.

Mama and Papa called me 'sensitive' and I knew they were only trying to be kind. Drew shook her head as she looked at me. I continued to pretend to be interested in my hair then at last she said something.

"Caroline," she said, "what do you know about these people?" She showed Caroline the photographs that we found in the attic. And from the look on her face she was shocked that we had those things. "Where did you get these?" Caroline wanted to know. "We found them in the attic along with these birth records," replied Drew showing her our parent's birth records.

"That door is always locked," said Caroline, "and there are only two keys. I have one and your parents have the other one. How did you get in there?" Drew and I glanced at one another. We were not going to tell on Lila and Dara so we told her a lie.

"Celia and I picked the lock on the door," lied Drew. Caroline eyed us suspiciously. She knew we were lying. "You know, girls," she said, "some things are better off left alone. You've put me in a rather awkward position here." "How so?" I asked her coming over to the table to sit down. "Well," she replied, "I told you two before that it's not my place to tell you anything about your family." Her answer might have sufficed before, but we had no intention of letting her off the hook so easily then.

"Come on, Caroline," said my sister insistently, "you've been with our family for a long time. We know that you know a lot about them. Why don't you just tell us? Nobody else will tell us anything." She was referring to our parents. "Celia and I are not babies anymore you know," continued Drew. Caroline was very calm. We looked at her waiting for her to answer us. I felt sorry for her in a way because we were putting her on the spot again, and she didn't deserve that.

"Are the dates on the birth records of our parents correct?" I asked Caroline. "If they are how can they be that old? Who are these other people in these photographs, and why haven't we ever been told about them? Are our parents really brother and sister as their birth records indicate?" Caroline sighed and looked at us because we had so many unanswered questions.

"Sweetheart," she began, "Richard was your mother's brother and so was Larry." "Then that means they were Papa's brothers, too. Right?" I asked her. "Yes, honey," she replied, "they were." She confirmed that our parents were indeed siblings. "So Danielle and our grandfather were their parents," asked Drew, "as well as the parents of Aunt Jada and Aunt Margeaux?" "Yes," answered Caroline. "How can these dates be right?" asked Drew looking at our parent's birth records. "If they are that makes them nearly two hundred years old but they don't look a day over forty."

"You girls have too many questions for me to answer," replied Caroline. "I will tell you again that it's not my place but your parent's place to answer them. I will tell you that Richard and your father were born before your grandparents were married, and Danielle Bellis-Carbell was your grandmother. You'll just have to talk to your parents about these things. Okay?"

"But why can't you tell us more, Caroline?" asked my sister becoming frustrated. "We know that you know. What about Uncle Marcus and Uncle Wilhelm, are they blood relatives, too?" "No," replied Caroline. She had a look on her face like none that we had ever seen before. She was upset, but not with Drew and I.

"Girls, listen to me carefully," said Caroline. "You're getting into something here and you have no idea about what problems you can create. I told your parents a long time ago and your grandfather, too, that the day was coming when you would start asking questions about them. In my opinion it was a mistake for your parents to have children. And the reason for that is something else you will learn eventually. I have a feeling about that. However, they insisted that they wanted to do it." She hesitated.

"No two children have more love on the face of this earth than you two do," continued Caroline smiling. "You have a right to know the answers to all of your questions. Unfortunately, I can't answer them for you because if I do it could have bad consequences for me. Do you understand what I am saying to you?" My sister and I looked at one another curiously. "No," I said. "What do you mean, Caroline?"

"Are you telling us that they would harm you, Caroline?" asked Drew in disbelief. She looked at both of us but said nothing. She reached for mine and Drew's hands across the table. "You know that I love you both very much. Don't you?" she asked us. We nodded our heads. "I don't think you should ask your parents about any of this stuff right now. Do you understand?" "Why?" I asked her. "It's just not a good time to do it," answered Caroline matter of factly.

"I know you have a lot of questions," she continued, "because you're young adults now, and it was inevitable. I don't think your parents can see that yet, but they will. You have to believe me. In time all of your questions will be answered. In the meantime I want you to relax, and be content with the love that covers both of you. Will you do that for me?" "Sure, Caroline," I said. Drew agreed.

"If your parents knew that you had these things," continued Caroline, "they would be very upset." Drew and I glanced at one another again. We would never tell on Caroline just as we would never tell on Lila and Dara. "I can't believe they would hurt you, Caroline," said Drew, "because they love you." She smiled at us and it was a smile that told us we couldn't have been more wrong. "Yes," she said, "but they love you more."

Caroline was telling us in a round-about way that our parents would have hurt her, or anybody else for that matter where Drew and I were concerned. We couldn't believe it. Whatever they were hiding from us had to be one hell of a secret. "Remember what I said," replied Caroline. "The right time will come just be patient. Okay?" We nodded. "Now," she continued, "you better do your homework. And you better hide these things you found inside the attic, too." She gave the photographs and the birth records back to us.

Caroline went back to reading the newspaper, and Drew and I started to get our school books together so we could do our homework. We would never repeat anything that Caroline told us because we loved her. She was very good to us, and we couldn't bear the thought of anybody harming her. Drew and I would never forgive our family if they ever harmed Caroline.

I got up to retrieve a school book. As I did I looked over Caroline's shoulder to see what she was reading in the newspaper. Three more bodies were discovered the night before in an old cemetery outside of town. And a number of people from Hardelle and nearby towns were still missing. One name in particular caught my eye. It was Alyson Merles.

Alyson was in my class at school before she dropped out. She was a year older than I was. She told me that she and her parents came from Wakling, the town that I was born in, but I didn't know it at the time. She and her family had to leave there she confided in me.

From all that Alyson told me her mother was a lot like Lila's and Dara's mother, Annabelle. However, it hadn't been the next door neighbor that she was fooling around with. It was someone very important, politically, and her parents foolishly tried to blackmail the guy. According to Alyson their plan backfired on them and they were almost murdered one night. After that they thought it was best to leave town so they came to live in Hardelle.

Alyson was an only child. She became a mother herself two years ago, and her little boy's name was Arturo. I thought that was a weird name to label a child with but she liked it so who was I?

Alyson was a wild one. She hung out at all hours of the night with different guys in our school as well as other guys. She drank beer, smoked marijuana and God only knew what else she did. She was tall and slender, and her hair was cut short in a nice style that I liked. A lot of the girls around our age were starting to go with the short haircuts lately. Also, she was known for the short, tight skirts and tight blouses that she wore. All of the guys liked her and a lot of older men did, too.

She tried a few times to get me to go out with her but I declined, because I knew she would end up in trouble one day. She was just too wild and now she was missing. Suddenly I saw something else and it was something that shocked me beyond words.

Under the previous story about the three dead bodies and Alyson Merles were the photographs of Randi Ames and Donnie Ross. After several months their partially decomposed bodies were found in an abandoned factory located behind our school. They had to be identified by their dental records because of the terrible condition that their bodies were in. The newspaper stated that they looked like they had been eaten alive. And both of their throats were ripped open nearly decapitating them.

I was truly sorry for what happened to Randi and Donnie, even after what they did to Drew and I. "They deserved what they got," said Caroline flatly. Drew and I looked at her a little taken aback. We couldn't believe she said that, and she noticed our stunned looks. "They hurt my girls!" she exclaimed quickly. "No one hurts my girls!" It still wasn't like her to be so cold and unfeeling.

I recalled the day when Drew and I came home from school bruised, and bleeding from the fight we had with Randi and Donnie. Caroline promised us that we would never have to worry about them bothering us again. *What made her say that?* I wondered. Evidently she knew something that we didn't. Because Randi and Donnie vanished after that, only to be found dead later. I thought back to the time when we lived in Sheriville, and I thought about Tommy Lee Stone.

I told Caroline who hit Drew with that stone and she told me that it would all be taken care of. A week later Tommy Lee turned up dead. Drew and I thought nothing of it at the time, but now we were older. It was easy to look back and see that whenever somebody hurt us, or threatened us in any way they would end up dead. At first I couldn't see how the Mackrey family figured into that scenario because they were kind to Drew and I, in the beginning that is. Then it dawned on me.

Millicent Mackrey, Lana's grandmother, never liked Drew and I. She called us 'demon spawn', Lana told us. We never did anything to her to make her dislike us, yet, she didn't like us just the same. She let us know it, too. I guess you could say that she was the matriarch of their family. All of them including Arnold, Lana's grandfather, did whatever she said. It made perfect sense. After all it was Millicent who had all of the money in their family.

She managed to turn everybody in their family against Drew and I, except Lana and Mavis, who paid no attention to her. They were told by their parents that because of Millicent they were not to bring Drew and I to their house anymore. So to keep down trouble we would meet them elsewhere whenever we wanted to be together. Truthfully, Drew and I were glad we were not welcome at their house anymore.

Millicent always gave us dirty looks. She would watch us closely, too, like we were thieves or something. She made us feel very uncomfortable, and I recalled my sister telling Caroline all about it, but only half-heartedly. It was no big deal to either one of us because Lana and Mavis were still our friends. No matter how Millicent and the other members of their family felt about us. Lana's family members became politely cool toward my sister and I after a while. Sadly, eventually Millicent managed to turn Mavis against us, too. But never Lana because she remained our friend.

CHAPTER THIRTEEN

"Do you think they will ever tell us anything about themselves, Celia?" asked my sister. "Or be willing to answer any of our questions?" She was referring to our parents of course. "I don't know, Drew," I replied, "maybe, maybe not. I have a feeling that the right time will come just like Caroline said. We just have to be patient that's all." We recalled the property deeds that we found inside the attic so we asked Caroline about them, too.

"Look at these deeds, Caroline," I said pushing them in front of her. "My, my," she said surprised, "you girls really have been busy. Haven't you?" "Did we ever live in any of these places?" asked Drew. Caroline looked over each deed carefully. "Yes, sweetie," she replied, "your family has lived in every one of these places." "Why did they move around so much?" asked Drew. Caroline sighed, folded the deeds and gave them back to us. "Your grandfather owned these properties for a very long time," she said. I noticed that she didn't mention Danielle's name regarding the deeds.

"Drew," she continued, "you were too young to remember anything about your grandfather. But maybe Celia might remember what happened to your family when they lived in Sheriville, and in Wesbury." "What happened to them?" asked my sister anxiously. "There were a lot of killings wherever your family moved to," said Caroline, "and they were always accused of those murders. Especially your grandfather though nothing could ever be proven against them. He wanted to keep his family safe and provide them with a place where they could always go. So he purchased homes in as many places as he could." "Were they in some kind of danger?" asked Drew becoming more curious. "Yes," replied Caroline right to the point.

"There were rumors that your grandfather was the last person to be seen with the people who were found murdered," continued Caroline. "What?!" cried Drew in disbelief. "Did he murder those people?!" "They never found the killer, honey," said Caroline. I could tell that she was holding something back from us. "He was blamed for the murders," continued Caroline. "And people in those towns were suspicious of your other family members, too. Whenever trouble came they would just leave town, and go to another place where your grandfather owned property. They've always had a place to go." "No wonder they moved around so much," said Drew.

"Oh, I wish you could remember your grandfather, honey," Caroline told Drew. "In Wesbury you were only five years old when he left the family." "I do recall a man who used to play with Celia and I when we were little girls," replied Drew. "That's right, sweetheart," said Caroline, "that was your grandfather." "Well," said my sister, "I don't believe he killed anybody. Did someone kill him?" Caroline hesitated.

"Those people in Wesbury," I answered. "I remember the night he left us." Caroline looked at me surprised. "Why, Celia," she said, "I didn't think you would remember that." "I do," I told her. "There was a bad thunderstorm and a lot of bodies were found. The people had been missing for a long time." "That's right, honey," said Caroline. "I'm really surprised that you remember that, Celia. I think your parents and the others believe you've forgotten it." "No," I assured her. "I haven't forgotten it."

"You told me that you didn't remember much about those murders, Celia," said Drew questioningly. "I know," I replied. "I just didn't want to say anything in front of Lila and Dara." I looked at Caroline. "They told us that their aunt was one of the victims." I told her. "I see," said Caroline. "Anyway after your grandfather left us," she continued, "your family left Wesbury and came to Hardelle. You've been here ever since and I don't foresee another move any time in the near future."

"Celia and I are thinking about following them one night," said Drew, "to see where they go and what they do." Caroline panicked suddenly. "No, honey," she said nervously, "y-you must never do that. Promise me that you won't ever do that." "But, Caroline," began Drew. "Promise me!" Caroline interrupted her. "Okay," said my sister. "You, too, Celia," she said looking at me. "Alright," I told her. "I promise."

Caroline got up and went into the kitchen to get our dinner started, and Drew and I knew the conversation was over. Caroline didn't want to answer anymore of our questions so we started to do our homework. "Why did she sound so scared," Drew whispered to me, "when I said we were thinking about following them, Celia?" "I don't know," I said softly. "Maybe she knows something that we don't."

"You know she does," replied Drew. "I didn't really promise her anything you know. All I said was 'okay'." "Well, I promised her," I said. "And I really don't think we should ever do that, Drew." She rolled her eyes at me.

I knew my sister. The day was coming when her curiosity would get the best of her. Our family members could've satisfied that curiosity but they weren't willing to tell us anything. Caroline didn't tell us all that she could have, but at least it was something. Secretly, I hoped Drew would forget about the idea of following our family members. However, all of my hoping would be in vain.

By the time we finished doing our homework that evening it was dinner time. We had just finished eating when we heard our uncles coming upstairs from the basement. "We ought to go down there, too," whispered Drew. "I sure would like to know what's down there. Wouldn't you?" "Sure I would," I replied. "But I'm not going to worry myself about it."

Suddenly I felt afraid for Drew. I prayed silently that she would push her eager curiosity aside. Caroline came into the dining room because she heard our uncles coming upstairs, too. "Remember what I told you, girls," she reminded us. "The right time will come."

They had been asleep all day and so had our parents and our aunts. Drew and I watched them as they came into the living room one by one, and they were dressed to go out. They kissed and hugged each one of us. "How are my girls this evening?" asked Mama. "Fine, Mama," we answered her.

She sat down at the dining room table with us. Papa kissed each one of us on our foreheads. Our house was alive with conversation and laughter. Yet, it wasn't long before all of them were out of the front door and into the night. Drew and I eyed one another then we looked at Caroline who was already watching us. It wasn't hard for her to imagine what we were thinking.

Although all of them had been asleep all day not one of them ate so much as a cracker before they left the house that night. Not even a sip of water touched their lips. It was incredible how they thought we wouldn't notice something like that. Caroline was right. Our parents couldn't see that Drew and I were young adults, and we noticed a lot of things that we never did before. They still thought of us as little girls. I felt sorry for all of them because they were in for a rude awakening.

"I'm going upstairs," said Drew after everyone else left. "Yeah," I replied, "I might as well go, too." "Are you feeling okay, Celia?" asked my sister noticing the sadness in my voice. "Yes," I said, "I'm alright." She went upstairs. I collected all of our school books which were strewn all over the table. Then I said good-night to Caroline and made my way toward the stairs. Suddenly I felt sad. *"What's wrong with me?"* I wondered. I reached the bottom of the staircase and was ready to ascend the stairs when I looked up.

There at the top of the staircase stood the shadowy figure of my grandfather. I saw the eyes that penetrated the covering around him. I stood at the bottom of the staircase frozen to the floor but I wasn't scared. Everything around me began to darken, and I was all alone again as I had been when we were in the attic that night. The darker everything around me got the more clearly I could see my grandfather. I realized he was pulling me inside the darkness with him, or maybe inside that covering with him, but I didn't know for sure. The sorrowful feeling left me.

As I stared at him a woman appeared next to him. She was beautiful and she smiled at me but she didn't say anything. I knew from her photograph that it was Danielle. She tried to take my grandfather's hand trying to pull him away from the stairs, but he wouldn't budge. He just kept looking at me. Danielle began to sob softly and they were heartbreaking sobs. I could feel the pain and the sadness of her spirit. Then I heard someone calling to me in the darkness.

"Celia! Celia, honey! Celia!" It was Caroline and she was shaking me gently but I couldn't feel a thing. "Celia! Snap out of it!" I kept staring at my grandfather whose dark figure was beginning to fade away right before my eyes, and Danielle vanished, too. I could neither move nor speak the entire time they were there, but I could hear Caroline's voice.

"Celia! Celia snap out of it!" she shouted at me. As suddenly as I was swallowed up by the darkness it disappeared just as abruptly. I stared at Caroline. "Celia, honey," she said, "what is wrong with you? You scared the shit out of me! You looked like you were in a trance or something." I shook my head as if I was coming out of a daze.

"I saw him again," I told her. "Who?!" she wanted to know. I started to sob softly. "Oh, honey," she said, "tell me what's troubling you. You were somewhere else. I was calling you but it seemed like you couldn't hear me." "I saw my grandfather again," I told her. "This time Danielle was with him and they were standing at the top of the stairs." "Oh no," said Caroline guiding me to the sofa. I sat down then Drew came downstairs.

"What's all of the shouting about down here?" she asked. "He was at the top of the stairs, Drew," I told her. I didn't have to tell her who I was talking about because she knew. "Danielle was with him," I continued. "She was crying then she disappeared and only he was there."

"I'm not going back up those stairs tonight," said my sister. She was truly frightened. "Calm down," said Caroline. "There's nothing and no one in this house that would ever hurt either one of you." It didn't matter what she said. Drew was scared and she refused to go back upstairs by herself that night.

Caroline fixed us a glass of her warm milk, secret recipe included. It had a soothing effect on us and we were asleep before we knew what hit us. We woke up in our beds the following morning. Caroline told us that Uncle Marcus and Papa had carried us upstairs to bed. "I see what you mean about that warm milk," said my sister. "I told you so,"

I replied. "I don't know what she puts in it but it sure does knock you out cold." "I'll say," she replied.

When we got downstairs that morning we didn't mention what happened on the night before, and neither did Caroline. It didn't matter anyway. Because by that time it was obvious that my grandfather wanted something from me, but what it was I didn't know. However, eventually I would find out.

CHAPTER FOURTEEN

I thought about everything that Caroline told Drew and I about our family. And I couldn't shake the feeling that our grandfather could've been capable of murder. From what I remembered about him he was very good to my sister and I. For that matter he was kind to all of us. We walked around in a daze after our talk with Caroline. Also, we tried to get around it but we couldn't. Because there was something very wrong about our family members. However, what it was we didn't know.

Drew began to talk incessantly about following them, and no matter how hard I tried I couldn't seem to dissuade her. I couldn't stop thinking about our grandfather either. I wanted to know why he was worrying me. Nobody else in our family ever saw him that I knew about, just me. *"Why?"* I wondered. *"What does he want from me?"*

There could have been an answer in the many papers we hadn't gotten to inside the attic. However, my sister and I noticed that a thick, heavy padlock was put on the attic door. We asked Caroline about that.

"Well," she said, "I suggested to your parents that they secure that door a little better. They don't know about you being up there, and it was merely a suggestion I made to them." "Why did you do that?" asked Drew flabbergasted. "Well, honey," replied Caroline, "it's better if you stay out of there. Don't you think? We don't want anybody getting into trouble because of their curiosity. Do we?" Then she winked at us.

We gathered that her suggestion to them was more for her benefit than for ours. She feared what would have happened if our family found out we had been inside the attic.

113

One night Drew and I were in our bedroom looking over the things we found in the attic, and we talked about our birth certificates. Lila told us that Doc B. told her that Wakling was a small town about fifty miles away from Wesbury. Also, he told her that there were a lot of murders there, too.

"I guess they think we're really stupid, Celia," said my sister. "Caroline knows what she is talking about. Doesn't she?" I knew what she was referring to. She was talking about our family. They still thought of us as little girls instead of young women. We had mature minds not the minds of little girls who would go on accepting things, and never questioning anything.

"It's an insult to our intelligence you know," continued Drew a little miffed. "Don't you think so, Celia?" "I do," I replied. "Well," she said, "I still say we ought to follow them one night." "I don't know, Drew," I said. "It doesn't seem like a smart thing to do." "Why not?" she asked me. "Don't you remember what Caroline said," I asked, "and how scared she got?" "I know, Celia," she replied. "But how else will we ever find out anything? All of these years we have watched them every end of the month, or so night after night going out in all kinds of weather. There is something going on here."

"I'm just as curious as you are, Drew," I said. "But I don't think we ought to follow them." "Well," she said, "I know how timid and scary you are so maybe I'll just go by myself." "No!" I cried. "Oh, Celia," she said, "stop being so chicken-shit. They'll never know a thing, trust me." My instincts kicked in then.

I did not like the idea of us spying on our family members. Somehow I knew it would be dangerous. So I decided that no matter what Drew did I would follow my own inner feelings, and have nothing to do with her little scheme. *"I wish something would happen to deter her from this foolish notion of hers',"* I thought. *"Anything!"* I didn't know it then but I would get my wish, at least for a little while. We talked for a long time that night before we went to sleep.

The following afternoon after doing our homework and helping Caroline with some of the housework we went upstairs to our bedroom. We looked over the photographs and the documents again. When Caroline called us for dinner I put the photographs that I had, my birth certificate and the deeds under my mattress, then got ready to go downstairs.

"I'll be down in a minute," said Drew. "You go on ahead." "Why?" I asked her. "What's wrong?" "Nothing," she replied. "I just want to look over my birth certificate again." She was truly fascinated with that document. "Okay," I told her, "I'll wait for you."

"Why do you think Mama chose a midwife and had us at home instead of in a hospital?" Drew asked me. "I don't know," I said. "But a lot of women do that you know." "Yeah," she said, "I guess you're right. It's probably better to have your baby at home huh?" "Yeah," I replied smiling. I didn't say anything to her, but as strange as our parents and the others were I would have been surprised if we had been born in a hospital. However, at home was the only place where Mama could've had us.

My sister put her birth certificate on top of her bureau dresser and we got ready to go downstairs. "Drew!" I cried. "What?!" she said. "Are you crazy?" I asked her. "You can't just leave that laying there like that. Suppose Mama and Papa decide to come in here for something when they wake up?" "We'll be back before then, Celia," she said calmly, "so calm down."

"I think you should be more careful than that," I scolded her. "Don't worry about it," she insisted. "We'll be back up here before you know it." "Well," I said, "at least turn the light off. That way if they do get up before we get back they'll know we're not in here." "Celia," she said, "will you please take it easy." She left the document where it was. We left the bedroom light on, too, and went downstairs for dinner.

We had every intention of going back upstairs to our bedroom that evening, but while we were having dessert Lila telephoned us. She told us that she and Dara were worried about Doc B. He hadn't come home from work and the office had been closed for hours. He told them he would be home early that day because he wasn't feeling very well, and they were very upset. She asked if Drew and I could come over so we could help them search for him.

"He's probably at Millie's house," I told Lila. "No," she said, "we already called her and she hasn't seen him since he left the office this afternoon." "Okay," I said. "We'll be right over." Drew and I quickly left to go over to their house. We never did go back upstairs to our bedroom that night.

We helped Lila and Dara look for their father, and as it turned out we didn't have to go out to look for him. Each one of us took a group of telephone numbers that were listed in his personal telephone book and called the people. It was easy because Lila and Dara had their own separate telephone line, and Doc B. had his own private line. When Dara got tired Lila took over, and when I got tired Drew took over. But nobody we telephoned had seen him. We never thought to call the local tavern.

In the meantime Millie came over to help us. "If he is somewhere drunk I'll kill him," said Dara angrily. "He could've at least telephoned us if he changed his mind about coming home early," said Lila. "Don't worry, girls," said Millie. "I'm sure he'll turn up soon."

After we tried for over an hour to find him Doc B. came home. He was so drunk that Lila, Dara and Millie had to help him out of his car, and they were very happy that he was alright. Therefore, the anger that Lila and Dara were feeling before disappeared. They thanked Drew and I for coming over to help them so we told them good-night, and set out for home.

On our way home Drew suddenly stopped walking and put her hand over her mouth. "What's the matter, Drew?" I asked her. She looked at me with wide-opened, frightened eyes. "What is it?" I asked her again. She took her hand away from her mouth and looked at me. Then it hit me like a bolt of lightning! "Oh no!" I cried. "I knew it! I told you, Drew, but you never listen!"

We remembered that we left the light on in our bedroom, and that her birth certificate was sitting atop her bureau dresser in plain view. By then we had been gone from home for three hours.

"How could you be so stubborn and stupid?!" I yelled at my sister. "All you had to do was listen to me for once and be more careful!" "I'm so sorry, Celia," she said softly. "I'm so sorry. I really am." It was too late for that. Because as soon as our parents awakened and saw our bedroom light on they would go in there to see what we were doing. They wouldn't miss seeing her birth certificate laying on top of her dresser. I was in a state of panic and so was she.

"How could you?!" I cried. "After all that Caroline told us! They'll see it and then they'll know that we've been upstairs in the attic, Drew!" "I'm so sorry, Celia," she said again. "I can't believe I did that." She sounded so pathetic and pitiful I felt badly for yelling at her like I did. She looked at me like she was going to break down and cry any minute. "It's okay," I told her. "You never know maybe Caroline went upstairs, and turned our bedroom light off." Of course I didn't believe that for a second. Caroline had absolutely no reason to go into our bedroom that evening.

We were half a block from Lila's and Dara's house when Dara happened to come outside to make sure that her Dad's car doors were locked. She saw us standing on the corner. "Hey," she shouted to us, "you two are still here? What's going on?" Then she called to Lila who came outside. So we walked back to where they were and told them what my sister had done.

"Oh shit!" said Dara. "Listen, Celia," said Lila, "whatever you do don't tell them that we helped you two please. Because we don't want any trouble." "We would never do that," said Drew adamantly, "and you have our word on that." We went back inside their house with them, and stayed there until ten o'clock that night too afraid to go home.

I thought about telephoning our parents just to see if everything was okay. But it was my cowardice making me think that way. Eventually Drew and I decided to go home and face our family. We had nowhere else to go anyway, and all the way home we were quiet.

When we got there our family members were waiting for us. By the way they looked at us when we came into the house we knew our worst fears were realized. It bothered me immediately that Caroline was sitting at the dining room table with tears in her eyes. The fact that she was responsible for us and she had been crying let us know that something had occurred while we were gone. All eyes were on Drew and I as we entered the living room.

CHAPTER FIFTEEN

Papa stood up and walked over to Drew and I. "Is everything alright with you ladies?" he asked us sarcastically. "Yes," we answered. "Are you sure about that?" asked Mama coming over to stand next to him. "Yes," replied Drew, "everything is fine. Why do you ask?" "We just wanted to be sure that's all," said Papa. "Where have you two been?" "We were at Lila's and Dara's house," replied Drew. "What's wrong with Caroline?"

Mama glanced at Caroline then turned back to us. "Nothing," she said smugly. "Well," I asked "why was she crying?" I was surprised at my boldness. "Nothing is wrong with her," said Papa. "Yet!" I don't know what came over me but when he said 'yet' I got angry.

My father stared at me as I stood in front of him and I stared right back at him. I wished he could've read my mind. Because he would've known that I wasn't afraid of him one bit. In fact, we had never been afraid of Papa. We had the kind of fear that grew out of respect. He expected sarcasm and problems from Drew but never from me and I think he was surprised. A few minutes later something he said let me know that he did know what I was thinking.

I looked at Caroline again and she smiled at me weakly. From the expression on her face I could tell that she was thinking, *"Good for you, Celia!"* I had never stood up to Papa before but I guess there is a first time for everything. Where Caroline was concerned I would have challenged him without a moment's hesitation. "I know what you're thinking, Celia," he said. "But what are you going to do?"

"You're not going out tonight?" Drew asked our parents. "No," said Papa still staring me down. "We've decided to stay home tonight in case there is something that you ladies might want to talk to us about." His remark was designed to make us uncomfortable but I did not flinch. And I still don't know what came over me that night.

"Why do you want to talk to us all of a sudden?" I asked him sarcastically. Our family members looked at me surprised. I'd had enough of them, their secrecy and their weird ways. And seeing Caroline's tears triggered something inside me, something I never knew was there.

"Why, Celia," said Mama, "you're not being a smart ass. Are you?" I looked at her but I said nothing as she stood next to Papa. "Come on, Celia," said my sister heading up the stairs. When I looked at Caroline again she dried her eyes. I looked at our parents and smiled half-heartedly. "Good night," I told them and headed for the stairs. When I said 'good-night' no one responded, and I didn't give a damn.

Our aunts and our uncles had not said a word the entire time. But I knew they were taken by surprise at my sudden surge of bravery just as our parents were. In my own way I wanted all of them to know that no harm had better come to Caroline. Because I would never forgive them if it did, and I would make all of their lives a living hell. Knowing how much they loved my sister and I it wouldn't be a hard thing to do.

Before Drew and I got into our bedroom our parents were right behind us. They scared the hell out of us, but I didn't let them know they had frightened me. I turned around and faced them. We had no idea they were there until we turned around to close our bedroom door. Our hearts fell to our stomachs.

"How did they get upstairs so fast?" I wondered in amazement. One minute they were downstairs in the living room, and the next minute they were right behind us on the second floor. We heard no movement at all to alert us to their presence, and it was spooky. Drew was visibly shaken and so was I. But I quickly regained my composure because I was not going to let them see that I was scared.

I saw a look in our parent's eyes that I never saw before, and it was a look of suspicion and distrust. Mama's hazel eyes were pitch black with anger and her complexion was darker, too. Papa's eyes were sinister- looking, and his face was filled with anger that he was controlling very well. Our parents loved Drew and I deeply but it did not seem like it then. They were like two different people we didn't know.

"You better shut your door," said Mama angrily. "Yes," said Papa, "and lock it. We wouldn't want anything to happen to you ladies." We couldn't believe those two people were our parents. Drew's shock was all over her face. Usually she was outspoken and brave but she was as quiet as a mouse. "Good night," I said to them again and again they didn't respond. So I closed our bedroom door while they were still standing there.

If we hadn't known better we would have thought that they wanted to do something to us. Something to make us sorry for searching around inside the attic. As soon as Drew and I entered our bedroom our fears were confirmed because her birth certificate was gone.

"My, Lord," I said. "What the hell is happening around here? What did they mean by that remark about not wanting anything to happen to us?" "I-I'm scared, Celia," said Drew nervously. "What do you think they'll do to us?" "Nothing," I told her. "Don't worry about it."

"Why is Papa calling us '*ladies*' all of a sudden, Celia?" she asked me. "Yeah," I replied chuckling softly, "maybe they've finally realized that's what we are. Huh?" She didn't think it was funny because she was frightened. Before we got into bed that night we did something we had not done in a long time. We locked our bedroom door, and we prayed.

We found the Bibles that Reverend and Miss Becka Daniels gave us and we read aloud from them. Drew and I couldn't believe our parents in a round-about way had threatened us. They didn't come right out and do it but they did it just the same.

We had never seen them the way that we saw them that night. They were like two strangers to us. I did know one thing for certain though. I didn't want to see one bruise or mark on Caroline when I awoke in the morning. If I did I vowed to make all of them pay. I didn't know how I would do it but I would.

"Do you know what, Celia?" asked my sister as we laid in our beds that night. "What?" I asked her. "I think they would've done something to us," she said still worried and frightened. "What do you think?" "I don't think so, Drew," I replied. "You know how much they love us." "Do they?" she asked me. "Of course they do," I replied. "It sure as hell didn't seem like it tonight," she said. And she was right because it hadn't seemed like it.

We laid awake talking softly that night and we agreed on one thing. Whatever it was that they didn't want us to know about them they were willing to hurt somebody to keep it a secret. We finally understood what Caroline meant when she told us if she revealed anything to us there could be bad repercussions for her. *"That's why she was sitting at the table in tears,"* I thought. *"They blame her for our being inside the attic."* Naturally they knew if my sister had her birth certificate we had other things, too.

I looked under my mattress to see if the photographs, the deeds, our parent's birth records and my own birth certificate were still there, but they were gone. Drew began to sob again because she was so scared. We were in trouble and so was Caroline. If they treated my sister and I as badly as they had it had to be worse for her.

"How could two people who love us so much turn on us so fast?" I wondered. "What is so terrible they have to hide it from us, Celia?" asked Drew through her tears. "What is it that would make them hurt Caroline or us?" I had no idea and I told her so. All I knew was that it had to be a terrible, terrible thing.

When we woke up the following morning we didn't smell the usual aroma of breakfast cooking in the kitchen. We ran downstairs to see if Caroline was alright but she wasn't there. Drew and I got dressed and went out to the guest house where she lived, but every window and door was locked. We called to her and rang her doorbell, but she never answered us. We wouldn't see Caroline for the next month.

I grew more angry at our parents and I didn't know what they did to Caroline. But I vowed that if they sent her away I was leaving, too. I was almost eighteen years old and I would be out of school soon. Although I was not considered by law to be an adult I would still leave home. And there was nothing that our parents, or anybody else could do about it. However, I did not want to leave Drew behind. And without a decent job, money, or a place to live I wouldn't be able to take her with me.

The month that Caroline was gone my sister and I, at my urging, avoided our family members. When it was time for them to awaken in the evening we went over to Lila's and Dara's house. And we would stay there until almost midnight. I wanted our parents to say something to us about it. Because then I would have an excuse to lash out at them, but they never said a word to us. I thought they might stay home and wait for us to come in. Yet, they hit the streets as usual and stayed out all night. So I held my anger against all of them inside me.

I thought about opening all of the shades on their bedroom windows just to be nasty, but my sister stopped me. I thought all of my timidity was gone because of the sudden courage that I felt. Yet, when another thunderstorm came I was just as scared as I had always been.

While Caroline was gone Drew and I made our own meals, although neither one of us could cook that well. We did our own shopping, too, with money that Caroline kept inside a safe located in our dining room wall. Everybody in our house knew the combination to the safe. We were glad not to have to see any of our family members but we sorely missed Caroline. "I wonder what they did to her?" asked Drew. "I don't know," I replied. "But I know she'll be back because they need Caroline, and so do we."

Things changed in our house after the night that our parents discovered we had been inside the attic. It would be more truthful to say that Drew and I changed. Our family didn't know it but we were more determined than ever to find out what they were hiding from us. *"What is the secret that they are willing to go so far to protect?"* I kept wondering to myself.

One evening before we left to go over to Lila's and Dara's house I checked on our sleeping parents, because my anger at them had abated by that time. It was the first time I had checked on any of our family members in a while. Drew was downstairs waiting for me. I was standing in the doorway of their bedroom staring at them.

Suddenly the darkness that was becoming familiar to me covered me, and covered the upstairs area where I was. I sensed that someone was watching me, and when I turned around there standing directly in front of me was our grandfather.

He looked so sad and he wasn't smiling at me like he usually was when I saw him. I couldn't move. He came closer to me and I wasn't afraid. Then out of my bedroom walked Danielle. She was holding my music box in her hands. Then she turned to face me.

"They didn't find this, Celia," she said to me sweetly. "And they won't because it is yours. I give it to you as a gift. So listen to it and it will tell you everything that you want to know." She smiled at me then she was gone, but our grandfather was still standing there watching me.

"Celia!" shouted Drew from downstairs. "What's taking you so long? They'll be getting up soon." I couldn't answer her then our grandfather spoke to me. "You have nothing to fear from your parents, Celia, honey," he told me. "They would never hurt you, or your sister. They were just upset that's all."

"Celia!" Drew shouted again. Then I heard her coming upstairs. Our grandfather disappeared and so did the darkness. "Celia!" shouted my sister standing in the middle of the staircase. "What are you doing? Let's go because it's getting dark." "Okay," I said softly. She was right. It was getting dark outside and our family members would be awakening shortly. "Hurry up," said Drew.

We ran down the stairs and out of the front door. When we reached the sidewalk the light came on in our parent's bedroom. We made it out of there just in time.

When we arrived at Lila's and Dara's house they were housecleaning. "You're just in time," said Lila when she opened her front door to us. "In time for what?" asked my sister. "We're cleaning out the basement," said Lila. "Since you two are here you can help us." "Sure," I said. We followed her into their cellar and it was loaded with junk. There was some old furniture, old clothing and many boxes that the previous residents had left behind.

Lila and I took one side of the room and Drew and Dara took the other side. "We'll get done a lot faster with all four of us working," said Drew. We loaded a lot of the old clothing and small items into trash bags to be thrown away. A lot of the things that were in boxes we left in there and put them out for the trash. Drew found another small box that was laying in a corner, then she opened it to see what was inside it.

"Hey, look at this," said my sister. We turned around to see what she had found. "Wow!" said Dara. "It's a Ouija board. I wonder who it belonged to." We could see it was very old. I had heard many stories about Ouija boards but I had never seen one before.

"I don't trust those things," said Lila, "because I heard they are evil." "That's just superstitious bullshit," said Dara. "Let's sit down and see if it really works." "I don't know, Dara," I said. "I agree with Lila. We should leave that thing alone because I've heard some bad stories about them, too." "You're all a bunch of punks," said Dara. "Come on it can't hurt anybody it's just a game."

Against our better judgment Lila and I pulled some chairs up to a small table with Drew and Dara. What we stumbled onto that evening took all of us down a road that we definitely never meant to travel. We had no idea how much pain and misery we were in store for because of us messing around with what we thought was '*just a game*'. Not once did the thought ever cross any of our minds that the previous residents of that house left that Ouija board behind for a reason.

CHAPTER SIXTEEN

The four of us began to play with the Ouija board. "Now," said Dara, "we have to put our fingers onto the pointer lightly, and it's supposed to answer our questions." "I've heard that these things harbor evil spirits and demons," whined Lila. She was very apprehensive about the board and so was I. However, we did as Dara said and put our fingers lightly onto the pointer.

"Let's ask it something," said Drew excitedly. "Like what?" I asked her curiously. She thought about it for moment. "I know!" she exclaimed. "Let's ask it about our family members, Celia! It might tell us what they're hiding from us." "Do you really believe that nonsense, Drew?" I asked her. "Well," she replied, "we can try." "Sure," said Dara, "it's just a game and it's supposed to be fun."

Dara and my sister were very excited about the Ouija board, but like Lila I was fearful of it. I'll never understand why I didn't follow my mind that night. Because all of us should have left that thing alone.

"I read somewhere that a woman was fooling around with one of these things," I told them, "and she opened a doorway to hell." I was still trying to convince them to leave the board alone. "She almost lost her life," I continued, "when a demon attacked her and her family. She had to burn the damn thing to get rid of all of the evil that she brought on her household. After all of that she still wasn't sure if the demon was gone, and they had to move." I might as well have been talking to myself. Because nobody other than Lila paid any attention to me.

"Are you going to be alright, Celia?" asked Drew noticing my nervousness. "No," I said. "I don't think we ought to bother with this thing." Lila agreed with me, but again Drew and Dara ignored us.

Hesitantly, Lila and I put our fingers onto the pointer with Drew and Dara. It was my sister who asked the board the first question.

"Ouija," she began, "what is the secret that our family members are hiding from us? And why do they act so strangely?" We waited for the pointer to move but nothing happened. "Good," said Lila relieved, "nothing is happening. Now can we get back to work?" She and I began to get up.

"Wait a minute," said Drew. "Celia, you ask it because maybe it doesn't want to answer me." "What makes you think it will answer me?" I asked her. "Just try it, Celia, please," she begged. "Remember that music box?" asked Dara. "It had some kind of power over you. So maybe there's something special about you, something you have and we don't." "I hardly think so," I replied chuckling a little bit. "Try it, Celia," she urged me. "Go on, Celia." said Lila. "Then we can get back to work." I sighed heavily. "This is ridiculous," I told them. Yet, I decided to humor them. So Lila and I placed our fingers onto the pointer again.

"Ouija," I said, "what is the secret that our family members are hiding from Drew and I? And why do they go out at night near the end of every month? What do they do?" "Good, Celia," said my sister. "I didn't think about that." "S-sh!" said Dara.

I really didn't expect anything to happen. But suddenly the pointer moved under our fingers, and not one of us was helping it. "Look!" cried Drew. "Be quiet, Drew," whispered Dara. The pointer began to move to different letters on the board and Drew called out each letter it pointed to.

The first word it spelled for us was 'n-o-s-f-a-r-t-u'. "What's that?" asked my sister curiously. "Nosfartu?" I said questioningly. "What in the world is 'nosfartu', Celia?" asked Drew again. "I have no idea," I told her. "But I also read that these things have a hard time spelling anything correctly." "So," said Lila, "what could it be?" "I guess we'll have to get a dictionary and look it up," said Dara. In the meantime the pointer was still moving under our fingers.

"It's spelling something else," said Lila, " look!" The next word it spelled for us was *'v-a-m-p-y- r'*. "What's that?" asked Dara anxiously. "Vampyr," said Lila. "That can't be right." We had read enough horror stories to know that the board was trying to spell the word 'vampire'. "That's crazy," said Drew. "The other word must be 'nosferatu'," I told them. The pointer proceeded to spell another word for us. It was *'m-u-r-d-r'* trying to spell out the word 'murder'. We were all stunned. "Vampires! Murder!" cried Lila astounded. "What the hell is going on here?"

"Do you mean it's trying to tell us that our family members are vampires, Celia?" asked Drew in disbelief. "It looks that way to me," I told her calmly. "Well," she replied, "you better try that again because that's just nuts. There is no such thing as a vampire and everybody knows it." Although all of us did know that I wasn't so sure anymore. I became more curious by that time. So I decided to ask the Ouija board another question.

"Ouija are you telling us that our family members are vampires?" I asked the board. We watched horrified as the pointer moved to the word 'yes'. "Oh no," said Drew. "I don't think I want to bother with this thing anymore. You were right, Celia. Who would believe such nonsense?"

I thought about all of the strange and mysterious things that our family members did. And about the things we found inside the attic. I said softly, "I would." "No, Celia!" cried my sister. "You know this thing can't be telling us the truth."

I saw the anguish in my sister's eyes and the stunned looks on the faces of Lila and Dara. "Think about it." I told her. "Everything would fall into place if we did believe it." My sister did think about it and it sounded crazy. "But how, Celia?" she asked me. "I don't know how," I replied. "Why don't you ask it?" Lila said to me.

"Ouija," I began, "how can our family members be vampires?" The pointer started to move again. It spelled out the letters *'D-a-n-e-l-l'*. "Danell," said Drew puzzled. "What is that?" "You mean..... who is that?" said Lila. "It's someone's name." We were all silent. Then suddenly my sister cried, "Danielle! Oh my, Danielle was a vampire!" I moved away from the table and away from the Ouija board after that.

"What's wrong, Celia?" Lila asked me. "I don't like this," I told them, "and I'm not going to ask it anything else. How did it know about Danielle?" "That's a very good question," said Lila. "It must be real, Celia, can't you see that? I would like to ask it something, too." She put her finger onto the pointer with the others while I stood back from the table.

"Tell me about Danielle, Ouija," said Lila. "What has she got to do with Celia's family members being vampires?" The pointer wouldn't move. Drew tried asking it the same question. Still, it wouldn't move. Then Dara tried but nothing happened, and everybody looked at me.

"It seems like it won't answer anybody but you, Celia," said my sister. "You must have some kind of power or something." I chuckled softly. "I can't imagine what it is," I said. "You ask it how Danielle has anything to do with this," said my sister. "And I'll bet it'll answer you." I didn't want to touch the damn thing anymore but they continued to persuade me. Even Lila who in the beginning felt the same way that I did about the board. Reluctantly, I sat down again and placed my fingers onto the pointer.

"Ouija," I asked it, "what does Danielle have to do with our family members being vampires?" Immediately the pointer began to move to different letters on the board. *F-i-r-t* it spelled out. "Firt," I said confused. "What the hell is that?" "First!" cried Lila. "It's trying to spell the word 'first'. She was the first one, the first vampire." "This is getting eerie," I said to them. "These things lie you know." "Well, Celia," said Lila, "if that's the case how did it know about Danielle?"

There was no way the Ouija board could've known anything about Danielle, so it had to be telling us the truth. "Continue on, Celia," urged Drew. "What do I ask it now?" I asked them. "Try to find out more about our family members," said my sister anxiously, so I continued. By that time I was just as curious as the others were. I wanted to know everything that the Ouija board could tell us.

"Ouija are you saying that Danielle was the first vampire?" I asked the board cautiously. The pointer wasted no time in pointing to the word 'yes'. "Was my grandfather a vampire, too?" I asked it, and again the board answered 'yes'. I even tried to trick the board after that. "Let's see if it really knows what it's talking about," I told the others. "What are you going to do?" asked my sister. "You'll see," I told her. "Ouija," I began, "what was our grandfather's name, and was he Danielle's husband?" I thought that if the board answered my question truthfully I would have all the proof that I needed to know if it was real or not.

All of us watched as the pointer proceeded to spell my grandfather's name, 'D-a-m-o-n', it spelled out. It was trying to spell 'Damion', and it answered 'yes' to the second part of my question. "Well," said Drew, "we sure as hell don't need anymore proof than that. Do we?" We took our fingers away from the pointer after that, and sat back in our chairs trying to take in all that the board told us.

"Vampires!" cried Lila in stunned disbelief. "Oh, Celia, that explains everything. All that we read in those papers we found inside your attic is true." "I never believed that vampires really existed," said Dara quietly. "Boy was I wrong." "Are you two going to be alright?" Lila asked my sister and I. "We have no other choice but to be alright," I said forlornly.

"We ought to confront them with what we know about them, Celia," said my sister. "No," I told her. "Why not?" She wanted to know. "Remember what Caroline told us?" I said to her. "She said that the right time will come and they'll have to tell us the truth." "Yeah," said Drew, "I remember. But I wonder what's going to happen to make them tell us the truth." "I don't know," I replied. "I'll bet Ouija knows," she said devilishly. "Why don't we ask it, Celia?" asked Dara.

The Ouija board would only answer me. Therefore, only my finger was on the pointer while the others watched in silence. "What will happen, Ouija, to make our family reveal their secret to Drew and I?" I asked the board. The pointer started moving under my fingers, and it guided my hand to the letters 'm-u-r-d-r' again. "Murder!" I cried. "Someone is going to be murdered, Ouija?" I asked it and the board answered 'yes'. "Who?" I wanted to know. It spelled out 'c-h-i-d'. "What is that?" asked Drew. We thought about it for a minute.

"Ouija," I said, "are you trying to spell 'child'?" The pointer moved to the word 'yes'. "Who is this child who will be murdered, Ouija?" I asked it. Then it spelled the letters 'f-r-e-n'. "What's 'fren'?" asked Lila curiously. "Are you spelling 'friend', Ouija?" I asked it and again it answered 'yes'. I panicked after that because Drew and I only had two friends, Lila and Dara. The pointer moved again spelling the word 't-r-t-h'. "Truth," I said, "we're going to find out the truth about something."

The Ouija board was telling us that Drew and I would learn the truth about our family members as a result of a 'friend'. However, that 'friend' had to do with me, and believe it or not my grandmother, Danielle. It was a 'friend' that I had not met yet. And a 'friend' whose ultimate goal would be to murder me. I would have no idea what was happening at the time. However, it was so strange to me how I knew that but I said nothing to the others about it. I kept it to myself, and continued to ask the board questions for their sakes. We didn't know it but the Ouija board had another surprise for us.

"Who will murder this friend of ours, Ouija," I asked the board, "and why?" The pointer started to shimmy under my hand. Then it abruptly stopped and wouldn't answer me. I guessed it felt that it had told me all I needed to know. But I repeated my question.

"Who will murder this friend, Ouija, and why?" I asked again. The pointer moved so quickly after I asked that question my finger came away from it. Then it began to move by itself. The four of us watched as it spelled out the letters 'M-a-r-c-s' and 's-p-y-n-g'. At first we couldn't figure it out then it dawned on me. It was telling us about an entirely different murder, a second murder.

"It's trying to spell 'Marcus' and 'spying'," I said. "Someone will be spying on Uncle Marcus," asked Drew in amazement, "and he's going to kill them?" "Let's not jump to any conclusions here, Drew," I told her. "What else could it be, Celia?" she asked. In my heart I knew she was right but I just did not want to believe it. I put my finger onto the pointer again lightly.

"Ouija," I asked, "who is this friend who will be spying on my uncle, Marcus? Are you saying that he will murder this friend?" After that was when we got the shock of our lives. The pointer spelled the word 'D-a-r' then it moved to the word 'no'. We didn't have to be rocket scientists to know who 'Dar' was. It was Dara that the Ouija board was telling us about. According to it she was the one who was going to be killed but not by our uncle. I noticed how quiet Dara got suddenly.

"I can't imagine what you would be doing spying on our uncle, Dara," I said curiously. "You don't even know him. Do you?" "W-what makes you think that I know your uncle, Celia?" said Dara shakily. "Are you sure about that?" I asked her suspiciously, because I had a feeling that she was lying to us. "O-oh, c-come on," she said nervously. "I-I d-don't know your uncle, Celia." I didn't believe her and neither did anybody else. I believed she did know Uncle Marcus. I started to recall the different things that Lila told me about Dara recently.

According to her Dara often went out at night alone. Doc B. would be asleep, or just too drunk to notice that she wasn't in the house. She wouldn't come home until near dawn sometimes. Knowing all of this I realized it was easy for her to have met Uncle Marcus. We knew for a fact that he liked the ladies. Dara was a beautiful girl that he wouldn't have missed seeing. I had to do something because Dara was lying through her teeth. Also, I sensed that she was in serious danger and didn't even know it.

"Ouija," I said, "is Dara the friend who will be murdered for spying on our uncle, Marcus?" "Celia!" cried Dara. "What the hell are you doing?!" We watched as the board answered 'yes' then we looked at her. "All of you are crazy!" she said getting a little upset. "And so is that stupid Ouija board. I'm going upstairs. I don't want to hear anymore of this nonsense." "You're the one who started this," said Lila. "It wasn't nonsense a few minutes ago and it could help you, Dara. Now do you know their uncle or not?" "No!" cried Dara heading upstairs. Strangely, she didn't want anything else to do with the Ouija board after that.

"You have to talk to her, Lila," I said. "Because she could be in terrible danger and she doesn't even know it." "You are probably right," said Lila. "But she won't listen to anything that I say, she never does." "Maybe I can talk to her," suggested Drew. She and Dara were very close. "Maybe she'll listen to you, Drew," I said. "Try to talk some sense into her because we know that she is lying. So convince her how dangerous the situation could get for her if this board is right." "Alright," said my sister. "I'll do my best."

She followed Dara upstairs. Lila and I hoped that Dara would listen to reason. Yet, my instincts told me it was already too late for Dara. But I pushed the thought out of my mind. I wanted to be sure we were right about Dara lying to us so I decided to question the Ouija board more. "Ouija," I began, "does Dara Birch know our uncle, Marcus?" The board promptly answered 'yes'. Lila and I looked at one another because Dara lied to us. "How does she know him, Ouija?" I wanted to know. The pointer spelled the letters '*l-o-v*'. "Is she in love with him?" I asked it and again the board answered 'yes'.

"How did she meet him?" I wanted to know. The pointer spelled the word '*p-a-r*'. We had to think about that for a moment. "The park," said Lila. "She met him in the park." "Do they still meet there, Ouija?" I asked and the board answered 'yes'. "Is Dara going to be alright, Ouija?" I asked it. Our hearts fell to our knees when it answered 'no'.

The pointer continued to move and it spelled the words '*g-r-a-t*'………'*d-a-n-g-r*'……'*j-e-l-o-s-y*'.

"Oh no!" said Lila. "Not my sister please, Celia, we have got to do something!" "Ouija," I began, "can we help Dara?" The board answered 'no' and Lila began to sob softly. I tried to console her but there was really nothing I could do. Dara was in danger. However, I was the only one who paid any attention to something else the board told us. It was telling us something about 'jealousy'. We had to convince Dara to leave Uncle Marcus alone. Then we heard Doc B. come into the house.

CHAPTER SEVENTEEN

"Hello!" he shouted. "Where is everybody?" "Hi, Dad," we heard Dara say to him. "Hi, Doc B.," we heard Drew say. Lila pulled herself together and we went upstairs. I carried the Ouija board with me because I planned to take it home with me since Lila and Dara didn't want it. Lila was afraid of it and so was Dara after it mentioned her and my uncle. But Drew wasn't and my fear of it had vanished.

I wanted to use it again when we got home. However, we had to keep our family members from seeing it. I knew it was the last thing that any of them wanted to see Drew and I with. Whatever their secret was they were desperately trying to keep it hidden, and they were fully aware of what Ouija boards could do. Lila and I greeted Doc B. when we got upstairs.

"How are you girls this evening?" asked Doc B. "Fine," replied Drew and I. "Are you and Drew having dinner with us tonight, Celia?" he asked me. "I guess," I told him. "We haven't been invited yet." "Of course you're invited," he said. Suddenly a worried look came upon his face as he looked at Lila.

"Lila, honey," he said, "are you feeling alright?" "Yes, Dad," she replied, "I'm okay." "Well," he said, "get your sweaters, jackets or what have you and let's go." "Go where, Dad?" asked Dara. "Out to dinner, Madam," he said playfully. He was in a very good mood.

"I'm going to pick up Millie," he continued, "and we're all going out for pizza. Are you ready?" Sure," said Lila half-heartedly. "Alright," replied Dara quietly. "Well," said Doc B., "don't everybody show any enthusiasm all at once because it might overwhelm me. What's going on here?" "Nothing," we told him. "Come on now." he said. "I know there's something wrong. So what is it? You girls know you can talk to me. Right?" "Dad, really," said Lila, "everything is fine."

"What's that you have there, Celia?" asked Doc B. looking at the Ouija board. "We found it in your basement." I told him. "It's a Ouija board." "Oh no," he said a little dismayed. "Listen to me, girls, I know I'm not your parent. But I really don't think you ought to be fooling around with that thing." "We were just going to have some fun with it that's all," I told him. He sighed deeply.

"I remember my sister and her girl friends having some fun with one of those things, too," said Doc B. "I found out after she was killed that it foretold her death." If Drew and I were not afraid of the board before we got a little nervous when he told us that. And more afraid for Dara because of what the board said about her and Uncle Marcus. Strangely, I could not get that word 'jealousy' out of my head.

I was going to leave the board there while Drew and I went out to dinner with them, and pick it up when we returned. But Doc B. told me to take it out of his house and get rid of it. Of course I had no intention of doing that. But he didn't even want it in his car with us. So since we couldn't leave it there, or take it with us we decided to go home.

"I'm really sorry, girls," Doc B. told my sister and I. "But I can swing by your house and pick you up after you get rid of that thing if you want me to." "No," I said, "that's okay. Maybe some other time we can go out to dinner with you." "Okay," he said, "we'll see you later on. Alright?" "Alright," we said. Drew and I were hungry. Pizza sounded very good to us after all of the make-shift meals we had been eating. But we wanted to keep the Ouija board so we set out for home.

When we got home that night we were met by the sweet aroma of something cooking in the kitchen. Caroline was back, and we were all over her when we saw her, so happy she had returned. There were no marks, or even a faint trace of a bruise on her body anywhere. And she looked well rested, too. "Caroline, where have you been?" We said to her excitedly. "We missed you so much."

From all that Caroline told us we surmised that her going away, at the bequest of Papa, was done as a punishment for us. As my sister and I had suspected they blamed her for our being inside the attic. When we asked her where she had been for a whole month she wouldn't tell us. All she said was, "Let's just say it was in my best interest to leave you two for a spell."

She told us that Papa had finally contacted her and asked her to come back. He told her he hadn't seen Drew and I since she had been gone. And he knew we were avoiding him and the others. I could feel my resentment toward our family members building up again. However, this time I decided to just let it go. Caroline was back and that was all that mattered. We heard noises upstairs after that.

"Are our parents home?" Drew asked Caroline surprised. "Yes, honey," she replied, "they are. And they probably heard you two come into the house. I hear they haven't seen you in a while so what have you been doing?" "We've been dodging them ever since you left," said Drew. "Oh," said Caroline with a smile. "I see." We heard our parents talking as they were coming down the stairs.

"Quick," I said to Drew, "hide the board." "Where?" she asked. "What board?" asked Caroline curiously. We showed her the Ouija board. She gave us a funny look then took the board from us, and put it underneath the kitchen sink. "You can get it later," she told us.

After they came into the living room Papa came over and stood in front of my sister and I. He was smiling at us lovingly. My sister smiled back at him but I didn't. He was very happy to see us, too. They remained at home that night because they were tired of us avoiding all of them. He kissed Drew on her forehead gently then he looked at me. "Will you let your Papa kiss you, Celia, honey?" he asked me eagerly. "Or are you still pissed off at us?"

My mother walked over to Drew and hugged her tightly. My parents were both watching me smiling. I nodded my head to my father, and he wrapped his muscular arms around me and hugged me tightly to him. "I love you, honey," he whispered into my ear tenderly. I thought he would never let me go. Mama hugged me, too. Their strength was astonishing. It was then I realized that it didn't matter how much I resented our parents for the things they did. I loved them both more than words could ever express, and I knew my sister felt the same way that I did.

The rest of our family members entered the room where we were. Caroline came into the room, too. Soon we were all talking with one another a mile a minute. We played music on the phonograph and we played games. Everything was back to normal, and it was as if nothing had ever happened. Drew and I forgot about the Ouija board and Caroline didn't remind us about it. Three weeks would pass by before I thought about it again.

Caroline told us later on that our parents knew about everything we found inside the attic. But they never questioned us about it, or said a word to us about it. Oddly, one morning when my sister and I woke up everything we found inside the attic was placed atop our bureau dressers. Our parents were using that as a way of letting us know they were ready to talk to us. Yet, we never questioned them and I will never understand why we didn't.

It was the beginning of the month when they remained at home in the evenings. So if we wanted to talk to them about anything we had ample opportunity to do it. I recalled what Danielle told me about the music box. She said it would tell me things I wanted to know if I listened to it. I was thinking about that when I suddenly remembered the Ouija board.

I went to the kitchen sink and looked underneath it for the board but it was gone. So I went to Caroline and asked her for it. Hesitantly, she went out to the guest house and got it for me. "I really wish you wouldn't fool around with this thing, Celia," she told me. "It's only a game, Caroline," I told her. "You have no idea what kind of trouble these things can bring on you, sweetheart," she continued. "Like what kind of trouble?" I wanted to know, already knowing the answer.

"Just promise me one thing," she said. "Alright, "I replied. "What?" "Never use it when you're alone," she told me. "Why?" I asked her. "Because," she replied, "they harbor the spirits of the dead who have done something evil in their lifetime. They're spirits that are trapped in this world for some reason, or another. All they want is an opportunity to entrap an unsuspecting person like you, or Drew. And they can do that best when the person using the board is alone. It's harder for them when there's more than one person using it at the same time. Sometimes there are good spirits in them, too. But like I said they're trapped in this world for some reason so you can't trust them." "Okay," I told her. "I promise I won't use it when I'm alone." *"She sure knows a lot about Ouija boards,"* I thought. It was some while later when Caroline confided in me, and told me her mother and some of her friends had been using a Ouija board, and it foretold her family's death. They thought it was fun, too. But shortly after that was when her parents, and her sister were killed in that car accident. It was after she told me that story when I truly believed all that the Ouija board told Lila, Dara, Drew and I.

While we were in our bedroom one evening I told Drew what Caroline said about the Ouija board. "It does make sense," my sister replied. "Did you tell her what it has already told us?" "No," I replied. "Good," said Drew. "Let's ask it some more questions about Mama and Papa." "How about Uncle Marcus and Dara?" I asked her. "We should be asking it about that. Don't you think?" "No, Celia." she said. "It told us she is going to die, but I still don't really believe it. Do you?" "Of course I do," I told her. "It's obvious these things don't lie about everything, Drew." I still couldn't get that word 'jealousy' out of my head for some reason.

My sister wouldn't believe anything the board told us about Uncle Marcus and Dara, but I did. Maybe she set up a mental block about that. But I knew it was going to happen, and we would be powerless to stop it. We set up the Ouija board and started playing with it.

Whenever my sister asked it a question it wouldn't answer her. "I don't understand why it will not answer anybody but you, Celia," she said. "You must have some kind of power." I laughed about that. "That's just ridiculous," I told her. Yet, whenever I asked the Ouija board a question it would promptly answer me. I even tried asking it a silly question just to see if my sister was right, and it answered me. "See," she said after the board answered me, "I told you so, Celia."

It was eerie and it unnerved me a little bit. "Why else won't it answer anybody but you?" she said. "Where would I get special powers from?" I asked her chuckling. "I'll just keep my finger on the pointer along with yours," she told me. "But you ask the questions." We began to ask the board more questions about things we wanted to know.

"Are our parents really brother and sister, Ouija?" I asked the board, and it answered 'yes'. That day I asked it a lot of questions regarding our parents, the photographs and all of the other things we found inside the attic. It revealed a lot of unknown things, too. And it confirmed everything about our family members that we had already suspected.

"It's a damn shame we didn't have this thing a long time ago, Celia," said Drew. "Look at all of the things that we could've found out. Let's ask it about Caroline." "What about her?" I asked. "Well," said Drew, "was she in love with our grandfather? And if so why didn't they ever get together?" When I asked it the board answered 'yes' she had been in love with our grandfather.

The second part of our question was answered by the board as the pointer tried to spell the word *'sadness'*. It was weird how my sister believed the Ouija board about everything else, but not about Uncle Marcus and Dara. It was almost idiotic to me. She must have had some kind of mental block about that.

"Hey, I know," said Drew, "let's ask it about Lila's and Dara's aunt, Selma Ann." "Alright," I said. We put our fingers lightly onto the pointer again. "Ouija," I began, "tell us about Selma Ann Birch. What happened to her and who killed her?" Suddenly and without any warning whatsoever the board flew into the air, and almost hit us both in our heads. It slammed itself into our bedroom wall as if someone we couldn't see threw it there. "Are you girls alright up there?!" Mama shouted to us from downstairs. "Yes, Mama!" I yelled. "We're okay! I just dropped something that's all!"

"What the hell just happened, Celia?" asked Drew a little shaken. "Don't ask me, " I replied still a little stunned. "The damn thing just went crazy." "It never did that before," she said. "It was only when you asked it about Selma Ann." "Yeah," I replied, "I know." "Shall we try it again?" asked Drew. "Sure," I said, "why not? I think we need to try a different approach though." "Like what?" she asked. "Let me think about it," I told her. It was apparent to both of us that Caroline was right. There was definitely a spirit that was trapped inside that Ouija board, but whether it was good or evil we didn't know. I began to think about a different way to ask the board questions concerning Selma

Ann, without upsetting the spirit that was inside the board. We set it up again and put our fingers onto the pointer. Also, we would soon find out why the spirit was so upset.

"Ouija," I said, "why did you get so upset just now?" Drew and I sat silently and watched as the pointer moved from one letter to the next. First it spelled the word *'l-o-v'* then it spelled the words *'t-e-e-r-s'*..........*'s-a-d-d'*........ and *'d-a-n-g-r'*. "It's telling us something about love and tears," said Drew. "There is sadness and danger, too," I added. "Who are you talking about, Ouija?" I asked the board. The pointer spelled *'S-e-l-m-a-n'*. "Selma Ann!" cried Drew. "It's telling us about Selma Ann, Celia!" "Are you talking about Selma Ann Birch, Ouija?" I asked the board. It answered *'yes'*. After that it proceeded to spell the word *'m-e'*. "Me?" said Drew frightened.

I put my hand over my mouth in shock and disbelief. "Oh my!" I cried. "What?" asked Drew. We stared at one another, and what had dawned on me was finally obvious to her. "No," said Drew, "that can't be." "Ouija," I said nervously, "a-are y-you telling us that *you* are the spirit of Selma Ann Birch?" Immediately the Ouija board answered *'yes'*. My sister and I moved away from it slowly because both of us became afraid after that.

We watched in silence as the pointer on the board continued to move by itself to different letters. *'D-o-n-t'*........*'b-e'*......*'a-f-r-a-d'*. "Don't be afraid," said Drew repeating what the Ouija board told us. "How did her spirit get inside that Ouija board, Celia?" she asked me as if I would know. "I have no idea, Drew, " I replied. However, the pointer on the board was still moving from letter to letter without us having our fingers on it.

'L-o-v-r'........*'p-a-n'*.......*'m-u-r-d-r'*. "Lover, pain and murder," said my sister. "I think she is trying to tell us about her murder, Celia." Suddenly the pointer stopped moving so we sat down, and put our fingers back onto it again. "Selma Ann," I said, "what are you trying to tell us? Are you saying that your lover killed you?" The spirit answered *'yes'*. "What was his name?" asked Drew. But nothing happened and she looked at me. "Why won't you answer anybody but me?" I asked it. The board spelled the words *'s-p-i-r-i-t-a-l'*.......*'p-o-w-r'*.

"What is that?" I asked confused. "Spiritual power," said Drew, "you must have some kind of spiritual power, Celia. I knew it because I told you so." "Is that it, Selma Ann?" I asked and the spirit answered 'yes'. I recalled my sister's last question to the Ouija board. "Are you ready for this?" I asked her. "Ready for what, Celia?" she wanted to know. "The answer to your question, Drew," I told her. She nodded her head remembering her question.

"Ouija," I began, "what was your lover's name and would we know him?" Drew looked at me anxiously and a little confused but I knew what I was doing. I asked the spirit in the board about something that I already had a gut feeling about. Furthermore, I already knew the answer to my question, but I didn't tell my sister that. The pointer started to move from one letter to the next under our fingertips.

'D-a-m-o-n'.........'g-r-a-d-f-a-t-h-r'. Once again we snatched our fingers away from the pointer as if we'd been burned by it. "Oh no," said Drew. "She was murdered by our grandfather, Celia." All we could do was stare at the Ouija board after that. Yet, its' answer didn't surprise either one of us. I suspected all along that our grandfather had something to do with Selma Ann. I began to suspect it right after Lila and Dara told us about her, and the mysterious boyfriend that she had in Wesbury.

In fact, secretly I suspected our grandfather, and the rest of our family members of all of the other murders that occurred there, too. I just never said anything about my suspicions to anybody. Our beloved family had not been suspects in all of those killings for no reason. It began to make perfect sense if everything the Ouija board told us was true, and by that time we knew it was. "My, Lord," I whispered to myself. "All of those poor people."

"What's wrong, Celia?" asked my sister breaking into my thoughts. "Are you alright?" "Yes," I told her. "I guess so." "I know," she replied somberly. "I'm just glad Lila and Dara don't know it was our grandfather who murdered their aunt." "Yeah," I replied, "me, too." As far as she knew only our grandfather was the culprit. She had no idea that the other members of our family were suspected of those murders, too. Then she began to think aloud about the other murders.

"Do you think the rest of our family could've been responsible for any of those killings, Celia?" she asked me. "I don't want to believe it, Drew," I replied. "I really don't." "Think about it, Celia," she said. "There have been a lot of murders everywhere we've ever lived. Right? At least that's what Caroline told us." "Yes," I said. "It is something for us to think about. It doesn't matter if we want to believe it or not."

Deep down in my heart I would never be able to accept the knowledge that our family members could be killers. Yet, I had always suspected that our grandfather might've been. Because there was just too much evidence that pointed in his direction but not our parents and the others. Even though Drew mentioned it she had a hard time accepting it, too.

"How can people be so loving and kind like our parents and the other members of our family?" she asked. "And be the most brutal killers on the face of the earth?" I remembered every horror story I had ever read. And nothing in any of them remotely resembled what was going on around my sister and I.

Vampires were supposed to be evil beings, the undead, demons from the pit of hell incapable of loving anybody. Our parents and the rest of our loved ones were nothing like that. Drew and I had to be mistaken in what we were thinking. And the Ouija board had to be wrong, too. The entities inside them did lie sometimes because I had read that somewhere. Still, in my heart I knew the Ouija board was telling us the truth about everything.

We heard somebody coming up the stairs. Our bedroom door was slightly ajar. So hurriedly we put the Ouija board under my bed and turned on the radio. Then there was a soft knock on our bedroom door.

"Come in," said Drew. It was Mama. "Hi," she said as she entered the room. "Hi, Mama," we replied. "What are you girls doing up here?" she asked us. "You're awfully quiet so there must be something good on the radio." We turned the radio on hastily so we had not bothered to turn the channel to anything worthwhile. There was a comedy program on. "A comic, huh?" said Mama surprised. She sat down on my bed. "Well," she said, "I like the comics. Come on, let's get cozy and listen to them together."

She propped up the pillows on my bed and laid back against them. Then she held out her arms and beckoned Drew and I to lie down on the bed with her. We laid down and snuggled against her breasts. She kissed us both on our foreheads and gently stroked our hair as we listened to the comics on the radio. It was a man and a woman.

"Remember how we used to do this when you girls were little?" asked Mama tenderly, and we nodded our heads. "You're getting to be young women now," she continued. "But you'll never be too old for me to hold you in my arms like this. Don't ever forget that. Okay?" "Okay, Mama," we replied softly then she kissed us again.

It had been a long time since our mother held us in her arms like that. We hadn't realized how much we missed it. Drew and I came to another realization that evening, too. It would never matter to our parents how old we were. Because in their eyes we would always be their little girls. Even if we lived to be ninety years old they would never see us any other way.

As we laid there in Mama's arms she continued to caress our faces and our hair and it was very soothing. I felt my eyes getting heavier and heavier. When I looked over at Drew she had fallen asleep. Mama kissed us again and I knew she was as disinterested in the comedians on the radio as we were. However, she was content just to lay there with us in her arms.

As I was drifting off to sleep I sensed some movement in the room. Papa came into our bedroom and kissed my sister first on the top of her head then me on the tip of my nose. "Good night, Celia, darling," he whispered softly. "Good night, Papa," I whispered back. After closing our bedroom door he laid down on Drew's bed and started listening to the radio, too. As I watched my father he smiled at me lovingly. Soon I fell asleep and had a strange, frightening and perturbable dream.

CHAPTER EIGHTEEN

"Katie!" A woman was calling to someone. "Katie, where are you? It's time to come inside now because it's getting late." In the dream I was a little girl sitting in a big backyard. And there were crisp, white sheets blowing in a warm, summer breeze on a clothesline. I looked at the dress that I had on and it was very old-fashioned.

In reality I had never owned a dress like that when I was a little girl. The woman kept calling to someone. "Katie Carbell," she said walking over to me, "what's wrong with you? Didn't you hear me calling you? Come on now and let's go inside." I recognized the woman. It was Danielle.

She looked just like she did in the photograph that we found of her inside the attic. She took me by my hand and gently pulled me to my feet. "You'll get your pretty new dress all dirty," she said brushing off my dress. "Your Papa is coming to see you, your sisters and your brothers today," she continued. "You want to look pretty for him. Don't you?" She was smiling at me tenderly. "Your grandparents are coming over, too," she continued. "And we're all going to have a nice dinner together."

When I came into the house other children were there. I saw my music box sitting atop the fireplace in the living room. It was playing the same sad tune. A young boy was laying on the sofa. "Katie," Danielle said to me, "why don't you help Margeaux while I dress your baby sister?" I recognized Margeaux as my aunt when she was a child by her light eyes, and facial features.

As I walked over to her I passed by a long mirror and saw my reflection. The little girl who looked back at me was not me. I was looking at my mother when she was a child. I knew it was her because she had the same long, black hair, hazel eyes and coffee-colored complexion.

A young boy came up behind me and pulled one of my long curls. "Ow!" I cried. "Ricky," said Danielle, "leave your sister alone." He had to be Richard Bellis our parent's brother, and he looked to be around twelve years old. Another young boy ran into the house after that, and tapped the boy laying on the sofa on his leg. "Get up, Omri," he said. "They're coming, Mama. I see them." "Okay, Larry, honey," said Danielle. Larry was our parent's brother and Omri was Papa as a young boy.

Instead of helping Margeaux I walked over to the living room window and looked outside. "Katie," whined Margeaux, "Mama said for you to help me." When I ignored her she began to dress herself. I felt another gentle tug on one of my curls. "Hey!" I cried again. "Larry," said Danielle, "please leave Katie alone." He looked to be just a little bit older than I was.

As I was looking out of the window I saw a horse-drawn buggy coming down the road toward our house. A man and a woman whom I guessed were our grandparents were in the buggy. However, I didn't recognize the man but I did recognize the woman as Selena Bellis from her picture. There was a young man sitting in the back of the buggy. As they came closer I knew it was my grandfather. They pulled in front of the house and the three of them got out of the buggy.

"Come on, children," said Danielle very happy to see the man and the woman. "Let's go meet them." She gathered all of us together. There was Omri, Richard, Larry, Margeaux, the baby I suspected was my Aunt Jada and I. As we opened the front door Selena had a big smile on her face as she held and kissed each one of us.

She was a stout woman with a beautiful brown complexion, long, curly, graying hair and hazel eyes. The man with her was her husband, Oliver. My grandfather stood on the front porch with Danielle while Selena and Oliver, who was a big man, took us in the house. I wondered what was going on.

Danielle had the dining room table set for dinner. There was a big baked ham in the center of the table, and lots of other different foods she had prepared. Selena and Oliver laughed and played with us, and we liked them because they were very kind to us. I could sense how much they loved all of us, too. However, I didn't know why Danielle and my grandfather remained outside. Then it was dinnertime.

"Come on, children," said Selena. "I'm going to fix dinner while your parents are outside talking." When we finished eating dinner my grandfather and Danielle were still outside talking. We had just started to play another game when Danielle ran into the house sobbing softly. After that everything got quiet.

My grandfather came into the house and there was one thing that I would never forget about him. He was a very handsome man, and there he was in my dream as handsome as ever. He came over to me and picked me up in his arms.

"Hello, Katie, darling," he said kissing me on my cheek. "Hi, Papa," I replied. "How is my girl?" he asked me. "Fine," I told him, then Margeaux came over to him. "Papa," she said, "pick me up, too." He held us both in his arms. Omri, Larry and Ricky stood back because something was wrong. My grandfather put Margeaux and I down then he walked over to where the boys were.

"Don't you boys want to talk to me?" he asked them. "Hello, Papa," each one of them said. "Do you fellows have something that you want to talk to me about?" My grandfather asked them again. They looked down at the floor then my grandfather hugged each one of them. Larry started to sob softly.

"Oh, son," said my grandfather, "everything will be alright, you'll see." "Will it, Papa?" asked Ricky. "Because it doesn't seem like it." "Damion," said Selena, "why can't you and Danielle work things out? She is your wife and there are the children to think about." "I know, Mama Selena," said my grandfather. "We're trying. But there's something coming between us, and Danielle knows what it is." Just then I learned that time does not exist in the world of dreams. Because without any warning the dream switched to a later period in time.

Suddenly I wasn't a little girl anymore but a full grown woman, maybe thirty years old or more. I was my mother and I was in bed with

Papa, who was my brother, and we were having sex. No one else was at home at the time because they had all gone over to Mama Selena's house. "I love you, Katie," said Omri. "And I'm going to marry you."

"We can't do that," I told him, or should I say Mama told him. "It's not right." "Who cares?" he said. "You love me. Don't you?" "Yes," I replied. I had to admit that the sex between us was great, or rather between my parents. However, I just couldn't get past the fact that their incest was morally wrong.

In reality I was seventeen years old and a virgin. I had read a lot of books about love and romance. And I heard the girls at school talking about it but I had no idea it was that good. I actually had a great deal of enjoyment in the dream. I could feel the wonderful love between my parents and it was so much deeper than sibling love.

Omri and I heard someone come into the house so we hurriedly put our clothes on. We heard people talking downstairs, too. And we recognized Danielle's voice but the man's voice was unfamiliar to us. It was obvious that they thought they were alone in the house.

"You can't stay here, Trevor," we heard Danielle tell the man. "Because Damion and the others will be home shortly, and I can't take the chance that my husband will catch you here." "What does it matter?" The man named, Trevor, asked her. "He knows about us anyway. I want to be with you forever, Danielle, so just say 'yes'. Please."

"What about my family, Trevor?" she asked him. "I couldn't bear to leave them and never see them again because I love them, and I love my husband." "Yes," said Trevor, "but you love me, too. At least you told me that you did. I can't let you go, Danielle. I just can't." After that everything got really quiet downstairs.

Omri and I assumed that Danielle and the man named, Trevor, were probably kissing, but it was quiet for too long. So we went to the top of the staircase where we could see into the living room and see what they were doing. Danielle and Trevor were on the living room sofa and her dress was pulled up to her waistline. I never saw Trevor's face but his hands were all over her. Then I saw him raise his head back and open his mouth. Yet, I still couldn't see his face and it was the strangest thing.

"No, Trevor," said Danielle. In disbelief Omri and I saw the fangs of an animal in Trevor's mouth where human teeth should have been and his eyes were blood red. He looked like a demon from the pit of hell. Omri quickly covered my mouth with his hand to muffle my scream.

We saw Trevor bite into Danielle's flesh like a hungry animal as she held onto him tightly. An expression of ecstasy was on her face as she moaned with pleasure. We couldn't believe what we were witnessing. Trevor was one of the undead, a vampire. And we watched in horror as they made love on the sofa in our living room. After that he left our home.

When Danielle got off the sofa Omri and I ran into our own separate bedrooms. We heard her come upstairs. I was peeking out of my bedroom door and noticed the puncture wounds that were in her neck. Then I heard her pouring water for a bath. When she was done she came out of the room wearing a nightgown with a high neckline that covered the marks on her throat.

"Oh no!" I thought. *"What is going on here and where did that monster come from?!"* I still couldn't believe what Omri and I saw that day. About an hour or so later my grandfather and the other members of our family returned home. I was still in shock from what happened earlier and so was Omri. But we didn't tell anybody what we had seen and I don't know why.

After that day we caught Trevor and Danielle together on many occasions, right there in our house, when my grandfather and the others were out. However, they never knew it. Also, to my amazement I could never see Trevor's face and it was so very peculiar.

Danielle began to sleep her days away after a while and she would ramble the streets at night. She kept her bedroom as dark as possible during the day, and she no longer slept with my grandfather. Our family heard many horrible rumors about people who were missing in nearby towns. And some of them were found mutilated and murdered. Omri and I began to think there was a connection between Danielle's night- ramblings and the killings that were happening. And we were not the only ones.

My grandfather found out that Danielle was seeing Trevor. Which was something everyone already believed that he knew about and had known about for many years. I recalled the first part of my dream when he told Mama Selena that *'there was something coming between he and 'Danielle'*. That something between them was obviously still there, and had been for all of those years from the time that I was a child until I was a grown woman. So I gathered the 'switch' in the dream was really that message to me. He confronted her about it and threatened to leave her if she didn't stop what she was doing. And I wondered what took him so long to do that.

My grandfather told Danielle that he would make certain that all of us left with him, too. It seemed so perplexing to me that all of us would still be living at home as old as we were. And none of us were married or had any children. My parent's brothers, Ricky and Larry, were ladies' men like my grandfather was. Margeaux and Jada had their share of men, too. And both of them were very beautiful women. They knew it, too. They didn't have time to settle down with just one man, and they rarely brought any of their men friends home. Although they lived in the house with us Ricky, Larry, Margeaux and Jada were rarely at home.

My brothers and sisters enjoyed the lives they were living, or should I say my aunts and uncles. It was only Omri and I who were the homebodies. Apparently, because we were involved in an incestuous relationship and a definite taboo in the eyes of society. No one in our household suspected anything for a long time, except my grandfather. Because once he caught Omri and I in bed together when he came home unexpectedly. However, he had much worse problems to worry about at the time.

Despite all of my grandfather's threats to leave her Danielle continued her illicit affair with Trevor. And the murders continued, too. She would leave the house every evening always returning home just before dawn. One morning my grandfather was waiting for her when she came home. There was a very bad thunderstorm that morning, too. They had a terrible fight that awakened everybody in the house and we listened to their horrible fight.

CHAPTER NINETEEN

"I'm leaving you, Danielle!" my grandfather told her with tremendous anger. "And you better believe I'm taking the rest of the family with me!" "No, Damion, please!" cried Danielle nearly in tears. "I won't let you leave me. I can't live without you and our family because you mean everything to me." "Yeah, we can see that!" My grandfather yelled nastily. "It's too late for that now. Isn't it? You've made your choice and it's not me and our family. I thought it would be over between you and that monster if I stayed around and became a husband to you. But you lied to me!" Danielle began to sob softly.

"He wouldn't leave me alone, Damion," sobbed Danielle. "I tried to break it off years ago. But you kept leaving me alone all of the time so you could run around with other women. What was I supposed to do? It's as much your fault as it is mine."

"So," said my grandfather indignant with rage, " it's my fault that you've become a hound from hell like him, huh? My family and I are in grave danger just being around you. Did you know that, or don't you give a damn?!" "No, Damion," sobbed Danielle harder. "I would never hurt you or our family. I just couldn't do that!" "You should've thought about all of that before," said my grandfather. He had absolutely no sympathy for her at all.

"You've made your choice, Danielle," he told her angrily, "and evidently it's him!" We assumed he was talking about the man named, Trevor. Danielle was sobbing pitifully still pleading with him not to leave her. But he didn't want to hear anything she had to say. She was one of the undead. He was afraid for himself as well as for us and rightly so.

"If you leave me, Damion," sobbed Danielle, "and take our family with you I'll die. I'll have nothing left, nothing!" "You're already dead, Danielle," said my grandfather disgustedly. "Don't tell me you didn't know that. We're living people and you have no part in our world anymore, no place among us. You're already dead!" "No!" she screamed hysterically.

Suddenly we heard a lot of thrashing around as if they were fighting. All of us jumped out of our beds and ran to the top of the staircase to see what was going on. We saw my grandfather laying in the middle of the living room floor. And there was blood coming from two puncture wounds in his neck. He looked very pale as if his body had been drained of every ounce of its' blood. Without even touching him we knew that he was dead.

We ran downstairs and stood in the living room where Danielle was staring at her in horror. She was covered with my grandfather's blood, and there was more blood running down one corner of her mouth. She had attacked my grandfather. There was a crazed look in her eyes that were blood red like Trevor's were on the day we saw him on our sofa with her. Before we knew anything Danielle lunged for all of us.

We ran in different directions trying to get away from her. But she was much too fast for any of us, and her strength was inhuman. I watched terrified as she attacked my brothers one by one. They tried their best to fight her off but it was useless. They were no match for her. In the end all three of them lay on the floor dead just as my grandfather did. Margeaux and Jada were sobbing hysterically because they were so terrified as Danielle began to move toward them both.

"No, Mama, please," sobbed Margeaux frightened out of her mind just as Jada was. I stood there frozen to the floor watching the whole ugly, horrifying scene unfold before me. I could not believe what was happening right before my very eyes. As she walked toward my mother's two sisters Danielle had tears in her eyes. She was covered in blood from her head down to her toes as she held out her arms to my aunts. "I am so sorry, darlings," she told them. "I am so sorry this had to happen. But I can't let you leave me. I just can't do that."

The two women tried to get away from her but Danielle was unnaturally fast. "I can't let you go," she said holding onto Margeaux and Jada tightly. "Don't you see that I just can't? I am so sorry but I can't." "No, Mama," sobbed Aunt Jada. "Please don't do this to us!" "Please don't, Mama," sobbed Aunt Margeaux in great fear.

Danielle was completely oblivious to their pleas as any monster would be. Aunt Margeaux and Aunt Jada fought for their lives to no avail. Danielle attacked them draining their beautiful bodies of every ounce of life while I looked on in horror. When she finished with them she laid them gently down onto the floor beside the others. Then she turned to me.

"Katie, darling," she said to me sweetly, "you know how much I love you. Don't you?" I started backing away from her. Because the thing that I saw before me was not my mother, or Danielle, Mama's mother, but a demon showing itself in her form. I glanced at the front door. *"If I can just make it outside,"* I thought, *"I will be safe because it's daytime and she won't come outside."* However, she caught my glance.

"No, honey," she said softly. "Don't run away from me, please. I love you so much." She tried to smile at me. It was a smile that was both sad and evil at the same time. As I moved toward the front door she moved, too. So I ran up the stairs.

"Come back, Katie, darling," said Danielle softly. I ran from room to room terrified, trying to find a place to hide from her, or some way to get outside into the day light where I would be safe. I started crying and I couldn't seem to stop. No matter where I ran I would run right into her. I was so scared! I was feeling my mother's utter terror because I did not want to die like my siblings and my grandfather had. I was shaking all over and found sanctuary inside a closet in the hallway upstairs, or so I thought. It didn't matter where I ran, or how fast I ran I could not get away from her unnatural ability to appear anywhere suddenly. It felt like I was a mouse caught in a trap, and there was nowhere that I could escape from the horrifying monster that at one time had been my mother.

I heard Danielle's soft footsteps approaching the closet where I was hiding. I tried to be very quiet and I was scared to even breathe. A loud crack of lightning made me shudder to the very core of my being. I heard her walk away from the closet door. I thought she was gone but it was only what she wanted me to think. When I peeked out of the door there she was standing right there. I had never known such fear in all of my life. Yet, I knew I was dreaming so I began fighting hard to wake myself up, and at last I awakened.

The dream seemed so real to me. My entire body was soaked with sweat, and I was still trembling with terror. I could hardly breathe and I was still laying in Mama's arms. Drew was still asleep. I looked at our clock on the dresser. Our parents looked like they were unconscious like they usually did during the day time. And in a way they were I guess. The room was almost pitch black. I nudged my sister gently to awaken her.

"Celia," she said groggily looking at me, "God, are you alright? You're sweating like a pig and you're shaking." "I just had a terrifying dream, Drew," I told her. "What?" she said. "What time is it?" "It's almost eight o'clock in the morning," I replied. "Let's get up and I'll tell you all about the nightmare I just had." "Okay," she said. "But let's not wake up Mama and Papa." "Don't worry," I told her. "They won't wake up no matter how much noise we make." "Huh?" said Drew confused. My sister refused to believe what the Ouija board told us that our parents were but I did.

Drew and I got out of bed and got our clothes together. "Drew, what Danielle did to all of them was so horrible." I told my sister. "And I saw it all in a dream." "What did she do, Celia?" asked my sister curiously. I was still trembling with fear as I got dressed and I couldn't seem to stop shaking. The dream, or rather the nightmare had seemed so real to me and I had never been so terrified in my life. "I'll tell you all about it when we get downstairs," I told her.

For the first time in my life I understood completely the sheer and utter terror that our family members had lived through. A ' *life*' had been forced upon them that none of them ever wanted and surely didn't deserve. Although our parent's incest was wrong they really did love each other very much and they adored my sister and I. So I could not bring myself to call them 'monsters'.

I was sure that many innocent people had been brutally murdered at their hands. They were trying to survive in a world that they didn't belong in anymore. And they hadn't belonged in it for a very long time.

Out of habit Drew reached for the cord to open the curtains on our windows. "No!" I cried. She was a little startled by my outburst. "What's wrong, Celia?" she wanted to know. "Leave them closed. Okay?" I told her. "Alright, Celia," she said with a puzzled look on her face. The Ouija board plainly told us what our parents and the others were. However, my sister still wouldn't believe it.

Just as she wouldn't believe that someone was going to kill Dara because to her it was all just a *'game'*. "I'll explain everything to you when we get downstairs," I said. She nodded her head. We left our bedroom and closed the door behind us.

When we got downstairs Caroline was making breakfast for us. "Good morning, sweeties!" she greeted us cheerfully. But when she saw my face she knew something was terribly wrong.

"Celia, honey," she said, "what's the matter with you? You look like you've just seen a ghost." "She had a bad dream," said Drew nonchalantly. "Oh, sugar," said Caroline, "why don't you sit down at the table and I'll fix your breakfast. Then you can tell me all about it."

Drew and I sat down at the kitchen table. Everything that Caroline prepared for us looked delicious but all I wanted was a cup of tea and a slice of toast. Still shaken from my horrible nightmare I had no appetite at all.

"That must've been some dream," said Caroline concerned. "It's been a long time since all you had for breakfast is a cup of tea and a slice of toast. In fact, it was the last time you were sick. Are you feeling alright, honey?" "No," I replied. "Not really." "Well," asked Drew, "what did you dream about, Celia?" She and Caroline were watching me waiting for me to answer.

"I dreamed about Danielle and a man named, Trevor," I told them. I will never forget the look of sheer shock on Caroline's face as long as I live after I told them that. Without asking her anything I knew that she knew all about Danielle and Trevor. And by my mentioning their names she had a pretty good idea about what I dreamed about, too. It was through her I learned that my nightmare was much more than that.

I had been transported backward in time to relive the horror that our parents, their siblings and our grandfather had gone through. When I finished telling my sister and Caroline about the terrifying nightmare I had I broke down and cried. The thought of what had happened to the people I loved so much was almost too much for me to bear. Drew had tears in her eyes, too. She was finally beginning to realize that what the Ouija board told us could really be true, whether she wanted to face it or not.

Suddenly I was covered in the darkness that always accompanied my grandfather again. When I looked he was standing right next to me stroking my hair gently. Caroline and Drew vanished, and there was no one else in the room except he and I.

"Don't worry, Celia, honey," my grandfather said to me. "I'm here and I won't leave you. Everything is going to be alright." Then I saw Danielle and I was filled with rage and anger toward her. "How could you?!" I cried looking at her spirit. "Your own children! How could you do that to them, and to our grandfather?!" She looked at me sadly. A lone tear rolled down her cheek and a sad, little smile was on her lips.

"Oh, Celia," she said, "you will never understand how I felt." "No," I said, "you're right I won't. How could you do that to them?" I heard a voice in the darkness and it sounded so far away. Somebody was calling to me and I felt someone shaking me gently.

"Celia! Celia! Snap out of it, Celia!" It was Caroline talking to me and shaking me. I squeezed my eyes shut. Then I shook my head as if to bring myself out of a trance. "Celia," said my sister a little afraid, "you were in a daze again like before. Are you sure you're okay?" I put my head down onto the kitchen table, and sobbed softly.

"Didn't you see him?" I asked Caroline and Drew who were looking at me strangely. "See who?" Caroline wanted to know. "Grandfather was here," I sobbed. "Oh no," said Drew. "Yes," I said wiping away my tears, "and so was Danielle." I looked at Caroline. "What was wrong with her, Caroline?" I asked. "Why would a woman destroy her own family?" Caroline sat down at the kitchen table with us. Then she told my sister and I a story.

It was a very sorrowful story about a beautiful woman who was deeply in love with her husband. Sadly, she was a very lonely and distraught woman, too. It was that loneliness along with much despair that drove her into insanity. And in her angst she became mentally and emotionally unhinged. It was total insanity that made her do a horrifying thing. A terrible thing which ended in the condemnation of herself as well as her husband and her children.

The truth about our family was coming for my sister and I. I could feel it. The Ouija board foretold that the 'truth' about them would involve a murder. As I said before I knew it was *my* murder. Someone would try to kill me. And it was someone who was coming my way in the guise of a 'friend'. I was the only one who had surmised that information from the Ouija board, probably because of my newfound 'special gift'. It gave me no details at all and I never said anything about it to the others. Yet, it was never out of my mind who would try to hurt me, or how it was connected to our family member's terrible secret. Somewhere in my future this 'friend' would approach me. I didn't know when or where it would happen. But I did know something I didn't know before. It had to be a man. But why he would want to hurt me I couldn't 'see'. It was a complete mystery to me. The strange thing was that I had no inkling about any of that until Caroline told us Danielle's sad story.

CHAPTER TWENTY

Danielle Bellis was our grandmother and she came to America with her parents in the mid-1700s. Her parents were Selena and Oliver Bellis. They came from a little town in France called Lairdeaux. Danielle was the only child they ever had. Her parents took her away from France because of her involvement with a man named, Trevor D'Aisane.

Originally, Danielle was to marry one of Trevor's brothers whose name was Nicholas. There was a terrible fight between the two brothers one day. Nicholas discovered that Trevor was trying to steal Danielle away from him. He pulled a knife on Trevor but Trevor got the knife away from him, and stabbed him with it killing him.

A woman by the name of Anisa had loved Trevor for many long years and she had a child with him. But when he met Danielle he left her. However, Anisa remained friendly with his brothers. She was very close to Nicholas and was devastated by his death. Also, she was heartbroken over losing the man she loved to another woman. Anisa played a tremendous role in Trevor's life as well as in Danielle's. Everybody in Lairdeaux knew her. But what they didn't know was that she had always been heavily involved in dark magic.

Trevor became an outcast in Lairdeaux after he murdered his brother. Their parents had been dead for many years and he had raised Nicholas and their youngest brother, Charles. People liked Nicholas a lot. He was very kind and fun to be with, and everyone in Lairdeaux was stunned and outraged about his murder. After the murder Trevor had a hard time in Lairdeaux because many people wanted him to go to prison for the murder. But Nicholas's death was ruled as an accident by the Magistrates of Lairdeaux. After that Trevor couldn't find any work because everyone in the town turned against him. Yet, he knew he had to find a way to survive.

His family never had a lot of money. However, they had a farm and managed to make ends meet. No one in Lairdeaux wanted anything to do with Trevor after Nicholas's death. Even his youngest brother, Charles, left Lairdeaux after the murder. Selena and Oliver Bellis felt sorry for him, and gave him a job as a hired hand on their farm.

All Selena and Oliver Bellis ever knew was that Trevor had killed his brother by accident over a woman. Unlike everyone else in the town they didn't know the woman that they had fought over was their own daughter, Danielle. Danielle was never in love with Trevor. Yet, she began to sneak around with him behind their backs.

When Anisa found out they were seeing each other she informed Danielle's parents about the affair. And told them who the woman was that the two brothers had fought so bitterly over. Selena and Oliver were furious with Trevor and they fired him. But it did not stop him from being with Danielle.

Anisa was desperately in love with Trevor but he never felt the same way about her. She couldn't make him leave Danielle and come back to her. So she set out to destroy both of them. She tricked Trevor into sleeping with her. Which was not a hard thing to do since most men think with their little heads instead of the big one. She got pregnant by him a second time hoping to force him into marrying her. And she made sure that Danielle and her parents knew about the second baby she was having by Trevor. The news spread throughout Lairdeaux like wildfire.

When Trevor found out about Anisa's wicked scheme he was outraged. He became more angry that she told Selena and Oliver about his and Danielle's affair. He told her that he would never have anything else to do with her, or the children. In her quest for vengeance Anisa invoked a vicious, and malefic curse upon his head.

Through the dark and nefarious magic that she practiced she summoned the most demoniacal force from hell itself, solely to attack

Trevor and him only, in his home one night. The only purpose of that necromancy, summoned for only that one night, was to turn Trevor into the worst of monsters out of hell. He became one of the undead for all eternity, a vampire, a blood sucker. He could only survive at night and on the blood of human beings. Anisa got her revenge on him and after that she left Lairdeaux. However, not before she forewarned the people in the town about Trevor. It was later learned that she met and married another man.

Lairdeaux became a place of death and despair for all of its' people as Trevor roamed the countryside seeking out unsuspecting victims. Danielle's parents as well as others in surrounding towns also found out what Anisa did to him, and most of the people who could left there. Yet, there were others who had no choice but to stay and try to survive. Although those who were left lived in constant fear they were determined to destroy Trevor before he could destroy them. And they sought him out but strangely he was never found.

Selena and Oliver feared for Danielle's safety and fled overseas to America. Still, eventually Trevor did find her. However, by that time she had met and fallen in love with our grandfather. They got married after a while and had a family. Yet, that did not stop Trevor from trying to rekindle his and Danielle's affair.

Danielle had not realized it in the beginning but my grandfather was a horrific ladies' man. He had always been that way. He had many women and was never the kind of man to settle down with only one woman. But she fell head over heels in love with him. A lot of women were in love with Damion Carbell for that matter, and he knew it. However, he never had any intentions on marrying any of them.

When he finally did marry Danielle they already had two children. Out of all of the women my grandfather had she was the only one dumb enough to get pregnant by him, twice. The first child could have been considered a mistake, but not a second child. She definitely wanted to trap him into marriage and in the end she did. Yet, what she did not know was that her plan would backfire on her very badly.

My grandfather took care of Richard and my father when they were born. He was a good father to all of his children. He just never wanted to marry anybody. When Danielle became pregnant by him the third time Selena and Oliver insisted that my grandfather do the right thing by her, and the children so he did. Still, Papa was over a year old when my grandfather married Danielle.

Trevor continued to pursue Danielle in spite of my grandfather, and my grandfather knew what was going on. But he was too busy running around with other women. At first he didn't care about his wife and Trevor. And it was through Selena that he found out what Trevor was after the birth of my aunt, Jada. He would have known a lot sooner than that if he had bothered to pay attention to his wife. She loved and adored my grandfather. Which is why she didn't bother with Trevor for many years after he found her in America.

My grandfather often left Danielle alone with the children, sometimes for days. After many years and out of great loneliness and anguish she started seeing Trevor again. She knew the thing that he had become. But she was so starved for love and affection she didn't care. He never harmed her, or her children. Yet, he was always ready and willing to do away with my grandfather.

Danielle would not let him touch my grandfather under any circumstances. In spite of the way he treated her she adored him, and could not bear the thought of anybody harming him. She made it clear to Trevor that if he ever touched my grandfather she would hate him for the rest of her life. Despite what she did to her family I knew Danielle must have had a kind heart and a good soul. The hurt my grandfather deliberately caused her did not affect her deep love for him, or for their family.

"She must've been a very loving person at one time," I thought. *"And she didn't deserve to be treated so shabbily, because nobody deserves to be treated like that."* Also, I thought about how it must have been a terrible tragedy to be in love with someone who did not love you the same way you loved them.

Eventually my grandfather decided to settle down and be a husband to Danielle. However, when he did all of their children were well grown, and she had been involved with Trevor for many years. Once my grandfather decided to settle down Danielle told Trevor she did not want to see him anymore. Also, that she and my grandfather were trying to get their lives and their marriage together. Needless to say, Trevor did not want to hear that.

Fearing that he was losing Danielle forever he turned her into what he was, one of the undead, a monster! Throughout all of those years only my parents and my grandfather knew the truth about Danielle and Trevor. The others never knew a thing until their lives were destroyed forever.

It did not take much for my grandfather to figure out what happened to Danielle after a while. She began sleeping all day and roaming the streets all night, always returning home before dawn. When he threatened to leave her and take the rest of their family with him, it was the very thing she always dreaded since her *'life'* of darkness began.

As Caroline told Drew and I the sorrowful story I started to feel sorry for Danielle. She had suffered through many long years of loneliness, despair, adultery and unrequited love. And over time it took a terrible toll on her already fragile mind.

My grandfather was ready to leave Danielle forever on the morning they had that terrible fight. Which I saw and heard in my nightmare because of the *'gift'* I did not even know I had. She viciously attacked him then attacked the rest of her family. Her state of mind was so deluded from all of the years of abuse she had gone through. She believed they would never be able to leave her if she turned all of them into what she was, and they would be together for all time.

In the end my grandfather hated her for what she did to him and their children, because she condemned all of them to a *'life'* of pain and torment. Everything Caroline told Drew and I that morning, except for the part about Lairdeaux, France was exactly what I had dreamed about.

According to Caroline, Danielle was unable to 'live' with my grandfather's hatred, and with the knowledge that she had doomed her own family. Therefore, one morning she failed to returned home after being out all night long. It was later that same morning that her skeletal remains were found on top of a hill where the sunlight never failed to shine.

She allowed herself to be destroyed. Also, she hadn't been *living* for many years like the blood-suckers in horror stories did, so her skeleton didn't turn to dust but remained intact because of that. I guess you could say that she was a '*baby*' vampire. Then Caroline said, "Your grandfather wasn't sure if it was true or not. But he heard that Trevor vowed to make him, and the rest of your family pay dearly for Danielle's demise, if it was the last thing he ever did." "How would he do that, Caroline?" my sister asked her. "I don't know for sure, honey," said Caroline. "But it sounded like he wanted to get some kind of revenge on your family because of Danielle. However, you best believe that your grandfather was always on the look-out for anything Trevor might try to do to his family."

When she said that I began to think it was the reason why my grandfather kept coming to me all of the time. To warn me that Trevor was coming to harm me, and that he may be the 'friend' that the Ouija board told me about. In the future, although at the time I didn't know for sure, my father would destroy Trevor. After that I would never see my grandfather again. However, I was wrong about what I was thinking because he did not stop *visiting* me. Therefore, it definitely had to be something else that he wanted from me.

"Your grandmother was a very lonely and pathetic woman," Caroline told Drew and I. "She was very sick. But truthfully she brought the heartache, and misery she suffered upon herself when her parents forced your grandfather to marry her like she wanted. It's a shame to say that but it's the truth. She was very much in love with him, and I believe in his own way he loved her, too. He just wasn't the kind of man that any woman would marry because he could never be faithful to one woman."

"I just can't understand why she had all of those children by him," said Drew bewildered. "Knowing what kind of man he was." "For the same reasons some women do the very same thing nowadays," replied Caroline matter-of-factly. "They mistakenly believe that the baby will help them hold onto the man. But you girls know it as well as I do, that a baby has *never* helped a woman hold onto a man, and it never will."

"Yeah," said Drew, "you're right about that. Because a couple of girls who go to our school did that." "What's that?" asked Caroline. "They got pregnant," said Drew, "and the guys were forced to marry them. Now they're in very unhappy situations, talk about a rude awakening."

"Evidently Danielle didn't believe that." said Caroline. "Because she truly believed that having the children would make your grandfather settle down with her. But she was wrong. He never stopped running around with other women until your parents, and the others were well grown." "That is so sad," said my sister. "Whatever happened to that guy, Trevor?" "Nobody knows," replied Caroline. "He just disappeared right after Danielle destroyed herself."

"How do you know about all of this stuff, Caroline?" I asked her curiously. "Your grandfather told me that story a long time ago," she replied, "when I asked him how he, and the others became what they are." "Wow," said Drew. "And that's when you learned about all of them?" "Yes, sweetheart," answered Caroline. "Because when you're living with people you tend to notice anything strange, or out of the ordinary about them. Naturally you begin to ask questions just like you two are beginning to do. He had to tell me something. I'm just glad and grateful he thought enough of me to tell me the truth, especially when he didn't have to."

"Did our parents and the rest of them hate Danielle, too, Caroline?" I asked her. "I am afraid so, sweetheart," she replied, "especially your Papa and his brothers." "No wonder he never mentioned any family he had," I said referring to Papa. "I just can't get over a mother doing what Danielle did. They didn't even have a choice in the matter. She just decided to destroy their lives."

"You have to understand, honey," said Caroline compassionately. "Her love for your grandfather, and her children was very great. She couldn't bear the thought of being without them. She became one of the undead. But keep in mind that she was already mentally unstable. And in her state of mind they were all being snatched away from her. She was part of one world and they were part of another one. And she just couldn't stand it."

"I wonder why they were all still at home anyway," continued Drew. "They were pretty old to still be living at home. Don't you think so?" "I just think the whole thing was horrific," I replied.

"Well," said Caroline, "one day when you girls fall in love, and have families of your own you'll understand how Danielle became so tragic. I guarantee it. It's a different kind of love from anything you've experienced in your lives so far. Because there's a bond between parent and child, or husband and wife that is sacred." "In the dream," I said, "I felt the terror that our parents and the others felt." Caroline squeezed my hand gently.

"Celia," she began, "you're a very special young woman." "How so?" I wanted to know. "You have the same unique power that people believed Danielle had." "Really?" I said. "Sure," said Caroline.

"You know," she continued, "psychic powers are usually passed down from one generation to the next. In your case it skipped over Katie and Omri and went to you, their child." "How about me?" asked Drew anxiously. "I'm sorry, honey," Caroline told her. "But if you had it we would've known about it a long time ago. However, we always suspected that Celia might have it since she told us about seeing your grandfather." Drew looked very disappointed. But in my opinion she didn't know how lucky she was. I sure as hell did not want the *gift*. Yet, according to what Caroline said I never had a choice in the matter.

"Listen to me, Celia," said Caroline. "How many times have you shrugged something off as being instinct, or coincidence?" "A lot," I told her. "Well," she said, "do me a favor. Will you?" "Sure," I said. "What is it?" "Pay closer attention to your instincts, or your intuition from now on," she continued. "Believe me, honey, it will help you and guide you in certain matters. Alright?" I nodded my head.

Caroline talked to my sister and I freely and openly about our family that morning and we were so grateful to her for that. When she left the kitchen to begin her work for the day we talked among ourselves. I couldn't forget how hard my mother fought for her life and how terrified she was in my nightmare. Caroline told us how our parents desperately wanted to live normal lives again. Therefore, over the protests of the rest of our family members, they decided to have Drew and I. They believed that through us they could live somewhat normally again.

Relying on a horror story that I read I never knew that the undead could create life. But I wasn't in a story because this was something that was very real in mine and Drew's lives. It didn't matter what some people said, or what some book said about the undead. My sister and I were living proof that a man and a woman involved in a sexual relationship with each other, no matter what they were, could produce offspring. To top that off Drew and I were born with no abnormalities whatsoever.

Our parents, our grandfather and the rest of our family adored Drew and I from the time we were born. And they loved us more and more as we grew older. By loving us so totally and completely it gave what was left of their human side what they needed to survive the horror they lived every day. I didn't think I could ever love our family members more in my whole life than I did right then. Also, I felt more sorry for all of them than I already did.

My sister and I recalled all of the grief we had put our parents through, and as we thought about their strange rules we began to understand them. It became clear to us why they did the things they did.

"All they've been trying to do all of these years," I said, "is to protect themselves and us." "Don't forget about any friends we have had," added Drew. I nodded my head in agreement with her. We felt like two, selfish, spoiled brats who thought about nothing and no one but ourselves. So we made up our minds to make things easier for our family, instead of harder for them like we had been doing for so long with our contumacious behavior.

CHAPTER TWENTY ONE

The school that Drew and I attended started having classes in the evenings once a week. You could earn extra credit in subjects you were not doing well in. There were classes for adults, too, who wanted to get their Diplomas. Drew, Dara, Lila and I all signed up for extra classes in the evenings. My sister and I were on our way there one evening when I began to feel strangely. I wasn't sick. It just felt like something was going to happen to me. However, I didn't know if it was something good or something bad.

Lila and Dara were not going with us that evening. Their grandparents were sick so Doc B. was taking them back to Wesbury for a visit. Lila and Dara loved their maternal grandparents, who had nothing to do whatsoever with their mother, Annabelle, their own daughter. It was something that involved her setting those two older people up to be robbed once many years ago. And they had not spoken to her since. They loved Lila and Dara very much and were very kind to them.

"Maybe your coming down with something, Celia," said my sister. "Yeah, maybe," I replied. When we got to school that evening she went straight to her class. I went to my locker to get the school books I had left in school that day. While I was retrieving my books from my locker I heard an unfamiliar voice behind me.

"I haven't seen you around here before," the man said. I turned around to see who was talking to me. And looked into the face of the most handsome man I had ever seen, other than my father that is.

"Hi," he said cheerfully. "My name is Vortre', and you are?" *"What an odd name,"* I thought immediately. "My name is Celia," I told him. "Well, Celia," he said, "I am very pleased to meet you. So what class are you going to?" I told him. "My class is just across the hallway from yours," he said. "Do you mind if I walk with you?" "No," I replied. "I don't mind.

Vortre' was tall, dark and handsome. He had dark brown hair that was cut closely around the sides and beautiful, light brown eyes. I could easily see he was quite a bit older than I was. Yet, for some reason he seemed out of place. Not just in the school, but like he was from a different time when guys were very mannerable and polite. A time and an era that my parents would have come from. He wore a small, pearl earring in one of his ear lobes and he dressed very nicely. He walked me to my classroom.

"Can I meet you when the class is over?" he asked me politely. "We can walk to the next class together if that is alright with you." "Okay," I told him. "If you want to." "Oh, I definitely want to," he said looking into my eyes. I was registered for two evening classes and so was Drew. However, I gathered as old as he was that he was there to get his Diploma.

I had never had a real boyfriend before. Yet, I could handle myself if things got out of hand with any guy. However, I knew that Vortre' would be different. Somehow I knew I wouldn't be able to handle him so easily. When he looked at me I melted under his gaze. It was like he had some kind of hypnotic power over me, or something. He never touched me, but if he had I knew I would have crumbled in his arms.

As we were walking down the hallway I noticed how other women and teenage girls were eying Vortre'. I smiled to myself because he was handsome. Also, I gathered they were probably thinking about how out of place he seemed among the rest of us like I thought. "I'll see you in a little while, Celia," he told me after I arrived at my classroom. "Alright," I replied. Then he went to his class.

After classes were over that evening Vortre' invited my sister and I to a nice little cafe. When he left the table to go to the mens' room Drew commented about him. "He sure is handsome," she said. "Where did he come from because I haven't seen him around here before?"

"That's the same thing he said to me," I told her. "He looks a lot older than us, Celia, just how old is he?" "I don't know," I said. "I didn't ask him."

Mysteriously, only she and I ate at the cafe because Vortre' neither ate nor drank anything. "Aren't you hungry?" My sister asked him curiously. "No," he replied. "I've already eaten, thank you." He was very polite, almost too polite.

Drew was suspicious of Vortre' from the very beginning. "I don't know, Celia," she said when we got home. "I don't trust him because for one thing he came out of nowhere." I gave him my telephone number and address when he asked me for them. He called me on the following evening just before our family members awakened.

He and I made plans to go to a movie that coming Friday night. "Do you want me to go with you?" asked Drew when I told her about it. "Are you kidding?" I asked her flabbergasted. "What kind of date is that where I have to bring my little sister with me as a Chaperone?" "Well," she said, "I hope you know what you're doing, Celia." I did not tell Caroline, or our parents about my date with Vortre'. In fact, I didn't tell them anything about him at all. I don't know why but I didn't.

Finally Friday night came. Vortre' and I went to the movies, and had a very good time. I told Caroline that I was going over to Lila's and Dara's house that night. They already knew about my plans. After the movie was over he and I went to the park. We were sitting on one of the benches talking when suddenly I had a feeling of deep dread, and I started to shiver. It did not go unnoticed either.

"What's wrong, Celia?" asked Vortre' concerned. "Oh, it's nothing," I told him. "You're trembling," he said, "and you look like you are scared to death. Are you sure you're alright?" "Yes," I lied. "I'm fine, thank you." Truthfully I was far from 'fine'.

I wanted to run home right then and there. But I knew Vortre' would think that I was crazy or something if I did. He put his jacket around my shoulders and kept his arm around me. We sat silently for a few minutes then he kissed me.

I had never been kissed so deeply before and I was out of breath when he let me go. He looked at me and I at him then he kissed me again. This time he pulled me closer to him and I felt his hand underneath my blouse. He began to massage my breasts gently, and it felt good. I didn't want him to stop. And I could tell that he was very experienced, because as old as I thought he was he had to be.

My nipples became hard and I felt a dampness where my womanhood was. Then his hand gently lifted my skirt and traveled upward toward my stomach. He pulled the front of my panties down, and placed his hand inside them as I squirmed under his touch. He took my hand and placed it onto his manhood, and I recalled the dream that I had when I was my mother making love to my father.

"Celia," Vortre' whispered tenderly in my ear, "let me make love to you." I wanted to but I was afraid. "I can't," I told him. "Okay," he said softly. "I know that you're scared but I can wait." His hand was still caressing my womanhood and my loins were on fire. "Love will be good between us," he told me softly in my ear. "I know it will, you'll see." I had no doubt in my mind about that. I felt so good that I almost forgot I was in a public place. Then I pushed him away from me gently.

"Alright," said Vortre' softly. "You'll let me know when you're ready for me." He kissed me again, putting his tongue inside my mouth all the way to my throat. I was gasping for air when he let me go. We sat there a little while longer then we stood up to leave. Standing next to the bench where we had been sitting was the dark-veiled figure of my grandfather. But I knew Vortre' could not see or hear him.

"Celia," he said to me, "go home right now. I'll follow you to make sure that you're safe." I could tell by the tone of his voice that he did not like 'Vortre' one bit. The startled look I had on my face was noticed by 'Vortre'. "What's the matter, Celia?" he asked me. "Nothing," I lied again. "You look like you've just seen a ghost," he continued. "No," I replied. "I'm okay. I just want to go home."

When we got to my house Vortre' kissed me good-night. "I'll see you tomorrow," he told me. "Okay," I said. Then he left and I watched him as he walked up the street. When he disappeared from my view I went inside the house. To my surprise my parents and the others were there. Papa was the first one to say anything to me.

"Celia," he said, "why didn't you tell us that you had a date tonight?" I didn't know what to say at first. I knew Drew had told him about

Vortre' because he probably questioned her about my whereabouts that evening. Neither one of us could ever lie to him because he could be so intimidating. My poor sister had no choice but to tell him where I had gone. She was sitting at the dining room table playing cards with our aunts, our uncles and Caroline.

"I don't know why, Papa," I said. "I guess I wanted to see if things worked out first." "Well," he said, "before you go out with this guy again we'll have to meet him. Is that clear?" "Yes, Papa," I replied. I said good-night to everyone and went upstairs to my bedroom. I was on cloud nine.

I didn't tell anybody that I saw my grandfather in the park with Vortre' and I. And it never occurred to me until much later, that if I had said something about it my family would've known something wasn't quite right about my date. After our date all I could think about was Vortre' and how good he made me feel. Still, I wondered why my grandfather was there, and why he sounded so angry with me.

It was more than obvious that my grandfather didn't like Vortre' and I wondered why. However, I would find out why. He knew Vortre' and a lot better than I would've ever guessed. As I laid across my bed lost in my thoughts Drew came into our bedroom.

"So," she said, "how was it, Celia?" I told her all about my date, and she confirmed my suspicions about what happened with our father. "Are you going to make love with this guy, Celia?" she wanted to know. I thought about it for a moment. "I guess so," I replied smiling. "You better be careful." she admonished me. "You need some kind of protection you know."

"I'm sure that a guy as experienced as I think he is has plenty of that," I remarked. "I guess you're right," she replied. "He looks so much older than us that he's probably had lots of women. You don't need any problems if you know what I mean, and neither do Mama and Papa."

Time passed by and I had been dating Vortre' for weeks. Yet, every time I wanted him to meet my family he had some kind of excuse why he couldn't do it. Papa was constantly on my case about it, too. He continued to let me see Vortre'. But I could tell he and Mama were getting more, and more concerned about the relationship. Although they never met Vortre' they didn't like him.

"There must be a reason why he doesn't want to meet us," Mama said to me one night. "What is his full name anyway?" "It's Vortre' Deasian," I told her. His name was pronounced 'dee-ah-see-an'. "Well, where does he live?" she wanted to know. "He lives near our school, Mama," I replied. "Hm m," she said thoughtfully, "that's strange. Because there's nothing around there but an old abandoned factory, a few empty houses and a lot of open field." I didn't tell her, or anybody else that every time I was with Vortre' my grandfather appeared.

I would never have told my parents that I had never been to Vortre's home, or met his family. Because they would've gotten even more suspicious of him. One day I asked him about his family and where he lived. "I'm all alone," he told me. "My parents died a long time ago and so did my brothers. I never like to go to my home or take anybody there." "Well," I told him, "why is it that you don't want to meet my family?" "People don't like me." he told me sternly. "So I stay to myself because I make out better that way."

Even though I thought it was very strange I never pressured him about it anymore. Yet, Papa stayed after me about meeting Vortre'. If I had been using my head instead of my heart I would've known something wasn't right about him. After a while all of my family members got suspicious of Vortre'.

Whenever I was out on a date with him my grandfather appeared covered in that veil of darkness. And I could sense that he was sad for some reason. He always told me to "go home, Celia, now." Then I would abruptly end our date and do as he said. *"I wish he would tell me what he wants,"* I thought.

I kept wondering why he was always there with us. Because it was as if he was protecting me from something, or someone. Once he and Danielle both were there and she was crying again. It didn't take much for me to know they were there for a reason.

There was something else strange about Vortre' because I only saw him at night. He told me that he worked during the day as a Mechanic at a garage in town. However, when I telephoned the place the owner had never heard of Vortre'. That was when I started to get suspicious of him. *"Why did he lie to me?"* I wondered.

Of course Drew told Lila and Dara about Vortre' and I, and they insisted on meeting him. Therefore, all of us went out one night to the movies and when the movie was over they went home. He and I went for a walk. We ended up at the old factory behind our school. I wanted to talk to him anyway. Because I noticed the way he had been eying Dara all night. When I questioned him about it he said, "Celia, you're not jealous are you?" "Of course not," I said indignantly. "Yes, you are," he insisted. "No," I said. "I'm not." "Yes," he said. "You are."

He wrapped his arms around me and kissed me deeply. Then he laid me down on some old blankets that were there on the floor and we made love. It was great! Afterward we laid there for a while and I fell asleep. But before I closed my eyes I saw the dark, shadowy figure of my grandfather.

Vortre' awakened me just before dawn and I was in a state of hysteria. "My parents are going to kill me!" I cried upset. "It's all my fault," he said. "I should have awakened you a lot sooner than this."

"Yes," I told him still upset. "A whole lot sooner!" Papa was going to go berserk. I was glad he would just be getting home himself and on his way to bed. But I would see him that evening. I knew he and my family would be very angry with me.

Vortre' walked me home and kissed me at the front door. It was almost dawn and he seemed to be in a great hurry for some strange reason. "See you later, Celia," he whispered. Suddenly the front door swung open violently and there stood Caroline.

"Celia, are you out of your damn mind?!" she yelled at me. Vortre' looked embarrassed. "How do you do, Maam?" he said to Caroline. "It's all my fault. I am sorry because I didn't mean to get Celia into any kind of trouble. My name is Vortre'." He extended his hand to Caroline and she politely but coolly shook his hand.

"Well, Vortre'," said Caroline visibly upset, "Celia is in big trouble. And if I were you I would get my ass back here tonight so you can talk to her parents, who want to meet you I might add!" "Yes, Maam," he said. "I'll try to do that." "You better do more than try!" said Caroline angrily. "Let's go, Celia." She held the door open for me.

We went inside the house and Vortre' left. As a matter of fact he literally ran up the street as I watched from our living room window.

"Good grief," I thought. *"Why is he in such a big hurry?"* Once we were inside the house Caroline really lit into me.

"What the hell is wrong with you, Celia?" she asked me. "I fell asleep, Caroline," I replied. She covered her mouth with her hand. "Oh, my Lord, no," she said. "You didn't.......!" I nodded my head. Then she put her arm around my shoulders. "Did he use protection, honey?" she asked me. "Yes," I replied. She breathed a sigh of relief. "Thank God," she said. "Just how old is that guy anyway, Celia?" "I don't know," I told her. "Well," she said, "he looks like he is much too old for a young girl like you."

"Celia, sweetie," she continued, "when Omri and Kate came home this morning and you weren't here they had a fit. I can't tell you how angry and upset they are with you. And I hope for your sake that this guy comes back here tonight. Because your father is ready to kill him and you. I mean that, Celia, he is just that angry, and so is your mother."

"What should I do, Caroline?" I asked her. "I don't think there is anything you can do, honey," she replied. "If Omri doesn't meet this Vortre' guy tonight you might as well kiss him goodbye." I didn't want to hear that. By that time I thought I was falling in love with Vortre'. I went upstairs to my bedroom and my sister was just coming out of the bathroom.

"Celia," she said, "where the hell have you been all night long? Mama and Papa came into our bedroom this morning and woke me up because they wanted to know where you were. I told them that I didn't know but I don't think Papa believed me. Where were you all night?" I told her what happened between Vortre' and I.

"What does it feel like, Celia?" she wanted to know. "It was everything that we've always read about," I told her smiling, "and more." "Wow," she said. "I can't wait until I find somebody. Dara is being intimate with her boyfriend, too." "Who is he?" I asked her. "I don't know," she replied. "He's so mysterious. Lila said that she and Doc B. met him once and they like him. But she only sees him at night like you and this guy, Vortre'." We stopped talking for a moment.

"It is kind of bizarre though," said my sister. "What's that?" I asked her curiously. "At school in physical ed the other day, Dara had two sores on her neck. But I didn't ask her about them. I hope that guy isn't the type that likes to put passion marks on you. She keeps complaining about how the light bothers her eyes lately. She's starting to wear a lot of things with high necklines, too." I began to wonder because it didn't sound like Dara at all. Usually the blouses and sweaters she wore were low-cut. In all of this I never once used my head to put two and two together.

I laid down across my bed and Drew went downstairs. I hated the idea of facing our parents that evening. I thought about leaving the house before they got up, then coming home late, but I knew Papa. I wouldn't escape him that easily. So I decided it was best to just face him and get it over with. And I hoped Vortre' would show up to meet them that night. I got my music box from the top of the closet and wound it up. As I laid there listening to the sorrowful tune I drifted off to sleep and had another dream.

In my dream I was standing in the middle of the floor of a huge house. It looked like I was in the living room and it was night time. "Come on, Katie, we'll be late and I'm hungry." It was Papa talking. And he was addressing me because in my dream I was my mother again. I couldn't see what I looked like because I didn't see any mirrors anywhere. But we were dressed formally.

He looked so handsome in the black tuxedo he was wearing. And I was dressed in an evening gown made of black chiffon and silk. It was a beautiful evening gown I had seen among the old clothing inside our attic. I had a lovely diamond bracelet on my wrist that I had seen inside the attic among the old jewelry. Papa got my coat. It was a gorgeous mink I had also seen inside the attic.

"Come on, sweetheart," Papa said to me. "Let's go!" In the dream we were going to a fancy, formal dinner party. "You look beautiful tonight," Papa said to me, or rather to Mama. Then he kissed me on the tip of my nose, which was something he always did to my mother in reality. When we got outside a limousine was waiting for us, and we were taken to another large house. There were lots of cars parked in front of the house and lots of people were inside the house.

A woman by the name of Adria greeted us at the front door. Immediately the name sounded familiar to me. I had heard it somewhere before but I couldn't remember where. "Omri! Kate!" she cried. "You're late! Come on in!" She took my coat. Then guided us to a table where there was a big bowl of what looked like punch.

"Have a drink before dinner," Adria told us. Papa filled two, long-stemmed glasses with the punch and gave one to me. As soon as I tasted it I knew it was blood. Surprisingly, it tasted very good to me, and I was amazed at myself in the dream.

Adria Dubois came from France. She was tall and beautiful like my mother and my aunts were. She had long, black hair that was curled all over and reached down to her buttocks. Also, she was dark-complexioned with big, blue eyes and full, red lips. I noticed that there were no mirrors in her house either. The walls were covered with paintings that depicted demons. I wondered what kind of dinner party it really was and what kind of person Adria was. I looked around the room at the other guests and that's when I saw him. It was Vortre'.

I was both shocked and surprised to see him there. He was dressed very handsomely and he was with a woman that I knew in the dream, but not in reality. Therefore, I knew that my mother must have known her. Her name was Louisa and she was very lovely. He was all over her, too. I realized that like my grandfather Vortre' was a ladies' man. But he couldn't have been Vortre'. Yet, he certainly could have been his twin. In the dream neither one of my parents liked him either. In fact, it would be safe to say they despised him.

"Come on everyone," said Adria. "Dinner is served!" She lead all of us into her big dining room. I was stunned to see three, young women and two, young men tied down to a table. They looked terrified as they struggled to free themselves from the thick ropes that held them down to the table. "We can begin whenever you're ready people," said Adria. "Don't be shy because this is a celebration." She happily reached for the arm of a young man who was standing beside her. "This is my wedding night!"

Everybody crowded around the five, terrified people laying on the dining room table, including Papa and I. We began to nibble and chew on the women and the men, draining them of their blood. And it was horrifying! We were oblivious to their screams as they were being eaten alive. *"My God,"* I thought. *"This is the dinner?"* And for us it was dinner.

I looked at the man who resembled Vortre'. He was like a wild beast as he ravaged one of the women laying on the table. I had to turn away because it was so bad. As I did I could see blood dripping down the front of my beautiful gown. Also, I felt it running down one corner of my mouth. Papa gave me his handkerchief so I could wipe my mouth. Suddenly I heard a man's voice speaking to me.

"See him, Celia," said the voice. I turned around quickly and my grandfather was standing there. He was covered by the veil of darkness as usual. Nobody else could see or hear him in the dream, only me. "See him," he said to me again. "Open your eyes, Celia, and see him for who and what he really is."

I was not surprised that my grandfather called me by my real name in the dream. Because he knew I wasn't my mother, even though nobody else in the dream did. He was looking in the direction of the man who looked like Vortre'. I realized my grandfather was trying to tell me something very important about him.

Suddenly there was no one else in the room but my grandfather and I, because everybody else had vanished. "Is that really Vortre', Grandfather?" I asked him. "He's not who you think he is, Celia," he told me. "The name is an anagram." I woke up with a start!

"Oh no!" I said as I laid there in my bed. Everything began to fall into place. I knew why my grandfather was always there when I was out on a date with Vortre'. I got up, got a pencil and a piece of paper from my drawer. Then I wrote Vortre's first and last names on the paper so I could unscramble the letters. I turned the letters in his name around many times. Finally to my stunned disbelief the name "Trevor D'Aisane" surfaced.

"Oh, my God!" I cried. "No! It can't be!" My grandfather had been there on every date I had with Vortre' to protect me. Trevor singled me out purposely because he knew who I was, and he knew my family. I remembered Danielle's sad story that Caroline told us. And about the revenge Trevor promised to exact on our family. It was also what the Ouija board told me about my murder. And about the "friend" that would come into my life.

Danielle told me to listen to the music box and it would tell me things. It did exactly what she said it would do. Vortre' was really Trevor D'Aisane, the monster who destroyed our family. Also, I realized he was the 'fren' that the Ouija board told me about. The 'fren' who would kill me.

I felt such hatred toward him from my parents in the dream. My grandfather stayed around Vortre' and I because he knew who he really was. Trevor was still trying to destroy our family. The Ouija board had warned me that he was going to kill me.

I realized how blessed I was to find out about him through the Ouija board, and the music box before it was too late. He could easily have murdered me. Or worse did to me what he did to my grandmother. The only reason he had not hurt me so far was because he was simply biding his time. Now since I knew who he really was he would never get the chance to harm me, or my family again. "I'll tell my parents about him tonight when they get up," I said to myself.

Mama and Papa would become hysterical knowing how close I had come to danger, and possibly death. Yet, they would react in a way that I never would've imagined. Drew and I would truly learn the brutal truth about our parents and the others. And in a way there would never be any doubt at all about what they were. It was more of the 'truth' that the Ouija board told us about.

CHAPTER TWENTY TWO

After Drew, Caroline and I finished eating dinner that evening we heard our parents coming downstairs. My sister and I were still sitting at the dining room table. "Good luck, Celia," said Drew. "Remember I'm on your side." I smiled at her and nodded my head. She didn't know that she was in for a surprise, too, just as they were.

Our parents came into the dining room and sat down at the table with us. "Celia," said Papa calmly, "if I don't meet this Vortre' character tonight you can kiss his ass good-bye. Do you understand?" I nodded my head in agreement with my father. "Honey," said Mama sweetly, "there's something wrong here because he doesn't want to meet us." I looked at both of them and smiled a sad smile.

"You are right, Mama," I said, "and so are you, Papa." They looked stunned. I knew they were expecting a fight from me. They stared at me as if I had lost my mind, or something, and so did my sister. "What's going on here, Celia?" asked Papa looking confused. I took a deep breath and let it out.

"I had a dream while I was napping earlier," I told them. "What about?" asked Papa. "Who is Adria Dubois?" I asked my parents. Neither one of them could hide the look of surprise that was on their faces. "How do you know about her?" asked Mama. "Who is she?" I asked them again. They glanced at one another. Mama was the one who answered me.

"Adria was the midwife I had when I delivered you and your sister," she replied. Then I recalled where I had heard that name before. It was on mine and Drew's birth certificates, but no last name was written.

"Tell us about your dream, honey," said Papa. I didn't know how to tell them that from the dreams I had about them I knew what they were, and *how* they became what they were. "It's the second dream I've had about you two," I told my parents. They glanced at one another again. Mama held my hand. Papa pulled his chair closer to mine and put his arm around my shoulders.

"Tell us about the dreams, sweetheart," Papa said tenderly. "What were they about? Don't be afraid because you know that you and your sister can tell us anything. Don't you? We love you and there is nothing for you to fear." "Yes," I replied. "I know that, Papa." Mama sat quietly. I think she had an idea about what I was going to say, and I believe Papa did, too. All I had to do was mention Adria's name.

I looked down at the dining room table. Papa lifted my chin with his finger and turned my face toward his. "What is it, honey?" he asked me softly. "Tell us please." My sister didn't say a word. But I could see that she was anxious to hear what I had to say, too.

"I dreamed that I was you, Mama, in both of my dreams," I said looking at my mother. "In the first dream I was a little girl. Then the dream switched to a later period in time and I was a grown woman. I was in love with Papa in the second part of the dream." I hesitated after that. "Go on, honey," Mama urged me. "I know Danielle was your mother, Mama and Papa," I told them point blankly.

Mama squeezed my hand gently and Papa began to stroke my hair. The surprise in their faces was gone by then. Of course they knew Drew and I already knew that because we read their birth records. "What else, sweetheart?" asked Papa gently.

"In the dream I saw how things were between Danielle and Grandfather," I continued. "And I saw how it was with her and the guy named, Trevor, too." My parents remained quiet. "He was a vampire," I blurted out. "And he turned her into one, too." "Yes," said Papa calmly. "Go on." I turned to my mother. "Oh, Mama," I said nearly in tears, "I'm so sorry for what happened to you, Papa and the others. It was so horrible! You were so scared and I saw the whole thing in my dream."

Mama got up and wrapped her arms around me. She sat back down and held me on her lap. I felt like a little girl again. I put my head onto her breasts. "It's okay, honey," she said soothingly stroking my hair. "It's okay." Papa put his head down onto the table then he looked up and said, "I want to hear the rest of it, Celia." I could feel tears forming in my eyes because I felt so sorry for them. Then I took a deep breath and wiped my eyes.

"Also, in the second dream," I began, "I met this woman Adria Dubois. She was having a dinner party at her house because she'd just gotten married, and you and Mama were there, Papa." I hesitated again. "There were three women and two men tied down to her dining room table. And she told everybody there that dinner was served. Everyone started eating those people who were lying on the table. It was terrible, Mama, because you two were eating those people, too."

"What?!" cried Drew in disgust and disbelief. "That wasn't a dream, Celia, it was a nightmare!" "S-s-sh!" Mama told her. "Is there anything else, honey?" asked Papa. I didn't know how to tell them the rest of the dream. But I knew I had to tell them.

"I saw the man named Trevor in the dream, Papa," I said slowly. "He was at the dinner party that Adria had, too." "Oh?" said Mama. "What was he doing there?" "I think he was invited just like you and Papa were, Mama," I replied. "He was a monster!" I felt the tears in my eyes again as I shook my head. I realized if I considered Trevor to be a monster what did that say about my own parents? I shuddered! "What else, honey?" asked Papa softly. I looked at them both and I had to say it so I blurted out, "He's the same guy that I've been dating."

My father's eyes widened in shocked disbelief! "How do you know that?!" he demanded to know. "Because Grandfather was in the dream, too," I replied. "And he told me that he was the same person. Also, that his name is an anagram. It is because I wrote his name down on a piece of paper, and unscrambled the letters. When I did the name 'Trevor D'Aisane' surfaced. I've known all along that something was wrong. Because every time we're out together I see Grandfather."

Papa got up so quickly he knocked his chair over onto the floor. He started pacing the floor frantically like a caged animal as Mama, Drew and I watched him. I could see the wrath and rage in his face. "How can that be, Mama?" asked my sister. "Wouldn't he be dead by now?" "No," said Papa angrily. "But after tonight he will be! How dare that bastard touch my child!"

I don't know how Papa knew that Vortre' and I had been intimate but he knew. I guess all parents can tell about things like that with their children. Both his and Mama's eyes were black with wrath.

As I looked into my mother's eyes they were as black as the night and filled with rage. Yet, she smiled at me tenderly. Papa left the dining room and went upstairs. We heard him getting dressed. He came back downstairs and said something to Caroline, our aunts and our uncles. But I couldn't hear what it was. Then he came back into the dining room. I was still sitting on my mother's lap with my head on her breasts. A wonderful feeling of relief washed over me because I was so glad to get everything off of my chest. The deep, dark secret that our parents and the other members of our family had held onto for so long was now out in the open.

I felt so relaxed that my eyes began to grow heavier and heavier with sleep. I could hear Drew and Mama talking to my father. Also, I heard Caroline and the rest of our family members talking, too. Their conversation was about Trevor D'Aisane. My father left the house after that and I fell asleep.

It seemed like I had just gotten to sleep when I felt someone gently shaking me awake. "Celia, wake up, honey! Celia!" It was my mother and I was still sitting on her lap. "Yes, Mama," I answered her groggily. "We're going to take you and your sister somewhere," she told me. "No, Mama," I replied. "I'm so tired and sleepy." "I know, honey," she said softly. "But this is very important because we want you and Drew to see something. Okay?" I nodded my head. "Come on, baby," said Papa gently helping me to my feet. My sister was already standing.

"Where are we going, Papa?" asked Drew a little excitedly. "You'll see when we get there, honey," he told her. "You better put their sweaters on them," said Caroline. "It's kind of cool out tonight, and we don't want anybody catching a cold." She kissed Drew and I on our foreheads. Our parents wouldn't tell us where they were taking us. However, I was sure that Caroline and the rest of our family members knew. Wherever it was we set out walking.

I was so tired and sleepy I could hardly think straight. Mama held mine and Drew's hands as Papa walked ahead of us. We walked until we arrived at the old, abandoned factory where Vortre' and I made love. It was very dark inside the factory. Although the electricity in the building was still on our parents kept the lights off. "Be very quiet, darlings," Mama whispered to Drew and I.

We sat down on an old sofa that was in one corner of the room while Papa stood by the window looking outside. It was as if he was on his guard for something, or someone. *"How does he know about this place?"* I wondered. I fell asleep again leaning on my mother's breasts as she gently caressed my face. She had her other arm around my sister's shoulders as we sat on the sofa quietly.

It seemed like I had been asleep for hours when my mother awakened me. I don't think my sister had ever been asleep because she was wide awake. "Look, Celia, baby," said Mama. Papa was holding my face toward his. As he looked into my eyes his own eyes were blood-red. He looked sinister and menacing.

"Get a good look at him," Papa said to me softly. "Because you'll never see him again." Then he moved away from me. When he did I could see Vortre' walking toward the factory through the open door. He had a young girl with him. They were laughing and talking with each other. That poor girl was blessed and she didn't even know it. Because she had no idea what Vortre', or rather Trevor planned to do to her. He didn't even get inside the factory good before Papa was all over him. The young girl screamed in terror and ran away as fast as she could.

The two men threw each other around the room like rag dolls as my sister and I watched in horror. Yet, Mama was very calm. Papa was much fiercer than Trevor was, and both men were extremely powerful. They fought for what seemed to my sister and I like hours, but in reality was only a matter of minutes.

Finally Papa held Trevor in mid-air with one hand around his throat. His eyes were blazing like two balls of fire. He was frightening! Trevor, using both of his hands, tried to free himself from Papa's grasp but he couldn't. I heard somebody screaming after that but it sounded so far away. Mama still sat calmly on the sofa. She never moved, or said a word.

"You destroyed my parents, my sisters, my brothers and I," Papa said to Trevor with great rage, "now you've come after my daughter. It was the greatest mistake you've ever made, and your last!" With one powerful blow Papa tore Trevor's head from his body. I was horrified!

He tossed Trevor's headless body across the room. After that he reached down to the floor, picked up a long piece of wood, and stuck it deeply into Trevor's heart. His body and his head both burst into flames and vanished. I could still hear somebody screaming and they were terrible screams. It was my sister because she was hysterical. I was in shock.

Papa walked over to my sister and picked her up in his arms. She was flailing her arms wildly in fear trying to get away from him. But he held onto her tightly. "No, no, honey," he whispered to her gently as he held onto her. "No, Papa loves you, sweetheart, s-s-sh, calm down now. It's okay, s-s-sh!" She began to sob softly as she started to calm down. She held onto Papa tightly still filled with terror. "Okay," he said to her gently. "It's alright now." Then he looked at me.

"No one will ever hurt you or your sister, Celia, honey," my father told me. "If anyone ever tries they will end up just like him. Never forget that." It was at that moment that Drew and I would never have to wonder anymore about what happened to Tommy Lee Stone, the Mackreys, Reverend and Miss Becka Daniels, or Randi Ames and Donnie Ross. Because we knew what happened to all of them.

I thought backward in time to the night of the Daniels' visit to our house. I realized that the Reverend and Miss Becka unfortunately stumbled onto something when they unexpectedly came to our home that night. But they never had a chance to tell anybody. They knew about our family members as soon as they came into contact with them. And they knew probably because of their spirituality more than likely.

Eventually talk would have been all over the town that something wasn't quite right with our family members. It was inevitable. And it wouldn't have taken long before the whole town would have become suspicious of them. Maybe even begin accusing them of having something to do with the missing people and the killings that were going on.

Our family members had to keep their horrible secret so they had to silence the Reverend and Miss Becka. I was sorry for that. They were really nice people and were always kind to Drew and I.

It took my sister and I quite a while to get over the shock of what we saw in the factory that night. But it really made no difference to us what our parents and the others were. We loved them and we knew they loved us. And there was nothing and no one that was ever going to change that.

Drew did cry herself to sleep in Papa's arms that night. Mama looked me in the eyes and said softly, "You will never see anything like that again, Celia, honey, neither you nor your sister. We love you both so very much. If anything or anyone threatens your well-being in any way we'll take care of the problem. Do you understand what I'm telling you?" I nodded my head because I understood perfectly.

However, my mother was wrong. Because neither she nor Papa could've known it and neither did Drew and I. But we would see something like that again, and it would be much much worse. The only difference would be that our parents wouldn't mean for us to see it. What happened to Trevor they wanted us to see. Yet, without a doubt they would've given up everything they had if they could've stopped us from seeing what was coming our way in the not too distant future.

"Come on," said Papa. "Let's go home." He carried my sister all the way home that night. After we got there he carried her upstairs to bed. Everybody was at home when we got there. They had already known about what was going to happen that night. I told all of them goodnight and went upstairs to bed.

CHAPTER TWENTY THREE

The following morning when Drew and I got downstairs Caroline had prepared a lavish breakfast for us. "Wow," said Drew. "What's the occasion, Caroline?" "Oh nothing special, honey, " replied Caroline. "I just wanted to make you girls something special this morning that's all." She fixed our plates and sat down at the kitchen table with us.

"Did you know what was going to happen last night, Caroline?" I asked her. "Yes, honey," she said. "I did because Omri told all of us before you left." "So what do you think about it?" Drew asked her. "I think Trevor D'Aisane finally got exactly what he deserved after all of these years," answered Caroline. "I had no idea who he was, and I stood face to face with him that morning on the porch."

"You mean……you met him?" asked Drew surprised. "It was when Celia had been out all night long. Remember?" Caroline asked my sister. "Oh," said Drew. "Well I never trusted him anyway and I told Celia that."

"Remember, girls," continued Caroline. "I told you if you would be patient your parents would have to tell you the truth about themselves. And it happened just like I told you it would. Didn't it?" "It sure did," said Drew. I agreed.

"Now," said Caroline, "let me ask you two something." "What?" asked my sister. "What do you think about all of this?" asked Caroline. We didn't have to think about it very long. My sister and I loved our parents and the others. It made no difference to us what they were and we told her so. Drew and I would never see them as monsters. All we could see was the love they had for us, and the love we had for them. Our hearts were entwined with one another's. We would never stop loving them, and we knew they surely would never stop loving us.

"Learning the truth about them wasn't as bad as we thought it would be," said my sister. "How do you feel about what they do to survive?" asked Caroline. We thought about that but only for a moment. We couldn't say that knowing they were the killers that everybody was looking for didn't bother us, because it did. I don't think anybody else would have understood how we felt. But my sister and I vowed to do whatever we could do to protect them. And we told Caroline that.

"All of the years of dealing with their strange and weird rules is understandable now," said Drew. "They do what they have to do to survive. It's really not their fault because they certainly didn't ask for this." "That's right," I said. "All of those rules were to protect themselves, and any friends we had not to hurt us." I thought about the Reverend and Miss Becka Daniels again, and I mentioned their murders.

"If only they had stayed away from our house that night," I said. "And not surprised us like they did they would still be alive." When I said that I noticed the sorrowful look on my sister's face. Because she felt responsible in a way for their deaths. But it really wasn't her fault. She had no idea what our parents and the others were. And neither did I before the Ouija board told us. Although we never really wanted to believe what the board said. Because who in their right mind would believe something like that?"

"It's alright, Drew," I said gently squeezing her hand. "You didn't know." "Thanks, Celia," she said with a forced smile. Yet, I knew she would live with their deaths for the rest of her life. No matter if she thought it was her fault or not. After that day we never mentioned the Reverend and Miss Becka's names again.

"Do your parents and the others know how you feel?" Caroline asked us. "No," I replied. "We haven't talked to them about it yet, but we will." "I'm glad," she said. "Because I know it will make them very happy to know how you feel." I recalled my grandfather, and I felt so sad for him. He was still a handsome, young man when his life was stolen from him. And he never had a chance to fully live and neither had the rest of our family members. They were trying to live their lives through my sister and I. Because through us they felt like they were still a part of humanity.

I had been determined to leave home after I graduated from school. But I began to rethink my decision. I didn't want to leave our family anymore because if I did who would protect them? Caroline needed a life, too. We had never seen her with a man as long as we'd known her, and she was still young and beautiful. As we sat around the kitchen table that morning my sister and I made some arrangements of our own. We suggested to Caroline that she start going out and have some fun.

"We can take care of our family during the daytime, Caroline," said Drew. "You need a life, too." She readily agreed with us. "You two girls are getting older," she said. "And you don't need me as much as you used to." It was all settled as far as Drew and I were concerned. However, we would regret making that suggestion to Caroline.

"Well," said Caroline, "let's not move too hastily here. Let me think it over and talk to your parents about it." "Sure," we told her. Then the telephone rang and Caroline answered it. "Hello," she said into the receiver. "Oh hi, Lila," she said. "How are you this morning?" There was a pause. "Yes," said Caroline. "Just a minute please." She called me to the telephone and I took the receiver from her.

"Hi, Lila," I said. "Celia," said Lila on the other end of the line," can you and Drew come over here and bring that Ouija board with you?" "Why?" I asked her. "What's the matter?" "It's Dara, Celia," she said. "I'm really worried about her because something is wrong with her. She sleeps all day and she can't stay awake in school anymore, when she goes that is. She stays out all night long with this boyfriend of hers'." "I thought you and Doc B. liked her new boyfriend," I said. "I'm beginning to wonder about him, Celia," said Lila. Suddenly I remembered the spirit that was inside the Ouija board.

"Oh yeah," I said to Lila calmly. "Guess who the spirit is that's inside that board?" "Who?" asked Lila. "It's your aunt, Selma Ann, " I told her. "What?!" she cried surprised. "She must've followed us from our old house, Celia." "How?" I asked her. "The Ouija board was already there at your new house when you moved in." "Yeah, I know," replied Lila. "But spirits travel, Celia. Didn't you know that?" I didn't know that. I continued to tell her about the spirit inside the Ouija board.

"Drew and I asked it one day who it was," I told Lila. "And she spelled out her name for us on the board." "Oh my," she said. "I wonder how her soul got trapped inside it like that." "I don't know," I said. "Oh well," said Lila. "How soon can you get over here?" "In about twenty minutes or so," I replied. "Where is Dara now?" "Where else?" said Lila.

"She's in bed asleep because she didn't come home until some time this morning." "That doesn't sound good," I told her. "Okay, we'll be over there shortly." "Alright," said Lila. "See you when you get here." We hung up.

When I got off the telephone I told Drew that Lila wanted us to come over and bring the Ouija board. And she was all for it because she enjoyed fooling around with it but I didn't. We got our jackets and the Ouija board. Then told Caroline where we were going and set out for Lila's and Dara's house.

After we got there we rang the doorbell and Doc B. opened the front door for us. I was glad we had put the Ouija board inside a bag. "Hey, girls," he said cheerfully. "How are you today?" "Fine, Doc B.," we told him. "Is Lila here?" He was always glad to see Drew and I because he liked us a lot. "Come on in," he told us. Then he called for Lila to come downstairs. "Hi there," she greeted us. "Hi, Lila," we said.

"Is your sister feeling any better, honey?" Doc B. asked Lila solemnly. "I don't think so, Dad," she replied. "I'll telephone the doctor if she doesn't get any better by tomorrow," he said. He was very concerned about Dara. "Come on," Lila told Drew and I. "Let's go upstairs so we can talk in my bedroom." We followed her upstairs and passed Dara's bedroom on our way to Lila's bedroom. She was sleeping soundly.

Her bedroom was almost pitch black. "She never kept her bedroom so dark before," said Lila concerned. I didn't want to say anything to alarm her. But I already had my suspicions about what was wrong with Dara. Her bedroom was just as dark as our parent's and our other family member's bedrooms were during the day. When we got to Lila's bedroom we set up the Ouija board. Needless to say when we began to ask it questions it would not answer anybody but me.

"Ask it about my sister, Celia," said Lila. "Ouija," I began, "tell me what is wrong with Dara Birch. Is she sick or something?" The pointer began to move from one letter to the next spelling out words for us. Panic gripped my heart as it spelled the word *'n-o-s-f-a-r-t-u'* again. "Nosferatu," said Drew. "That's what it told us before about Mama and Papa. Remember, Celia?" I nodded my head 'yes'. The pointer continued to move.

'G-r-a-t'........'g-r-a-t'........'d-a-n-g-r' it spelled out. "Oh no," said Lila. " My sister is in great danger, Celia!" "Are you the spirit of Selma Ann Birch?" I asked the Ouija board and it answered 'yes'. We kept our fingers onto the pointer. It was very hard for Lila because she was so upset by then. "What is the great danger, Ouija, for Dara Birch?" I asked the board. And the pointer began to move again.

'P-a-n'........'t-e-e-r-s'.........'s-a-d-n-s-s' it spelled. "Pain, tears and sadness," said my sister. "Oh no," said Lila her eyes filling with tears. "My Dad can't handle another tragedy, Celia. It would crush him." Drew put her arm around Lila's shoulders. "Go on, Celia," she said. "Ouija," I said, "tell me more about this pain, tears and sadness. Is it for Dara, or for her family?" We watched the pointer move again. *'P-a-n'........'t-e-e-r-s' ....'d-e-t-h'* it spelled out. "Is it for Dara, or for her family, Ouija, tell me," I said.

All of a sudden the Ouija board flew into the air as it did on the day my sister and I were using it in our bedroom. It slammed itself against each one of the four walls of Lila's bedroom. Then it flew through the air almost hitting us. Finally, it crashed against another wall and landed on the floor. We were afraid to touch it after that.

"Is everything alright up there, girls?!" Doc B. shouted from downstairs. "Yes, Dad," Lila told him. Drew was the only one of us who was brave enough to pick the Ouija board up and put it back onto the table. "Let's continue," she said to Lila and I. "I don't know, Drew," I said. "Maybe it wants us to leave it alone." "No," said Lila. "We have to know about Dara, Celia."

All of a sudden Lila started looking around the bedroom like she suddenly sensed that something, or someone was in the room with us. Then she closed her eyes. "It's alright, Aunt Selma," she said quietly to someone Drew and I could not see. "It's okay," she continued. "I'm not afraid anymore so you can tell us the truth." My sister and I were frightened. Because we could not see anybody then Lila opened her eyes and looked at us. "Okay, Celia," she said. "She'll answer you now." Drew and I had no idea about what had just happened. But we knew somebody other than Lila was there in the room with us.

As soon as we put our fingers onto the pointer again it began to move. It spelled out different words for us. 'D-a-r'.......'i-n'.......'l-o-v-'.......'M-a-r-c-s'.........'d-a-n-g-r'..........'t-o'.........'l-a-t'........'n-o-s-f-a-r-t-u'........'d-e-t-h' it spelled. Selma Ann was telling us in no uncertain terms that Dara was going to die. We didn't know what to do then Lila started crying.

"You've seen her at school," she sobbed speaking to my sister and I. "She looks so pale and sickly lately and she can barely stay on her feet during the day. Half of the time she doesn't even bother going to school anymore. Whatever is going to happen to her is happening right now." We tried to comfort her but there was really nothing we could do.

The room became ice cold, and the three of us shivered violently from the icy chill that came out of nowhere, and engulfed the room. Each one of us felt the hairs on our forearms and the backs of our necks standing on end. Then the room began to grow darker and darker. At first I thought it was my grandfather but it wasn't. We looked around the bedroom. And the spirit of a young woman appeared to us standing in one corner of the room. I knew she had to be Selma Ann. Drew started to scream but I quickly put my hand over her mouth, and my arm around her shoulders.

"Be quiet, Drew," I whispered in her ear. The spirit looked very distraught then it spoke. "Lila," said Selma Ann, "there is nothing you can do for Dara now. She has allowed Marcus to control her completely. She is under his power now so there is no hope. However, another one stalks her, too. And one who is extremely dangerous. By this time tomorrow Dara will be dead." Then the spirit vanished after that.

"Oh, God, no," said Lila starting to sob again. "Who was that woman, Lila?" asked my sister frightened half out of her mind. "Don't be scared," sobbed Lila softly. "It was my aunt, Selma Ann. Did you hear what she said? My sister will be dead tomorrow. We have to do something. I wasn't sure it was your uncle that she's been seeing. But remember it told us that before?" Drew and I said nothing because truthfully there was nothing we could say.

"It's Walker," said Lila. "He is really your uncle, Marcus. We have to do something, Celia." She was looking at me pleading with her eyes for me to do something to help Dara. "What can we possibly do, Lila?" I asked her. "I don't know," she sobbed. "But we have to do something. We can't just let him kill her." It eluded all of us that the board had told us that Uncle Marcus would not kill Dara.

"The spirit said there is no hope for Dara," said my sister sadly. "I don't know what we can do, Lila." Then I remembered what Selma Ann said. She told us that there was another person stalking Dara, someone who was extremely dangerous. *"Who can that be?"* I wondered. *"And why are they stalking Dara?"* I thought about going to my father.

"Maybe he can stop Uncle Marcus from hurting Dara!" I thought. Of course he would want to know how we knew it was Uncle Marcus that she was seeing. And we would have to tell him about the Ouija board. Furthermore, I knew there would be a fight between them. In the end I decided not to go to Papa. And it was something I would regret for the rest of my life. Because instead of going to him for help we tried to handle the matter ourselves.

"I know what we can do," said my sister. "What is that?" I asked her curiously. "We can follow her tonight when she goes out," she continued. "There you go again, Drew," I said. "You're always wanting to follow somebody. I told you it is dangerous to do that." "Well," she replied, "it's better than just sitting back and doing nothing, Celia. At least if we're there and he sees us he might not hurt Dara." But I didn't say anything because I figured maybe it was wrong about that one thing for some reason, and I don't know why. Maybe it was because Dara would be with my uncle and he was just the logical person who would harm her. There was no one else's name that the board ever mentioned.

"It always puzzled me how she met your uncle in the first place," said Lila. "Don't you remember what the Ouija board told us before, Lila?" asked my sister. "What was that?" asked Lila anxiously. "She met him in the park one night. Remember?" said Drew. "Oh yeah that's right," answered Lila. "I don't know how I could've forgotten about that."

Lila and Doc B. had no idea that Dara's new boyfriend they liked so much, and my uncle were one and the same person. The Ouija board, or should I say Selma Ann, gave us more details about the way they met when I asked it. And I was not surprised by what her spirit told us.

According to Selma Ann it happened one night when Dara left Lila at home and was coming to our house. On her way she stopped at the store. After leaving there she decided to take the long way to our house which meant going through the park. There she met Uncle Marcus and she never made it to our house that night. From that point on Uncle Marcus wined and dined her. She told him she knew us and that she was a friend of ours. But obviously it made no difference to him. And that was a strange thing. Drew and I had gotten a clear understanding from our parents as well as our other family members that our friends were off limits to all of them. *"Something is just not right here,"* I thought. Yet, I kept my thoughts to myself.

Whatever power my uncle had over Dara she was powerless to resist it. Then I thought, *"Maybe she doesn't want to resist it!"* It was only a matter of time before he made her like he was. But someone else was going to kill her. Either way she would be dead like Selma Ann told us.

The Ouija board had spelled out another word for us regarding Dara and Uncle Marcus. It mentioned that same word before, but I just could not connect it to what we were concerned with at that time. Later on it would become crystal clear. It was the word *'j-e-a-l-u-s-y'*. *"What does it mean?"* I wondered to myself. *"And how is it connected to this?"* When I mentioned it to the others none of us had any idea how jealousy figured into the scenario. Therefore, we shrugged it off. And it was another mistake because I should have asked Selma Ann more about that, but I didn't.

While we were in Lila's bedroom again we asked Selma Ann what happened to her and she told us. It was pretty much the same thing that was happening to Dara. She had fallen in love with a man named, Damion. And they saw each other for weeks before he attacked and murdered her.

All she had lived for, she told us through the Ouija board, was to be by his side. Because she was very much in love with him. However, one night she caught him with another woman and it infuriated her. But there was nothing that she could do about it. So she followed him and the woman that he was with and confronted him. That was when my grandfather killed them both.

I didn't have the heart to tell Lila that the 'Damion' the spirit was telling us about was our grandfather, and neither did Drew. It wasn't hard to figure out that at first our grandfather had not intended to harm Selma Ann. However, when she caught him with another woman, whom I assumed was a potential victim, he had no choice but to kill her. He was not willing to let that poor, unsuspecting woman go free in order to hold onto Selma Ann. Therefore, she had to die, too. And it was so very sad.

I began to recall the taunts from other children when my sister and I were little girls. We never knew why they said our family members were killers, too, just like our grandfather was. And we never knew why people always turned on us, and we always lost our friends. We wondered for many years why people said such ugly, hateful things about us and our family. Now at last everything was falling neatly into place for us.

It was a horrible thing to know that the only two real friends Drew and I ever had, other than Lana Mackrey, had always been connected to us in a terrible way. Our grandfather had caused them a lot of pain and heartache. Now our uncle, or someone else would bring them more pain and heartache. I was lost in my thoughts and didn't hear my sister talking to me.

"What are you thinking about, Celia?" asked Drew, noticing the far-away look that was in my eyes. "Nothing much," I lied to her. "So," said Lila forlornly, "what are we going to do?" "I don't know, Lila," I replied. "I really don't know." Dara awakened that evening while Drew and I were there and came into Lila's bedroom where we were.

"Hey, there!" she said to us cheerfully as she came into the room. "What's going on?" The change in her was so dramatic it startled all of us. She was a far cry from the Dara we saw during the day time in the past few weeks. Because she would be almost lethargic during the day. Suddenly she was the usual Dara, full of energy, but she was very pale.

"I see you're still fooling around with that Ouija board," she said to us. "Want to join us?" Lila asked her hopefully. "No," she answered flatly. "I'm getting ready to go out." "Oh?" said Lila. "Where are you going? We'll come with you." "No," said Dara. "This is a private party. No third wheels are allowed."

"Please?" pleaded Drew. "No, Drew," replied Dara adamantly. "I'll see you tomorrow. I'm going downstairs to see what Dad is up to." "I smelled something cooking, " Lila told her. "So he has probably tried to get some dinner together for us." "Alright," she said heading down the stairs.

Lila told my sister and I that Dara hardly ate anything anymore. It was a tremendous change from a girl who could gobble down two large cheeseburgers, a large order of French fries and a large milkshake for lunch. However, if she had not been eating she certainly didn't look like it. Because I couldn't see where she had lost any weight. She was just so pale-looking.

All kinds of things began going through my mind at the time. Because I just couldn't figure out that word 'jealousy' that the Ouija board kept telling us about. And it was so strange how no one else paid much attention at all to it. But I knew it had to mean something. Strangely, I began to think back to the night we saw Uncle Marcus with that strange, young woman we had never seen before on our front porch, and Aunt Jada let them both inside the house. Drew and I were so stunned by that. I knew there was only one person who would be jealous of Uncle Marcus and that was Aunt Jada. There was no one else although she certainly didn't act like it on that night. Or was it someone who just didn't like Dara?

According to Selma Ann it was Dara who was in great danger from a very dangerous person. I just couldn't figure it out. And it was something that really bothered me because I knew the board didn't tell us that for no reason. When I did find out what it meant I knew my world would definitely never be the same again because it was a great shock to both my sister and I.

We heard Dara talking to Doc B. downstairs. And we could tell she hadn't stopped to eat anything because she was continuously talking to him. We heard her tell him that she was going out for a while and she would be back around eleven o'clock that night. From the sound of his voice he was very happy that she was feeling much better.

"If we're going to do anything, Celia," said Lila, "we better do it now." "You're right," I replied. So we decided to do what Drew suggested and follow Dara. We put the Ouija board back inside the bag and got ready to go downstairs. But before we left Lila's bedroom the cold chill returned and it was stronger than it was before. All three of us shivered again from the sudden coldness that came into the room. "I don't know about this," I told Lila and my sister. "Maybe Selma Ann is trying to warn us not to do this." "But we have to, Celia!" cried Lila. "We can't let anything happen to my sister!"

I felt so sorry for Lila. Despite all we had been told by the spirit of her dead aunt she still believed we could help Dara. Drew believed it, too. When the coldness in the room lifted after a few minutes and the room became warm again we got up and went downstairs to the kitchen. When the doorbell rang a few minutes after that Dara went to answer it and it was Millie at the door.

"Why, Dara," she said happily, "you're looking very pretty this evening. You must be feeling a lot better. I'm so glad." "Thanks," replied Dara. "I'm going out for a while now so I'll see you later on, Millie." She hurried out of the front door. Drew, Lila and I went to the front porch and watched Dara from the window to see what direction she was going in. When she got about a block away from their house we set out to follow her, and sure enough we ended up in the park.

Dara sat down on one of the benches as if she was waiting for somebody, and after a few minutes Uncle Marcus stepped out of the shadows. She stood up, took his arm and they walked away together.

Then out of the corner of my eye I saw another person standing in the shadows, and it was a woman. I knew she was following Dara and my uncle, too. "Did you see that?" I asked Drew and Lila. "See what?" they asked me in unison. "There was a woman there," I told them. "And I think she's following Dara and Uncle Marcus, too." "A woman?" said Lila surprised. "I wonder who she is?" "I don't know,

I said. "But I saw her." "I didn't see anybody," said Drew. "She was there," I insisted.

Drew and Lila never did see the woman but I did. It was so dark I could not see her clearly, but I knew it was a woman. "Alright," said Lila anxiously. "This is it so let's stay far enough behind them so they won't see us." We started to walk in the same direction that my uncle and Dara had gone in, as well as the strange woman that I saw. Then suddenly everything began to grow dark around me. "Oh no," I said softly. I could see nothing inside the darkness. And I was all alone again like before because Drew and Lila had suddenly vanished, and my grandfather appeared. He had the same dark covering over him like always. Yet, I still saw those penetrating eyes of his.

"Celia," he said to me, "don't do this because if you do you will be sorry. And you might see something that you and your sister should never see again. I told Marcus to leave your friend alone. I warned him, honey. For reasons you have no idea about yet. There is nothing you girls can do for your friend because she's already dead." "No!" I cried. "No, no, no, Grandfather, please, help us!" My legs gave out and I fell to my knees sobbing softly.

"Grandfather, please!" I cried. "Don't let him hurt our friend, please! Don't let anybody hurt her! Please do something!" "I'm so sorry, Celia, honey," he told me quietly and sadly. Then he was gone. I could hear my sister calling to me in the darkness that was beginning to fade away.

"Celia, what's wrong?!" Drew asked me worriedly. She and Lila both helped me to my feet but I still could not see anything clearly right away. Then everything was bright suddenly and I looked into the faces of Lila and my sister who were staring at me confused. "Didn't you see him?" I asked them. "Didn't you hear him? He was standing right there." I pointed to where my grandfather had been standing.

"We didn't hear or see anybody but you, Celia," said Lila. I realized again that once I was inside the darkness with my grandfather no one could hear anything he said to me, and I couldn't see anybody but him. "He was here," I said with great sadness and nearly in tears.

"Celia, stop it!" cried Drew becoming frightened. "He was here, Drew," I told her quietly. "I think he was trying to stop us. He doesn't want us to follow Dara and Uncle Marcus." Lila sighed. "I think you're right, Celia," she said sorrowfully. "Because now we don't know what direction Dara and your uncle went in. We were busy watching you. You scared us for a minute."

"I asked Grandfather to help us," I told them. But I didn't tell them what he said to me. "Well," said Drew, "maybe he will help us." I didn't say anything but I knew that was not going to happen. The three of us sat down on a bench and all of our hearts were heavy.

"I just don't understand why he only comes to me and nobody else in the family," I said speaking about our grandfather. "Well," said Drew, "I'm glad he never bothers me. I had enough when we saw Selma Ann. Maybe it's like Caroline told us, Celia. You have special powers like a sixth sense, or something and none of the rest of us have it. That's why he only comes to you. And don't forget the connection with him that Aunt Jada told you about a while back." "I guess so," I replied a little forlornly. "It's obvious that he's around you for a reason, Celia," said Lila. "And in time I have a feeling you will know why." Lila didn't know how close she was to the truth and neither did I.

"I think he's trying to tell me something," I continued. "Or maybe protect me from something like it was when I was seeing Vortre', or rather Trevor. I just don't know." "It could be that," said Drew. "But did you forget you were seeing Grandfather long before that Vortre' guy came along, Celia?" She was right of course. "I would like to know just where Dara is right now," said Lila changing the subject on us. "I'm really getting worried."

"Well," said Drew, "there is one thing for sure. Our uncle is the last person we saw her with." "That's right," replied Lila. We sat in the park for a long time that evening, and we were very worried about Dara. Our plan to follow her and Uncle Marcus was foiled by the appearance of my grandfather, and I knew it was on purpose. Also, I still couldn't get that strange woman out of my mind.

Around eleven o'clock we decided to call it a night and we hoped Dara would be alright. "I heard her tell Dad she would be home by eleven o'clock," said Lila. "So maybe she's already at home." However, I knew from what my grandfather told me that Dara was not at home and she wouldn't be coming home ever again. I wanted to cry so badly because I felt so sorry for our friends but I held back my tears. Then Drew and I walked Lila home.

"I know I will not be able to sleep tonight if she's not home," Lila said sadly when we got to her house. "Well," I replied, "we're going on home now and we'll say a prayer for Dara tonight. Okay, Lila?" "Thanks a lot, Celia," she said. "I really do appreciate that." "I think everything will be fine, Lila," said Drew. "I sure hope so," replied Lila half-heartedly. "See you guys later." We waited until she got inside her house then my sister and I headed for home.

That night Drew and I did say a prayer for Dara although I knew it would do no good. All of our fears were realized on the following morning when Sheriff Jackson knocked on our front door. He wanted to question my sister and I about Dara because they found her body in the woods that morning. It had been drained of all of its' blood and she was decapitated. She had to be identified through her fingerprints and a birthmark that she had on her left leg. However, her head was nowhere to be found.

CHAPTER TWENTY FOUR

My sister became hysterical when she heard the news about Dara and I went into shock. Even though our grandfather and Selma Ann had already told us what was going to happen to her. I thought about Lila and Doc B. and the pain that they must have been in. Caroline did her best to console Drew and I but it was useless. I ran upstairs to our parent's bedroom. Because we needed them at that time more than we had ever needed them before. I screamed at them.

"Wake up, Mama!" I screamed. "Wake up, Papa! Please, wake up!" Of course they didn't wake up. I became angry with them after that and started pounding on their chests with my hands. "Wake up! Wake up I said!" I was shouting at them. "Don't you know what he has done?!" I was referring to Uncle Marcus murdering Dara. And I began to sob bitterly because I didn't realize it at the time. But I was more hysterical than my sister was.

Caroline came upstairs and pulled me away from my sleeping parents who were oblivious to the fact that I, or anybody else was in the room with them. I heard my sister sobbing heartbreakingly in our bedroom. Caroline held me tightly in her arms.

"Come on, honey," she said tenderly. "It's going to be okay." "Why don't they wake up, Caroline?!" I said sobbing and hysterical! I was out of my mind. And I didn't realize it because the fact that our parents could not have awakened completely left my mind.

"They're never around when we need them, Caroline," I cried hysterically. "They never are, never! Why did they ever have us?! Why did they bring us into this world and bring all of this hell onto our heads?! Dara was our friend and Uncle Marcus killed her! He knew she was our friend, Caroline! But he didn't care because Grandfather told me so!" I saw the look of disbelief on Caroline's face.

"What are you talking about, honey?" she asked me calmly. "He killed our friend, Caroline!" I cried. "We saw him with her last night in the park! And he's been seeing Dara for a while now! She started getting pale lately and sleeping in the dark all day like our parents and the others do! She would be out all night long with him!" I was ranting and raving like a madwoman.

"Alright, sweetie," said Caroline still trying to calm me down. "We will get to the bottom of this, you'll see." She rocked me in her arms. "He killed our friend, Caroline," I sobbed softly. "Uncle Marcus did it." I couldn't stop sobbing. "We followed Dara to the park last night," I continued. "She met him there and they walked off together. But we didn't have a chance to follow them because Grandfather came to me. He said that he told Uncle Marcus to leave Dara alone."

As I looked at Caroline I saw the tears in her eyes, too. She had grown very fond of Lila and Dara. Our parents had a rule that our friends were never to be harmed by any member of our family. And it was set in stone. Caroline knew that, too. She told my sister and I to lay down for a while.

"I wish they would all just die," sobbed Drew angry and upset. "Oh no, sweetheart," said Caroline quietly. "You don't mean that. You're hurting right now, that's all." "Why do they keep hurting us, Caroline?!" asked my sister completely unstrung with tears running down her face. "Why?!" Caroline just smiled a sorrowful smile at her. "Honey," she said solemnly, "they're not trying to hurt you or your sister. You know that. They love you both very much and when your parents awaken I'll tell them what Celia told me. I know Omri will take care of this, believe me." I didn't like the sound of that. But as much as I loved Uncle Marcus I hoped my father would beat the hell out of him for what he did. Or did he do it?

"You know, girls," said Caroline matter-of-factly, "it just might be that Marcus didn't do this, and someone else did." "We saw him with her, Caroline!" cried Drew. "Just let us get to the bottom of this. Okay?"

said Caroline. "There might be more to this than meets the eye. I have to tell you both it does not sound like something Marcus would do, especially knowing Dara was your friend." Suddenly, I recalled the mysterious woman I saw in the park when she said that.

She was hiding in the shadows, too. And she was following Dara and my uncle. "There was someone else there last night, Caroline," I said. "What?" asked Caroline surprised. "Who?" "It was a woman," I told her. "But I couldn't see her clearly." "Alright," she said. "I'll be sure to tell that to your parents, too. Because it could be very helpful in finding out just who did this."

Caroline fixed Drew and I some of her warm milk and gave us a small white pill to take with it. Before we knew anything we were sound asleep. I awakened around eight o'clock that evening and our parents were in our bedroom. Papa was sitting on the side of my bed, and Mama was sitting on the side of my sister's bed. They were gently caressing our faces and our hair. My sister was still sleeping.

"Hi, sweetheart," said Papa lovingly when I opened my eyes, and Mama smiled at me. "How are you feeling, honey?" she asked me. My eyes were swollen from all of the crying I had done. My mother came over and knelt down by the side of my bed. "We heard about your friend, sweetie," she said softly. "And we want you to know that we're going to find out what happened. Alright?"

"It was Uncle Marcus," I told them flatly. "She's been seeing him for weeks now, and last night we followed her to the park. We were going to follow her and Uncle Marcus but Grandfather stopped us."

"Yes," said my father. "Caroline told us all about that." "Also," said my mother, "she told us something about you seeing a woman there." "Yes," I replied sadly. "I don't know who she was because I couldn't see her that well. And the others didn't see her at all." "I would like to know who she was," said Papa. "What are you going to do, Papa?" I asked him.

"Celia, honey," he said, "did I ever make you or your sister a promise that I didn't keep?" "No, Papa," I answered. "Well," he continued, "I'm not about to start now. So I promise you both this will be taken care of. Okay?" "Okay, Papa," I replied.

"Celia," said Mama, "you know that we love you and your sister so very much. Don't you?" The words that came out of my mouth after that surprised me and our parents. "Is it enough anymore, Mama?" I asked her with my voice barely above a whisper. Our parents looked a little stunned because they were not expecting a response like that from me.

"Why do you ask us such a thing, sweetheart?" asked Papa curiously. "Because," I said, "I just don't know if it's enough for us anymore, Papa." "Oh, honey, no," said Mama. I could see the hurt in both of their eyes. "What are you saying to us, sweetheart?" asked my father. I hesitated as our parents were looking at me waiting for an answer.

"Why did you have Drew and I, Mama?" I asked my mother curiously. Papa sighed and moved closer to me. He began to caress my face again. "Oh, honey," said Mama. "We wanted you both so much." "But why?" I asked her again. She and Papa glanced at one another. "We needed you," she replied in a condoling voice. "So we could bring some kind of happiness into our '*lives*', sweetheart. And that's all you and your sister have ever given us."

"Then," I began, "why can't Drew and I be happy, too?" "Aren't you happy with us, honey?" asked my father. "Sometimes," I replied. "But other times we're not so happy. What you and Mama are has always affected Drew and I and it always will. Don't you understand that? For us to have normal lives you two have to have normal lives, too. It's great to have Caroline around but we still need you."

Papa put his arms around me and Mama put her head down. I thought I saw tears in her eyes. Then I felt something wet on the back of my neck and realized my father was crying. He held onto me tightly while Mama began rubbing my back gently. "I love you and your sister so much, Celia, honey," said Papa as he looked into my eyes. Neither Drew nor I had ever seen our father cry.

"If you and your sister only knew how much we love you both," said Papa in a solacing voice. "Your mother and I can't help what we are. I wish to God we could but we can't. We didn't ask for this '*life*' if you want to call it that. It was forced onto all of us by our mother. So we had to have you and Drew, or we would have destroyed ourselves a long time ago. You two are what keep all of us going from day to day and without you we don't want to exist. Can you understand that, honey?"

"Yes, Papa," said Drew who had awakened and was listening to our conversation. "But you need to understand us, too. Celia and I are normal young women and we need to live normal lives like other young women do." Mama put her arms around my sister and my father released me. "What do you think we should do for you both?" he asked us.

"I know you do not want to hear this," I said to my parents. "And I don't want you to be upset, but I need to leave home when I graduate from school. I'll look for a job so I can support myself of course." "And I need to go with her," added my sister. "I don't think we're ready for that," said Papa. "So how about if we just let you live normal lives here with us?"

"It wouldn't work, Papa," I told him. "We've been trying to do that all along. And you have to admit it yourselves that all children grow up and leave home sometime. We'll never have any friends or boyfriends if we don't leave here."

Our friends were never to be harmed. But in light of what happened to Dara we didn't know when their urge for blood would become too overwhelming for them. It was a huge risk for us to take with the lives of our friends.

Drew and I felt as if we could minimize that risk by not having our friends around our family. And if my sister and I lived on our own away from them we wouldn't have to worry about it. We were willing to stay at home and take care of our family so Caroline could have a life, but that didn't seem like such a good idea anymore. Furthermore, we still had school to think about. Of course our parents didn't see things the same way we did.

"Celia," said Mama, "I know you and Drew are almost grown women, and I don't think your father and I wanted to see that before, but now we do. Yet, we just can't let you go that easily. Believe me we know how you must feel because you're afraid that sooner or later one of us might not be able to control ourselves, especially after what has happened to your friend. I thought she was reading my mind but I wasn't sure. I had read books about vampires. And according to all of them they could read and control people's minds.

"Ever since you were little girls," began my mother, "we have made it a priority to know who your friends were. We do that to make sure we never go near any of them, and that goes for all of us." "Something went wrong this time," Papa said to Drew and I. "So please give us a chance to find out just what happened." "Then," said Mama, "let us show you both that we can be better parents to you. Will you give us a chance to do that? We would do anything to keep you from leaving us." There was so much love in their eyes for Drew and I.

"Our family," began Papa, "has always believed in the family staying together. And no one ever has to leave the family home unless they want to." When he said that Drew and I knew why all of them were still at home with my grandfather and Danielle when they should've been out on their own.

We did feel sorry for our parents and the others because they couldn't help what they were, and we knew that. We were tired though. Tired of never being able to recall walking with them in the sunlight, or having them teach us how to ride a bicycle, or how to roller skate, or drive a car. All of the things other parents did with their children our parents had never done with us.

As much as they adored Drew and I their love didn't seem like it was enough anymore. Papa looked so forlorn and so did Mama. They made a vow to my sister and I that night that they would make things better for us. No matter what they had to do so we could be happy and content with them. They told us about the way their '*lives*' were. Also, about the things they had done to survive for nearly two hundred years. And they told us about the others as well. It was all so incredible.

Uncle Marcus and Uncle Wilhelm were brothers. And they were the two sons of the woman named, Anisa, who had lived in Lairdeaux, France as well as the sons of Trevor D'Aisane. Drew and I were surprised because Caroline had not told us any of that. Therefore, we guessed she didn't know. However, our parent's hatred of Trevor did not affect the way they felt about our uncles.

Anisa's last name was 'Anderson'. She was unmarried when she had her first child who was Uncle Wilhelm. When she got pregnant by Trevor the second time she left Lairdeaux. After that she met and married a man with the last name of 'Walker'. She was pregnant with Uncle Marcus at that time which is why the two brothers had different last names.

Our parents confirmed everything that I dreamed about Danielle and what she did to all of them. I still couldn't get over the fact that a mother would destroy the lives of her own children. But it was true. Our parents had only known what it was like to live normal lives for a short time. Because their lives were literally 'stolen' from them by their own mother.

It was Uncle Marcus's and Uncle Wilhelm's misfortune to fall in love with Jada and Margeaux. Neither one of the men knew what the women really were when they met them. Nor did they know about their father, Trevor. They didn't know anything about what their mother did to him either. When they found out about our aunts it was too late. Aunt Margeaux and Aunt Jada had fallen in love with each of the men. And it was only a matter of time before they made their lovers into what they were.

We asked our parents if our uncles resented our aunts for what they did to them. All they did was smile without giving us an answer. Which was all the answer we needed and we would find out later that they did. Uncle Marcus's resentment against Aunt Jada for what she did to him was worse than Uncle Wilhelm's. What the Ouija board told us came true. Trevor came after me in the guise of a 'friend' to harm me eventually, and we saw our father destroy him. We had no doubt at all after that about what our loved ones were. The death of a child our friend, Dara, forced our parents to sit down and tell us everything. And it was more of the 'truth' that the board spoke of.

My sister and I had a long talk with our parents that night. Afterward Papa said, "I'm going downstairs to have a talk with Marcus. I'll have Caroline bring you girls some dinner. Okay?" "Okay, Papa," we replied. "You just rest and take it easy," he continued. "And your mother is going to stay with you for a while." He kissed Drew and I on our cheeks and kissed Mama then he left our bedroom.

Caroline fixed dinner for us and brought it upstairs to our bedroom. Then we noticed it was very quiet downstairs. "Is Omri still downstairs, Caroline?" my mother asked. "No, Kate," replied Caroline. "He asked me where Marcus was and I told him he had gone out." A worried look came upon Mama's face.

"I do hope he is patient with Marcus," said my mother worriedly, and with a great deal of concern in her voice. "Because somehow I don't believe he is responsible for this." "But he was the last one we saw with her, Mama," said my sister. "I know that, honey," she said. "But sometimes things are not what they appear to be. I truly suspect it was someone else who killed your friend."

"But who?" asked Drew and I anxiously. "Oh," replied Mama. "I have my suspicions about that. Especially since you said you saw a woman there, Celia. I'll just wait and see what happens before I blame anybody. Don't worry because we will find out what happened to your friend."

Although we were not very hungry my sister and I forced some food down. Caroline and my mother were still talking when we finished eating. Then we laid back down in our beds. I started to drift off to sleep again and so did Drew.

The following morning my sister and I decided to visit Lila and Doc B. to pay our respects. That morning we did something else we never did before. We went into our parent's bedroom and kissed each one of them on their foreheads. As we watched them sleeping we realized just how vulnerable and helpless they were lying there. When we got downstairs Caroline was in the kitchen.

"How are my girls this morning?" she asked us as we came into the room. "We are okay," said Drew. "Did Papa find Uncle Marcus last night?" I asked her. "Yes, honey," she said. "He did." "What happened?" asked my sister. Caroline pulled up a chair and sat down between us at the table as we nibbled on some sausages and eggs she cooked. "Honey," she began, "Uncle Marcus is no longer with us." "What?" I cried and Drew looked stunned. "Why?" she asked. "What happened?"

"I wasn't there," said Caroline. "But they tell me that a fight broke out between your father and your uncle. Let's just say that your father won the fight. Alright?" "Is Aunt Jada alright?" I asked. "Is she still here?" "Yes," replied Caroline. "For now at least." "What does that mean?" asked my sister. "It means," replied Caroline, "there is no telling if she will stay here with us since her husband is gone now." "Where did Uncle Marcus go?" asked my sister anxiously. "He probably went to hell," said Caroline sarcastically.

In a round-about way she was telling my sister and I that my father destroyed Uncle Marcus. But I had a problem believing that and I didn't know why. Maybe because I knew that they loved each other. "He did tell your Papa that he didn't murder Dara though," added Caroline. I thought about the strange woman that I saw in the park again. In the back of my mind I knew she was the one who killed Dara. Although Uncle Marcus was the last one that we saw her with.

After all of the years I had known my uncle it was hard for me to believe that he would have murdered Dara. I had been feeling from the beginning that something wasn't quite right concerning the relationship between them, and that something was amiss. *"Could Uncle Marcus have been in love with Dara?"* I wondered.

Drew and I felt sad after hearing about Uncle Marcus. "Listen," said Caroline noticing the sad looks on our faces, "don't be sad for Marcus because he knew Dara was your friend, and evidently he didn't care. He broke the golden rule for this family. And that is to never bother any of your friends. So don't feel badly for him feel badly for Dara and her family." She was right of course. Already my sister and I missed Dara terribly and in the days to come we would miss our uncle, too.

The Ouija board told us about Dara being in love with Uncle Marcus but it never told us that he was in love with her, too. Drew and I would learn more about that from someone that we least expected. I couldn't seem to get the strange woman that I saw in the park out of my mind. *"What if it wasn't Uncle Marcus who murdered Dara?"* I began to think. *"What if Mama's consensus is right?"*

When Drew and I finished eating our breakfast we told Caroline we were going over to see Lila and Doc B. "Very good, darlings," she said. "Please give them my condolences. And if there is anything that I can do for them tell them to let me know, please." "Alright, Caroline," I said. "We will." Then my sister and I left.

CHAPTER TWENTY FIVE

When our parents and the other members of our family awakened that evening my sister and I were sitting in the dining room playing a game with Caroline. Our parents came into the dining room where we were and kissed each one of us on the cheek then sat down at the table with us. "Did you go over to your friend's house today?" asked my mother tenderly. "Yes, Mama," I replied. "How are they doing?" asked my father. "They're not doing so good, Papa," said Drew sadly.

"Did Caroline tell you girls what happened to Marcus?" asked Papa. "Yes, Papa," I replied. "We are very sorry, darlings," he said, "for everything that's happened." "We know that, Papa," said my sister. I noticed that my mother still had that worried look on her face.

"What's the matter, Mama?" I asked her softly. She squeezed my hand gently. "I'm almost certain that we've made a terrible mistake here," she replied. "Even so," said Papa, "Marcus wasn't blameless here, Katie. Because if it wasn't for him none of this would have happened."

Immediately it struck me as rather strange that my father said that. Because it was as if he knew something that nobody else did, not even my mother. I knew he and Uncle Marcus must have talked before the fight broke out and I couldn't help wondering what they talked about.

"Why do you suspect that someone else killed Dara, Mama?" I asked my mother. "We told you Uncle Marcus was the last one that we saw her with." As soon as I said that I recalled the mysterious woman again. But I didn't say anything else to them about her. "This whole thing just doesn't feel right to me," said Mama shaking her head confused. "Because I know Marcus wouldn't have done this." She was steadfast in her belief that he was wrongfully accused of Dara's murder. And I was beginning to believe she might be right about that.

My parents wanted to know when Dara's funeral was so they could go with Drew and I. We were glad about that because we desperately needed their support. I knew they had thought about our conversation in our bedroom that night and they were making an effort to be there for my sister and I.

They told us that we could stay home from school until after the funeral if we wanted to. We were happy about that because our minds were not on school anyway. And we wanted to spend some time with Lila.

The rest of our family members went out that night but our parents stayed home with Drew and I. Not only did they remain home that night but for many nights after that. However, around midnight after Drew and I went to bed we heard them retreating downstairs to the basement. They would be down there for hours, too. My sister and I were still very curious about what was down there.

Sheriff Jackson conducted the usual investigation into Dara's murder. Hers' was different from all of the others because her body was found intact but her head was missing. He and his Deputies were determined to catch the killer. But no matter what they did they got nowhere and their investigation turned up nothing at all. It felt very strange to Drew and I because we knew who the killer was. However, even though Dara was our friend we couldn't tell anyone.

I thought about Uncle Marcus a lot before Dara's funeral and vengeance had long been gone from mine and my sister's hearts. I was overwhelmed sometimes with guilt whenever I would think about all of the poor families in the towns where we had lived whose loved ones were brutally murdered. It was hard for Drew and I. Yet, when we thought about our beloved parents and our other family members our love far out-weighed that guilt.

One day I was on my way to Lila's house when I ran into, Jennifer, Lana's aunt and I was so glad to see her. "Why hello there, Celia," she said to me cheerfully when she saw me. "How are you? I haven't seen you or Drew for quite some time." "I am fine," I told her happily, "and so is Drew. How are you doing, Jennifer?" "Oh well," she replied, "I'm okay. I just take one day at a time you know. That's all any of us can do. Right? Alvin is home now." "That's wonderful," I said. "And how is Lana doing?" Suddenly her face fell and she looked very sad.

"Oh, Celia," she said, "I haven't talked to you or your sister in such a long time. And there's been so much going on in my life so I guess you haven't heard the news." "What news?" I asked her dreading what she was going to say. "Lana killed herself, Celia," she said solemnly. My mouth dropped open in shocked disbelief. "It happened about a month ago," continued Jennifer. "What?!" I cried stunned. "Lana is dead?!" I couldn't believe it, not Lana!

"Yes," continued Jennifer sadly. "She hung herself in her room at the asylum with some bed sheets she tied together." "Oh, God, no!" I said. "I'm so sorry to hear that, Jennifer, because Lana was my friend." "I know," she said. "But don't feel too badly about it, Celia, even though she was your friend. I know she is much happier now and in a much better place. I don't think she would've ever gotten over the tragedy you know."

I could still hear Jennifer talking to me about Lana but my mind was in a daze and she sounded so far away from me. "Are you alright, Celia?" asked Jennifer concerned. "Y-yes," I stammered. "I-I'll be okay, Jennifer. Thank you for telling me about Lana and I'm so sorry to lose my friend." "Celia," began Jennifer, "I believe we lost Lana long before this. Don't you?" I nodded my head slowly. "There was one thing that was really strange about her suicide though," she continued. "W-what was that?" I asked her still shaken. "She wrote one word all over the walls of her room with some lipstick that one of the Nurses gave her." "W-what word was that, Jennifer?" I asked calming down a little.

"Well," replied Jennifer confused, "we never could figure it out and we still can't. But the word she wrote was *'vampire'* all over the walls of the room." I nearly fainted when she said that but she caught me. "Are you sure you're okay, Celia?" she asked me. All I could do was nod my head a little. "I-I h-have to go now, Jennifer," I told her nervously. "S-so I-I'll see you around."

She looked at me concerned as I slowly walked away from her. "Okay," she said. "See you around, Celia, and tell Drew I said hi." It was then I knew that my family members murdered Lana's family and Lana did see Aunt Margeaux that night. It was the reason she was so frightened when she saw her again on that Thanksgiving eve. *"Oh, my God!"* I thought. *"My God!"*

When I arrived at Lila's house I was still very shaken up from the startling news about Lana's death. I broke down and cried right there on Lila's front stoop. After I rang the doorbell she answered the door. "Oh, Celia," she said when she opened the front door and saw me, "everything is going to be alright. I know my sister is at peace now because she was always troubled you know." She thought I was crying over Dara and I let her believe that.

"Come on in," she said guiding me inside her house. "I'll make us a nice hot cup of tea. Okay?" I nodded my head wiping the tears from my eyes. She lead me into the kitchen. "Where is Drew today?" she wanted to know. "She decided to stay home," I told her. "I can't say that I blame her," replied Lila.

"I'm glad there aren't many people here today," she continued. "I guess that's because the funeral is tomorrow night. My mom had the audacity to telephone me and said she would be at the funeral. I really don't care if she comes or not. And I hope she knows that she's going to pay for what she did to my sister and I." We sat down at the table with our tea. Doc B. was in the living room talking to some people who came over to pay their respects.

"You know, Celia," said Lila, "I hate to say this and I hope you do not take it the wrong way." "What is that?" I asked. "I'm glad your Dad took care of that bastard uncle of yours," she said. "I know he got just what he deserved and I only hope he suffered as much as Dara did." I had told her that Papa beat my uncle up and threw him out of the house......nothing else.

I wanted to tell her my mother felt that my uncle was innocent and that somebody else killed Dara. Also, that I suspected he had really been in love with her and she with him. More and more I was beginning to think Mama was right and that Uncle Marcus had not murdered Dara. I did understand how Lila felt though. I would have felt the same way if it had been my sister.

"Did you want to go with us to Mr. Darwood's tonight, Celia?" Lila asked me. "Yeah, sure," I replied. "If nobody would mind." "Who would mind?" asked Lila incredulously. "She was your friend." I stayed with Lila and her father all that day and when Mr. Darwood came to get them that evening to take them to the funeral parlor I went with them. It was a tradition for families to see how their deceased loved one looked just before the funeral service.

In the beginning Doc B. decided on a closed casket funeral for Dara because of her head being missing. But he changed his mind a few days later. Sheriff Jackson received a telephone call from the Sheriff in the next County when some children who were playing in the park came across a trash bag that had blood on it.

Out of curiosity the children looked inside the trash bag and inside it was the head of a woman. And it was Dara's head. I didn't understand why her killer tore off her head and discarded it nearly twenty miles away from where her body was discovered, nobody did.

The funeral was to be held at the church where Drew and I used to go. Reverend Bernard Dykes was glad to help Doc B. out by letting Dara be laid out there. And it didn't matter if they ever attended the church or not. Of course he asked Doc B. for a small donation.

Reverend Dykes took over the congregation after Reverend Daniels was murdered. He always wondered why Drew and I never came back to the church. And whenever he saw us he would tell us how much we were missed by everybody and urged us to return. We would make him an empty promise that we would come back knowing we had no intention of ever going back there. Because to us it just wasn't the same without the Daniels'.

Reverend Bernard Dykes was a young Pastor like Reverend Daniels was. He was only thirty eight years old but he was fiery. Everybody who knew him knew he loved the Lord. Also, it was known around town he had been going with the church secretary, Eliza Sams. And rumored that their affair began while he was the Associate Pastor under Reverend Daniels.

Reverend Dykes was fairly handsome, well over six feet tall and slender. A few of the choir members said they smelled alcohol on his breath many Sundays that Reverend Daniels let him preach. When he dressed in his regular clothing no one would ever guess that he was a Minister. He had no family in Hardelle anymore and he had never been married.

Eliza was seen leaving his living quarters right next door to the church on several occasions late at night. There were rumors that she and her husband, Tony, were getting a divorce. And the rumor about her being pregnant by the Reverend was all over Hardelle. Then suddenly everything got quiet. There were no more rumors about Eliza and Tony getting a divorce, or about her being pregnant by the Reverend. I figured that some jealous woman had nothing else to do but spread a nasty rumor like that. And a lot of women in town were jealous of Eliza because she was very pretty.

She and her husband attended the church together on a regular basis. They had been married for over a decade and she was expecting their first child. It was many years ago that Eliza told a lot of people in Hardelle that Tony was sterile. I think it was just more jealousy toward her because that rumor wasn't true either. And she never told anybody that about her husband. The rumors died away eventually like they usually do. Yet, in spite of that there was still suspicion among a few people that she was carrying the Reverend's baby.

For a long time Eliza Sams was known as the town tramp. She was very pretty, medium height and she had a 'knock-out' figure. Her hair was dark auburn mixed with a little gray although she couldn't have been more than thirty five years old. She was very lively and out-going and she wore short skirts and tight blouses, both of which were too tight for her and unbecoming for a married woman.

When Eliza Marton married Tony Sams people stopped calling her nasty names. Poor Tony had been in so many fights over her that his face looked a little bit like a road map from all of the scars he had. Still, he was a tall, good-looking, young man. Eliza calmed down quite a lot since they got married. Except for the rumored affair with the Reverend she reminded me of Alyson Merles.

We arrived at the funeral parlor and my heart was in my stomach. Lila began to sob before we even got inside the building so Doc B. put his arm around her shoulders. "We don't have to do this right now, honey," he said to her, "if you don't want to." "It's okay, Dad," she sobbed softly. "I'm okay. " Then she reached for my hand. After we got inside the parlor Mr. Darwood guided us to the room where Dara's body was laying.

Mr. Darwood was a little elderly man who looked to me like he was tired all of the time. He was one of five Morticians in Hardelle and his wife, Ellie, helped him at the parlor. I'd heard he was too cheap to hire anybody to help him. He, his wife, his six children and fourteen grandchildren all lived in Hardelle. But his own children wouldn't help him at the parlor because he hardly wanted to pay them anything. He was very compassionate though and everybody in town liked him and his family.

His wife, Ellie, short for Eleanora was a big woman who adored children. She was a lot more spry than her husband was, too. The children in Hardelle would often come to the parlor to visit with her and to talk to her. She would feed them plenty of milk and cookies and show them around the parlor telling them what she and her husband did there. When Drew and I were little girls we used to visit Miss Ellie, too. She was very kind, not only to children, but to everybody who knew her.

Miss Ellie would tell us stories about her childhood and they were fascinating stories, too. A lot of the time I think she made them up just for entertainment purposes. She told us that she and her family lived on an Indian Reservation when she was growing up. She told us many interesting stories about her Native American ancestors, too. Mr. Darwood, however, hardly ever talked at all. We entered the room where Dara's body lay and she looked beautiful.

She was dressed in a lovely pale blue negligee with matching slippers on her feet and it had a very high collar on it. Miss Ellie fixed her hair so that it laid softly around her face. You couldn't tell that her head had been torn from her body. Mr. Darwood told Doc B. that a net would be placed over the casket for the funeral. Therefore, we knew her head was just sitting atop her shoulders.

The net would be there to prevent anyone from touching the body. A corsage was on her right wrist. It had the words 'beloved sister' on a tag that was attached to it and a silver plaque across the front of the gray casket read: 'Beloved Daughter'.

There were a lot of beautiful flowers surrounding the casket. I smiled when I saw a big bouquet shaped like a heart that was sent by the Bellis family. We stood there looking down at Dara for what seemed like a long time but it wasn't. Lila kissed Dara on her hand and Doc B. kissed her on her forehead. "Good-bye, darling," he said then he and Lila both broke down and cried. I cried, too. It was so heartbreaking.

As I stood there looking down at my friend's body I recalled the day that Drew and I first met her and Lila at the Teen Center. *"Would she still be alive today,"* I wondered, *"if we had never met?"* Our two families were connected by some strange twist of fate. Selma Ann knew it but no one else other than Drew, our family and I did. As long as I would know Lila and Doc B. I would keep it that way, too. I began to recall all of the horror stories that I read about vampires.

According to the stories I read the poor unfortunate victims of vampires ended up as one of the undead themselves. I wondered if Dara would indeed stay dead. And I wondered why, out of all of the ravaged victims, she was the only one whose body was found intact but her head was taken. Then I remembered something else that I read, too.

The victims of vampires would never return from the dead if their heads were separated from their bodies. Whoever killed Dara had not torn her apart like all of the others. Those people couldn't come back because they were left in pieces. But for some reason Dara's killer had not really wanted to kill her I surmised. As incredible as it seemed I sensed that her killer had some compassion for her and whoever it was felt they *had* to kill her. It didn't make any sense to me at first but as time passed it would. I suddenly realized, *"Uncle Marcus didn't kill Dara!"*

I began to get the uneasy feeling that Dara had gotten herself involved in something that she shouldn't have. At first nobody else noticed the big silver crucifix that was attached to the lid of her casket then Doc B. did.

"Where did that come from I wonder?" he asked. "I don't know, Dad," replied Lila. "I thought you might have requested that it be put there." "No," said Doc B. "Why would I do that?" He turned to

Mr. Darwood who was standing there with us. "Do you know where that crucifix came from, Arthur?" he asked Mr. Darwood. "It was in a package I received in the mail the other day," said Mr. Darwood. "And it had instructions with it that it should be placed inside your daughter's casket."

"I got a telephone call confirming if I received the package," continued Mr. Darwood. "But they wouldn't give me their name. The only thing they wanted was for me to make sure that the crucifix was attached to the lid of your daughter's casket. They said that they were a friend of your daughter's and they wanted to make sure she rested in peace. It was a very odd thing but I figured you wouldn't mind." "Oh really?" said Doc B. "Yes," replied Mr. Darwood. "The caller was a woman but I didn't recognize her voice. Do you want me to leave it there?"

"It's just a gesture of kindness I think, Dad," Lila told Doc B. "Maybe you're right, honey," replied Doc B. "Yes, Arthur," he said, "you can leave it there." "It was kind of strange," continued Mr. Darwood. "How is that?" asked Doc B. curiously. "Well," began Mr. Darwood, "the woman who called me on the telephone specifically told me to make sure that the crucifix was facing your daughter when the lid of the coffin was closed." When he said that I knew that someone in my family had sent the crucifix to him. And that same family member called him on the telephone to make the strange request.

By the time Mr. Darwood dropped me off at my house that night I was feeling very distraught. When I got inside the house our parents were in the living room talking. Caroline was out at the guest house and Drew was upstairs in our bedroom laying down. "How are you, sweetheart?" asked Papa kindly. "I'm alright, Papa," I replied. "Where have you been, honey?" asked Mama. I told them where I had been. I told them about Lana, too. Strangely, they didn't seem surprised by that news.

My mother got up and put her arms around me. She held me tightly to her. "Are you alright, sweetie?" she asked me tenderly stroking my hair. "Not really, Mama," I admitted. Then I felt tears in my eyes.

I didn't think it was possible. But throughout mine and my sister's terrible ordeal our parents managed to shower more and more affection on us and that night before I went to bed I talked to them. I let them know that my sister and I had made a decision. We would stay with them instead of leaving home and they were very happy to hear that.

The following day I was nervous and jittery and Dara's funeral was to be held that night. I thought it was just apprehension about the funeral. My sister was very quiet that day. Caroline left us alone and went about her daily household chores. When dinner was ready none of us wanted anything to eat.

Around six o'clock that evening we started getting ready to go to the funeral. Our parents and our other family members awakened an hour later. They were all going to the funeral with us, that is all but Aunt Jada.

I was insulted by that. However, I shrugged it off because I guessed she was still upset about Uncle Marcus. "Are my girls going to be alright tonight?" asked my mother just before we left for the church. "Yes, Mama," we replied. "We'll be alright." Then we set out on our walk to the church.

It seemed like my sister and I were walking the last mile. I wondered if it was how a condemned prisoner must feel on their way to the execution chamber. Papa kept his arms around our shoulders the whole time and Mama walked quietly beside us. When we got to the church our family members went no further than the vestibule while Caroline, Drew and I went into the sanctuary. Everyone was crying and it was a very sorrowful affair.

Doc B. had to be held up by two male Nurses when he walked to the front of the church to view Dara's body and Lila couldn't stand on her own at all. It was horrible! After viewing Dara's body Drew, Caroline and I joined the rest of our family in the vestibule and we were filled with grief. Yet, having our parents there meant a great deal to my sister and I. To this day I believe it was the only reason that we held up so well. The next morning at the cemetery it was worse for Drew and I.

They started lowering Dara's casket into the ground. I would never hear her voice again, or see her beautiful face, or laugh with her ever again. My sister and I needed our parents at the funeral the night before. But believe me we needed them at the burial, too. It was the final step when we knew Dara was gone forever. Although we had Caroline it just wasn't the same as having our parents there with us.

To my surprise at the cemetery Lila held up very well but Doc B. was a total basket case and I felt afraid for him. I didn't think he would ever be the same again. I never did see Annabelle, Lila's mother, and if she had been there I know Lila would have pointed her out to us. Millie tried her best to console Doc B. but he was inconsolable. As we stood around the grave site the sun which had been shining brightly disappeared and dark clouds came out of nowhere. It started getting darker and darker.

Reverend Dykes was still praying when we heard the first rumblings of thunder. They became louder and louder as he prayed over Dara's grave then the lightning came. A few drops of rain began to fall and people started opening their umbrellas. Drew and I had none because we had not bothered to listen to the weather report that morning, however, Caroline had hers'.

She stood between us and opened her big umbrella as it started raining a little harder. I always believed that if it rained on a person's new grave their spirit went to heaven so I figured Dara had made it in. Of course I had no way of knowing if what I believed was true or not. And I don't know where I even got that notion from. It was just something I always believed.

We were all throwing our one little flower atop Dara's casket as it was being lowered into the ground when the storm became more fierce and the sky was almost black. I felt a gentle breeze on my face as if someone unseen hurriedly passed by me and someone touched my hand lightly. I looked over to my right and there stood my grandfather, covered in that veil of darkness, that I came to know so well but no darkness covered me.

I could tell he was looking down at the casket as it was being lowered into the earth then he turned to me. He alone was covered in that darkness. Usually he pulled me into it with him but not that time. "Don't be afraid, Celia, honey," he told me. The thunder and the lightning grew more fierce and I couldn't move.

I wanted to say something to Drew and Caroline who were busy watching the proceedings but I couldn't speak either. Also, I was not aware that I was trembling. "Are you alright, Celia?" Caroline asked me. I nodded my head. She looked in the direction where my grandfather was standing but she couldn't see him so she turned back to the proceedings.

"Listen to me, Celia, honey," said my grandfather. "Marcus didn't murder your friend." Quickly I turned around to face him. Caroline looked at me again then turned back to the proceedings. "It was not Marcus," my grandfather said. "He was blamed for something he didn't do, Celia. He was there when it happened but he couldn't have stopped it." Then he hesitated and after that he abruptly changed the subject.

"You've learned many things, Celia," my grandfather continued, "and there are more things to come for you and your sister. There is something about me you will learn soon and something about Jada and Marcus." After saying that he was gone and I gasped. "Celia," said Caroline turning to look at me, "I think we had better go home because I don't think you're as alright as you claim to be." She was right.

We had planned to go over to Lila's and Doc B.'s house with everyone else after the burial was over but we changed our plans. The storm ceased as suddenly as it began and the sun came back out shining as brightly as ever. Strangely, I wasn't afraid like I usually was.

When we got home I told Caroline and Drew all about seeing my grandfather in the cemetery and I told them what he said to me. "My God!" cried Drew. "That means we blamed Uncle Marcus for nothing." "No," said Caroline. "It means he wasn't the killer but he's still just as guilty because I know there must have been something he could've done."

"That's not what Grandfather told me, Caroline," I said. "Because he said that Uncle Marcus couldn't have stopped it." "Well," she said, "it's over now so there's no need to keep going over it."

What our grandfather said stayed on the minds of Drew and I. *"Maybe there is a reason why Uncle Marcus couldn't have stopped Dara's murder,"* I thought. "I can't imagine," replied Drew, "why Uncle Marcus wouldn't have been able to stop Dara's killer, Celia. Can you?" "No," I replied. "Not really." Neither one of us said anymore about it after that. But it didn't stop us from wondering about it.

"What do you think Grandfather was talking about, Caroline," I asked, "when he said there is something else that I will learn about him?" Caroline looked at me and smiled. "I suspect that whatever it is he wants from you, honey," she said, "he is ready to tell you, you will know." "Where did they bury Grandfather, Caroline?" asked Drew. "There was nothing to bury, sweetie," replied Caroline. "Why not?" asked Drew. "Sweetie," said Caroline, "you know what your grandfather was. Right?" "Yes," replied my sister a little confused.

"Well then," continued Caroline, "surely you're not surprised that there was no body to bury. Are you? After all he was well over a hundred years old so truthfully he 'died' a long time ago." "Like in the horror stories we've read huh?" replied Drew. "Yeah," chuckled Caroline. It was amazing how Drew and I came to accept what our family members were so nonchalantly.

I started thinking. And I recalled that none of our family members, or Caroline ever said that our grandfather was destroyed when they talked about him. They always said that '*he left*' or that he was '*gone*' which to me was not the same thing as being destroyed. Aunt Jada was the only one that I recalled ever saying that he was murdered and that the people in Wesbury killed him.

"Was he really destroyed?" I asked Caroline curiously. "Celia, honey," she said, "it seems like everything is coming out into the open now so just wait. Remember I told you to be patient when you were curious about your parents. Didn't I? Well, I'm telling you again to be patient because all of your questions will be answered. The truth always comes out." She smiled at me. As one of the undead our grandfather must have had many powers and he could create any illusion that he wanted to. But why the dark covering all of the time? What was it that he was hiding?

I realized that there must have been something that our grandfather wanted me to know. In the cemetery that day from what I could make out it looked like his hair was white. *"But that's ridiculous,"* I thought. *"Because that would mean he has aged and that's impossible for the undead."* He was concealing something but I did not know what it was. And I felt that the dark covering was an illusion for my benefit. I asked myself all kinds of questions but I had no answers. And I found myself looking forward to the next time that he would 'visit' me.

It was then that I told Caroline and my sister about our grandfather always being covered in a dark veil when he came to me. Drew thought nothing of it but Caroline said, "You never mentioned that to me before, honey." "Do you know what it means, Caroline?" I asked her anxiously. "It has some significance for sure," she told me. Then she thought about something for a moment.

"You know," she began," I remember reading a book about vampires when I was younger. And in that book vampires always came to those they loved in their lifetimes covered in a veil. It was a covering for them to hide themselves so their loved ones wouldn't be afraid of them. When there was no more fear the covering vanished and the creature was seen in its' true form. Not only by one particular family member after that but by all those they loved in life." "I don't understand," I said confused.

"Well," continued Caroline, "the unfortunate soul who had existed as one of the undead couldn't rest in peace because a loved one was still holding onto them, and they stayed around that loved one. They protected them and comforted them in bad times. And it was their love for that person that covered them and shielded them. Also, there was something their dear one feared and they associated that fear with the departed soul. As long as that fear was alive the spirit remained earthbound to 'cover' its' loved one. It was simply a matter of the beloved one letting go of their fear." She hesitated then said, "You could say that 'love' is the covering you've been seeing, Celia."

For years I had feared thunderstorms because subconsciously I associated them with our grandfather's trouble and his leaving us when I was a little girl. So in a way I understood what Caroline was talking about. At last I knew what our beloved grandfather wanted from me. He wanted me to let him go. And he was letting me know that I had nothing to fear from the thunderstorms because they had nothing at all to do with what happened to him.

Yet, that was my fear but it was not the only reason that our grandfather was always around me. There was another reason for him being around me that should have been obvious to all of us. He was there to help me through something. And I in turn could help my sister but I just didn't realize what it was at the time, and neither did anybody else.

What happened to our grandfather and our family members in Wesbury would have happened anyway. It didn't matter if there was a thunderstorm that night or not. Because it was inevitable just as things were to change for my sister and I as we grew older. It all would have happened anyway and no one could have stopped it.

I didn't know if I could let my grandfather go because I still loved him. In the cemetery that morning I felt no fear when the storm came out of nowhere. I had to let him go but he would have to help me do it because he had been with me for so long. After all of the years that he had been gone I finally knew that there was something very important I needed to know and understand. He was there to help me as I grew older for reasons I could never have guessed. He was not the only one that I had to let go of and I was not the only one who had to learn to let go of someone. A change was coming for Drew and I. A great change that concerned our entire family.

Many things had happened to my sister and I, especially after I turned seventeen years old. There was no way that Drew and I could have known how much things were going to change for us. But our grandfather was there to help me through those changes. Caroline came through for me again and our grandfather was right because I did learn something about him.

He told me there were more things for me to learn. I began thinking back to the night I first saw him when I was twelve years old. I didn't see him anymore after that for five years but he began to 'visit' me more after I turned seventeen. My sister and I were becoming young women. And he knew we would discover the dark and terrible secret that our family members harbored. However, because of love so deep and dear that I saw portrayed by that beautiful covering over him, he was there to help us through another stunning realization that had not yet occurred to any of us but should have. Also, I didn't know what it was that I was to learn about Aunt Jada and Uncle Marcus that he spoke about.

CHAPTER TWENTY SIX

Two weeks after Dara's burial Lila returned to school and Doc B. went back to work. They seemed to be recovering well from such a great and tragic loss. Drew, Lila and I became even closer and we decided to get rid of the Ouija board. We buried it in the woods just outside of town where Dara's body was found.

We thought it was appropriate to bury it there since it foretold her death. Furthermore, we didn't want it falling into any other poor, unsuspecting person's hands. No one had to tell us there was a reason why the people who previously lived in Lila's house had left it behind. We never wanted to see it again and we were quite sure that the previous owners of the house had felt the same way. We buried the spirit of Selma Ann with it, too. Because Doc B. stopped pining over her after that. He never mentioned her name again.

Things were almost back to normal in our household. Drew and I still missed Uncle Marcus and we knew Aunt Jada missed him, too. We could see it in her eyes and she became a little distant toward all of us. Often while our parents and the others were out at night she would return home and retreat to her bedroom. One night my sister and I decided to have a talk with her so we knocked on her bedroom door.

"Come in," she said softly and we entered her bedroom. "Aunt Jada," I said, "do you mind if we come inside and talk with you?" "No, honey," she replied sweetly. "I don't mind at all." We sat down on the side of her bed. We had no idea what to say to her and there was an awkward silence in the room at first.

"What did you girls want to talk to me about?" Aunt Jada finally asked us. Drew and I could not think of anything to say so as if she was reading our minds my aunt said, "You want to know how I feel about losing my husband. Don't you?" We nodded our heads. "I've waited," she continued, "for someone in this family to ask me how I felt about all that's happened and nobody would, not even my own sisters." She had tears in her eyes when she said that but she quickly regained her composure.

"Drew and I didn't think you would want to talk to anybody, Aunt Jada," I said. She got up and sat down between my sister and I on the bed and put her arms around our shoulders. "Sweetheart," she said, "there is absolutely nothing on earth that would ever make me not want to talk to my girls." "So," said Drew, "how do you feel about what's happened?" Aunt Jada sighed heavily.

"You know," she began, "when your parents told us that you knew the truth about all of us we were surprised that you took the news so well. I mean…..let's face it, it's not every day that two normal, young women like yourselves find out that their family members are creatures of darkness, but you still loved us anyway." "Of course we do, Aunt Jada," I told her. She hugged us tightly. Then she told us how she and Uncle Marcus first met.

She told my sister and I that he was not a vampire when she met him but that she made him that way after she fell in love with him. She wanted to be with him and him only. My mother had already told us that. Aunt Jada continued to tell us how over the years she was always afraid. "Afraid of what, Aunt Jada?" My sister asked her curiously and my aunt hesitated.

"I stood by for years and watched," said my aunt, "as my husband did whatever he had to do to survive. Including wining and dining many beautiful women right under my nose." We could see the tears in her eyes again. I recalled the strange woman that Drew and I saw on our front porch that evening and it seemed like such a long time ago.

Aunt Jada continued to tell us how she knew there was always the chance that Uncle Marcus would find somebody else and leave her. Someone that he would want to make as he was, one of the undead. She told us she was always fearful that the day would come when she was no longer enough for him. And it came when he met Dara. *"My God!"* I thought. *"I was right. He was in love with Dara."*

Aunt Jada told my sister and I that although he did love her Uncle Marcus resented her for what she did to him. She told us that it was the same way with Aunt Margeaux and Uncle Wilhelm. However, Uncle Wilhelm was never the kind of man who had eyes for other women like Uncle Marcus did. He only did what he had to do to survive.

They were brothers, yet, they were very different from one another. Aunt Jada told us that as Uncle Marcus's resentment toward her grew their marriage began to deteriorate and she felt helpless to do anything about it.

Uncle Marcus let her know many times that if and when he found somebody else he was leaving her. Unfortunately along came Dara. Before Aunt Jada said anything else I knew that she was the mysterious woman I had seen in the park that evening. Yet, the real shock was still to come and my sister and I were totally unprepared for it.

"Things hadn't always been that way between us," continued Aunt Jada. "Sometimes he would go out and get our prey while I stayed home." The way that she spoke about human beings as 'prey' unnerved me a little bit. Again I recalled the poor woman that we saw on our front porch with Uncle Marcus. And Aunt Jada let them inside the house that night.

"I can't remember you ever staying home, Aunt Jada," said Drew, "while the others were out." "Oh yes, honey," said my aunt. "I would be in the basement and you just didn't know it." "He would bring people back here to our house?!" I asked astonished. Aunt Jada gently stroked my hair. I couldn't believe that people had been killed right there in our house.

"Oh my!" said my sister looking at me. I was thinking the same thing that she was. Because we didn't have to wonder anymore what was downstairs in our basement. And just the thought of what our aunt told us began to sicken us. I believe she could tell by the disgusted looks on our faces, too. She had a crooked little smile on her lips and it was a smile of sympathy, sympathy for Drew and I. I started to feel more anger toward my grandmother, Danielle.

"I'm so sorry, darlings," said Aunt Jada. "But you were born into a family of beasts. We tried for a long time to talk your parents out of having any children. But they wouldn't listen and all of us were very apprehensive about your births. We didn't know how you would turn out. And Kate fed on the blood of mammals during both of her pregnancies." She was referring to warm-blooded animals.

"We thought you would be born deformed or something," she continued. "But to our joy you were born normal and healthy and we were overjoyed. No two children could've been more loved and welcomed than you two were."

"Is that why you and Uncle Marcus and Aunt Margeaux and Uncle Wilhelm never had any children," I asked her, "because you were afraid?" "Yes," said Aunt Jada. "But after you two came along we didn't need to worry about it anymore because you're our children, too. Margeaux and I changed just as many diapers as your parents did. Also, we were up for many late night feedings." She chuckled softly as she recalled her happy memories.

"It just goes to show you," continued Aunt Jada, "you can't believe everything that you read in books about the undead. Because you two are living proof that love overpowers everything in existence and with that nothing is impossible."

"As you grew up you helped us realize what it was like to be normal again and to be a normal family," continued my aunt smiling. "We're so sorry for what happened to you and the others, Aunt Jada," said my sister. Then my aunt hugged us again. "It's okay, honey," she said. "My mother was a very tragic and emotionally distraught woman, but now I know." She hesitated again. "Now you know what, Aunt Jada?" I asked her. "I know how she felt when she knew she was losing the man she loved," she replied looking downward.

"What do you mean, Aunt Jada?" I asked her. Quietly she moved away from us and rested against her pillows. "I know how she must've felt," said my aunt with despair in her voice, "when she knew she was losing her husband forever." My sister and I were puzzled. "You mean..... you were losing Uncle Marcus?" asked my sister. "Is that what you're telling us, Aunt Jada?" She looked at my sister and I but she didn't answer us and she didn't have to.

It was obvious from all she said that my uncle was leaving her for Dara. But Drew still had not caught onto what she was really telling us. "How were you losing him?" I asked her already knowing the answer. But I asked her that for my sister's sake not my own.

Aunt Jada looked down at her hands then she looked at Drew and I. "He was leaving me for another woman," she said. "And I couldn't let that happen you know. I just couldn't. If he left me I would've destroyed myself a lot sooner believe me. I would've been happy to join my father in the hereafter." My heart started pounding frantically and I saw my sister beginning to tremble. It was then I realized for certain that our grandfather had been destroyed.

"What is it that you're trying to tell us, Aunt Jada?" I asked her again for my sister's sake and dreading what I knew we were going to hear. "Celia," she said, "you and Drew are big girls now so surely you can read between the lines when someone is telling you something." "No," I said. "I don't understand what you're trying to say." "Yes, you do," she insisted. "You know Marcus didn't kill your friend. I know you do because Kate knows and so does Omri and the others."

It seemed like a house had just fallen on my sister and I. "Oh, no, no!" cried Drew looking at my aunt in wide-eyed disbelief. "No, Aunt Jada! No!" Although I knew what my aunt was going to tell us I was still shocked. And I realized what Selma Ann's spirit was trying to say to us through the Ouija board when it spelled out the word 'jealousy'. My aunt was so overwhelmed with jealousy because of Dara taking Uncle Marcus away from her that she was enraged when she killed her. My uncle probably tried to stop her from hurting Dara but he couldn't because of her fierce rage. My sister and I knew about that rage, too. Still, I believe his being there was the only reason why her body wasn't ripped to shreds like all of the others. Then Aunt Jada continued speaking to us.

"We knew that your friends were off limits to all of us," continued Aunt Jada. "Always. And none of us wanted to face your father's wrath for any reason but Marcus was my husband. You must understand that. Don't you?" "You could've come to us, Aunt Jada," said Drew nearly in tears. "You didn't have to kill Dara because we would've talked to her.

Why? Why?" My aunt reached for my sister's hand but Drew ran out of her bedroom.

I sat there on the side of the bed staring at my aunt in shock. I did not want to believe it but I knew that it was true. She murdered our friend and I was filled with rage and anger toward her for what she did.

"Celia," said my aunt, "you talking to your friend wouldn't have done any good trust me. Because Marcus had her completely under his power and nothing you said or did would have made any difference, nothing. And you should know something else, too." "W-what is that?" I asked her with my voice beginning to crack.

"Your father didn't destroy Marcus," said Aunt Jada. "He left me because I killed that girl. He chose to separate from all of us and go his own way so you see I lost him anyway." "Dara was our friend, Aunt Jada," I told her becoming very upset. "She may have been your friend, Celia, honey," said Aunt Jada softly, "but she was my enemy."

Slowly I got up and backed out of her bedroom. I could not stop staring at her. After all of the years that I had loved the woman I saw before me I began to feel hatred toward her. And I didn't know the monster that I saw before me. I left her bedroom closing the door behind me and I felt numb all over.

Drew was sobbing as Caroline held her in her arms. I looked into her eyes and saw that she as well as the rest of our family already knew what Drew and I were just finding out. Nobody had bothered to tell us because they knew we would be extremely upset and we were.

Aunt Jada on the other hand couldn't live with the guilt that she felt. All along she wanted to tell us the truth. At last we gave her the opportunity she needed to do that. I sat down in a chair in the living room. However, my aunt was right when she said that talking to Dara wouldn't have done any good because we did try to no avail.

"It'll be alright, Celia," said Caroline. "And it is good that you and Drew know the truth now." I wanted to break down and cry but the tears just wouldn't come and Drew couldn't stop sobbing. A few minutes later Aunt Jada opened her bedroom door and came out of her room dressed to go out. She looked at my sister and I and smiled weakly.

"I want you girls to never forget that I loved you very much," she said to Drew and I. "And I always will. I never meant to hurt you like I did. You're like my own children and I hope you can forgive me some day." She left the house after that. The image of her that night and the words she spoke would remain with us for the rest of our lives, because we would never see our beloved aunt again.

Caroline didn't say anything else to Drew and I. She sat down in the living room with us silently as we tried to take in what had happened. My sister cried herself to sleep. I told Caroline good-night and went upstairs to my bedroom. As I laid down across my bed the tears that I wanted to come so badly still wouldn't come. Eventually I drifted off to sleep and had another dream.

In my dream I was standing in a large field covered with beautiful red and white roses, Aunt Jada's favorite flower and her favorite colors. There was a big white cat there, too. It had big, green eyes and a golden locket around its' neck. It walked over to where I was standing and sat down in front of me. Its' big, green eyes looked right into mine. Also, there was a stream there that had the clearest, bluest water in it that I had ever seen, and the sun was shining brightly.

Standing under a tree in the middle of the field were Aunt Jada and Uncle Marcus, and they were holding each other's hands and smiling. Across the stream in the other direction I saw Dara. She looked beautiful all dressed in white as she smiled at me, too. She waved good-bye to me then turned around and walked away.

When I looked toward the tree again Aunt Jada and Uncle Marcus were waving good-bye to me, and I waved back. Then they turned around and walked away still holding one another's hands. The cat had vanished but it left behind the golden locket that it had around its' neck. I was there in that beautiful field alone. When I woke up it was morning. I looked over at Drew who was sound asleep. So I guessed Papa, or Uncle Wilhelm had carried her upstairs to bed.

There at the foot of my bed on the bedpost hung Aunt Jada's golden locket. Ever since I could remember she never took it off. And she told my sister and I that it was a birthday gift from her mother on her twenty first birthday. Without thinking I put the locket around my neck then I checked on my parents. After that I went downstairs.

Caroline was sitting on the sofa. "Look, Caroline," I said showing her my aunt's golden locket. "I found Aunt Jada's locket hanging on my bedpost this morning." "I know," said Caroline calmly. "She left it for you, honey, early this morning while you were asleep." "What do you mean '*left it for me?*' I asked her.

"She's gone, sweetheart," said Caroline. "Gone where?" I wanted to know. "This morning," she replied, "for the first time in many many years your aunt went up to Sires Hill to watch the sunrise." "What?!" I said stunned.

Sires Hill was a place where you could sit and look over the whole town, and it was nothing but wide open space. If Aunt Jada was there when the sun came up she had deliberately destroyed herself. It dawned on me what she said to us the night before when she told Drew and I that if my uncle left her she would've destroyed herself a lot sooner, and glad to join our grandfather.

She had already planned to go up to Sires Hill that morning. I realized that if she destroyed herself and Uncle Marcus was in my dream with her that something had happened to him, too. I felt light headed and knew that somewhere deep inside himself my uncle must have still loved my aunt. Because they were certainly together in my dream but Dara was by herself in the dream. I gathered that Uncle Marcus, who was ever the ladies' man to the very end, couldn't have been that serious about Dara if he was with Aunt Jada.

Caroline kept me from falling to the floor. She sat me down in a chair. "She couldn't go on anymore, honey," she told me tenderly. "We have all known it was going to happen sooner or later. Because it wasn't only Marcus's leaving her, but the fact that she hurt you and Drew. She loved you both so much. It was like she had hurt her own children and she just couldn't stand the pain anymore. She wasn't going to do anything until she told you both the truth and that's why she waited."

The tears that I wanted to come so badly before and would not come now came in a flood. I thought my heart had broken in two. Aunt Jada did a horrendous thing but we still loved her dearly. I thought I would die of heartache and sorrow as Caroline held me in her arms. I cried bitterly.

She confirmed that our parents already knew it was Aunt Jada who murdered Dara because she admitted it to them. Our family said their good-byes to her during the wee hours of that morning while Drew and I were asleep. They were very sad Caroline told me. However, it was something my aunt felt that she had to do. She didn't want to go on any longer in a 'life' where she was doomed, and she wanted peace.

My tears finally stopped and I walked over to a chair by the livingroom window and sat down. I looked outside because it was strangely quiet. Then I recalled the dream I had about Aunt Jada, Uncle Marcus and Dara. "You have found peace, Aunt Jada," I said softly. "You have at last and so has Uncle Marcus. I forgive you and I will always love you, too."

Aunt Jada and Uncle Marcus came in a dream to say good-bye to me and so had Dara. My aunt and my uncle were together just like she wanted. I couldn't help but wonder if Uncle Marcus really would've left Aunt Jada, or would he have left her only for a little while and come back to her. I hated the thought. Yet, something in the back of my mind told me that Dara had died for nothing. It was something that none of us would ever know for sure since all three of them were dead. I truly hated to believe that all Dara was to my uncle was something to play with for a while.

When Drew awakened that morning Caroline and I told her about Aunt Jada. She wept bitterly, too. As angry as she had been with our aunt she forgave her, too, just as I did. After I told her about my dream about them she didn't feel so badly anymore. We would miss our aunt terribly because she was like a second mother to us. And we would never forget Aunt Jada. The youngest of our aunts, the prettiest and the most fun. My sister and I laid around the house that day dealing with the grief in our hearts.

Caroline fixed us a light supper that evening but we hardly ate anything. "Did you get a chance to speak to our parents yet, Caroline?" asked Drew. "You know......about what we talked about?" She was referring to our conversation about her having a life of her own. "Yes I did, honey," said Caroline. Then she hesitated.

"Well?" said my sister anxiously. Caroline took a sip of the cocoa that she was drinking. My sister and I watched her waiting for an answer. Again we were completely unprepared for what was coming.

"I was going to wait until a later time to tell you girls this," began Caroline. "Tell us what, Caroline?" asked my sister. "Well," she said, "your parents and I had a long talk about you two the other night." "And so?" said Drew. "I have decided and so have they," she said, "that you girls are right and I do need a life of my own. As I said before you two don't need me as much as you used to." We didn't like the sound of that. And we knew something was coming that we didn't want to hear.

"So what have you decided?" I asked her. "I'm going home, girls," said Caroline matter of factly. "What?!" cried Drew and I. "What do you mean?" asked Drew. "You are coming back. Aren't you?" She just smiled at us. "No, honey, " she replied. "I'm not coming back." We were totally taken by surprise.

"You mean.....you're leaving us for good, Caroline?" asked Drew in shock. Caroline nodded her head smiling. "But why?" I asked her. "Why do you want to leave us?" She held each of our hands. "Don't look at it that way," replied Caroline. "I'm leaving so I can travel and see some of the world. It's time now and I want you two to be happy for me." "How can we be happy about you leaving us?" asked Drew with tears in her eyes.

"Oh, honey," said Caroline. "You're young women now. And soon you'll be finding lives of your own, you'll see. There's a great big world out there. And it's waiting for you two and for me." "I don't understand why you have to leave us to do that," pouted my sister. "You can travel and come back. Can't you?"

"No, sweetheart," said Caroline. "You two don't need a baby sitter, or a housekeeper anymore because you can take care of yourselves, and you have your parents. They love you both so much." "Did they suggest that you do this?" I asked her. "No, they did not," she answered. "In fact, they feel the same way that you two do. But it's something I need to do."

"I still don't understand," replied Drew. "You always told us that you loved us." "I do, honey." said Caroline. "You know I do." "Well," said my sister, "how can you just pack up and leave us?" "You may not be able to fully understand it right now," said Caroline. "But one day you will, believe me." We didn't think we could stand anymore sorrowful news. But in the near future there was more to come for my sister and I.

In my heart of hearts I did understand why Caroline had to leave us. She had put her life on hold for many years just for Drew and I. And she had a right like anybody else did to find happiness for herself. I didn't want her to leave just as the rest of our family didn't. But it was true. She really had no reason to stay on any longer. It was time for her to go just like she said.

"When are you leaving?" I asked her calmly. "Right after your birthdays," she replied. "That's not that far away," said Drew flabbergasted. "That's right, sweetie," said Caroline. "As a matter of fact I'll be leaving soon after yours, Drew."

My birthday was coming on May 20th and my sister's was on June 1st. At least Caroline would be with us for Memorial Day. We made a big deal out of holidays in our house, and I couldn't imagine a holiday without Caroline. Then I started thinking about our grandfather.

Silently I thanked him for bringing Caroline into our lives and that we had her for so many years. I thought about what he told me in the cemetery on the day that we buried Dara. I was learning more and more about our family. First it was him then Aunt Jada and Uncle Marcus like he said then Caroline. I couldn't help but wonder who or what was coming next. I didn't have to wonder long.

I heard our parents getting up and I heard Aunt Margeaux and Uncle Wilhelm stirring. I went upstairs to my bedroom to fix my hair. As I stood in front of the mirror I saw my grandfather but when I turned around he was not there. There was no veil over him when I saw him either and he was smiling at me. His hair was gray and he had aged considerably.

"How can that be possible?" I wondered. He didn't look anything like the man in the photograph that Aunt Margeaux showed me, or as he looked in my dream, but it was him. *"Why is that 'covering' gone now?"* I wondered to myself. And I wondered how I was able to see him in a mirror. I couldn't deny it any longer. There was definitely something that he was trying to tell me. When I was done fixing my hair I went back downstairs.

CHAPTER TWENTY SEVEN

Our parents, our aunt and our uncle were in the dining room with Caroline and Drew and they were laughing and talking with one another. I told all of them about seeing my grandfather again. "He knows you are sad, honey," said Aunt Margeaux softly. "And he just wants to let you know that he is with you, that's all."

When we were alone I told Caroline that my grandfather had no dark veil over him when I saw him and that he looked as if he had aged when I saw him in my mirror. I was so confused. "He's been earthbound for so long," said Caroline. "It's the only reason I can think of why his spirit looks like it has aged. You're seeing him as he would have been if that terrible thing had not happened to him, and he had been allowed to live out his natural life. Whatever has been troubling you all of these years is passing away now I think." "I don't understand," I replied.

"Celia," she said, "you're finally letting him go just like you don't need me anymore it's the same thing with him." "I wasn't aware that I ever needed him," I told her. "Celia," she said, "if you will only be honest with yourself you never really believed that your grandfather is gone, in body that is." "No," I replied. She was right because I never believed it until Aunt Jada said it. I knew he wasn't what you would call 'alive' anymore and what I always saw was his spirit. "Why did I see him in my mirror?" I asked Caroline curiously. "That," she said, "I don't know. But don't worry. Okay?" I nodded my head. Then my mother came into the kitchen.

"What's going on in here?" she wanted to know so I told her what I told Caroline. She hugged me tightly. "Caroline is right, honey," she said. "You're finally releasing him." "I don't know how I could see him in my mirror, Mama," I said. "Because I can't see you, Papa, or the others in a mirror." Which believe it or not was something that my sister and I never noticed until after we learned what our family members were. "You saw him because you wanted to see him, Celia," said Mama. "You must have been thinking about him." Lately I was always thinking about my grandfather.

"You are a very special young woman, honey," said Caroline. "Don't you remember that I told you that before?" "Yes," I replied. "I remember." "Now you know it's really true. Don't you?" said Mama smiling. I didn't say anything then she kissed me on my cheek.

"Celia," said my mother, "you have the same 'gift' that my mother had. You know things that other people don't know. And sometimes you can 'see' things that others cannot see." I never told any of them but as far as my 'gift' was concerned I certainly could have lived without it.

All we could think about was Caroline leaving us and it made Drew and I very melancholy. One evening as the entire family sat in the living room my sister and Caroline started putting up decorations for Valentines Day.

With all that had happened I had no holiday spirit and usually all of our decorating would have been done already. But here it was almost Valentines Day and we were just decorating the house. I sat down on the sofa watching them and Papa turned on the radio. They were playing love songs.

"Celia, how do you feel about Caroline going away?" my father asked me. I told him how my sister and I felt about it and he was not surprised. "Well," he said, "Aunt Margeaux and Uncle Wilhelm are leaving us, too." "What?!" cried Drew and I stunned. "Yes," he said. "Around the first of next month they're leaving for France." Drew turned to face our aunt and uncle. "Are you coming back?" she asked them. "No, sugar," replied our aunt, "we're not coming back."

Drew threw the decorations that she had in her hand to the floor and stormed upstairs sobbing. "Oh, Drew," said Aunt Margeaux compassionately, "please come back, honey." "Let me talk to her," said

Mama heading up the stairs behind my sister. "You come too, Celia, honey. Because there is something that I want to talk to both of you about." I followed her up the stairs.

Once we got inside our bedroom Mama laid down on Drew's bed and told us to lay down with her. She gently wiped Drew's tears away and as we laid there she held us in her arms and began to talk to us. "Remember that we told you girls we would make things as normal as possible around here for you?" she asked us.

"But, Mama," said Drew sniffling, "we don't want our family to break up and they're all leaving us." "It's their decision, sweetheart," replied Mama, "not your father's and mine. They need to go and I don't think it would be fair to try to keep them here. Do you?"

It wasn't fair to them if they wanted to leave. Mama talked to my sister and I for quite a while that night. And she helped us understand why Caroline, Aunt Margeaux and Uncle Wilhelm had to leave us. I thought I understood about Caroline but I really didn't. However, after Mama talked to us it was all very clear.

We had known and loved Caroline for many years and after all of those years she was still in love with our grandfather. By staying with our family she felt closer to him and by loving us she poured onto us all of the love that she wanted to give to him. It was very odd, but in a way she and I were in the same situation because neither one of us wanted to let him go. Now she was finally able to do that just as I thought I was.

"Aunt Margeaux and Uncle Wilhelm should've had a life of their own together apart from the rest of us a long time ago," continued Mama. She told us that ever since they were young women her sisters looked up to her and clung to her, especially after what Danielle did to all of them. While Mama was talking to us we decided to ask her about other things we were curious about.

"What happened to your other two brothers, Mama?" I asked her. "Larry and Richard?" I wanted to ask our parents about those two men for a while but I didn't know how to do it.

"My brother, Larry, was destroyed," said Mama, "many years ago when we lived in Treylor." She told us how Uncle Larry was betrayed by a woman that he fell in love with, and her name was Savannah Reilly.

She was very pretty and also very married. Uncle Larry convinced her he thought to spend the rest of her life with him so she told her husband that she was leaving him for my uncle. Also, she told him what my uncle was and of course he didn't believe her.

Her husband found out that she was telling him the truth when he came after my uncle to fight him one night. And it was Savannah who stopped my uncle from killing him. After that Savannah's husband got a gang of his buddies together and when Uncle Larry least expected it Savannah lead them to where he was during the day time.

Savannah's husband and his friends destroyed my uncle. And after that my mother and our aunts killed Savannah, her husband and all of his friends who were involved in my uncle's destruction. I thought that was terrible, and I felt sorry for the uncle that Drew and I had never known. It gave me another reason to resent Danielle and what she did to all of them.

"I think my brother, Ricky, is still out there somewhere," said Mama sadly. "I don't know for sure because I haven't seen or heard from him in over ten years now." "Have we ever seen him, or Uncle Larry, Mama?" I asked her. "Yes, honey," replied Mama, "you've seen your Uncle Ricky because he stayed with us for a long time when you were around three years old, then he left us. He never told us where he was going, or if he would be coming back. And in my heart I believe that something has happened to him." "Why do you say that, Mama?" asked my sister.

"Well," said Mama, "he would've come back to see us by now." "So you think he might have been destroyed, too?" I asked her. "I am afraid so, honey," she replied sadly. "Did he have a woman, too, Mama?" asked Drew. My mother chuckled softly. "He certainly did, honey," she said. "In fact, quite a few of them. He was a lot like my Papa, a real ladies' man." "What about Uncle Larry?" asked Drew. "Was he a ladies' man, too?" "Oh, yes," answered Mama. "He certainly was. But Savannah seems to be the only one that he was stuck on for some reason."

She told Drew and I all about our family openly and honestly that night, and we didn't go to sleep until the wee hours of that morning. She made us feel a lot better after our talk, too. Later that evening Lila came over to see us. She ended up spending the night with us and finally got to meet our family. They liked her a lot and she liked them. It was a real turning point in mine and my sister's lives.

Soon we were standing on the dock waving good-bye to Aunt Margeaux and Uncle Wilhelm as their ship left for France. It was a very sad and tearful farewell, too. Drew and I would miss them very much and they promised to write to us but they never did. My sister and I were glad that Caroline was there and our parents, too. She wanted to be with us when Aunt Margeaux and Uncle Wilhelm left us.

A few days after our aunt and our uncle left Drew and I ventured downstairs to the basement to look around. It had been thoroughly cleaned out and we could still smell the odor of the disinfectant that was used. There was nothing down there but a few empty boxes, and no trace of whatever had been down there when our uncles used it for a sleeping quarters.

That night our parents awakened and decided to go out for a while. It was unusual for them because it was near the beginning of the month. But then a lot of things had changed in our household. They decided to have a small party for Drew and I to make us feel better after all of the sad news that we had gotten. They wanted to do something to try to cheer us up. It was scheduled for that coming Friday night which was two days away.

Caroline was making all of the preparations for the party. It would be the usual get-together with only the family. Except this time our aunts and our uncles would not be there. However, to our surprise our parents invited Lila, Doc B. and Millie to the party. Caroline went out to the guest house to get some party favors that she bought. And Drew and I watched as our parents left the house that night.

My sister hurriedly got up and started to put on her jacket then she headed for the front porch. "Celia," she said, "you can sit there if you want to but I'm going to see just where they are going." "Drew," I said, "are you crazy? What do you think you're doing?" "What does it look like?" she said. "I'm going to follow them tonight and don't try to talk me out of it."

"You can't do that, Drew," I told her. "Just watch me," she said. "I want to see where they go and you don't have to come with me if you don't want to." She knew as well as I did what our parents were going to do. It was macabre and against my better judgment I went with her. It was the greatest mistake that we could have ever made.

When we got outside we saw our parents two blocks away and they were headed in the direction of the park. We stayed far enough behind them so they would not see us. There was a car parked just outside the gates to the park and a couple of teenagers were sitting inside it. It was obvious to us what they were doing.

We could see that the boy had his hand inside the girl's blouse and they were kissing one another passionately. We didn't know where our parents had disappeared to because we didn't see them anywhere. But what we saw after that would be burned into our memories, even into our souls for the rest of our lives.

Papa stepped out of the shadows and he took his fist and bashed the top of the teenager's car in, then Mama came out of the shadows. She went around to the other side of the car and tore the passenger door completely off of its' hinges with one hand. Drew's mouth fell open in shock and so did mine. We couldn't believe what we were witnessing. What my sister and I saw Papa do to Trevor D'Aisane was nothing compared to what we saw him and my mother do to those two teenagers that night.

We watched from a distance in horror as our parents snatched the two helpless teenagers out of the car. They attacked them viciously and it was horrifying. Drew and I were petrified! Mama bit into the young boy's throat deeply nearly decapitating him. And Papa bit off both of the young girl's breasts right down to the chest bone. We watched in utter terror as they literally ate those two teenagers who never even had a chance to even cry out for help.

We saw my father pull the arms off of the young girl's body. I couldn't stand to see anymore and neither could my sister so we ran home as fast as we could. The horrible scene was etched into our minds forever.

Before we got inside our house Drew and I had to vomit. We made it to our front yard. Caroline came outside to see what was wrong with us. "Oh my," she said when she saw us. "What's the matter with you two?" We were shaking uncontrollably and we couldn't speak. A worried look came upon Caroline's face then she took us inside the house.

"Where did you girls go?" she wanted to know. "I came back to the house and you were gone." All we could do was stare at her then somehow she knew. I don't know how she knew but she did.

"Please don't tell me that you followed your parents out of here," she said. "Because you promised me you would not do that!" She was yelling at us but all we could do was stare at her. "Oh my dear, God!" she cried. "How could you do that?! You promised me you would not do that!" She sat down on the living room sofa and started smoking a cigarette nervously.

We sat down beside her on the chair. She was silent for a few minutes and just kept shaking her head sadly. Drew and I still couldn't speak. It felt like our tongues were glued to the roof of our mouths then finally Caroline said something.

"If your parents ever find out about what you've done," she began calmly, "it will destroy them. Do you understand that?" We didn't answer her. "I know you are in shock right now," she continued, "because of what you've seen and you deserve to be. Do you realize what you've done? Your parents would never be able to face you again. Do you understand what that means?" Then at last I found my voice.

"Oh, Caroline," I said still shaking, "it was so horrible! Those poor kids! You wouldn't believe……" "Yes," she said angrily cutting me off, "I would believe it. But did you hear what I just told you and your sister?!" "Y-yes," I replied sheepishly with my voice shaking. "You can never ever tell anybody about what you've seen," said Caroline. "You'll just have to live with it for the rest of your lives."

I started to sob and so did my sister. "What have we done?" cried Drew sobbing. "Oh, God, what have we done? How can we ever live with what we've seen?"

"What made you two do such a stupid thing?!" asked Caroline still angry. "You did something that you will suffer for terribly, believe me." "It was all my fault," sobbed Drew. "Celia didn't want any part of it. It was all my fault." Caroline had no sympathy, or compassion for either one of us because she was very angry and upset with us for what we had done.

"There is no use crying about it now," she told us very aloof. "You just couldn't leave well enough alone. Could you? Even after things were getting better around here for both of you? You just would not listen so now you will pay for your idiocy forever."

"We didn't mean any harm, Caroline!" said Drew. "We never imagined that we would see anything like that!" Caroline chuckled sarcastically. "I find that very hard to believe, Drew," she said. "Especially since you know what your parents are through no fault of their own. Just what did you expect to see?" "I don't know," sobbed Drew sorrowfully. "I'm so sorry I ever did it because I can't get it out of my head."

She was right about that because I couldn't get that terrifying scene out of my head either. "It will never go away!" Caroline said angrily. "And if you love your parents and I know you do, you will never let them know what you've done, never!" "How can we act like nothing has happened, Caroline?" I asked her looking for some kind of hope, or compassion from her. "That's your problem!" she almost spat at me. "But you better find a way to do just that! And for the rest of your lives!"

Although she was extremely upset with us Caroline fixed us some of her warm milk to calm us down. After that she walked out of the room leaving Drew and I alone. She felt as though we should suffer for what we did and in a way we agreed with her. We would regret what we had done for the rest of our lives for sure.

We were only fooling ourselves and I think that Caroline knew that, too. Because there was no way that my sister and I would be able to live with our dark secret. We didn't know how soon the day was coming but we would have to tell somebody about it. It was either that or go insane. And in the end what we did would hurt both of us very badly.

Needless to say, it put a tremendous damper on the party that our parents had for us two days later to cheer us up. It was all that Drew and I could do just to get through it as best as we could. Mama and Papa sensed that something was bothering us. And they thought it was only our being hurt because our family was breaking apart.

I wanted to break down and cry whenever I looked at our parents. They would smile so lovingly at my sister and I. I had to fight back the tears whenever I thought about how Drew and I had blatantly betrayed them.

Caroline kept up a good front, too. She never let on to anybody what we had done. We felt like we had hurt the two people in the whole world who loved us more than life itself and we had. We were very happy when everything was over and everybody went home after the party was over.

As we laid in our beds that night I heard my sister sobbing quietly. My tears rolled silently down the sides of my face and onto my pillow. I laid there looking up at the ceiling listening to my sister's heartbreaking sobs until I fell asleep. I don't know what time our parents came upstairs that night to kiss us like they usually did.

CHAPTER TWENTY EIGHT

Drew, Caroline and I went about our normal, daily routine. Caroline did talk to us about our problem although she had no sympathy for us whatsoever. Believe me we were grateful to have someone to talk to about it. We did our best to stay cheerful around our parents, too. But Mama wasn't fooled. She knew there was something bothering us.

"Celia," she said to me one evening, "are you feeling alright?" "Sure, Mama," I lied to her. "Well, you know that you girls can talk to me. Don't you, sweetheart?" she asked. I looked into her trusting eyes and they were so filled with love. "Yes, Mama," I replied solemnly. "We know that." "Well, then, "she said putting her arm around my shoulders, "why don't you tell me what's bothering you and your sister." I looked into her loving eyes again. There was no doubt that she could read our minds if she wanted to. And the only reason she didn't do it was out of fear of what she would learn.

"If only she knew how badly I want to talk to her," I thought. I desperately wanted to tell her that Drew and I saw her and Papa that night when they killed those two kids. "Celia?" she said breaking into my thoughts. She had a questioning look on her face. "I'm alright, Mama," I lied to her again. "Nothing is wrong with me." She felt my forehead to see if it was too warm thinking I might have a fever or something.

"You're not sick. Are you, honey?" she asked me. "No, Mama," I said. "Well," she said smiling "there is definitely something going on with you and Drew, and I will find out what it is you know." "I'm really fine, Mama," I insisted. "Really I am." I could tell by the look on her face that she didn't believe me for one second. I went into the living room and turned on the radio but I could feel her eyes on me watching me.

She sat down at the dining room table where my sister was directly in front of her. She covered Drew's hand with hers'. "How about you, honey?" she asked my sister. "I'm okay, Mama," said Drew sounding like she wanted to break down and cry any minute. I prayed that she wouldn't break down. My mother got a strange look on her face after that. She knew something was wrong and that both of us were lying to her. Then Papa came downstairs.

We could get away with lying to our mother easily enough but I prayed silently that our father wouldn't question us. He kissed me on the cheek and kissed Drew then he kissed Mama on her forehead. "How are my ladies this evening?" he asked us. "Fine, Papa," replied my sister and I.

"I think there is something troubling our daughters, Omri," Mama told Papa as he sat down in the dining room. My heart fell to my knees. *"Oh no!"* I thought. "Really?" replied Papa curiously. "Come in here, Celia, honey," he told me. Slowly I got up from my chair and went into the dining room. "Sit down," he told me and I did as he said. "Look at me," he said to Drew and I. We looked at him as he looked deeply into our eyes.

"Now," said Papa, "I want to know what is bothering you two and do not tell me 'nothing' because your mother and I have been watching both of you. You've been moping around here for a reason, and I want to know what it is." Neither my sister nor I said a word then Caroline came into the house.

"Caroline," said Papa, "I know that the girls talk to you about everything so you tell me because they will not. What is bothering them?" Caroline's eyes widened in surprise and that was a mistake if you were dealing with Papa. Any sign of surprise, fear or apprehension was a dead give-away to him that something was amiss.

"Well," began Caroline as Drew and I looked into her eyes. And our parents caught the look of panic that I know showed on our faces.

"There have been a few boy problems that I'm aware of," Caroline lied to him. Drew and I breathed a sigh of relief.

"Is that what this is all about?" asked my mother surprised. However, she really didn't sound all that surprised to me. "Oh, sweeties," she continued, "we can talk about it if you want to." "A lot of the guys that you girls like are not going to be what you expected," said Papa. "But it will be alright, you'll see."

They fell for Caroline's outright lie. I was surprised that Papa did, or so we thought he did. Drew and I smiled. We were glad as well as relieved because Caroline always came through for us. Papa started talking to us about men, boys and sex which were all of the things that parents usually talked about with their children. Although in my case it was a little late. But we listened anyway as if we were genuinely interested. We already knew about the things he was telling us.

When the conversation was over we began to play a game with our parents. I would never know until some time later, but our parents had not believed Caroline. They just didn't bother to press the issue. The following morning we thanked Caroline for helping us out of what we knew could've been a problematic situation. "Yes," she said. "But I won't be around much longer so who is going to help you two then? Believe me you're no match for your parents." She was right about that. But for the time being Drew and I had a reprieve.

My sister and I went out of our way to put on a cheerful act for our parents. But Mama kept a watchful eye on both of us. I would still catch her watching us when she thought we were not looking. Caroline eyed us, too. But we were careful not to let the anguish that was in our hearts show on our faces. However, it was more than obvious that our parents were not reading our thoughts because they went along with the farce that Drew and I were putting on. It was very clear to both of us that they would've been reacting very differently if they knew what we were really going through just as Caroline pointed out to us.

Drew and I missed our family members so much but things did seem to get better for us at home. It felt more family-like with only our parents and us. To our surprise we began to feel glad for Caroline, too. We were happy that she was finally going to find a life for herself. And as each day passed by we seemed to feel better about her leaving us.

My mother did all that she could do to keep Drew and I cheery and happy. And for no reason at all she baked us a carrot cake which was our favorite dessert. I was surprised because I had never seen Mama cook anything before. Instead of going out in the evening like they had been doing for years they stayed home with us, at least until midnight, or until after Drew and I went to bed.

Things were really changing just like our parents promised us they would. Yet, all of the heartache and sadness was not over for Drew and I. Weeks after we spied on our parents Caroline left us forever and we thought we would never stop hurting. It seemed like the end of the world.

Caroline chose to catch an evening train to Kingstown so our parents could be there with Drew and I to see her off. From Kingstown she was scheduled to go on a Caribbean cruise three days later. "I'll miss my girls," she told Drew and I as we stood on the train's platform with her. "I love you both very much and I always have and I always will."

"We know that, Caroline," said my sister sadly. Then she hugged and kissed us. "Will we ever see you again?" I asked her but all she did was smile and said, "If you don't just know that I will always be with you in spirit." She hugged and kissed our parents, too.

"We'll miss you, Caroline," Mama told her with tears in her eyes. "You're a part of this family you know." "I know, Kate," replied Caroline. "Take care of my girls. Okay?" "You know that we will," said Papa smiling. "Have a good life, Caroline, because you certainly deserve it." Then she turned around and walked toward the train to get on board, and we watched her as she boarded the train.

She waved good-bye to Drew and I from the window after she found her seat on the train. I could hardly see anything because my eyes were filled with tears. Our friend was gone. And no matter what she said we knew that we would never see her again. Life for my sister and I had definitely changed. And we didn't know how we would ever make it without Caroline in our lives anymore. The train began to move and we stood on the platform until it disappeared from sight. Our parents held Drew and I all the way home and we cried all the way there.

We had been home for an hour or so when our parents told us they were going out. Drew and I watched them from the porch window as they walked up the street holding each other's hands. They were going in the direction of the park again. We knew what was going to happen to some poor, unsuspecting person, or persons. And that knowledge made us feel worse than we already did.

"I don't know if I can keep holding this in, Celia," said my sister referring to the dark secret that we kept. "Now that Caroline is gone I feel like I'm going out of my mind sometimes." "Me, too," I replied. "But all we have to do is remember what she told us. We can never tell anybody, or let Mama and Papa know that we saw them that night, never."

Drew decided to read a book in the living room and I went upstairs to our bedroom. I got my music box from the top of the closet and wound it up. As I listened to the sorrowful tune that it played I laid down on my bed staring at the ceiling. "Celia!" I heard a man's voice call to me and it startled me. There in the doorway of my bedroom stood my grandfather.

There was no dark veil or covering over him and his hair was not gray as it had been before when I saw him. And I was not afraid. He looked young and handsome. "What do you want, Grandfather?" I asked him glad to see him. "You know what I want, Celia, honey," he replied. "No," I said. "I don't." "Yes," he contradicted me. "You do. And I can't leave this world until you're able to release me and realize the truth. You won't need me anymore, honey." "I just don't understand, Grandfather," I told him. "Because I don't know how to release you." "Of course you do, honey," he said. "You're already doing it just as you're letting all of the others in the family go."

"All you and Drew have now are your parents," he continued. "And that's the way it should have always been. With all that you know you have to accept what is true and move on with your life. And your strength can help your sister. Can you accept the truth about what we were? Just ask yourself that question because there will be an answer for you." I was a little puzzled and as suddenly as he appeared to me he was gone. *"What is he trying to tell me?"* I began to wonder.

"Celia," said Drew standing in the middle of the staircase, "who are you talking to?" "It was Grandfather again," I told her. "Oh no," she said. "What did he want?" I told her what he said to me. "I just don't get it," she said as she came up the stairs and into our bedroom. "There was no covering over him this time either and he looked like he did when we were little girls," I said. "Well," replied Drew, "remember Caroline said that was because you were letting him go, or something?"

"Maybe I am accepting the truth," I thought. *"But I thought I had already done that."* Drew and I were getting older and I would be out of school soon and looking for a job. I would have a life of my own. My sister and I were not little girls anymore and we wouldn't be needing our parents as much anymore either. I already knew that. Since Caroline was gone in a way we were already on our own. At last I thought I was seeing everything clearly, or so I believed. What my grandfather wanted me to see was there all along. However, I was looking in the wrong direction for the answer. I started to feel more sorry for our parents all of a sudden. Because they would be forced to see what my grandfather had been telling me about, too. I don't understand how none of us ever saw it, only our grandfather. Maybe it was our love for one another that kept all of us so blinded.

Drew and I talked for a while. Around two o'clock that morning we went to sleep and that was when the nightmares began. Not only the nightmares but my sister started walking in her sleep at night.

It was the same nightmare over and over again. It was always dark and there was thunder and lightning. Somebody would be chasing me but I could never see who it was. And I heard someone's voice saying, "Can't you see it yet, Celia?" I would be terrified and when I started to scream I would wake up. Every time I had that nightmare when I awakened my grandfather was there then he would vanish.

It didn't matter what time of the day it was either. I could be napping in the afternoon, or asleep in my bed at night and the same nightmare would come. It occurred one night and when I screamed in the dream I was actually screaming in reality. Our parents were at home that night and heard me and suddenly they were in our bedroom.

"Celia! What's wrong, honey?!" cried Papa a little shaken up. He was gently shaking me awake. "What is it, honey?!" he asked again visibly upset. "What is it?!" Mama knelt down beside my bed and my sister was sitting up in her bed. "I had a bad dream," I told them. "And it's the same one that I've been having over and over again." "Tell us about it, sweetheart," said Mama calmly. So I told them about the nightmare.

"I wonder what it is that they want you to see, honey?" asked Mama curiously. "I don't know, Mama," I replied. "Is it a man's voice," asked Papa, "or a woman's voice?" "I don't know," I told him. I couldn't tell whether the voice in the nightmare was male or female.

Our parents stayed with Drew and I in our bedroom that night. My mother got into bed with Drew and I and Papa laid in my sister's bed.

I had to admit it. I did feel safer with our parents in the room with us. And they did the same thing every night after that for the next week. The nightmares stopped but that's when Drew began walking in her sleep at night.

One night while our parents were in our bedroom with us a lot of commotion in the room awakened me. When I opened my eyes I saw them standing in the middle of the floor and Drew was standing in the hallway. She looked confused as if she didn't know where she was.

"Drew," said Mama softly, "come back to bed, honey." My sister looked at her as if she didn't know who she was. "Come on, sweetheart," said Papa gently taking my sister by the hand. He guided her back to her bed. Then she laid down, closed her eyes and went back into a sound sleep. It was like nothing had ever happened and the same thing occurred after that for several nights.

When Drew began sleep-walking one night our parents followed her. She got out of bed and in her pajamas and bare feet walked downstairs and out of the front door. She headed toward the park and our parents followed her. They didn't awaken her because they read somewhere that if you did that the person who was sleep-walking could die from shock. Drew stopped at the park gates and looked around as if she was wondering which way to go next.

Without startling her our parents lead her back to the house, up the stairs and back to her bed. She closed her eyes and that was that. Our parents were frantic! They knew something was wrong but they didn't know what it was. Mama ran from the room sobbing softly and Papa promptly followed her downstairs. For the first time in my life I heard my parents quarreling.

"What's wrong with our girls, Omri?!" I heard Mama asking Papa angrily. She was very upset. "I don't know, Kate," replied Papa sadly. "Maybe it's something that we've done to upset them." He didn't know how close he was to the truth. "Oh yes," said Mama sarcastically, "as if we haven't done enough to them already."

"What is that supposed to mean?" asked Papa. "You know exactly what it means!" said Mama angrily. "I told you that I didn't think it was wise for them to see what you did to that bastard, Trevor. Didn't I? But no-o-o you knew it all and I didn't know what I was talking about!" "Kate," said my father, "what are you talking about? What happened to Trevor would've bothered them back then when it happened not now all of a sudden!"

"Oh yes," continued Mama still angry, "and Caroline leaving us. I told you that I didn't like that idea either. Didn't I? You know how close the girls were to her, Omri, and all of this started right after she left us!" They went on for about a half an hour with my mother blaming my father for whatever problems Drew and I were suddenly having. A little while later everything downstairs got quiet so I got out of bed and tip-toed to the middle of the staircase to see what they were doing. I could hear moaning and what sounded like kissing.

I saw our parents on the living room sofa making love and I was shocked because I didn't think they did that anymore. But there they were locked in each other's arms in a passionate embrace. They were still in each other's arms when Drew and I came downstairs that morning. And since we couldn't awaken them we got a blanket and put it over them. I was glad they were not completely naked and we kept the downstairs as dark as possible all that day, too.

Drew and I talked about my nightmares and her sleep-walking. In the end we surmised that her walking to the park in her sleep had some significance to the night we saw our parents murder those two teenagers. In fact, it wasn't hard to figure out that the nightmares and the sleep-walking had something to do with our dark and terrible secret.

After what Caroline told both of us there was no way we could tell our parents what was really bothering us. "God, I miss Caroline!" I told Drew. "Yeah," she said. "Me, too." We didn't know what to do and we had no one that we could talk to about our problem. Our parents couldn't go on standing guard over us every night either.

We could see no solution to our dilemma and our parents were at their wits end so they hired a Psychotherapist for my sister and I. Dr. Wilma Tangee made house calls in the evenings so it was perfect for them.

Dr. Tangee wasn't much older than Caroline was and she was very nice. Wilma, as she told Drew and I to call her, was medium height and brown skinned. She had dark brown eyes and hair and she was very professional. She had a wonderful sense of humor, too, and we liked her a lot. It didn't take her long to figure out that the problems my sister and I were having had something to do with our parents. My mother was not surprised by that but my father wouldn't accept it.

"We've always shown our daughters nothing but love." Papa told Wilma emphatically. "So you have to be mistaken." "I understand how you feel, Mr. Bellis," said Wilma. "But I'm telling you this from my own experience because I've seen this many times. Your daughters have seen, or heard something that has had a tremendously negative impact on their minds. Something that has upset them both very badly and you are their parents and the closest people to them. So it has to have something to do with you, either both of you or one of you. If you think about it hard enough maybe you will discover what it could be. It doesn't have to be a big thing because it could just be something very minute."

"I don't think you know what you are talking about, Doctor!" Papa told Wilma rather nastily. "What could they have possibly seen us do, or heard us say that was so terrifying for them?" "I don't know, Mr. Bellis," said Wilma. "But I would like to try to find out if you will let me." "What do you mean *try?* asked Papa.

"Well," began Wilma, "I don't want you to get your hopes up too high because sometimes I don't always have success in these kinds of cases. We may never know what has happened to them. But there are medications that can help them if therapy doesn't work. What it boils down to is their willingness to tell me, or anyone else what is on their minds. I have to tell you that up front." "So," said Papa, "in the meantime our girls will just go on having violent nightmares and walking in their sleep. Is that it?" Wilma didn't say anything because I guess there was nothing else she could say. During the entire conversation between her and my father Mama said absolutely nothing. I believe my mother was so desperate by that time about what was wrong with my sister and I that she was truly considering reading our thoughts. It was something that I knew she really didn't want to resort to. Yet, in spite of everything she never did that.

Wilma asked my father if she could stay with Drew and I for a while in order to be around us more. And of course he denied her request. She couldn't understand why he did that but we did. I think it made her suspicious, too. Because Drew and I caught her a couple of days later snooping around the guest house. She was looking in one of the guest house windows. We were just coming home from school and she was only supposed to come to our house in the evenings.

"Wilma!" I said sneaking up behind her and startling her. "O-oh, hi, girls!" she said nervously. "What are you doing here?" I asked her. She was at a loss for words for a moment. "Please don't tell your parents that I was here. Okay?" she said to us.

"Don't worry," said Drew. "We won't. What are you looking for?" Wilma sighed. "Can I ask you where your parents are during the day?" she asked us. "I never see them in the day time." Drew and I glanced at one another.

"They are usually *out* during the day," I told her. "They're in around seven o'clock in the evenings and I know they told you that." "Oh," said Wilma. "Yes. Do they work?" "No," said Drew. "Well," she said, "maybe you'll be honest with me then." "How is that?" asked my sister. "Tell me what you two saw, or heard that has affected both of you so badly," she said.

"What makes you think that we've seen, or heard anything terrible at all?" I asked her. "Oh come on, honey," said Wilma sweetly. "I've been in this business for a long time and I know that both of you have seen, or heard something horrifying. Please just tell me what it was because I can help you but you have to trust me." My sister and I were silent for a moment.

"We saw two people get killed one night," Drew blurted out and Wilma was stunned! "Oh, my God!" she cried compassionately. "No wonder, you poor things! Did you know the people who were murdered?!" "No," answered my sister. "But we know the people who killed them." Wilma's mouth fell open in shock. Drew and I were laughing at her on the inside and I was fully aware of what my sister was doing. She was toying with Wilma.

At least it was a way for us to tell somebody our terrible secret. And we thought Wilma wouldn't believe us but she did. We were just fooling around with her trying to be smart asses but what we didn't know was that our actions that day would bring us a lot of pain, despair, anguish and grief in the near future.

"Did you tell the Sheriff about this?" asked Wilma still stunned. "No," said Drew. "Why not?" asked Wilma in disbelief. "Because he wouldn't have believed us," replied my sister. "Nobody would." "I don't understand," said Wilma puzzled. "Well," continued Drew, "the killers were our parents because they're vampires." The expression on Wilma's face after that turned to one of disgust and anger.

"Look you two," she said holding back her anger at us. "I'm here to help you not to hurt you, and I do not appreciate being made a fool of or being lied to." "See," said Drew. "I told you nobody would believe us." Wilma sighed again. "Alright," she said. "Whenever you're ready to talk to me I'll be around but right now I'm going back to my office. So maybe I'll see you and your parents this evening. If not I'll be back tomorrow night. Okay?" "Sure," said Drew. "Okay," I replied.

Then she got into her car and drove off and Drew and I went inside the house. We had a good laugh over what happened with Wilma, too. Yet, our laughter would turn to bitter tears of sorrow before too long.

The following evening Wilma came to our house. She talked to our parents never once mentioning what my sister and I said about them. We were very glad about that, too, and we were still laughing about it. Strangely enough after we told Wilma the truth my nightmares and Drew's sleep-walking suddenly stopped.

Our parents were thrilled! We thought they would have no more need for Wilma after that but they did. Papa asked her to continue to talk to us in case there was something that we wanted to talk about with her and not with them. He kept her on a retainer basis like some people kept lawyers. Throughout all of this I noticed that my mother was very quiet. And it was as if she was changing in some way. I couldn't explain the change that I was seeing come over her. But secretly I think she was picking up on mine and my sister's thoughts. She just never said anything to anybody about it.

After a while Wilma was almost like another Caroline to Drew and I although no one could ever take Caroline's place in our lives. She had been like a mother to us as well as our friend but Wilma simply became a friend. She was not allowed to come to our house during the day and she just could not understand that. However, every evening as soon as it got dark she was there, except on the weekends. We liked her company, too. Also, we found out that she had been treating Doc B. ever since Dara's untimely death which is how my parents found her in the first place. After that time passed by and nothing eventful happened.

CHAPTER TWENTY NINE

I went to my high school dance a month before graduation with a guy who went to our school named, Billy Darson, and it was something! I thought I would never want to go but things had not only changed for Drew and I inside our household and with our family, but we became more outgoing and friendly with the other students in our school. Billy was my first real high school date and I went with Lila and her date. We had a wonderful time and it was something we would never forget.

Not long after that it was graduation day and graduation day for Lila as well since we were in the same grade. My prayers were answered when it was announced that the ceremony would be held at night. My parents would be able to attend and they were very excited and happy about it. "My baby is graduating from school," said Papa proudly. He and my mother were so proud of me.

Neither one of them ever graduated from school they told us. They dropped out at a very young age simply because they got tired of going.

When I walked down the aisle on graduation night with my Diploma in my hand my parents were beaming. When we got home that night we had a party to celebrate. They invited Lila, Doc B., Millie and Wilma. It was at the party that Doc B. and Millie announced that they were going to get married and everybody congratulated them. It was a wonderful evening.

I laid in bed that night after everything was over and thought about how I had not been 'visited' by my grandfather in a while. *"Suppose I never see him again,"* I thought. I mentioned it to my sister when she came to bed. "He could be gone now, Celia," she said. Yet, I didn't believe that.

During the wee hours of that morning there was a terrible thunderstorm and it awakened me but to my surprise I was not afraid. *"Maybe Aunt Margeaux and Caroline knew what they were talking about,"* I thought. After all of the years of being scared my fear of thunderstorms was now gone so I went back to sleep and slept like a baby.

I awakened again later that morning and my grandfather was standing at the foot of my bed. He was looking down at me smiling. "It will all be over soon, Celia, honey," he told me and again he vanished. I had no idea what he was talking about. *"What will be over soon?"* I wondered. There was no veil or covering over him that time either.

I went out looking for work and found a job right away. It was as a Receptionist in one of the attorney's offices in town. I worked with one Secretary and two lawyers.

Lionel Frank and Harris Sky were elderly gentlemen who were very nice and easy to work for. They had been practicing law in Hardelle for nearly thirty five years and did a good business as criminal attorneys. Also, they were working closely with the Sheriff regarding all of the unsolved murders that had occurred, too. Every potential client was screened in case they might have known something about the murders. Personally, I found the cases that they handled very interesting.

The number of shop-lifting cases and robberies they handled was surprisingly large. I never knew there were so many thieves in Hardelle and in the neighboring Counties. There was one case where a guy tried to hold up a gas station with a toy gun.

The Attendant at the station believed he had a real gun and gave up all of the money that he had, but the robber was caught right away and Mr. Sky was representing him in the case. I discussed my job and the people that I met in the office with our parents, Drew, Lila and Wilma. Lila had decided to go to nursing school in a nearby County. However, we still saw one another regularly.

I felt strange one day as I sat in the office listening to the two attorneys discussing the murders in Hardelle and other towns. The rate at which the murders occurred had suddenly dropped dramatically. Of course they did because there were only two killers left.

"I don't think they will ever catch those murderers," said Mr. Frank. "I tend to agree with you, Lionel," replied Mr. Sky. "But we can always hope." I thought sadly, *"I wonder what you would think if you knew what I know."*

While people were being slaughtered Drew and I managed to keep ourselves totally aloof from the murders. We completely buried the knowledge that our parents were the killers into our subconsciouses. But we would never forget what we saw on the night that the two teenagers were brutally attacked and killed.

One day at the office I saw the file on the two murdered teenagers. The Sheriff happened to drop it off so Mr. Sky could look it over. The girl was only fifteen years old and the boy was seventeen years old. *"My God!"* I thought sorrowfully. *"They were younger than I am."* I felt terrible for their families because the boy had lived with his mother and he had three younger siblings. His father died when he was eight years old from cancer and the girl had lived with both of her parents and she was an only child.

I put the file on Mr. Sky's desk and I couldn't help the deep feeling of sorrow that I felt for those two families. I couldn't stop thinking about them either. It was those feelings that must have ruptured something in my subconscious mind because without warning the nightmares returned.

That same night I woke up screaming at the top of my lungs. "Celia," cried Drew who was awakened from her sleep when I screamed. "Are you alright?!" I heard our parents at the bedroom door and I didn't even know they were at home. Papa came into the room first and snatched me up from my bed and held me close to him.

"Oh, honey," he said soothingly stroking my hair. "What is it?" "Oh, Celia," said Mama who was right behind him. "Is it the nightmares again, sweetie?!" I nodded my head. "Oh no," said Papa with a concerned look on his face. He rocked me back and forth in his arms and I felt like a little girl again. He whispered comforting words into my ear as I laid my head against his chest.

"Maybe it's that job, sweetheart," said Mama softly. "You're always hearing about murders and criminals all of the time and it's not good." I didn't say anything but I knew that my reading the file on the two teenagers that day had triggered something in my subconscious mind. My job was not the cause of my problem.

"I'll call Wilma and tell her to get over here," said Mama reaching for the telephone in our bedroom. "She's probably in bed asleep by now, Mama," said my sister. "I don't care if she is or not," said Papa angrily. "Call her, Kate, and tell her to get her ass over here right now!" "Alright, Omri," replied Mama softly. "But I still think it's that job." Mama dialed Wilma's telephone number. I could see that something was on my mother's mind and it wasn't anything about my job no matter what she said.

"Papa," said my sister, "Celia has been on that job for a while so it's unlikely it would bother her after all of this time. Don't you think?" "Maybe, honey," he told her. "But I'm not going through this again." I listened to my mother talking to Wilma on the telephone then she hung up. "She's on her way over here," she told my father. "Good!" he said. Then I laid back down in my bed. Wilma arrived about a half an hour later and came upstairs to my bedroom.

"Oh, Celia," she said. "You've been doing so well and you haven't had a nightmare in a long time. Is something bothering you?" "Not that I know of," I lied. "Is anything going on at work that you haven't told anybody?" she asked me. "No," I replied. "Maybe she ought to think about quitting that job," said my mother. But there was something different that I saw in her eyes.

She was absolutely convinced that my job was the cause of my nightmares coming back. And totally oblivious to the fact that I was having them before I ever started working there, or so I thought she was convinced. I think it was just something that she desperately wanted to make herself believe. "No, Mama," I told her. "I like my job and I don't want to quit." Our parents asked Wilma to come downstairs with them so they could talk to her.

"We'll be back soon, sweetheart," Papa told me. "And we'll be staying in here with you two tonight. Okay?" "Alright, Papa," I said and Drew nodded her head 'yes'. He, Mama and Wilma went downstairs to talk after that. Our beloved parents walked out of our bedroom that night and out of our lives forever. Because it was the last time that we would ever be with them.

We heard Wilma and our parents talking softly downstairs but we couldn't hear what they were saying. Then suddenly we heard my mother scream, "Oh no! Oh, God, no!" Drew and I jumped out of our beds and rushed down the stairs to see what happened. As long as we would live we would never forget the looks on our parent's faces when we saw them for the last time.

"Oh, no! No! No!" Mama cried with tears running down her face as she looked at Drew and I. Papa looked like he was in a state of shock as he turned to face us. "We are so sorry," he said to Drew and I and his voice was barely above a whisper. "We are so so sorry, babies," he continued. "Please, please forgive us. Please."

"What?" I asked wondering what had happened. Mama ran from the house but Papa just stood in the middle of the living room floor staring at Drew and I with one lone tear rolling down his cheek. Then he smiled a sad smile. My sister and I would never forget the look on his face as long as we lived.

"We would never hurt you," Papa said. "You know that. We've always loved you more than anything in this world." "What is it, Papa?" asked Drew cautiously. "What?!" He walked past us without saying another word and out of the front door.

"Oh no!" cried Wilma. "You girls were telling me the truth! Weren't you?!" "What are you talking about, Wilma?" I asked her. She shook her head sadly then she started to sob a little. "I have to get out of here," she said to my sister and I. "And I will not be coming back here. I had no idea that you were telling me the truth about your parents murdering two people." Both mine and Drew's mouths dropped open in stunned shock.

"What did you do?!" cried Drew yelling at Wilma. "Did you tell them what we told you?!" I asked her with panic stabbing at my heart. She smiled a weak, sad smile and nodded her head. I could see that she was sorry for what she did as well as fearful. "How could you do that?!" cried my sister. Wilma ran from our house after that. Needless to say, we never saw her again and we heard she left town after that.

Jokingly, she told our parents everything that my sister and I told her, all about seeing them on the night that they murdered those two teenagers. I panicked! We had to find them because I recalled what Caroline told us. That if they ever found out what we saw they would never be able to face us again. She told us that it would destroy them. Wherever our parents were they were in grave danger but I didn't know it was already too late.

Drew and I got dressed then we set out to look for our parents. We searched all over town but we could not find them. Drew became angry and bitter toward Wilma. But I told her it was not Wilma's fault because it was our fault. Something that we did as a prank had backfired on us.

The sun was just showing the top of its' head when Drew and I got tired and went home. We desperately hoped our parents would be there but when we got there the house was empty. We looked in each bedroom and in the basement but they were nowhere to be found. It was obvious by then that they had not come back and we were scared. The first place I thought about was Sires Hill and I mentioned it to Drew.

"Why would they go there, Celia?" she asked with her eyes welling up with tears. "We have to go there and see if they are there, Drew. Okay?" I told her. "And if we hurry we can stop them." "Stop them from doing what, Celia?" asked my sister becoming more upset. All I had to do was look at her and she knew the answer to her question.

"No!" she cried. "I won't go there because they are not there! No!" She was becoming hysterical by then. "Drew," I shouted, "snap out of it and let's go!" She started crying so I put my arm around her shoulders.

"Come on," I told her gently. "I know everything will be alright. Okay?" "It will, Celia?" she asked looking to me for reassurance. "Sure it will," I told her. "You'll see." I had to tell her that because if I hadn't she would've become even more hysterical than she was. "O-okay," she said nervously through her tears. "O-okay."

We hurried out of the front door and down the street toward the Hill. On our way there a great dark cloud came out of nowhere and engulfed us. It seemed to swallow us up. "What's this?!" asked my sister becoming frightened. And I knew it was our grandfather. Sure enough there he was standing directly in front of us.

"Who is he, Celia?" asked my sister a little alarmed. "It's Grandfather, Drew," I told her. "Oh no!" she cried. "There's something wrong!" She was panicking. "Don't be afraid," said our grandfather. "It's all over now." "What's all over, Grandfather?" I asked him but he ignored my question. "We always loved you girls very much," he said to us. "And we always will. But there was no way that we could've stayed with you. So just remember how much you were both loved and go on with your lives." Then he smiled the sweetest smile that I had ever seen.

Drew seemed to calm down a little when he smiled at us and she could see him at last. He told us 'good-bye'. And as he turned around and walked away from us the darkness that had engulfed us disappeared. Our grandfather's spirit faded away as we watched him walk away from us and I knew he was gone forever. The sun was beginning to shine brightly. "We have to hurry, Drew," I said taking her by the arm.

When we reached Sires Hill the sun was high in the sky and when we got to the top of the Hill all we saw were two mounds of burnt ashes. Drew screamed and crumbled to the ground in a fit of heart wrenching sobs and I couldn't stop the tears that were flowing freely down my face. Our parents had destroyed themselves and my sister and I wanted to die, too.

We were so distraught I believe if either one of us had any kind of weapon on hand we would have used it on ourselves. Caroline was right. Our parents could never have faced either one of us again knowing that we saw them kill two innocent people. The deep devastation that Drew and I felt was unbearable but being the oldest I had to get myself together for her sake as well as my own.

Drew and I sat down by the two piles of burnt ashes there on the Hill and held onto one another. And her tears mingled with my own. After a while she laid down on the ground next to the ashes and went to sleep. I had to do something because I couldn't let what was left of our beloved parents remain there on the Hill like that. We took off our sweaters that we had on and I scooped up Mama's ashes first with my hands and placed them inside my sweater then folded it. Then I put

Papa's ashes inside Drew's sweater and folded that. I said a prayer for both of them.

I asked God to remember how kind and good our parents were to Drew and I. Also, I asked Him to remember that they had never asked for the 'life' that was forced onto them and I knew that He heard me. He had blessed my sister and I with two wonderful, loving parents and a wonderful family.

Any Being Who would do that certainly knew that those two people did not belong in hell, no matter what they had done. I was sure that He had not forsaken them and that their souls were finally free and at peace. Slowly, and heavy with sorrow Drew and I walked home carrying our parent's ashes in our arms.

CHAPTER THIRTY

Once we arrived home I made Drew lay down then I found two antique urns inside the attic. I put my mother's ashes into one of them and my father's ashes into the other one. Then I telephoned Lila and Doc B. and told them about our parent's *deaths*. Naturally, they asked me a lot of questions and I told them a lot of lies. I told them that they had died on the day before that from heart failure and they had already been cremated.

Doc B. never knew much about our parents and I felt that he didn't need to. Lila, on the other hand, had known about them because of the Ouija board. Yet, in dealing with her own grief over Dara she had completely forgotten what it said about them. Furthermore, she met our parents under normal circumstances and liked them. So neither she nor anybody else would've guessed what they really were. Except for the Daniels' and they were dead.

After I got my sister calmed down I called Lila and asked her to come over because I wanted her to stay with Drew while I went to see Mr. Darwood. She came right over and I left for the undertaker parlor carrying my parent's ashes with me.

I asked Mr. Darwood if he would bury our parent's ashes and I told him the same lie about their *deaths* that I told Lila and Doc B. "I'm so sorry to hear about your folks, Celia," said Mr. Darwood with compassion. "I didn't know them but judging by you and your sister I'm sure they were very nice people." I thanked him for his kindness.

"Usually you can hold onto the ashes yourselves," he continued. "That way your loved ones are always with you." "Our parents will always be with us anyway, Mr. Darwood," I told him. "And I want a full memorial service for them if you do not mind. I have enough money for the services and for the burial, and I want a nice headstone for them, too." "Of course, dear," he said. "I'll do whatever you and your sister want."

I gave him our parent's ashes and left. I guessed he had heard many strange requests in his business so mine was not that unusual. However, I knew it was rather strange to have a memorial service and a burial for some ashes. But it was what Drew and I wanted for our parents.

When I got back home that afternoon I told Drew and Lila about the arrangements I made for our parents and my sister broke down again. Many weeks after the burial I found out that she held a lot of guilt inside her regarding our parents, especially because of what she told Wilma. I tried to reassure her that none of that mattered anymore. They had cherished both of us and that is what really mattered. All they ever wanted was for both of us to be happy with them. Still, it was a long time before she stopped crying over them.

Drew and I passed out funeral notices to everybody in Hardelle although nobody knew our parents. A lot of the kids we went to school with came to our house to pay their respects and so did a lot of people in town. Even Harris Sky and Lionel Frank came to pay their respects. My sister and I truly appreciated everyone's kindness. Especially since except for Lila, Millie and Doc B. none of them had ever met our parents.

A few days before the funeral Drew and I gave our house a thorough cleaning. We got rid of all of the black curtains and dark shades. And we had all of the bedrooms re-painted in bright, cheerful colors. I kept a lot of my mother's clothing and gave some to Drew. Some I gave to Lila and Millie because my mother always had wonderful taste in clothing. A lot of my father's things I gave to Doc B. since they were about the same size, and the rest I donated to The Community Basket.

I found two photographs of our parents that were taken before their 'lives' of darkness and had them enlarged and placed next to their urns at the memorial service. I asked Reverend Dykes if we could have the service at his church. He was eager to help us and said 'yes'. Also, he volunteered to do the best that he could do in giving a Eulogy.

On the night of the service the church was packed and I was surprised since our family never bothered with the people in town. But I knew that people came because of Drew and I, even Jennifer came.

We didn't think we had any tears left to shed but we did. All we had to do was remember all of the love that our parents had showered on us.

I realized that God had indeed forgiven our parents when we were in the cemetery on the following morning for the burial. A beautiful ray of sunlight shone directly on the two urns as they were being put into the ground and another ray of sunlight shone directly on Drew and I alone. Everybody in the cemetery marveled at that and so did we. One golden ray of sunlight that only covered the urns, and one that only covered Drew and I.

After the burial was over and all of the people were gone Drew and I sat down in our living room and looked around the big, old house. "We really don't need all of this room anymore. Do we, Celia?" asked my sister. "No," I said. "Not really." I had saved a lot of money from my job and our parents and our grandfather left us well off financially so we could afford an apartment of our own if we wanted one.

Also, we had many other houses in other Counties that we could have moved to. But we decided to stay in the house where we had spent most of our lives and where we had been happy.........most of the time that is. Also, it held a lot of wonderful memories for us. Drew stayed in our bedroom and I took over our parent's bedroom. It was the first time that each one of us had a bedroom all to ourselves. We could have always had that but we chose to sleep in the same bedroom with each other.

It took my sister and I a long time to accept our parent's deaths. However, time seemed to pass by quickly and soon Drew was going to her own graduation. She cried during the entire ceremony and I knew she was thinking about our parents, Caroline and the rest of our family. "I wish they were here, Celia," she told me. "They are here, Drew," I replied. "They are."

It didn't take her long to find a job after her graduation. Then she changed her mind about the job and decided to go to college in a neighboring state. I only saw her on holidays and during semester breaks. I don't have to tell you how lonely it was in that big, old, Victorian house by myself.

After a while I decided to advertise for Boarders. I would rent out the extra bedrooms and the guest house. Also, I rented the other homes that we owned. I was very lonely without my sister but Lila and I talked very often before she decided to leave Hardelle. I don't think she ever got over Dara's death and just wanted to get away. However, whenever she visited Doc B. and Millie she would spend some time with me. I would have to hire somebody to do the cooking for me because it was something that Drew and I never learned how to do…..well at least not that good.

The first person to answer my ad for a Boarder was a handsome, young man who was newly divorced named, Raphael Lander. He was three years older than I was and he had custody of his three year old daughter named, Beyda. She was a sweet little girl and we all hit it off right away. Raph, as he wanted to be called, let me know after some time that he was attracted to me so we started dating.

I liked him a lot and he liked me, too. He was a kind, intelligent, gentle, soft-spoken man who loved and wanted a peaceful life and it was the same thing that I wanted. As time went on we fell in love with each other.

Six months after we met we were talking about marriage. I had to think long and hard about that because after all I was not yet twenty years old. I didn't want to get married too young and end up regretting it. I wanted a marriage just like the one that my parents had. However, if people ever knew they were brother and sister they would've shunned them. Still, theirs' was a beautiful marriage.

I took all of the photographs of our family members that we found inside the attic and had them enlarged to wall-portrait size. I put them in lovely handmade frames and hung them on the walls in the living room and dining room. And I filled the house with mirrors, too. I left everything else in the attic there.

After I finished I stood back and observed all of the changes that I had made in the house. Our parents and the others would've been so pleased because they always wanted to live normally but couldn't.

Mine and my sister's lives had undergone a great transformation beginning when I was seventeen years old. As I look back to that year I realize it was the beginning of my sister and I learning the *'truth'* which would affect our lives forever. And not just our lives but the lives of all of our family members as well. Even though they refused for so long to accept it. When our parents found out what Drew and I saw them do that night I believe they knew that they could not deny it any longer.

Everything that happened to us was inevitable and our grandfather always knew what was coming, even if none of the others wanted to see it or not. I was so glad he had been there for me in spirit. And he was there from the time that I was twelve years old to help me through it all.

Drew and I started visiting our parent's grave at least twice a year and when I'm done here I'll visit hers'. She passed away five years ago and I still miss her very much because she was always my best friend. Now here I am eighty eight years old leaning over the patch of earth where our parent's ashes lay buried for so long. Reliving all that happened to my dear sister and I. And I've been here for quite a while reminiscing.

"Are you ready to go yet, Great Grandmom?" It was my granddaughter's son, Omri, talking to me. He would be going off to college soon. "I'm almost ready, Omri," I told him. "Okay, Great Grandmom," he said. He went to join the other members of my family. He is one of my eight great grandchildren and they are all so young and filled with the zest for life. I felt tears in my eyes as I turned around to look at all of them there in the cemetery. I smiled to myself as I recalled my precious memories.

I thought about Aunt Margeaux and Uncle Wilhelm because we never heard from them again and we never knew how to contact them. I refused to believe that they forgot about Drew and I. Therefore, I realized painfully that something must have happened to them in France, or on their way there.

I thought about Caroline, too. We received a letter from her a year after she left us. She met a nice guy and was going to marry him. He was in the Military and stationed overseas in Brazil which was where they were going to live. Drew and I wished great happiness for her and we did write back to her to tell her about our parents. She wrote back to us telling us how sorry she was. Although she never said it we knew that she was not surprised by what happened and we never heard from her anymore.

That was nearly seven decades ago. As I looked at my parent's grave stone I smiled. Mr. Darwood and many other people in Hardelle thought Drew and I were out of our minds after they read what we had printed on their headstone. But we didn't care.

It was a nice sized, beautiful, blue, marble stone and the letters etched into it were carved in solid gold. It read: *'Omri Antoine Bellis, born August 30th, 1764, Died August 29th, 1932 and Kathleena Carbell-Bellis, born July 23rd, 1767, Died August 29th, 1932. Beloved parents of Danielle Cecile Bellis (Celia) and Druann Kathleena Bellis (Drew).*

They died long before they chose to destroy themselves thanks to Danielle. We never did know what day, or year that it happened but we did know their birthdays. And we were not ashamed to let others know, too. The whole town for generations to come would be talking about that headstone. And it was something that Drew and I would always laugh about privately. We didn't care what anybody thought, or said because we wanted the true date of our parent's births on their tombstone. Their torment was over and they didn't have to put on a charade anymore because they were free.

I recalled the day that my grandfather came to me and told me that *"it would all be over soon"*. I didn't understand what he meant by that at the time but later on it was all clear to me. He meant that it would all be over for our parents and they wouldn't have to suffer any longer in the *'life'* that they had been doomed to. They tried to hold onto what little 'real life' they had because of Drew and I. However, as our grandfather said, it couldn't have gone on much longer and for reasons that our parents and our family members never even considered because they loved us so much. But our grandfather always knew. I guessed that he tried to make them see the *'truth'* but they refused because their love for us was so strong. Whenever I remember the Ouija board I realize that when it was telling us about *'the truth'* it encompassed everything.

All of the truth that was to come for Drew and I, not the bits and pieces like we thought at that time.

My sister and I were part of a world that our parents and the others could never be a part of again, no matter how hard they tried. In our hearts my sister and I knew that our beloved parents had finally accepted that truth on the day that they destroyed themselves. You see……..my sister and I would've continued to age but they would not have because they couldn't. And eventually it would have been a problem for all of us.

One year and eight days after we buried our parent's ashes I was laying on the living room sofa and I fell asleep and had a dream. In the dream I was standing on what looked like a seashore and a ship filled with people was going out to sea. All of the people were standing on the back of the ship waving good-bye to me.

I saw our grandfather, our parents, our aunts and our uncles and with them were two strange men I didn't know. I realized that they must have been the two uncles that Drew and I never knew, Richard and Larry. Danielle was there, too. And she was holding my grandfather's hand. I guess they had all finally forgiven her for what she did to them.

I never told Drew about that dream until nearly twenty years later because it took her so long to get over our parent's *deaths,* many many years. By that time she had been married to my brother in-law, Edmond Carlton, whom she met in college for years, and was expecting her second grandchild. Edmond died of a massive heart attack ten years before Drew died. However, she had four, beautiful children, six grandchildren and fourteen great grandchildren. Strangely I never had another dream about our family members and I have dreamed about Drew only once since she died.

None of mine and my sister's children were ever shocked, or astounded by what was on our parent's gravestone. Because we told all of them about our parents and our other family members, and we told our husbands, too. Of course at first they found it hard to believe. But over time they knew we were telling them the truth. I guessed they could tell because of the light in our eyes as we told them the story. The great light that was the wonderful love that our parents and family members showered on Drew and I all of our lives. They believed us although no one else would have. And they have been passing our story down to the rest of the family about the wonderful grandparents, great great grandparents and great aunts and uncles they would never know. Just try to imagine anyone passing down a story like mine and my sister's to their descendents.

"Mom, are you alright?" It was my son, Raphael, Jr. "Yes, honey," I told him. "I'm okay." "Well," he said, "we're going over to visit Dad. Are you ready?" "Sure," I said. "I'm ready." My husband, Raph, has been dead for twenty years and like my sister he just went to sleep one night and never woke up. Yet, I have always been surrounded by my children, grandchildren and great grandchildren so I was never lonely. I looked down at my parent's grave again and smiled. I knew it would be the last time that I would visit them because it wouldn't be long before I would see them all again. I haven't been feeling well lately. And every time I look up I see my husband's spirit beckoning me to come with him. "Come on, Celia," he says to me. "It's time for you to go now."

"Here, Mom," said my son taking my arm. "Let me help you." I saw Beyda waving to me. "Come on, Mom!" she cried. "I'm coming, sweetheart," I said softly. "I'm coming." She and her husband were expecting their third grandchild in the Spring. I didn't say anything to her, or the others but I knew that I wouldn't get to see that one come into the world, unless God allowed me to. Yet, somehow I didn't think He would.

Our parents and the other members of our family may not have been able to live out their lives like they wanted to but they certainly would live on. Mine and my sister's children, grandchildren and great grandchildren were living proof of that. I would go to my own grave as my sister did thanking God for the wonderful love that *'covered'* us all of our lives. And the *'veil'* that enabled my wonderful grandfather to give me the strength that I needed. The *'covering'* that had always been his great love for my family and I.

"THE END"

www.ingramcontent.com/pod-product-compliance
Lightning Source LLC
LaVergne TN
LVHW041905070526
838199LV00051BA/2495